Lead Me Home

Theresa Hupp

Copyright

ISBN for paperback edition: 978-0985324421

ISBN-10 for paperback edition: 0985324422

Rickover Publishing

Lead Me Home

Copyright 2015 by Theresa Hupp
Second printing January 2018

Cover illustration adapted from *The Cliffs of Green River, Wyoming Territory*, oil on canvas painting by Thomas Moran, 1875, Cincinnati Art Museum.

Map of the Oregon Trail from *The Ox Team or the Old Oregon Trail 1852-1906*, by Ezra Meeker, Fourth Edition, 1907.

Artwork for the covered wagon icon used in this book created by Jay Reinhardt.

Dedication

This book is dedicated to my parents, Tom and Mary Claudson. They read an early draft of this novel, but they did not live to see it published.

My parents encouraged me in my writing and supported me in everything else in life. They earned my love and gratitude.

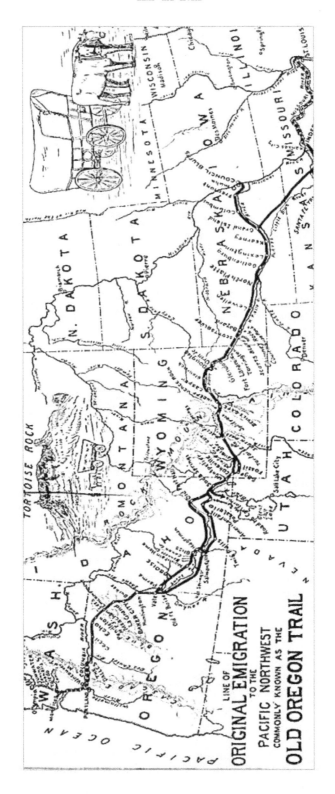

Chapter 1: Arrow Rock

*March 24, 1847. I killed a man today. The Bible says
thou shalt not kill. How did it come to this?*

Mac McDougall looked up from his journal. He had awakened this
morning in a warm cabin on the steamboat *Aurora*. Now he shivered
beside a smoldering campfire, only a tarp protecting him from the cold
Missouri spring. An unknown baggage of a girl slept at his feet.

And he had killed a man.

Mac had traveled a month already, hundreds of miles, before boarding
the *Aurora* at St. Louis several days earlier. Then the boat steamed up the
Missouri River toward Independence through a storm that pounded rain on
deck and shore.

The morning had dawned bright after days of dreary skies. Valiente,
Mac's black Andalusian stallion, pranced and whinnied, eager to escape
the confines of the boat. When the *Aurora* docked beneath the cliffs of
Arrow Rock, Mac decided to ride horseback to an upstream port while the
sidewheeler churned up the next stretch of river.

"You'll reach Waverly before we do," the steamship captain told him.
"Thirty-five miles by road. Two day ride, easy. Sixty miles on the river,
and we stop at ports to trade."

Mac packed food and the journals he'd kept on his travels thus far. He
strapped on his holster and pistol and lashed his rifle to his saddle. All the
men in the West were armed, and Mac was glad of his experience as a boy,
hunting with his grandfather.

He urged Valiente up the bluff above the river. From the top, he smiled at the rolling hills around him—wanderlust filling his soul. He'd been to law school, but the law could wait, despite what his father said. When Mac read of the explorer John Frémont's travels to Oregon Territory, he decided to see the western land for himself. Of course, there were other reasons to leave Boston, but Mac wouldn't dwell on those. Not now.

He rode along the muddy main street of Arrow Rock, passing a few small shops that lined the boardwalk. A dog lounged on the porch outside a dry goods store. A blacksmith shop stood down the road with a stone tavern opposite.

At a storefront with a wooden shingle advertising a post office, Mac dismounted and hitched Valiente to a rail. After entering the store, he bound his journals with brown paper and twine and mailed them to Boston. Then he walked Valiente to the smithy and asked the farrier to check the horse's shoes.

"One of those Ay-rabs?" the man asked, picking up a front hoof.

"No, he's Andalusian, a Spanish horse. More docile than most stallions." Mac wiped his hand across his face, sweating in the hot smithy.

"Where you headed?"

"Oregon."

The farrier completed his inspection of Valiente's hooves. "Shoes look good. But he's an awful fine mount to put on the trail. He's no pack mule." He slapped the horse softly on the rump.

"He can go the distance." Mac handed the man a few coins.

"Thank you, sir. And good luck."

Mac led Valiente across the street and tied him outside the tavern. When the horse snuffled at his shirt pocket, Mac chuckled and pulled out a sugar candy.

Inside the tavern, a girl folded linens behind a tall table. Scrawny thing, with soft blue eyes and wavy brown hair pulled back from her face. Her calico dress was tight on her, but neat and clean. No ruffles like his mother and sisters-in-law wore.

She glanced up, not quite meeting his eye. "Can I help you?"

"You serving dinner soon? I'm looking for something other than steamboat food."

"Noon," she said. "Roast chicken. Nothing fancy, just plain home cooking."

"Sounds fine."

She skittered out of the room.

Hearing a cough behind him, Mac turned and saw two men in the corner. The older of the two sat on a stool. He was neatly dressed, and a worn holster rode his hip like he'd been born with it. The younger man, wearing a polished new holster, lounged against the wall.

The older man squinted. "Howdy, stranger," he said. "Passing through?"

"Yes, sir," Mac said.

"How long you here for?" The man's eyes narrowed further.

"Just dinner. I'm Caleb McDougall." Mac held out his hand.

"Isaac Johnson." The man stood to shake Mac's hand, then gestured at the younger man. "My son Jacob."

A clock sounded twelve, and a dinner bell rang. Mac followed the Johnsons into the dining room, where a long table was laid with several settings. A bar sectioned off the far corner, shelves full of bottles behind it. Apparently, Mac and the Johnsons were the only customers. They sat themselves at one end of the table.

The girl Mac had seen earlier brought in a tray that must have weighed half of what she did. She set it on a side table, and moved platters of steaming food to the dining table—chicken, green beans seasoned with ham and onions, fresh baked bread, pickles, and relishes. Clinking dishes and flatware broke the silence while the three men loaded their plates.

As the girl put the last dish on the table next to Jacob Johnson, she gasped. The young man's arm circled her waist. She stiffened, slid away, and scurried to the kitchen. Mac frowned at Johnson's familiarity, but he didn't know enough to interfere, so he kept quiet.

During the meal the older Johnson man—Isaac—asked Mac where he was from. When Mac replied, "Boston," Isaac asked where he was headed.

"Oregon," Mac said.

"You ridden all this way?" Jacob Johnson asked.

"Took the train from Boston to Syracuse. Horseback to Pittsburgh," Mac said. "Then steamships—down the Ohio, then up the Mississippi, now up the Missouri. I'm on the *Aurora* from St. Louis to Independence."

"We seen a fair number of emigrants pass through," Isaac said. "But you don't look like you need no free land."

"I'm not planning to stay," Mac said.

"Why you going then?" Jacob asked.

"Adventure," Mac replied with a grin.

The girl returned to remove empty platters and plates, glancing furtively at all three men. As she lifted a large dish beside Jacob, the young man put his arm around her again and pulled her close. "Have you missed me, Jenny?" he asked.

"Don't," she whispered, blanching as she sidled away.

"Fetch me and Jacob some ale, girl," Isaac ordered.

Jenny hurried to the bar. The two men grinned. She came back with two pints and handed them to the Johnsons.

Jacob emptied his mug and asked for another. When Jenny returned with more ale, Jacob ran his hand down her arm. She slapped him lightly.

Isaac sniggered. "You should be more friendly."

Jenny rushed out of the room, and the two men laughed.

"Son, go after her," Isaac said.

Jacob shrugged. "There's time."

"She doesn't seem to welcome your attentions," Mac said, unable to stay quiet any longer.

Isaac sipped his ale. "Just the innkeeper's stepdaughter. A mousy little thing. But she's welcomed us in the past, if you know what I mean."

Mousy didn't describe the girl, Mac thought. She was about fourteen and timid, but would have a pleasing face, if she weren't so skittish. She'd grow into her looks. But contrary to what Isaac said, she didn't seem to welcome the Johnsons.

A gray-haired man with a beard entered the dining room. His suspenders held up trousers over a large paunch. "Dinner's over. What else you want?" he asked.

"Same as last time, Peterson," Isaac said. "As I recall, you had a taste for it yourself."

Peterson shook his head, beard quivering. "Don't want no trouble."

"No trouble for us," Isaac said with a smirk.

Jenny returned with a rag. She wiped the table, but kept as far away from the men as she could.

Mac toyed with his hat. He should be on his way, but it felt wrong to leave the girl with the Johnsons. "May I have a pint of ale also?" he asked.

Jenny went to get it. The older Johnson patted her buttock as she passed. She shied away. Isaac followed her and put an arm around her shoulders while she poured Mac's ale. Peterson tugged on his suspenders and left the room.

Mac stood. "The lady is trying to serve my drink." He wanted to say more, but he didn't know the relationship between Jenny and the men.

"You'll get it, mister." Isaac let Jenny pass, and she handed Mac the mug of frothing ale.

Mac sipped his pint until it was gone, then paid for his meal. The two Johnson men whispered between themselves. One chortled.

Jenny flinched at the rude laughter as she took Mac's money. She gave him a quick glance. "Are you sure I can't get you another pint?"

"No, thank you." Mac hesitated, uncomfortable leaving her alone with the men, but not wanting any part of a problem he didn't understand. He tipped his hat at her. "I have a long ride ahead."

He stepped outside and took a deep breath of the early spring air. A fine day for riding.

A shout and a scream behind him interrupted his thoughts. He ran back into the tavern. Another scream sounded from the dining room, and he raced toward it.

Jacob Johnson had Jenny crushed against his chest. Her sleeve was ripped. Peterson, the heavy man, pulled at Jacob's arm. Isaac had his pistol drawn and yelled, "Let my boy be!"

"Leave the girl alone!" Mac shouted.

Isaac pointed his gun at Mac. "You keep out of this, mister."

Mac drew his own pistol and aimed. Two shots reverberated. A bullet slammed into the wall next to Mac's head. Isaac fell to the floor.

Mac froze. He'd shot the man.

Jacob pushed Jenny away and dropped beside his father. "You killed my pa!" Jacob pulled his gun and fired. A splinter flew from behind Mac.

Before Mac could respond, another shot rang out from across the room. Jacob fell writhing on the floor, holding his arm and moaning.

Mac turned. Jenny cringed behind the bar with a rifle in her hands. Peterson stood silently beside her.

Mac ran to the Johnsons and kicked their guns away. Isaac's eyes were open, staring but unseeing. Dead. Mac's stomach lurched.

Jacob thrashed and sobbed, blood seeping from his left arm. Alive. At least the girl wouldn't have a death on her conscience, Mac thought. And her shot had saved his life.

Peterson grunted as he knelt heavily beside Jacob. He pressed the boy's wound with a handkerchief.

"You killed my pa, you bastard," Jacob said to Mac through chattering teeth. His body shook. "You'll pay."

"Is there a doctor in town?" Mac asked.

Peterson ran a hand through his gray hair. "Girl, go get Doc Morgan."

"He's in Jonesboro," Jenny replied. "Mrs. Whittaker's confinement."

"Then get some towels to stop this bleeding," Peterson said. "And fetch the blacksmith to cauterize the wound."

Jenny brought towels and dropped them at Peterson's feet. "I'm not doing anything more." Her voice quavered. "You know what he was going to do."

"Shouldn't someone call the sheriff?" Mac asked. "I killed one man. You shot another, and I'll be damned if I see him dead, too."

Peterson glanced at Mac. "You just killed the sheriff. This boy bleeding here is the deputy. I reckon we'll need the federal marshal. Could be days before he gets here."

Mac sank into a chair. "Hell," he said. "Why did the sheriff pull his gun on me?"

Peterson shrugged, and Jenny stared at the floor.

"What's your role here?" Mac asked Peterson.

"I'm Bart Peterson. It's my tavern. You'd best leave. You shot in self-defense. I'll tell the marshal." Peterson looked at Jenny. "You'll say the same, won't you?"

She nodded.

"Go," Peterson said.

Mac turned for the door, eager to leave the gruesome scene behind him, but wanting to do the right thing. In the doorway, he looked back at Jenny and the men. Jacob was still—he must have passed out. Peterson continued to stanch the wound. "The marshal won't come after me?" Mac asked.

Peterson shook his head without looking up.

Mac hurried to Valiente and unhitched the horse. His hands shook. He'd never killed a man before. He leaned his head against the stallion's neck. The horse's warm flesh comforted him.

As Mac mounted Valiente, Jenny ran out of the tavern. "Wait!" She hesitated, then said, "Take me with you."

Mac stared at her.

Jenny grabbed the back of the saddle, raising her other hand to Mac. He took it without thinking. She swung up behind him. "Ride!" she urged.

Chapter 2: Jenny's Story

Mac kicked Valiente, and they cantered through town. To his surprise, no one shouted, no one followed. Soon the town was out of sight. Mac slowed Valiente to a walk.

The violence in the tavern troubled him, and he didn't know what had prompted it. He needed to reach the *Aurora* by the next afternoon, but first he had to decide what to do with the girl. "Where do you want to go?" he asked.

"Where are you going?"

"Waverly. But I can take you home first."

"Not home."

"Then where?"

"Waverly will do. I can't stay in Arrow Rock."

"Why not? Peterson said the marshal would agree we shot in self-defense. Waverly's two days from here. I can't take you that far. It wouldn't be proper."

"I don't care." Jenny's voice was no more than a whisper.

Mac shrugged. If she didn't give him another option, he'd have to take her to Waverly. "Your name's Jenny. Jenny what?"

"Geneviève Calhoun."

"Where do you live?"

"Farm outside Arrow Rock."

"I should take you there. Won't your parents worry?"

He felt her shake her head against his back.

"Why'd the sheriff pull a gun on me?" Mac asked.

"I don't know."

"You work for Bart Peterson? The tavern owner?"

12

"He's my stepfather. Mama married him last year."

"What happened to your father?"

"Suffered a fever not long after we moved to Missouri. Never really recovered. He died last year." She sighed. "I surely miss him."

She spoke with a slight Southern accent. "Where are you from originally?"

"Louisiana, where Mama grew up." That explained the Southern accent and the French name. "Papa bought land nearby, but lost it. We moved to Missouri when I was eight. Then Papa died. Mr. Peterson runs our farm now and keeps the tavern in town."

"Why won't you go home?"

Jenny shook her head again.

They passed farm houses on hills along the dirt road, some fairly prosperous, surrounded by fields of new corn, cotton, and hemp. As the afternoon heated and the sun shone on their faces, they encountered an occasional cart or solitary rider. Mac tipped his hat at the people they passed, who nodded in return.

By late afternoon storm clouds rolled toward them and a cold wind blew. It started to rain. Mac hunched into his leather jacket and pulled his hat lower on his forehead. "There's an oilskin in my saddlebag," he told Jenny. "Put it on to keep the rain off."

As daylight faded, Mac steered Valiente into a clearing off the road by a small stream. "We'll make camp," he said. "Go on to Waverly tomorrow. Need to be on the road at sunup to catch the steamboat."

Mac unsaddled Valiente and let him graze, hobbling his hooves with a length of rope. He tied a tarp to a low branch on an oak tree at the edge of the clearing. "This'll keep most of the rain off," he said.

He started a fire in front of the tarp. The wood hissed and smoked until the flames caught, but finally Mac felt heat push the cold away. He pulled hard tack and coffee out of his saddlebag and boiled water. "It's not as good as your dinner at the tavern," he said smiling, "but we won't starve."

Jenny hesitated, then took his offering.

Mac tried to make conversation as they ate. Jenny said little and watched warily as he moved about the camp. After supper he handed her the saddle blanket. She shied away like a spooked pony.

"Take it," he said. "I have a coat, and you don't. It'll get cold. Maybe rain again."

Mac checked Valiente's hobbles, then said, "Don't mess with him. He's skittish in the mornings, particularly around strangers."

Jenny tensed when Mac sat beside her. Her skirt swished as she moved as far away from him as possible while remaining under the tarp.

He took a blank journal out of his saddlebag and began to write. About the shooting. The girl. His hopes for the journey. After putting away the notebook, he lay down, huddled in his jacket, and slept.

Mac woke to the sound of water dripping. Rain pooled on the tarp above him and oozed through. His wool trousers were damp, and the smell of wet, charred wood from last night's fire wafted in the cold air.

At the sound of a shrill whinny, he bolted upright. Jenny was bareback astride a rearing Valiente. The hobbles lay on the grass between his prancing hooves.

"God damn it," Mac shouted as he ran toward Valiente, "I told you not to touch him!"

To her credit, Jenny didn't fall, but clasped the stallion's mane and bridle tightly. She looked relieved as Mac grabbed the bridle. Valiente pawed the ground, but didn't rear again. Mac held him with one hand and helped Jenny dismount with his other arm.

As she slid down, Mac caught her against him. She'd seemed like such a little thing at the tavern, but in his arms she had more substance than he'd thought. She stumbled into the bushes, retching.

"Are you hurt?" Mac asked when she returned.

"No," she gasped.

Mac allowed his temper to flare. "What in hell's name possessed you to ride him?" he yelled.

She hung her head.

"Damn it! I told you to leave him alone. Where in blazes were you going?"

"Away."

Mac grabbed her arm. "Were you stealing my horse or trying to kill yourself? What's going on?"

She didn't speak for a long time. Mac waited her out, keeping his hand like a vise on her arm.

"I'm expecting."

She couldn't mean what he thought she meant. "Expecting what?"

"A baby."

She did mean what he'd thought. She was too young. Mac dropped her arm. "Where's your husband?" he asked.

She trembled. "I'm not married. I don't know who the father is."

Shocked, Mac said, "Forgive me, but you don't look like the kind of girl who'd take up with several men."

She blushed and slumped to sit on the wet ground.

Mac waited for her to say more. He didn't want to ask again.

Jenny looked up at the trees above them where a robin sang. She spoke, stumbling over her words. "Three months ago. Before Christmas. At the tavern. The Johnsons came. Both of them. For dinner."

She stopped. Mac sat beside her.

"Jacob stared at me. Sheriff asked him if I was pretty. Jacob didn't say anything. Then his father asked, had he ever . . . had he ever been with a woman. Jacob turned red. Sheriff laughed."

Jenny plucked one green grass blade, then another and another before she continued. "After they ate, Sheriff asked for a room. Mr. Peterson gave him a key. Sheriff pulled Jacob up the stairs behind him. Asked me to bring them whiskey."

She kept plucking the grass. "I told Mr. Peterson I didn't want to. He said do what Sheriff asked. Take the bottle upstairs. So I did."

Jenny stared at the clouds and wiped her hand across her forehead. The hair bristled on Mac's neck as he waited for her to continue.

"I knocked," Jenny said, still looking skyward. Her voice was so soft Mac barely heard her. "Sheriff opened the door and pulled me in. He took the bottle. Pushed me toward Jacob. 'Have at her, son,' he said."

Tears streamed down Jenny's face. "So he did. I fought, but Sheriff held me down." Her white knuckles brushed her cheek.

Her pain was palpable, but Mac didn't dare touch her.

Jenny took a shuddering breath. "Then the sheriff. While Jacob held me. I tried to fight, but there were two of them."

At that, Mac did reach out, but she flinched, so he pulled his hand back. She sobbed, but had more to say.

"When they were through, and laughing, I sat up. Mr. Peterson was in the doorway. Watching. Sheriff said it was his turn. So he did. I couldn't do anything, couldn't stop it."

As a child, Mac had seen a kitten stoned by other boys. He'd nursed the cat back to health and cared for it until it died of old age. He'd seen callousness and evil—maybe even caused some, given why he'd left Boston. But Jenny's story angered him more than anything in his experience. Maybe killing Isaac Johnson had been God's will after all. Maybe Jacob should have died as well. And Peterson.

"Now you're with child," he said when her sobs lessened.

She nodded.

"Who knows?"

"Mammy Letitia, my old nurse. She guessed. She told Mama yesterday morning. Mama thinks it's the boy on the neighboring farm."

"Shouldn't you tell your mother the truth?"

"About Mr. Peterson? I can't. Mama's having a baby, too. In a couple of months. She's seen him looking at me. She said I was wicked."

Mac stared at Jenny. "Your mother thinks it's your fault?"

She looked at the ground.

It could be true, he thought. His mother had dismissed a servant girl in similar circumstances. "What will you do?" he asked.

"Just take me away," Jenny said. "Please. I can find work."

Chapter 3: Independence

Waverly was smaller than Arrow Rock—only a few shops and a tavern. Mac couldn't leave Jenny there. The *Aurora* was already docked and loading cargo, and Mac arranged for a room on the riverboat for Jenny.

Jenny balked. "I've never been on a ship. I can't swim," she said, hanging back on the shore.

"It's a big boat," Mac said. "You'll be safe." He escorted her to her cabin. "Here's your room."

"I can't pay."

"Don't worry."

It took three days for the *Aurora* to steam the sixty miles to Independence. Jenny stayed mostly in her cabin and kept away from the railing when on deck.

Mac watched the boat's hubbub and wrote in his journal:

> *March 31, 1847. By day the* Aurora *crewmen stoke the engine and watch the current for snags. By night they keep guard, crooning softly to themselves. We stop each day at towns along the river. Dockhands, mostly Negroes, haul boxes and bales of cargo. There's a rhythm to the work. Will wagon travel be so pleasant?*

At last they reached Blue Mills Landing, the port near Independence where wagons left for Oregon, California, and Santa Fe. Blue Mills was smaller than the bustling wharves of Boston, but wilder. The chaos and commotion fed Mac's sense of adventure. He had Valiente saddled and ready to disembark when the gangway connected.

"Let's ride to town," he said to Jenny. "We'll fetch my belongings later."

Mac pulled her up behind him, and they rode the three miles to Independence. Horses trudged in both directions on the main street, hauling carts laden with boxes, barrels, and lumber. Men shouted and swore at their teams and cracked their whips. Horses whinnied, mules brayed, oxen bellowed. Wagon wheels squeaked, chains on oxen yokes rattled.

"I didn't know Independence was so big," Jenny said weakly as a wagon rumbled past.

Mac grinned. "It's small compared to Boston."

They passed a blacksmith's shop, heat emanating from the fire inside. Mac boarded Valiente at the livery. He and Jenny continued on foot. Two old men sat on barrels outside a tavern arguing politics. A Mexican walked beside a mule loaded with bundles.

An open shop door revealed racks overflowing with merchandise. Women hurried along the boardwalks, children in tow. Near the Court House, a little girl with a parasol darted out of a store. She was about the age of Mac's nieces in Boston, and he smiled at her.

A yeasty scent wafted out of a bakery. Jenny stared in the window.

"A sweet?" Mac asked. She smiled and followed him into the shop.

"Two buns," Mac said to the woman behind the counter. He handed her two pennies and sat with Jenny at a table in the corner, savoring the sugary taste of the pastry.

"What next?" he asked.

"What do you mean?"

"I'll be in Independence for a while. Need to join a company headed to Oregon and buy provisions. Then I'm leaving. What will you do?"

Jenny shrugged. "Don't worry about me."

"You need a room and work. What can you do?"

"Cook. Clean. Wait tables."

"Maybe now," he said. "But what about when your time comes?"

"I can sew."

Mac frowned. "Do you know anyone in Independence?"

"I can take care of myself," Jenny said, lifting her chin.

"Tavern across the square needs help," the woman behind the counter said. "The Black Rooster. Their girl got married last week. Went to California. They might give you room and board."

Mac thanked her and ushered Jenny outside. They dodged a cart as they crossed the road, then walked to the Black Rooster and entered the tavern.

"I'd like a job, sir," Jenny said to a man wiping glasses behind the bar. "I worked in a tavern down river."

The man scrutinized her. "You're a tiny thing. Can you carry heavy trays?"

"Yes, sir." Jenny nodded. "I can cook, too."

The man glanced at Mac. "You her husband?"

"Friend."

"I run a family business," the man said, leering. "Maybe the saloon by the river could use another working girl."

Mac turned on his heel and pulled Jenny along with him. "She doesn't need that kind of work," he said over his shoulder.

Back on the boardwalk, Mac said, "I'll stay at a boardinghouse while I'm here. I'll get you a room, too."

"I don't have any money."

Mac didn't want to feel responsible for Jenny. But he couldn't abandon her, not after running from his Boston problems. He shrugged. "You saved my life in Arrow Rock, shooting the Johnson boy. That's worth a few days lodging."

They found a boardinghouse. "May I have two rooms?" Mac asked the proprietress, Mrs. Jenkins. "For my sister and me."

Mrs. Jenkins raised an eyebrow, but said only, "One week's rent up front."

Mac paid. He left Jenny in her room, retrieved Valiente, and returned to the dock to arrange moving his belongings to a warehouse. He would purchase equipment and provisions before he started west—but first he needed to find a wagon company.

For the next two days, Mac visited stores and taverns, searching for a company headed to Oregon. He took his copy of John Frémont's report, which he had purchased in Boston the winter before. The book showed the route Frémont had traveled to Oregon in 1842, with extensive notes about landmarks, water, and grazing conditions. This might be an adventure, but Mac wasn't a fool—travel in the West could be dangerous.

He wanted a knowledgeable wagon captain, but soon learned anyone could lead a company. Many men wanted to charge a captain's fee, but Mac didn't trust most of them. He had more experience in the wilderness than these men had.

Finally, at one tavern a grizzled Army veteran talked about taking families to Oregon. "I saw it in forty-two with Captain Frémont. Wild country," the man said. "Mostly men looking to escape their troubles. Few white women, so men took up with squaws." The man looked weathered, but spoke knowledgeably. "The land is bountiful and free. Just needs Christian family folk to settle it. I'm emigrating with my family."

"You went with Frémont? Are you following his route?" Mac asked.

"Close as I can." The man squinted at Mac, pulling on his gray whiskers. "Franklin Pershing. Who might you be?"

"Caleb McDougall."

"You married?" Pershing's voice boomed, even in the crowded tavern.

"No, sir. I've seen Frémont's book. I want a company as well managed as his. I'm not staying in Oregon. I'll return to the States next year."

"Why in tarnation would you travel two thousand miles on a lark?" Pershing asked. "I ain't taking adventurers. You want to settle, come with me. But get yourself a wife first." He turned back to his whiskey.

Mac left the tavern disappointed and returned to the boardinghouse. He wrote in his journal:

March 30, 1847. I found a Captain Franklin Pershing who traveled with Frémont and is headed for Oregon. He's the man I want leading me, but he only wants families to emigrate. How can I change his mind?

Pershing was the only wagon master Mac met who had traveled the trail. The next day Mac argued with Captain Pershing again, but the man was firm. "I'm just taking family men. People to settle the West. Find a good woman in these parts, if you want to join my company."

That afternoon Mac found Jenny in the boardinghouse parlor with Bart

Peterson.

"Your mother wants you home," Peterson said as Mac entered the room.

"She's not going with you," Mac said, moving beside Jenny. After what Jenny had told him, his fists itched to punch the portly man's jaw.

"That's for her to say," Peterson said.

Jenny hid behind Mac.

"How'd you find her?" Mac asked.

"You said you was going to Independence. All's I did was ask around." Peterson held out a hand to Jenny. "Come on, girl."

She shook her head.

"Your mother needs you." Peterson grabbed Jenny's arm.

At that, Mac threw the man against the wall, one hand squeezing Peterson's fat neck, the other fist ready to strike. "She's not going with you," he said again, this time through his teeth.

Jenny shied away from both men. "I won't go. Tell Mama I love her."

"Get out," Mac said, shoving Peterson toward the door.

Peterson looked from Mac to Jenny. "Seems you're a whore after all," he said. He stormed out of the house, slamming the door behind him.

Jenny's face was white and her hands shook.

Mac led her to a chair. "I see why you can't go home."

She nodded, biting her lip.

Mrs. Jenkins pulled Mac aside after supper. "What're you going to do about the girl? I heard the argument this afternoon. She ain't your sister. None of my business why she won't go home. But she can't stay here."

"She doesn't have anywhere else to go," Mac said.

"You brought her, she's your responsibility." Mrs. Jenkins wagged her finger at him, like his old nurse had done when he was a boy.

"She just tagged along." He knew Mrs. Jenkins was right, but he didn't want the obligation.

"You know she's in the family way?" Mrs. Jenkins asked.

He nodded.

"I can't keep her here." Mrs. Jenkins was adamant.

Mac spent a sleepless night. He'd behaved dishonorably in Boston and yearned to escape his guilt. Now he'd killed a man and assumed an obligation to Jenny. And the best wagon captain he'd found wouldn't have him. His adventure to Oregon was already a struggle.

He saw only one solution—a way to solve both Jenny's problems and his desire to join Pershing's company. He would have to take her with him.

The next morning he found Jenny alone by the fire, mending linens for Mrs. Jenkins. "What will you do when I'm gone?"

She shrugged. "I'll manage."

"And when the baby comes?" Mac asked gently.

"I don't want it." She trembled. "Maybe it will die. Or I will."

Mac turned away and looked at the fire. Her response confirmed his decision, though he'd fought against it all night. He could not let her do harm to herself or the child. "You have to come with me," he stated.

Jenny stared at him. "I can't go to Oregon."

"Well, you can't stay here," Mac said. "I found a captain who's been to Oregon and back." He paused. "There's just one hitch. He wants married men in his company."

Jenny's eyes widened with dread. "I can't marry you," she whispered.

"I didn't say we were getting married. But I'll tell Captain Pershing we are."

She stood. Her sewing fell to the floor. "It's wrong to live a lie."

"I can protect you better if people think you're my wife."

Mac worked feverishly for the next two weeks to prepare for the journey. He persuaded Pershing that he and his bride would be ready to leave by mid-April. He found a carpenter to build a wagon of aged hickory for two hundred dollars. He purchased tools and provisions.

He dickered over the price of oxen. "You'll need at least six," he was told. "Eight's better. Mountains wear 'em out."

"I've heard mules are faster," he said.

"Maybe. But they're stubborn. Oxen'll do whatever you want. And they need less water."

He bought eight oxen for twenty-five dollars each.

Every storekeeper in Independence recommended provisions for the journey. He compared their lists with what he'd read in Boston. Soon barrels and sacks of food and extra wagon parts filled his rented warehouse stall. He chalked a space on the floor the size of the wagon bed, and wrestled with his supplies, piling boxes and barrels on top of each other. Damn it, he thought as he worked, how would it all fit?

Mac was lucky to afford the warehouse. Most emigrants camped in fields outside town, covering their provisions with tarps. Animals grazed near the camps creating a muddy, odiferous mess.

Finally, he wrote in his journal one evening:

> *April 14, 1847. We leave tomorrow at dawn. God willing, we will travel safely in Captain Pershing's hands.*

Chapter 4: Setting Out

Jenny sat in the parlor stunned after Mac announced he would take her to Oregon. Pretend to be his wife? She wanted to scream at him that she couldn't go, she wouldn't go. But what were her choices? She refused to return to Arrow Rock. She had no work in Independence. Mrs. Jenkins didn't want her in the boardinghouse.

Mac had been kind so far. That didn't mean she wanted to go to Oregon with him—married or merely pretending to be. He was a man, after all—large and fearsome. Still, he was the only person who had shown her compassion since she'd been raped. A part of her had thrilled when Mac's strong arms had grabbed Bart Peterson, though she hated being the cause of any violence.

All day Jenny deliberated. But she had no choice—she had to go with Mac, even if the journey killed her. At least she wouldn't be alone.

When Mac returned that evening, he dumped bolts of calico, a cloak, and a sunbonnet on the sofa where she sat. "You have two weeks to make some clothes. We leave on the fourteenth. I've ordered a wagon and joined with Captain Pershing. Twenty wagons in his party."

"I can't be ready in two weeks." She panicked at the thought of actually leaving Missouri.

"I'll help," Mrs. Jenkins told her. "You'll be ready."

Blown like a dust mote, Jenny had no choice.

Jenny spent her days sewing with Mrs. Jenkins. The women made two loose blouses and two skirts with drawstring waists. Mrs. Jenkins assured

24

her the garments would fit until the baby came. The dress Jenny had worn from Arrow Rock grew tighter every day.

Mac was away most days. Buying provisions, he said, though she didn't know what he bought. She hoped he knew what he was doing. Not that she could be any help.

One evening Mac asked her, "Do you know how to read and write?"

She nodded. "The sisters in New Orleans taught me. And then Papa."

He handed her a small bound journal. "I'm keeping an account of my trip," he said. "You should, too."

"Who will care what I write?" she asked.

"You might find some comfort in it."

In her room that evening she thumbed through the blank pages. Their emptiness gave her no comfort. She was sick every morning from a pregnancy she abhorred. Only Mac's kindness kept her from loneliness, shame, and destitution.

Maybe certain disgrace in Arrow Rock would have been easier to face than the unknown wilderness. But at the thought of Mr. Peterson, Jenny shuddered. She had to follow Mac.

She dipped her quill in ink and wrote:

Friday, April 9th—In six days I start for Oregon. Will I survive?

On the Sunday before they left, Mrs. Jenkins took Mac and Jenny to church. "You need the good Lord's blessing for your journey."

Jenny choked back a sob as she tried to sing the familiar hymns.

"Plenty of folk leave homes and kin behind," Mrs. Jenkins said, patting her arm. "You'll be fine."

When they returned to the boardinghouse, Mrs. Jenkins handed Jenny a bundle. "Muslin. For the baby," the older woman said. "And a Bible for you to record its birth."

Tears welled in Jenny's eyes. She stammered her thanks.

"I stuck in a little piece of lace. Make yourself a collar," Mrs. Jenkins said. "You'll need something elegant living among the heathen."

On her last night in civilization, Jenny wrote in a shaking hand:

Tuesday, April 14th—We leave tomorrow. Mrs.

Jenkins has been kind. Now, only God can help me.

Wednesday morning, while the dew still sparkled, Mac assisted Jenny onto the wagon bench, and they pulled away. She looked back, her stomach roiling from sickness and fear. Mrs. Jenkins waved from the porch.

They joined Captain Pershing and his company at the outskirts of town. Mac introduced Jenny to the sturdy, whiskered man.

"You ain't very big, Miz McDougall, are you?" Pershing shouted.

Jenny's face burned. It was wrong being called "Mrs. McDougall." "Call me Jenny," she said.

Surrounded by bellowing oxen, barking dogs, and yelling children, Mac steered the wagon into line. The caravan plodded down the road toward Kansas Territory. Some people walked, some drove their mules from the bench, some hid in wagons. Animals strained with their loads, and mothers warned children to keep away from hooves and wheels.

That first day Captain Pershing rode back and forth alongside the wagons issuing warnings. "You'll tip over at the first big hill," he told one family, making them rearrange furniture, barrels, and bushel bags.

He inspected the teams. "Mule'll be dead before the Platte, if'n you don't keep that harness from chafing."

Jenny watched from the wagon. The swaying made her bones ache, but she didn't want to talk to anyone. Mac told her the wagon ahead of theirs belonged to a doctor and his wife from Illinois. When they stopped at noon, she met Captain Pershing's wife and seven children, ranging from two young men almost Mac's age to a toddler.

By sundown, the wagons arrived at Cave Springs, thirteen miles from Independence. "I wish we'd made better time," Mac said. "But Pershing says we shouldn't push it. This is the last settlement in the United States. Tomorrow we reach Kansas Territory."

The emigrants laughed and sang as they prepared their first evening meal. Mac showed Jenny how to cook over a campfire. "I used to camp with my grandfather," he said. She knew so little about him.

With his instructions and her sidelong looks at women bent over neighboring fires, she managed to fry beef and bake an apple cobbler in a Dutch oven.

"Make your bed in the wagon," Mac told her after supper. "It's flat on top of the crates. I'll sleep underneath."

Jenny awoke the next dawn when Mac poked his freshly shaven face in the wagon and touched her shoulder. Startled, she gasped and pulled her blanket to her chin.

"Sorry," he said. "We need to get moving. I'll hitch the oxen. You fix coffee and biscuits."

She dressed quickly, holding back her nausea until she clambered down and ran outside the wagon circle. Mac had started a fire, but it burned too hot. The biscuits she baked scorched before she knew it. When Mac returned, she handed him a plate. "I'm sorry," she said, choking back tears.

Mac looked at the black pellets. "Where's the honey?" he asked.

She gave it to him, along with a mug of coffee.

He chuckled. "We both have a lot to learn. Took me an hour to yoke the oxen. They won't move unless I slap them."

As they packed to leave, a drizzly fog settled over camp. Jenny couldn't tell if the mist rose from the ground or fell from the sky. The twenty wagons filed onto the road.

Rain drummed on the canvas cover all morning. Jenny rocked along inside the wagon. The motion made her nausea worse, but she'd get wet if she stuck her head outside. Mac donned an oilcloth cloak and rode Valiente beside the lead ox.

The only trees grew along creeks and next to isolated houses. Fewer farms dotted the open land the farther they traveled from Independence.

In late morning they reached the Blue River, swollen from spring rains. The road led straight down one bank and up the other. Deep, muddy ruts showed where previous wagons had crossed. It was a small obstacle for a man on horseback, but the first significant water the wagons had to cross.

"Line up," Captain Pershing called.

Jenny looked at the rushing stream. Her stomach spasmed in terror. "You know I can't swim," she said to Mac.

"It's only waist deep," Mac said, shaking his head. "Stay in the wagon.

Warn me if the load shifts." He guided the oxen into line.

When their turn came, Mac drove the team into the stream. "Hang on," he told Jenny. She clutched the wagon box and peered ahead.

The teams' pace didn't falter as they splashed into the river, though one ox bawled. Swift water rose against the wheels. Jenny gripped the wagon box as it rolled unevenly over sunken rocks. She sighed in relief when nothing spilled, and Mac led the oxen up the muddy west side to high ground.

Others were not so fortunate. A shout rang out as a bag of flour floated downstream before sinking.

"Why didn't you tie that down?" Pershing yelled.

"Seven years bad luck," a woman wailed when a mirror splintered into shards. Jenny shivered.

The rain ended while some of the wagons were still crossing. The doctor's wife ambled over to Jenny. "Why don't we walk a spell?" she invited.

Jenny smiled and climbed down.

"I'm Elizabeth Tuller," the older woman said. "From Springfield, Illinois."

"Geneviève Calhoun . . . McDougall now, I guess," Jenny said. "Call me Jenny. Mac told me your husband's a doctor."

Mrs. Tuller nodded. "I suspect you'll be looking for his help sometime along the way."

Jenny felt her face flush. "Is it obvious?"

"Child, when you've been bringing babies into the world as long as Doc and I have, it's easy to see."

"Do you have children?"

Mrs. Tuller paused a long moment. "We had three boys. All dead now. Two died as children. Fever. The oldest was crushed by a horse last fall. The doctor couldn't bear to stay on our farm after that. All I have left is the rocking chair where I held them as babes. And memories."

"I'm sorry," Jenny whispered.

"The Lord's ways are mighty strange," Mrs. Tuller said. "Taking the young and sending old men on a fool's journey." She shook her head. "Menfolk run from their troubles. Can't face their grief."

Jenny had run from her own troubles, but couldn't escape them. She'd only found more. She wondered for the first time whether Mac was running from anything. He hadn't talked about his life in Boston. But then, she hadn't asked him.

Despite the Blue River crossing, they made better time that second day. In late afternoon they stopped at Lone Elm campground in Kansas Territory. A single tree rose above the prairie. Beyond the open field the horizon stretched vacant to the west. Jenny smelled fresh grass, already trampled by hooves and wagon wheels.

After supper she asked Mac. "Why are you going to Oregon?"

Mac's blue eyes squinted toward the sunset. "I like new places. Nothing newer than a country that's never been settled."

"Don't you have family?"

He nodded. "Parents. Two older brothers and their families."

"Don't you miss them?" After two days on the trail, Jenny already missed her home, despite the circumstances under which she'd left.

"I'll go back when I'm ready."

Chapter 5: Across Kansas Territory

Shortly before noon the third day, the trail split. A small wooden sign bore two arrows—one pointed south to Santa Fe, the other north to Oregon. Mac grinned. They were in Indian Territory now.

"Last chance for Santa Fe," Captain Pershing shouted. "But we're Oregon bound."

Through the afternoon, the wagons crawled along the ridges of low hills and splashed through valley creeks. The ground was wet and the wild grasses fragrant.

Mac rode Valiente beside his lead ox to guide the team. Jenny walked with other women, talking with Captain Pershing's oldest daughter. He couldn't remember the girl's name. He had enough trouble remembering who the men were.

He knew the doctor, Abram Tuller, a somber man, who spoke plain common sense. Captain Pershing, of course, and his oldest son Ezekiel, a few years younger than Mac's twenty-four. Several farmers whom Mac couldn't yet name, and a Negro carpenter named Tanner. All with families, as Pershing had demanded.

The day after Mac had told Jenny he was taking her to Oregon, he'd found Pershing sipping whiskey in the tavern again. "You said if I had a wife I could join you," he'd told the captain.

Pershing narrowed his eyes. "You married now?"

"I will be when we leave." The lie came more easily than Mac had thought it would.

Pershing nodded his agreement, and Mac bought enough food and supplies for Jenny, throwing in a blue sunbonnet as his last purchase.

He was surprised she hadn't argued more about the journey. So far, she worked without complaint on the trail. Didn't talk much, though. Mac hoped their fellow travelers wouldn't ask many questions. He and Jenny hadn't agreed on a story. She didn't seem like a good liar, and he wondered if their ruse would hold up. He hoped it would last until it was too late for Pershing to send them back.

"That hill have a name?" Mac pointed at a rise ahead of them.

"Blue Mound," Pershing said. "Marks the Wakarusa crossing. Take your purty wife to the top. Nice view."

Mac rode over to Jenny, who now walked with Mrs. Tuller. "Want to climb the hill?"

"Who'll watch the wagon?" Jenny asked.

"I'll walk by your team a spell," the doctor's wife said. "Doc's minding ours. You two go on."

Mac pulled Jenny up behind him on Valiente.

"The prairie goes on forever, doesn't it?" she said when they reached the top.

"Sure does. There's the Wakarusa." Mac waved at a narrow ribbon of water. "Kaw's in the next valley. Can't see it yet."

"So many rivers," she whispered. It seemed the Blue River hadn't cured her fear.

That evening he wrote:

April 16, 1847. Camped on the Wakarusa. Tomorrow we cross.

It rained during the night, and the river rose three feet. In the morning Mac and the other men stood on the bank staring at the churning brown water.

"Can we cross?" someone asked.

Pershing pulled at his beard. "We'll have to float the wagons," he said. "Lighten the loads first."

The travelers unloaded half their belongings, floated the remainder across in the wagons, emptied that portion, and returned for the rest of their provisions. Ferrying their goods across took the whole day. Men and women alike were tired and dirty by evening. Mac saw Jenny wobble in fatigue and wipe a hand across her forehead.

"We'll stay here," Pershing ordered, after the last wagon crossed.

"Stay?" complained a farmer named Samuel Abercrombie. "We ain't gone nowhere. Got to move faster, if'n we want to reach Oregon afore winter."

Pershing shook his head. "Slow and steady. Some days we'll make good time. Not today. Dry out your belongings tonight. I'd planned to rest on Sundays, but not tomorrow. We'll have a prayer and a song, then head out."

Mac sat beside the fire that evening and wrote,

April 17, 1847. Wakarusa crossing took all day. The wilderness beckons, but it is hard work getting there. Men grumble at Pershing—for some, he moves too slowly; others want him to take a Sabbath rest. He has a rough manner, but knows what he's doing.

Mac's breath steamed in the frosty morning air. His muscles were sore from yesterday, and he still wasn't used to sleeping on hard ground. After breakfast the travelers followed Pershing in a prayer and "Amazing Grace." Jenny's voice rang out sweet as a meadowlark's before it caught on the last verse, "And grace will lead me home."

Later Mac walked with her beside their oxen. "We ought to have a story about how we met," he said quietly.

"What?" She stared at him in surprise.

"Someone will ask. We need to tell the same story."

"More lies." She sounded resigned.

He didn't like lying either, but they were committed now. "We can say we met in Arrow Rock where you lived. That's not a lie."

"All right."

Mac glanced at her. "No need to talk about killing anyone. Or running away."

She nodded.

"Just . . . we met, we fell in love, we married."

"Love." She sighed.

"Well, isn't that how it's done?" Mac tapped his whip on the lead ox's rump to get the team moving faster.

"How what's done?"

"Getting married."

"Sometimes." Jenny smiled. "Mama and Papa loved each other. But she married Mr. Peterson to have a man to run the farm."

Mac shrugged. "My parents get along well enough, I suppose." He'd never thought about their relationship. He'd done what they told him, until he discovered they weren't as well-meaning as he'd thought. Then he'd left.

In the afternoon the sun shone warm, the grasses dried, and many emigrants walked ahead of their wagons. Mac easily spotted Jenny in the new blue sunbonnet he had bought her. Most of the women wore drab browns or faded pinks.

He rode over beside her. "Want to ride a while?" he asked.

She nodded, and he pulled her up behind him. The horse pranced a few steps, then settled back into an easy gait.

"Are you getting to know the other ladies?"

"A few," Jenny responded. "Mrs. Tuller's very nice. So sad, though. All her children dead."

"Maybe that's why the doctor's so solemn."

"And Mrs. Pershing," Jenny said. "I've walked with her and her daughters Esther and Rachel."

"Esther's about your age."

Jenny nodded. "She seems older. Then sometimes she's so silly."

"Silly?"

"Oh, you know," she said, blushing. "About boys."

Mac grinned. "Is she sweet on someone?"

"Daniel Abercrombie. His father Samuel's a farmer from Tennessee."

"Good lad, Daniel."

"Lad?" Jenny laughed. "He's almost as old as you. Old enough to be thinking about marriage."

Chapter 6: Crossing the Kaw

Tuesday, April 20th—Camped on the Kaw. The river rages from spring run-off, its water muddy as the pigpen back home. A hundred or more wagons waiting to cross.

Jenny's hand shook as she looked up from her notebook and gazed at the river. They had traveled three days since the Wakarusa and now waited in line at the Kaw ferry.

The journey thus far had been slow. Jenny had bounced in the wagon until her bones ached or walked through tall grass that caught in her skirt. She amused herself for hours watching a solitary tree on the horizon, imagining what animal it resembled until she drew near enough to see individual leaves.

Now she faced the tedium of waiting. The Kaw ferry was nothing more than two dugout canoes covered with a log platform. It carried just one wagon at a time, rocking as the current pushed at the canoes.

Men shouted as they pulled each wagon onto the ferry with ropes. Then two Indians at the stern dug into the river with long, thick hickory poles to push the craft across the river. Two more Indians pulled on a guide rope tied to both shores to keep the ferry from floating downstream.

Jenny had seen Indians in Missouri, but these men were wilder. They wore beads and feathers with mismatched plaid shirts and trousers and spoke only broken English.

"One dollar a wagon," the ferry master shouted. "Pay me when your wagon gets in line."

"Dollar here, dollar there," Samuel Abercrombie griped. "If I had so many dollars I wouldn't be going to Oregon. Ain't there another way?"

"There's a ford a few miles upstream," Captain Pershing said. "But no telling 'bout the spring currents. River bottom could be scoured deep."

The Pershing company opted for the ferry, but several men decided to swim their teams across, rather than pay the ten cent per head fee.

"The ferry doesn't look very steady," Jenny said to Mac.

He smiled down at her. He was so tall. "Why are you so afraid of the water?"

"*Mon oncle*," she said. "Mama's younger brother. He threw me in the bayou when I was small. I was choking before Papa pulled me out."

Jenny lay awake most of the night. The crowds waiting to cross never quieted down. The sun was high before their turn came. The ferry master ordered them into line, marking his notebook as each paid.

"*Allons-y*," he cried. "*Vite! Vite!* Move quickly!"

Jenny stared. "*Vous parlez français!*"

"*Oui*," the man replied. "Joseph Papin, mademoiselle, *à votre service*."

"I'm not French," Jenny said. "But my mama is. From Louisiana."

"And I, mademoiselle, am French Canadian," Papin said. "Come. I help you myself. For you, *café* with my wife in my home." He led Jenny toward the ferry. Mac followed, frowning.

"Who are you, monsieur?" Papin asked.

"Her husband," Mac replied.

"Such a young girl, married. *Tant pis.*"

"I need to stay with my wagon," Mac said. "Will she be safe?"

"As if she were my daughter. I will escort her myself."

Papin helped Jenny onto the log ferry and sat her on a barrel with a formal bow. "Do not worry, *ma petite*. Very safe. No one drowned this year." Papin untied the boat and shoved it off. "Take her to Josette," he told the Indian ferryman.

Jenny clutched the barrel tightly as water swirled against the dugouts underneath. The Indian polemen levered the boat toward the landing on the far side.

Oxen, cattle, and mules swam beside the ferry, churning the muddy water into a roiling froth. Her stomach lurched at the smell of rotting plants and manure. A calf squealed and went under, kicked by the hooves of larger animals.

One edge of the ferry platform dipped beneath the water. Jenny screamed when waves washed toward her feet. The Indians thrust all their weight against their poles to level the boat. As the platform righted, water sloshed back into the river between the logs.

"Do the poles ever break?" Jenny's voice quavered.

One Indian flashed a smile of white teeth against dark skin. She wondered whether he understood or merely reacted to her fear.

When they reached the north side of the Kaw, another Indian lifted Jenny off the logs. She pulled away, frightened by his rough grasp, but without his help her shoes slipped and squelched as she tried to walk up the slimy bank.

The ferryman shouted at a woman with light brown skin on the shore, "Josette, Joseph say give girl coffee."

The woman beckoned. "Come," she said. "It is quieter in the house." She led Jenny to a low wood-framed building. Inside, she motioned Jenny to sit at a small table, then put a pot on the stove to boil. "I am Josette Papin," she said, in French-accented English.

"Geneviève . . . McDougall. Do you speak English or French?"

"Both," Mrs. Papin said. "I am French Canadian and Kansa Indian, but I speak English."

Jenny stared. A squaw! But Mrs. Papin was dressed like anyone else—calico dress, hair pulled back in a large black bun. And the house looked like many in Missouri.

"Isn't it . . ." Jenny searched for the word. Did Indians think like she did? "Isn't it wild here?"

"We are on Kansa land. My home. How can it be wild?"

A baby cried from a cradle across the room. Mrs. Papin smiled. "My son. You will have a son, too, I think."

"Why do you say that?" Jenny asked.

The woman laughed. "Every mother wants a son to care for her when she is old."

Jenny hadn't considered whether her baby would be a boy or a girl. She tried not to think about it at all, and refused to contemplate raising a child by herself.

Mrs. Papin handed her son to Jenny and turned to pour coffee.

The infant was dressed only in a long shirt. Jenny held him awkwardly. She had never held a baby before. His dark eyes stared back at her solemnly. She lifted him to her shoulder. He smelled of milk and moss, and his hair was damp with sweat. "He's beautiful," she said.

"Of course." Mrs. Papin smiled, then rummaged in a cupboard. "Here," she said, holding out a piece of soft leather. "For your child's first moccasins."

"Thank you," Jenny said.

After drinking coffee with Mrs. Papin, Jenny left the house and watched the other wagons in the Pershing company cross on the ferry. Three men on horseback plunged after a lost barrel that rolled out of one wagon. Men worked feverishly to rehitch teams and move the wagons away from the riverbank.

It took until late afternoon to reassemble wagons, animals, and provisions on the north shore of the Kaw. As the last wagon climbed away from the river, Mac came to get Jenny. She thanked Mrs. Papin and caressed the baby's cheek as she left. She hoped her child would be so sweet.

"Move out," Captain Pershing shouted. "Next company needs the space."

They plodded two miles along the Kaw through grassy bottomland. Mac trudged beside the lead oxen through deepening shadows. He stumbled over a rock and swore softly. He was so muscular that Jenny thought he could never tire, but he must be weary now.

She climbed down from the wagon. "I'll walk by the team," she said. "You rest."

Chapter 7: Company Rules

April 21, 1847. Crossed the Kaw. One family lost a chair when the ferry tipped. Jenny is French, or partly so, and speaks the language better than I do.

"Things ain't dried out from yesterday," a farmer named Hewitt grumbled to Mac as they rounded up their teams in a cold rain. After less than two weeks on the trail, Mac could hitch his oxen in half the time it took the first day.

"Listen up," Captain Pershing told the men, his hands on his hips. "We're deep in Indian territory now. Best work together instead of arguing."

"I thought this was a Christian group," someone called out. "Why didn't you keep the Sabbath last Sunday?"

"It's two thousand miles to Oregon." Pershing thrust his bearded jaw forward. "I can't molly-coddle any greenhorns. At the Kaw I met another captain. Man named Dawson. We talked 'bout divvying up our groups based on speed." He squinted at the men. "We'll rendezvous with Dawson at Potawatomie tomorrow night. Decide what you want to do."

When they left camp that morning, Doc Tuller walked next to Mac. "What does Pershing mean about splitting up?" the doctor asked.

"Men are complaining," Mac replied. "Those herding cattle can't move as fast as those without. Slower wagons don't want to eat the dust of those ahead. Some folks want to rest on Sundays, others to press ahead."

Tuller shook his head. "These men ain't used to taking orders. Farmers are independent cusses. Pershing's an Army man."

"So they make each other mad." Mac grinned.

"You're a lawyer, right?"

Mac nodded. "Haven't set up a practice yet."

"Speak up when we palaver, lad. You're young, but you seem to work hard and have some sense. Maybe you can help us get along."

The doctor's praise warmed Mac as he strode beneath driving rain. He'd started this trek as a lark, but had taken on a duty to care for Jenny. Maybe he'd earn a voice among the men. His father and older brothers had never thought much of what he had to say.

Foul weather continued all day. That evening they stopped near a small creek. Mac wondered how far behind the company from Westport was.

April 22, 1847. Made twelve miles. Talk is of splitting up. Each man eyes the others, wondering if we will still be together tomorrow.

Ominous low clouds hung in the sky the next morning. Mac left Jenny walking beside the wagon and rode Valiente.

"How you like Pershing?" Samuel Abercrombie asked him. Abercrombie, from Tennessee, was related somehow to Daniel Boone and acted like he knew everything. Most likely, he didn't. Abercrombie's older son Douglass was married with two daughters. The younger son, a grown lad named Daniel, was unmarried. The family had two wagons crammed full of possessions.

"Pershing knows the trail," Mac said. "That's my concern."

Abercrombie spat tobacco juice. "There's more to being captain than knowing which way's west. I seen Indians fight the Tennessee militia. You trust Pershing to fend off savages?"

"I'm hoping we won't have any fighting."

"Oh, there'll be fighting. Me and my boys can shoot, but we can only do so much. Need the whole company behind us. Don't you worry 'bout your little wife?"

"Of course," Mac said. "But I'm more concerned about the terrain and weather than Indians."

"Got to worry about it all, boy."

Jenny and Mac ate their noon meal with the Tullers. "You want to stay with the cattle or move faster?" the doctor asked.

"Faster, I hope," Mac said. "Only two families here have cattle."

The doctor rubbed his chin. "Aye. Hope those folks take a liking to the Dawson company."

Through the afternoon Mac talked with many others. Some men wanted the strength of a large company, others wanted speed. Some mentioned resting on the Sabbath, but as one man said, "If we git to Oregon, there's years to make square with the Lord. If we're caught in snow come fall, we die."

Shortly before dusk they arrived at the Potawatomie reservation. The Indian treaty land didn't look any different than the wide expanse of Kaw valley prairie they had crossed.

"They say Jesuits are starting an Indian school," Pershing said with a snort. "But ain't no sign of black robes yet."

As the last light of day ebbed, the Dawson wagons straggled into camp. It took them an hour to settle, herding a hundred head of cattle behind them. Their wagons creaked with unbalanced loads, pots and tools clanging from ropes on the sides. The Pershing company looked sharp in comparison.

After supper the men of both companies gathered. Pershing passed a bottle of whiskey around the circle. "As I said in Independence," he began, "this here's a family train. We'll do what we can to keep the Sabbath, but I won't let that slow us down. We'll go at my pace and stop when I say." He scratched his bearded chin, looking at Abercrombie. "Anyone can't follow orders shouldn't stay with me."

"I got folks moving cattle to Oregon," Jem Dawson said. "We'll travel a mite slower, but there's plenty of time afore winter. So anyone wants to follow me, be glad to have you. By the same token, any in my company wants to go with Pershing, no hard feelings."

"What kind of watches will we have?" Abercrombie asked, handing the whiskey bottle to Mac.

"Platoons of four or five wagons each," Pershing said. "With a sergeant over each group."

"Why's that?" Mac asked.

"So's the same folks don't eat dust every day," Pershing responded. "Platoons will rotate the lead. I'll call our starts and halts each day, choose the campsites, set the guards." He took the bottle from Mac, gulped a swallow, and belched. "For now, my sons and me will scout, but I'll assign more men to scouting if need be."

"We want about twenty wagons to follow each of us," Dawson said. "Any fewer, and we can't defend ourselves."

"We'll divvy up based on speed," Pershing said. "I'll take the fast group. Dawson'll take those with herds or who need to travel slower."

Who would agree to travel slower? Mac wondered.

"Dawson and I are walking out toward the prairie. Line up behind the man you choose. If the split ain't close to even, he and I'll make the call." Pershing turned on his heel and marched away.

Mac watched the two captains stride out of camp, then followed Pershing. Samuel Abercrombie was next to him, and Dr. Tuller not far back.

"So you'll go with Pershing?" Mac asked Abercrombie.

"I ain't fond of him, but I'm for speed."

The men from the Pershing company with cattle headed after Dawson, as did a farmer with a large family including elderly parents.

A short distance from camp, Pershing counted the men following him and tallied their wagons. "Twenty-two. Lost three families with six wagons. Picked up five families, eight wagons among them." He nodded. "No need to swap any with Dawson. Next step is electing sergeants. Need five. Any volunteers?"

"I'll do it." Abercrombie stepped forward.

"I nominate McDougall," Dr. Tuller said.

"Ain't he kind of young?" Pershing squinted at Mac.

"He's a lawyer. Can keep order," Tuller said.

"Who from the Dawson group?" Pershing asked. "Ain't playing favorites."

A mustached man waved his hand. "Josiah Baker. Been second to Dawson since we left Westport."

"All right. Abercrombie, McDougall, Baker. How 'bout Mercer and Hewitt?" Pershing pointed at two farmers. "You five divvy up the remaining wagons. McDougall, put my family in your group."

Sounded like Pershing didn't think he could handle a platoon. Mac shrugged. So be it. His group ended up with his own wagon, Pershing's two, the Tullers, and the Negro carpenter Tanner, who was the last to be assigned.

"Sergeants, set some rules. McDougall, write 'em down. We'll go over them tomorrow." Pershing took his bottle and walked back to camp.

April 23, 1847. We reorganized our company, and I am a sergeant. What would my father think? Probably not much more than Pershing does.

Chapter 8: Prairies and Rivers

Jenny walked with Esther Pershing ahead of the wagons. The scent of grass and wild thistles tickled her nose. A lark warbled, and she looked up to see a pair of birds dancing across the clear sky. "It's a pleasure to be in front of the wagons, not in their dust," she said.

"Aye," Esther said. "And a fine view ahead."

Jenny wondered if Esther meant the blossoming prairie or Daniel Abercrombie striding several yards in front of them.

"Let's walk with Daniel." Esther lifted her skirt and sprinted through the grass. When she reached the young man, she clutched his arm and gestured toward Jenny.

"Morning, Miz McDougall," Daniel said, when Jenny caught up.

"Call me Jenny." It was silly for Daniel, who was about nineteen or so, to call her "Mrs. McDougall." Particularly when that wasn't her name.

Esther giggled. "Jenny's way too little to be so proper. Why, she's younger than I am."

Esther stepped away from Daniel as her mother approached. Several young children trailed behind Mrs. Pershing.

"Nice morning, ain't it?" Mrs. Pershing said.

"Mighty nice." Daniel tipped his hat. "I was about to ask Esther and Jenny to climb the hill over yonder." He gestured at a mound to the north.

"You and Esther take the young'uns," Mrs. Pershing said. "Jenny, would you walk with me?"

"Yes, Mrs. Pershing."

After Daniel and Esther led the children away, Mrs. Pershing said, "Captain tells me you and Mr. McDougall were married in Independence." Her voice was cold.

43

Jenny blushed and nodded.

"Mrs. Tuller says you're in the family way."

Jenny nodded again.

"When you expecting?"

"September, ma'am."

"Captain Pershing ain't aware of your condition, most likely. Or he might have had a thing or two to say to Mr. McDougall about joining this company."

Jenny was silent.

"My concern, girl, is my children," Mrs. Pershing said. "I don't want them seeing or hearing anything indecent. Esther in particular. She's silly enough already. You keep quiet on when you was married. I'll make sure Captain Pershing don't spread it about."

"Yes, Mrs. Pershing." Explaining wouldn't help, Jenny decided.

"Don't give me any cause to regret being charitable," Mrs. Pershing said, her mouth a thin line. "I have to protect my family."

Jenny lifted her face to the warm sunshine. Would she ever be rid of that day in December? "How old are your children, Mrs. Pershing?"

"Let's see." The chill left the older woman's voice. "Ezekiel's twenty—we call him Zeke—and Joel eighteen. Captain sure is proud of them two. Then there's Esther at fifteen. Rachel's twelve. David and Jonathan—the twins—are ten. Ruthie's eight, and little Noah four."

Jenny glanced at Mrs. Pershing, then looked away.

Mrs. Pershing gave a short laugh. "Yes, girl, I've another babe coming in July." Her expression saddened. "Captain's left me alone so much. Twenty-one years in the Army. We've rarely spent more'n a few months at a time together. He's only been home for one of my confinements. I told him last year he wasn't leaving me no more. So now we're all going to Oregon." She sighed. "Who knows what'll become of us?"

By midafternoon black clouds roiled on the western horizon as the wagons lumbered into a shallow valley. "Better stop," Captain Pershing yelled. "Storm's coming." Jenny could barely hear him over the wind.

They circled the wagons and herded the horses in the middle, oxen nearby. As they finished, hail started to fall, small at first, but soon in chunks of ice as large as Jenny's fist. The travelers scurried into their wagons.

Animals bellowed, crowding close to avoid the sharp crystals. Valiente stuck his head under the raised wagon cover, frustrating Mac's attempt to lower the sides. The canvas tore as Mac and the horse struggled. Jenny grabbed at the frayed edges.

"Missouri thunderstorms aren't this bad," Jenny said. "Here there's nothing to slow the wind."

The hail didn't last, but rain continued to pour in diagonal sheets. Thunder rumbled across the prairie, lightning flashes coming nearer and brighter until they seemed right overhead. Huge drops bounced everywhere. Even the oxen bawled in fear. Horses and mules raced about the circle panicking. Jenny tried to hold the wagon cover together and got as wet as if she'd been out in the rain.

"She's loose," a man cried. Glancing out the back of the wagon, Jenny saw a gray mare race across the prairie, highlighted by bright lightning.

"Don't let the rest follow," another man shouted. "We'll never catch 'em!"

Mac and other men ran into the rain, holding their hats against the wind. They soothed the horses before more could escape.

Pershing rode up as Mac climbed back in the wagon. "Need extra guards," the captain said. "Four men riding circuit. Two hour shifts. Set the schedule for your platoon."

Mac took the first watch, leaving Jenny to mend the soggy wagon cover. She tried to sew an oilcloth over the hole Valiente had torn, but as she worked rainwater pooled in the oilcloth and trickled down inside the wagon. So she covered the food sacks with a blanket and hoped the caulking on the flour and sugar barrels held.

Too wet to cook. She ate a cold biscuit and set two more aside for Mac.

Jenny shivered in the damp wagon, despite her wool cloak. She pulled out her journal, but it was too dark to write. Mac had told her never to light a candle in the wagon, for fear of fire.

For hours lightning flashed eerily on the empty prairie followed by thunder crashing all around her. Jenny tried to get comfortable, but she was cold and wet. How had she come to this place? So far from home. Alone. She wept.

A faint flutter moved her belly. It passed, then came again.

The baby. It must be. Her baby kicking. Maybe she wasn't alone. Jenny pressed her hand to her stomach and smiled.

The next morning the sun shone, the sky bearing no sign of the prior night's storm. But everything in camp was drenched, the grass in the wagon circle uprooted by panicking animals' hooves. It was Sunday. Captain Pershing declared a rest day, but Mac and other men went out searching for the missing mare, not returning with her until afternoon. Those left in camp assessed the damage to wagons and provisions and cleaned up as best they could.

After supper the company made music. Fiddlers played the Oregon song and someone sang:

> *To the far, far off Pacific sea,*
> *Will you go, will you go, dear girl with me?*
> *By a quiet brook, in a lovely spot*
> *We'll jump from our wagon and build our cot!*
> *Then hip-hurrah for the prairie life!*
> *Hip-hurrah for the mountain strife*
> *And if rifles must crack, if we swords must draw,*
> *Our country forever, hurrah! hurrah!*

Jenny was headed for the far Pacific, but she didn't see much hip-hurrah about prairie life. Would she even make it to Oregon? And her baby? Her hand cradled her belly as she sat by the fire.

Monday they plodded through more rolling prairies and arrived at the Red Vermillion River in late afternoon. A French Canadian named Louis Vieux ran a ford across the river, charging a toll for his Indians' assistance.

Early Tuesday morning the emigrants forded the stream. Like the Indians at the Papin ferry, the tribesmen wore a mix of leather and cloth. In a patois of Pawnee, English and French, they somehow communicated with the emigrants. Pershing's men and the Indians worked together to brake the wagons with ropes to lower them down the steep banks.

Jenny waited near the bank for Mac to tell her what to do. She wouldn't cross until she had to.

When most of the wagons were across, Mac lifted Jenny on Valiente behind him, and they rode across the river. She trembled when her feet hit the water. She tightened her arms around Mac and buried her head in his broad back until Valiente made it up the far bank.

Walking beside the wagon Wednesday morning, Jenny wondered if she would ever get used to river crossings. Now that she'd felt the baby move, she worried about her child as well as herself. If she wanted the baby to live, she had to stay alive, too. It was too late to change her decision to leave Missouri. Now she had to survive the journey.

The prairie rolled on, waves of grass swaying in the breeze. The trail climbed away from the Kaw, though from hilltops Jenny could sometimes see the river behind them. Birds sang, perched on tall grass stems or from the occasional scrubby tree.

Wednesday night they camped beside the Big Vermillion. Jenny stood with Mac, Captain Pershing, and his sons Zeke and Joel as they studied the river.

"Must be seventy yards wide," Mac said. "And fast. See the eddies?"

"Tricky crossing." Pershing pulled at his beard.

Children played on the riverbank, carving their initials into cottonwoods. "If'n I don't make it," one of the Pershing twins said, "At least someone will know I came by here."

Jenny smiled. "Carve my initials, too," she said. "Who knows how far we'll get?"

The boy laughed. "I was just fooling," he said.

"Carve my name," she insisted. "You may not be afraid, but I am."

April 28th—I fear tomorrow's crossing, but nothing seems to bother Mac.

When they lined up the wagons in the morning, Jenny sat on the bench. Her stomach was nauseated, and not because of the baby.

Mac walked over with Zeke Pershing, the captain's oldest son. "Zeke'll sit with you," Mac said. "I'm riding Valiente near the lead team. I thought you might want company."

Jenny smiled at Zeke, who climbed up beside her. "Hang on," he said, tapping a whip on an ox's back.

They rolled forward faster than Jenny thought prudent. She closed her eyes and gripped the bench, whispering a prayer.

A woman ahead of them shrieked. "My baby!"

Jenny opened her eyes and saw a small child in the water downstream. She screamed and clutched her belly.

A man dove into the water, went under, and came up splashing as he flailed toward the tot. Mac abandoned the oxen and turned Valiente toward the rescue.

Zeke thrust the whip at Jenny and jumped into the river.

Jenny hugged the switch close. The oxen bellowed, thrashing in the water. Mac glanced back. "Keep going, Jenny," he yelled. "Don't stop."

Jenny's stomach rose to her throat as she cracked the whip over the oxen and shouted. The wagon lurched from side to side over the rocky bottom. She peered at the men in the water, but couldn't see the child.

When Jenny reached the far bank, she sighed in relief. Someone grabbed her oxen and led the wagon to dry ground. From the safety of shore, Jenny gazed into the churning brown current. Mac, still in the water on Valiente, held a small body over his shoulder. Zeke floated alongside, grasping Mac's saddle. No trace of the other man. Jenny whimpered in fear.

Valiente climbed out of the river, Zeke staggering behind. A woman— Mrs. Purcell, whom Jenny didn't know well—seized the child from Mac. A little boy, about four years old. "My baby!" she cried.

Doc Tuller laid the boy on the ground, pounded on his chest, stopped, then pounded again. The tot puked up water and began crying when his mother clasped him to her breast. "Thank you," Mrs. Purcell whispered to the doctor, burying her face in the boy's wet hair.

Then she froze. "Charles?" she said. "Where's Charles?"

"That your husband, ma'am?" Zeke asked. "I couldn't get him. He went under."

The woman wailed, clutching her child, who cried harder. Her keening turned to screams.

Mrs. Tuller gently took the boy away. "I'll get him dried off," she said.

Mrs. Pershing and Jenny assisted Mrs. Purcell into her wagon. "Does she have other children?" Jenny asked Mrs. Pershing over the sobbing woman's head.

"Two. They're with my brood. I'll get 'em."

Jenny embraced the woman until Mrs. Pershing brought back two children—a girl around eleven and a boy of eight. Eyes large and solemn, they rushed into their mother's arms.

Jenny stepped away. She found Mac at the water's edge staring downstream, along with the doctor and several others.

"They found his body," Mac said. "Two men are bringing it back now."

Thursday, April 29th—Crossed the Big Vermillion. Mac and Zeke Pershing saved a child, but the boy's father, Charles Purcell, drowned, leaving his wife and children alone. Tomorrow we bury him on this God-forsaken prairie. What would I do without Mac? Yet I have no hold on him.

The next morning men dug a pit and collected stones to protect the buried body from wild animals. Then the emigrants gathered around the gravesite.

"The Lord is my shepherd; I shall not want," Captain Pershing began. Jenny barely heard the familiar psalm. How many more would they bury before Oregon? She feared for herself, for her baby, for Mac.

After the psalm, Pershing cleared his throat. "Lord, into your hands we commend the soul of our brother Charles, who gave his life for his child. May he dwell with you forever. Amen."

Mrs. Purcell sobbed into a handkerchief. Her older two children's faces were pale. "Where's Pa?" asked the little boy who had almost drowned with his father.

"He ain't coming with us no more," his sister said.

Chapter 9: North to the Platte

Mac rode with Zeke Pershing beside the wagons, grass brushing their horses' bellies. "Shame we couldn't save Purcell," Mac said.

Zeke sighed. "I grabbed the child. Thought Purcell could take care of himself."

"Doc says he probably hit his head on a rock."

"You worry about Miz Jenny?" Zeke asked.

"Jenny?"

"You're mighty lucky. She's a purty girl. I'd worry if she was mine, 'bout something happening to me."

Mac didn't know what to say. "I suppose I worry."

"I ain't found a girl yet I'd want to marry. How'd you know she was the one?"

"I guess I just knew." The lies might get harder along the way, Mac thought.

The wagons headed north through low rolling hills. "We get to the Big Blue tomorrow," Pershing said at the noon halt. "Last big river afore the Platte. The Blue's a trial to cross."

Mac joined Samuel Abercrombie's hunting party in the afternoon, and they shot several antelope. By the time they dressed the meat and returned to the wagons, it was dark.

Jenny smiled at the fresh provisions. "I can simmer a stew on coals through the night," she said. "We'll eat it hot in the morning and cold at noon. Save the loins to fry tomorrow night. I'll make enough for the Purcells."

While Jenny added water and spices to the meat, Mac wrote:

April 30, 1847. Buried Charles Purcell this morning, our first death. Yet I am grateful for a solid wagon, a full belly, and pleasant company.

"Today we'll reach Alcove Springs, this side of the Big Blue," Pershing said in the morning. "Stay there for the Sabbath tomorrow, and cross on Monday. If'n the water's not too high."

When they reached the Big Blue at midday, the current swirled around rocks high up the banks. "Can't cross here," Abercrombie said.

Pershing squinted. "This ain't the crossing. This here's Blue Rapids. Alcove Springs is a few miles upriver."

Through the afternoon the wagons lumbered along the river. Near dusk they reached a spring under a stone overhang. Clear water spilled over the rocks, with thick grasses growing in soft earth near the stream.

"It's so green," Jenny said. "The flowers are starting to bloom." She knelt and scooped a handful of water. "Mmm," she said after sipping. "Tastes good. And cold."

At dawn the next day, after a quick breakfast of stew, biscuits, and coffee, Mac set out with another hunting party, despite the Sabbath. Pershing said they'd more likely find buffalo on the far side of the Blue, so the hunters splashed across on horseback.

"We'll scout the trail, too," Pershing said. "Not much water through here, so we'll have to stick close to the Blue till we cut north to the Platte."

"I'm after a buffalo," Abercrombie said. "Scout all you want, but don't hold me up."

Pershing pulled his beard. "No need to get testy. If there's any buffalo about, they'll be near the river."

The men rode until the sun was midway over the horizon.

"Look," Daniel Abercrombie said. "Ain't those buffalo chips?"

Pershing dismounted and scuffed the dung with his boot. "Yep. Old, though. No telling if they're still around."

They found fresh dung farther on. In the next valley a herd of buffalo grazed. "Must be a thousand," Mac said, awed by the huge number of massive beasts.

Samuel Abercrombie spat. "Let's go."

"Careful," Pershing said, holding out a beefy arm. "Buffalo are fast." He pointed out a canyon to the south. "We'll drive 'em that way. Need some men to sit at the end of the valley, ready to shoot when they jam up in the narrow. Rest of us'll ride down both sides of the valley, herding 'em ahead of us. Wait till I wave my hat to start."

Abercrombie grumbled, but agreed to lead the party of shooters.

"For God's sake, don't get in front of the buffalo. They'll mow you down in a stampede. Don't get caught in the crossfire," Pershing said, jamming his hat down on his head. "And don't shoot more'n two or three. Whole company can't carry or eat any more afore the meat spoils."

The men rode quietly into position. At Pershing's signal, the herders yelled and galloped forward, sending the buffalo into the narrow ravine, dust flying behind them—a melee of noise and confusion. Abercrombie's men started shooting. Several buffalo dropped.

When the surviving beasts stampeded away, the men found five dead animals. "Need to butcher 'em here," Pershing said. "Can't carry the carcasses back to camp. We need a wagon."

"I'll go," Daniel Abercrombie said.

"Bring more men back to help."

Later Daniel returned with an empty wagon and several men to butcher and load the meat. It was supper time when the weary hunters returned to camp. The whole company dined on fried buffalo steak, then parceled out the leftover meat, arguing over who had shot the animals and who should get which cuts.

May 2, 1847. Killed our first buffalo. Magnificent beasts and good eating. While we hunted, others caught turtles at the spring. We ate well tonight— buffalo steak and turtle soup.

Rain fell Monday morning. Mac hunched into his jacket and pulled his hat low on his forehead. The Big Blue was rising, but still passable.

"Need to get moving," Pershing said, scratching his whiskers. "Water'll come up fast."

The first wagons crossed easily, but the river lapped at the wagon beds of the last in line. Mac steered the Purcell wagon across, Mrs. Purcell and her children fearful and sobbing. Then he returned for Jenny and his own wagon.

Jenny's white knuckles gripped the bench. "Still afraid?" he asked, heading the oxen into the water.

"I'll think of poor Charles Purcell all the way to Oregon." She gasped when the muddy river surrounded the wagon, but they crossed without mishap.

The land past the Big Blue was a treeless plateau, which they traveled for three days. Buffalo chips were plentiful. At first, the children laughed while gathering the chips for fuel, but soon they complained when chancing upon a still damp, smelly patty.

On the third day Mac met with Captain Pershing and the other platoon leaders. "We cross dry land tomorrow," Pershing told them. "Twenty-five miles to the Platte. No water."

Mac relayed the news to his platoon and to Jenny. "Fill up all our water barrels tonight," he said.

Pershing called reveille when the sky was barely gray. While the men hitched the wagons, the women handed out biscuits. No time to brew coffee. The company set out for the Platte before full light, heading almost due north across a highland with views for miles in every direction. The rising sun lit dewdrops on the tall grasses.

"Is that another wagon train?" Jenny asked, pointing at a procession of wagons four abreast approaching from the east.

Mac nodded. "Must be the trail from St. Joseph," he said. "Pershing said the trails meet near the Platte."

"So many people. All headed for Oregon." Jenny shook her head. "How can they all want to travel so far?"

"Adventure." Mac smiled.

They stopped for a brief noon meal. Jenny ladled a bowl of cold turtle soup for Mac. "It'd be better hot. But the onions flavor it."

"Fills me up," he said. "That's what counts. Still a long way to the river."

In late afternoon a voice from the front of the train shouted, "Platte!"

Mac kneed Valiente ahead to see, then cantered back to Jenny. "It's enormous," he said. "Broad as the ocean. At least two miles wide."

The blue sky darkened into gray, and the setting sun reflected off the wide expanse of water, glistening red and silver. "It's wider than the Mississippi," Jenny said to Mac when the wagons arrived at a ridge overlooking the river. "Will we have to cross?"

"Not here," Mac said. "We travel along the Platte for days. The ford's upstream. It's not deep. Wide, but shallow. Don't worry."

The animals stomped and bellowed to get to the water.

"Don't let 'em run," Captain Pershing shouted. "Hold 'em steady. Can't have 'em breaking a leg."

Mac spurred Valiente to walk by the lead oxen. He pulled hard on their yoke to keep them in line.

Thursday's long trek to the Platte wearied everyone. Mac was glad when Captain Pershing decided to lay by on Friday, but others complained.

"We need to move along," Abercrombie argued to Pershing. "That St. Joseph group, their teams'll eat all the grass, if'n they get ahead of us."

"There's grass enough," Pershing said. "Besides, if we wait, we won't vie with them for the better campsites."

Abercrombie snorted. "Sleep in their trash, you mean." He strode off to his wagon.

Only sparse cottonwoods grew along the banks of the broad Platte. "Looks like the sea on a calm day," Mac said.

"Don't be fooled," Pershing said, scratching his whiskers. "Looks big, but it ain't. Full of quicksand. Barely drinkable. Not sure it could float a canoe. That's Grand Island out yonder, but ain't nothing grand about any of it."

"But the river leads us to Oregon?"

Pershing nodded. "Seems to be its main purpose on God's earth. Warn your platoon about the quicksand. Don't let nobody near the water alone. And guard the animals, or they'll sink faster'n you can get a rope around 'em."

Mac spent the morning inspecting equipment and provisions. So far, no serious wear on his wagon. One side plank had cracked, and he talked to Tanner about replacing it.

"No good wood 'round here, Mr. McDougall," Tanner said. "Need hardwood. Oak or ash."

"I have extra boards. Man in Independence told me to bring some."

Tanner shook his head. "Save 'em for when somethin' serious breaks."

"If you think that's best. How's your family holding up?" Mac asked.

"Doin' all right, Mr. McDougall. Doin' all right. Wife don't like the dust and all, but I've told her won't be no dust in Oregon." Tanner grinned. "Sure hope I'm right, or I'll be hearin' 'bout it the rest of my days."

"And your sons?" Tanner had two small boys.

"They ain't never had so much fun. Botherin' ever'body in camp."

"Put them to work," Mac said with a smile. "They can tote water for the women. But don't let them near the river without you or their mother nearby. It's dangerous."

"Yes, sir. We'll keep 'em busy."

After the noon meal Mac hunted near camp. He only shot a few quail, but Jenny was happy when he brought them back to camp.

"Larger game's been run off by all the people," Pershing told him later. "Two more companies arrived today."

"Where are they from?"

"All over," Pershing said, shaking his head. "Group downstream's from Indiana. Over yonder's from Missouri."

"Makes you wonder what they think they'll find in Oregon, doesn't it?"

Pershing frowned at Mac. "A better life. Ain't that what we all want?"

"Of course," Mac said. He sometimes forgot the rest of the company was heading to Oregon to stay.

After supper as the sinking sun turned the river from silver to gold, Mac wrote:

> *May 7, 1847. On the Platte. Wide and smooth, but I'm told the sands will suck down an ox until it drowns. Full of dirt, but not enough to grow anything. Is this really the path to a better life, as Pershing believes?*

Saturday the emigrants arose to sunshine and traveled along the south bank of the Platte in good spirits. Mac left Jenny to tend the wagon and rode Valiente to scout with Captain Pershing. At midday they met a group of Army surveyors.

Pershing greeted Lieutenant Montgomery, the officer in charge, whom he knew from his military days. "What's the Army doing here, Lieutenant?" Pershing asked.

"Washington's decided to move Fort Kearny." Montgomery snorted. "Just built the blockhouse last year, but now the generals say it's too far east. We need to be farther west to protect emigrants from Indians."

"Any skirmishes this year?" Pershing asked.

Montgomery shook his head. "Indians mostly want trade. Stole a couple horses from one wagon company, but that's it. But Washington says to move, so I'm surveying. Come next year, the Army'll be somewhere near here."

"Army never changes." Pershing grinned. "I'll leave young McDougall here to mark a campsite while I go back for the wagons." Pershing gave a half-hearted salute to Montgomery and rode off.

Mac marked space for their wagons to circle that night, making sure it had good access to the river. He hobbled Valiente and walked over to the surveyors.

"What makes a good fort location?" he asked Montgomery.

"Water, good visibility, close to the trail. We've been riding along the Platte for two weeks looking at sites. We'll make our report and let the generals decide. When they choose, we'll lay out the plan for stockades and buildings." Montgomery squinted at Mac. "Pershing said you're a college man. Why are you going to Oregon?"

"To see new lands."

"Thought Pershing was settling families in Oregon."

"My wife is with me," Mac said.

"Staying in Oregon?"

"I'll decide once I get there."

Montgomery shrugged. "Long trip if you're not planning to settle."

The wagons reached the campsite in late afternoon. Another company had also camped nearby. There was not enough wood, so the children gathered buffalo chips. There were plenty of those, though no sign of live beasts.

Pershing announced the next day—Sunday again—would be another day of rest.

"God damn it, we laid by yesterday." Abercrombie threw his hat on the ground. "You just want to jaw with Montgomery."

Pershing squinted. "Go on, if you want. But the rest of us are staying."

After supper the emigrants and the soldiers congregated. Bottles of whiskey circulated, and the group talked and laughed.

As the sun set two fiddlers played. They started with "Rock of Ages" and other hymns, moved on to "Coming Through the Rye," then to "Durang's Hornpipe" when the call came for dancing.

Mac smiled as Daniel Abercrombie bowed in front of Esther Pershing and offered her his hand. Jenny's foot tapped to the music. When the next song began, Mac leaned over. "Shall we dance?"

She shook her head. "Don't know how."

"I'll teach you," he said, standing and pulling her up. "Come on. It's easy."

She was tense in his arms, watching her feet.

"Relax," he said. "Just move where I take you."

She glanced at him. In the flickering firelight he saw her bite her lip.

"Close your eyes," he said.

They fluttered shut for a moment, and her rigid back began to relax. Then she stumbled. He caught her, but she pulled away.

"I can't," she said, and hurried to their wagon.

Mac watched the dancers after Jenny left. Daniel sat beside him. Esther spun by, dancing with one of the soldiers.

"Esther sure is purty, ain't she?" Daniel said.

Jenny was prettier, Mac thought, though Jenny never flirted. "Lots of pretty girls."

"Why's she spending time with the soldiers? I'd dance with her all night."

"Tell her, not me," Mac said, getting up. "Think I'll turn in."

He spread out his bedroll under the wagon. No sound from Jenny above him. He remembered her body softening briefly in his arms as they danced. Yes, Jenny was prettier than Esther.

Chapter 10: Roadway of Nebraska

Sunday, May 9ᵗʰ—Prayers this morning. Now I shall spend our day of rest sewing shirts for the baby. Mac is hunting again.

Jenny laid out the muslin Mrs. Jenkins had given her on top of a barrel. Mrs. Tuller sat in the rocking chair she had brought from Illinois. "This all you have, child?" Mrs. Tuller asked.

Jenny nodded.

"Not much preparation for a first baby."

"No, ma'am," Jenny said. "We decided very suddenly to make the journey."

Mrs. Tuller frowned. "But surely . . . ." Her voice trailed off. "No matter." She smoothed out a piece of cloth and marked where to cut with a piece of charcoal. "We'll make the shirts big to last a while. Baby won't mind."

Mrs. Pershing walked over with a pile of clothes in her arms and her younger children trailing behind. "I have mending," she said. "These young'uns rip something every day. And I'll cut down Zeke's and Joel's shirts for the twins."

"Got any scraps?" Mrs. Tuller asked. "Jenny needs diapers."

"Gracious, girl!" Mrs. Pershing said. "Don't you have rags of your own?"

Jenny shook her head. "No. Though maybe I will by the time the baby comes."

"Not enough." Mrs. Tuller laughed. "Never enough diapers. We'll ask other folks to save their rags for you, too."

"How many do I need?" Jenny asked. She hadn't realized caring for a baby would be so hard.

"Depends on how much washing you want to do. I boiled 'em clean every day." Mrs. Pershing sighed. "Thought I was done after Noah. But here I am again."

Mrs. Tuller stared at the horizon with tears in her eyes. Perhaps she was remembering her dead sons.

Esther sauntered over in late morning with a piece of embroidery in her hands. "I don't much care for fine work, but there's nothing else to do." She sighed and plopped down beside Jenny.

"You mean because young Daniel's out hunting," her mother said.

"Ma!" Esther's cheeks reddened.

"You do right to blush, girl," Mrs. Pershing said. "You spend too much time with that fellow."

"Daniel seems like a nice young man," Mrs. Tuller said.

"Maybe," Mrs. Pershing said, sniffing. "Too soon to tell."

The women cooked the noon meal and fed the children. Some of the older boys played in the Platte, walking across it with a rope to measure its width. "Be careful," one mother said. "Remember the quicksand."

Zeke Pershing returned from the hunt in midafternoon. "Killed eight buffalo," he told the women. "We're butchering 'em in the field so's the Army wagon can haul back the best pieces. Pa says be ready to pack the meat."

"So much for keeping the Sabbath," Mrs. Pershing said, sighing. She stood heavily and trudged to her campsite.

The women boiled water to cook the tougher cuts of meat and sharpened knives and saws to cut haunches into roasts.

When the hunters returned, Mac brought Jenny a heavy bundle. "I shot one," he said. "Made a trade with the Army cook—the raw skin and half the meat for a cured hide he had. Now you have a buffalo robe."

Jenny's lips curved in delight as she smoothed the wooly hide. "Thank you," she said, beaming up at Mac. He was kind, even if she was scared of him at times.

The emigrants worked by firelight to butcher the carcasses.

"It's a shame to throw away so much," Jenny said. "We only have space to keep the best cuts."

"The wolves will eat what we leave," Mac said. "Nothing in the wilderness gets wasted."

Jenny spread the buffalo robe under her bedding that night. It smelled musty but was soft and warm. She smiled again as she snuggled into Mac's thoughtful gift.

Monday Jenny awoke to pounding rain. She wanted to stay burrowed in the buffalo hide, but dragged herself out of the wagon and started breakfast. Mac was busy with the oxen, his hat pulled low on his forehead.

"One ox has a sore hoof," he said. "I'll have to herd that pair unhitched today. Can you drive the wagon?"

Jenny nodded. "How long before he can pull again?"

"Don't know. Good thing the land's flat. The other six can handle the wagon fine. But I can't trust the loose pair not to wander."

Jenny sat on the wagon bench with the buffalo hide around her shoulders. The heavy skin kept most of the water off her skirt, but her sunbonnet funneled rivulets down her back. She gave up trying to stay dry and sat in the pouring rain, whip ready to tap the team to keep them in line.

Even short one pair of oxen, she kept up with the other wagons easily. Some families only had four oxen or mules, though most had six, and Mac and the Abercrombie wagons had eight.

At noon Mac offered to switch places with Jenny and let her ride Valiente and herd the loose team.

"I'm all right," she said. She'd spent her morning alone worrying how she would care for her child by herself in Oregon. And whether she would love a child conceived in hate.

She missed her mother, despite the poor terms on which they had parted.

That night Jenny wrote:

> *Monday, May 10th—Mac gave me a buffalo skin which kept me warm all day. The fresh meat tastes mighty fine. Made 18 miles today, despite rain and missing one yoke of oxen.*

Rain continued on Tuesday, and the lame ox was no better. Jenny's back and legs ached from sitting in the jolting wagon, but she kept driving, lost in her thoughts. She fretted about what others would think when they learned she and Mac weren't married. Someday they would pay the price for lying, she was sure.

She watched antelope in the distance grazing in the rain without a care. She wished she had as few troubles as the antelope.

In midafternoon the Dempsey wagon pulled out of line, followed by the Tuller wagon. "What is it?" Jenny asked Mac.

"Mrs. Dempsey's confinement," he said. "The Tullers are with her."

"In the rain?" Poor Mrs. Dempsey giving birth in the wilderness. For the first time Jenny wondered where she would be when her baby came—another worry.

The downpour eased in late afternoon. When the wagons stopped in a small ravine running into the Platte, children gathered buffalo chips, but found only rain-moistened patties. Jenny started her campfire with grass, then slowly added the chips, which smoked and stank.

Another company with two French Roman Catholic priests was camped nearby. Most of the Pershing group refused to speak to the black robes, but Jenny said, "I'll pray with you." She and her baby needed all the prayers they could get. The priest blessed her and prayed with her in French.

Mac asked her afterward, "Are you Catholic?"

"My mother is," she said. "Papa wasn't. We attended Protestant services in Missouri, but Mama taught me the French and Latin prayers."

Mac smiled. "Boston's the same," he said. "Most folks are Protestant. But the Papist church is growing. I figure God listens to all of us."

"Sometimes it doesn't seem so," Jenny said. God hadn't heard her prayers the day she'd been raped. Now she had a baby coming. And a dangerous journey ahead.

As Jenny finished washing the supper dishes, the Dempsey and Tuller wagons pulled into camp.

"A beautiful little girl," Mrs. Tuller told Jenny.

But when Jenny went to see the baby, it was red-faced and mewling, not like the solemn Papin boy. "How sweet," she told the proud Mrs. Dempsey, worrying again about whether she would love her own child.

Chapter 11: Indian Trouble

Early morning sunshine woke Mac on Wednesday. The lame ox had improved enough to hitch to the wagon. Mac enjoyed the travel west along the Platte, through a wide valley with rolling hills to the south. Their company made good time and passed three other groups. Thursday brought them more of the same.

Each day Samuel Abercrombie took a few men hunting while the wagons rolled along the river.

"Don't know why he's always hunting," Pershing grumbled to Mac. "Buffalo will be around for weeks yet. Don't need more meat."

Abercrombie returned Thursday evening with a bloody haunch tied to his saddle. "Shot five antelope," he said, gesturing at his companions with similar loads. Flies buzzed around the new kills. "Fresh game again tonight."

"What'd you do with the rest of the meat?" Doc asked.

Abercrombie shrugged. "Indians'll take our leavings. Unless wolves or coyotes get there first."

Mac ate the buffalo stew Jenny had made and listened to Abercrombie boast from across the campsite, "Mighty fine antelope steak!" The man was hard to take.

> *May 13, 1847. Abercrombie delights in plaguing Pershing. Can they travel all the way to Oregon together? Making good time—over 30 miles in two days.*

Thursday night shots woke Mac from a heavy sleep. "Indians!" a man shouted. Women and children shrieked inside the wagons. He grabbed his rifle and joined others milling around camp.

"I seen 'em," Lennox, a farmer from Ohio, said. "Indians herding our horses in front of 'em. Look." He gestured at a gap in the circle. "Wagons ain't chained together."

"God damn it," Pershing said. "I've told you fools every night to check. Who was on guard?"

"Me," Lennox said sheepishly. "Musta dozed off."

"Christ!" Pershing said. "How many horses gone?"

"Five. Near as I can tell," Lennox said.

"Two of 'em's mine," said Polk, a man in Baker's platoon.

"Saddle up!" Pershing ordered. "We'll track 'em down."

"Jesus," Samuel Abercrombie said. "It's pitch black, and my horse was rode hard yesterday."

"If you'd stay near the wagons, he'd be in better shape." Pershing turned away from Abercrombie. "There's plenty of men without you."

Abercrombie cursed, but saddled his mount with the others.

Pershing sent men east, west, and south. "Hope they didn't go north," he said. "But I doubt they'd cross the Platte at night."

Mac rode south all night with Pershing, Polk, and four others. The sky was clear, the air cold.

Shortly after dawn they crested a sandstone hill to find a small Indian camp in the ravine beyond—about thirty makeshift huts clustered near a corral holding a dozen or so Indian ponies and five larger horses. Mac wondered how Pershing planned to retrieve the horses without getting shot.

"I see my mounts," Polk said. "Let's go!"

"Not so fast." Pershing held up a calming hand. "Only seven of us, and a slew of Pawnee. We'll walk down friendly-like."

"Ain't no friends of mine," Polk muttered. "Stole my horses."

They rode slowly downhill toward the Indian village. The dwellings weren't much—scraggly tree limbs covered with mismatched animal skins. Ten Pawnee men rode out to meet them, wearing hide shirts decorated with porcupine quills, bird feathers, and animal claws. One man's headdress sported a white wolf's tail hanging down the side. A necklace with a bear claw circled his neck. The chief, Mac thought.

"You have our horses," Pershing said, gesturing toward the Indian's corral.

"No." The wolf tail swung back and forth as the chief shook his head.

"They were taken from our camp last night."

"No take. Found on prairie."

"They're ours."

"In Pawnee corral."

"We'll pay," Pershing offered.

"God damn it," Polk said, pulling out his rifle. "They're horse thieves! I ain't paying to git my own mounts back!"

Two Pawnee flanking the chief pointed their guns at Polk. The chief raised his hand to hold his men back. "How much?" he asked.

"One blanket for each horse," Pershing said, ignoring the brandished weapons. His Army experience had made him a steely devil, Mac decided.

"Horse worth more."

"You've only had 'em one night."

"Gun, too," the chief said.

Pershing shook his head. "No guns. I'll throw in a knife." He took out his Bowie knife and handed it to the chief. "Good knife."

Polk spat in disgust. Mac eased his hand toward his rifle, just in case.

The chief touched his thumb to the blade. He turned to his men and said something in Pawnee. All but the two braves beside him turned and galloped back to camp.

The chief nodded at Pershing. "We bring horses your camp. You give blankets. I keep knife now." He and the remaining two braves followed the others.

Polk snorted. "They know where our camp is. They took 'em."

"Most likely," Pershing said. "But we'll get our horses back, and nobody gets shot. It was our damn fault for not securing the wagons."

The sun beat warm on Mac's back as the men returned to camp. He was impressed Pershing had negotiated for the horses without violence. He hoped the meeting in camp would go as well.

"Each man that lost a horse needs to give a blanket," Pershing ordered. "Polk, need two from you."

"I got just one blanket for each of my family," Polk said.

"Then find someone with extras and trade." Pershing folded his arms across his chest.

Polk cursed, but went to his wagon and returned, throwing two blankets down at Pershing's feet.

The Indians rode into camp, herding the horses. Pershing gave the Pawnee chief five blankets, and added a small bag of tobacco. "Keep away from our camp," Pershing said.

Abercrombie snorted and spat. "They'll come begging every night, if'n you treat 'em nice. Indians only understand buckshot."

"Double guards tonight," Pershing ordered. "And stay awake."

May 14, 1847. Spent the morning chasing horses. Bought them back from the Pawnee, thanks to Pershing's steadiness. Only made ten miles after noon.

The next day began with damp drizzle. As they got underway, a party of Indians rode along the crest of the hills south of the Platte. Mac pointed them out to Pershing.

"Stay close to the wagons today," the captain said. "Pass the word."

Mac sat with Jenny through the rainy morning, Valiente tied behind the wagon.

"Weren't you scared of the Pawnee yesterday?" Jenny asked.

"Some," Mac said. "But Pershing handled it well."

"Daniel told Esther that Captain Pershing gave them too much for the horses."

"What's a few blankets?" Mac said. "Horses are more important."

"I suppose," Jenny said. After a moment she continued, "Every tribe we see seems stranger than the last. Less civilized."

"Not used to white folks, I guess," Mac said. "Pershing says the Pawnee roam the prairie. The village we saw was a temporary camp."

"Will they follow us?"

Mac pointed to the Pawnee riders on the hill crest. Still following.

Chapter 12: South Fork of the Platte

Saturday, May 15ᵗʰ—Even after we lost sight of the Pawnee, I felt them staring at me as I fixed supper.

More cold rain fell Sunday morning beneath heavy, dark clouds. "No point in laying by," Pershing decided. "Women can't wash. Men can't hunt with Pawnee nearby. We'll move on."

The emigrants bundled into their wagons and headed along the Platte. Jenny sat in the Tullers' wagon for company, leaving Mac alone. The doctor drove while the women sat under the cover, sharing Jenny's buffalo robe for warmth.

"Listen to the children," Mrs. Tuller said. Jenny heard shouting and laughter from other wagons. "They need to run, even in the rain. But Captain won't let them, not with Pawnee around."

The women tried to sew, but couldn't in the jostling wagon and dim light. "Can't open the cover, because of the rain. And can't light a lantern for fear of fire," Jenny complained.

Mrs. Tuller put away her mending. "You've plenty of time to sew for your baby. How you feeling these days?"

"I'm past the sickness," Jenny said. "I feel it moving."

Mrs. Tuller smiled. "What a blessing."

"I don't know the first thing about rearing a baby." Jenny worried about more than tending her child—could she even love it?

The older woman laughed. "You'll learn."

"What was the hardest part for you?" Jenny asked.

Mrs. Tuller's face stilled. "Seeing 'em sick. Nothing I could do. And the constant fear. Fear they'd get hurt. Fear they'd die."

"I'm sorry," Jenny said. "I didn't mean to make you remember your loss."

"Memories are all I have, dear. I don't mind."

The doctor coughed from the wagon bench.

At noon they stopped for a quick meal. Jenny fried buffalo meat and flapjacks over a smoky fire made of chips dried and stored before the rain hit. The lean meat left hardly any grease for the flapjacks, which stuck to the skillet and burned.

Jenny huddled in her wagon during the miserable afternoon, until Esther ran over to the backboard. "May I join you?" Esther asked.

Jenny smiled and nodded. She called for Mac to halt the oxen so Esther could climb in.

"Tomorrow," Esther whispered to Jenny. "Will you walk with me and Daniel?"

"If it's nice," Jenny replied.

"I'll bring Rachel or Ruth, so you have someone to stay with you."

"Where will you be?"

Esther's eyes sparkled. "Walking ahead with Daniel. How'm I going to get him to declare with other people around?"

"Declare what?"

"That he wants to marry me! How'd you get Mr. McDougall to ask you?"

Jenny looked to see if Mac was near, but he was walking by the lead ox. She didn't know what to tell Esther. "It just happened."

"Didn't you know he would?"

Jenny shook her head. "I was very surprised." That much was true.

"Well, I won't be," Esther said. "Ma says the Lord helps those who help themselves."

"You've only known Daniel a month." Jenny couldn't imagine wanting to be married.

"He's handsome enough, ain't he?"

"His father's a tyrant."

Esther shrugged. "I ain't marrying his father."

"What do your parents think?"

The older girl shrugged again. "I haven't asked 'em. Of course, Daniel will have to ask Pa. But Pa'll let me do what I want."

"And your mother?"

"Ma wants me married."

After supper the rain let up, and a rainbow shone in the distance. Jenny spread out wet blankets and towels, hoping they would dry before sunset.

Sunday, May 16ᵗʰ—A wretched rainy day. Tomorrow I will walk with Esther, though I wonder at her foolishness.

The sun shone Monday morning in a sharp blue sky. Jenny packed her dry blankets and towels back in the wagon.

"Want to ride Valiente with me?" Mac asked. "You were cooped up all day yesterday. Zeke'll mind our wagon."

Jenny smiled. "I told Esther I'd walk with her, but I could ride a while first. If the Pawnee are gone."

"No sign of them. I thought we'd look for buffalo. You haven't seen the herds yet, have you?"

"Not any big herds. Just strays along the river."

Mac pulled Jenny up behind him, and they rode south over the green hills along the Platte. At the crest, they looked down into the valley beyond and saw thousands of buffalo grazing before them.

"So many!" Jenny exclaimed. Some of the beasts frolicked on the prairie, rolling like clumsy horses. Two young bulls pawed at the ground in mock battle.

As Jenny and Mac sat on the hilltop, hunters rode into the valley, culling several buffalo away from the herd. Shots rang out, and one of the young bulls dropped.

"Are those our hunters?" Jenny asked, ducking her head into Mac's back.

"Probably Abercrombie," Mac said. "We'd better move away. Buffalo might stampede." He turned Valiente down the hill, but not before more buffalo bellowed in pain and fell.

"What do you think of the Abercrombies?" Jenny asked.

"Samuel thinks he knows more than he does. Argues about everything. I haven't spent much time with Douglass, but Daniel's a good lad. Why?"

"Esther's sweet on Daniel."

Mac snorted. "Esther's not sweet on anyone but herself."

"You don't like her?"

"She's silly. Don't know why she can't be less giggly. Like you."

"Maybe she has more to giggle about," Jenny said. She thought Esther was flighty, too, but she defended her friend to Mac. After all, she wished she could act foolish once in a while.

When they returned to the wagons, Jenny told Zeke she'd drive the team. Mac took Valiente off to the hunt. "I'll bring back some meat," he told her. "Might as well get it while we can. We'll be leaving the South Fork of the Platte soon. Fewer buffalo then."

After the noon meal, Jenny sought out Esther. "Are we walking?"

"Where were you this morning?" Esther asked.

"Riding with Mac."

"I wanted to walk in the morning. When it's cool. Don't know if Ma will let me now." Esther pulled at her braid. "You ask her. She's nicer to you."

Jenny didn't think Mrs. Pershing was particularly nice to her, but she did as Esther asked. "Could Esther walk with me a spell?" she asked. "Mac's hunting, and I have to tend our wagon."

Mrs. Pershing frowned. "I seen you girls whispering," she said. "Don't know what you're cooking up. Esther, take a couple of the young'uns. Give me a rest."

"We'll take the twins and Ruth, Ma," Esther said. "Rachel can help you with Noah."

Mrs. Pershing stood wearily, rubbing her back. "All right. But stay close. Could be Pawnee around."

Esther called the ten-year-old twins and eight-year-old Ruth. The boys ran beside the girls, yelling wildly.

Ruth put her hand in Jenny's and whispered, "Thanks, Miz McDougall. Ma's been cross all morning."

They walked beside Jenny's wagon. Soon Daniel Abercrombie rode over, his face sweating.

"Afternoon." Daniel tipped his hat, looking at Esther.

"Oh, Daniel, you're so dirty," Esther said. "Go wash up. Then come walk with me."

"Might need to help Pa again." He rode off.

Esther sighed. "I guess he won't propose, at least not today."

"There'll be other days," Jenny said. "We have months until we get to Oregon."

Chapter 13: Crossing the South Fork

May 17, 1847. Reached the first ford on the South Fork of the Platte today, where Pershing crossed with Frémont in '42. Abercrombie wants to cross later. He shoots a buffalo almost daily, taking only the tongue and steaks. The rest of us salvage what we can.

Mac set aside his journal and watched Jenny wash dishes. She let the sediment settle in one bucket, then poured the water into a wash bucket, humming as she scrubbed. Mac couldn't make out the tune.

She hadn't been any trouble so far, except for her fear of rivers. She worked as hard as older women, even Mrs. Pershing. She didn't complain, at least not to Mac. In fact, she was the quietest female he'd ever known.

He should tell her Pershing thought the Platte crossing would be easy. Mac's oxen were in good shape now, the one recovered from its bad hoof, and all of them feasting on succulent spring grass. If Jenny weren't so afraid, the crossing might even be a lark.

"We'll cross the Platte in a day or so," he said.

Jenny looked up with wide eyes. "So soon?"

"We could cross here. But Pershing says we'll travel on this side another day."

"It's so big."

"Nothing will happen."

Jenny cradled her stomach. Mac was embarrassed to ask about her pregnancy. "Are you all right?" was the closest he could manage.

"Just nervous."

The next morning continued sunny and warm. Mac and Josiah Baker scouted ahead with Captain Pershing. Around noon they met another emigrant company fording the river. Children shouted, men yelled and cracked their whips, animals brayed, the water churned. But despite the commotion, the group wasn't having any difficulty.

"Let's see how it looks," Pershing said. The three men turned their horses into the water and splashed across the mile-and-a-half wide river.

"Never reached my horse's belly," Baker said as they reached the north side.

"Me neither," Pershing said. "We can ford the wagons easy enough. No need to float 'em."

"As long as the teams keep moving," Mac said. "I stopped once, and Valiente started to sink in the quicksand. Scared him."

Pershing nodded. "We'll post men in the river. They need to keep their mounts moving whilst they hurry the wagons along."

They returned to the south bank and found the company. Mac saw Jenny walking with Esther and Daniel beside one of the Abercrombie wagons. "Who's with our team?" he asked, dismounting.

"Zeke," Jenny said.

Mac frowned. "You shouldn't impose on him."

She glared, hands on her hips. "He offered. And Esther begged me to walk with her."

"Esther has plenty of company." Mac gestured at Esther and Daniel, who had walked ahead.

"Her mother doesn't like her to be alone with Daniel."

"For good reason," Mac said. He walked Valiente beside Jenny until they reached their wagon. "Thanks," he said to Zeke. "We'll handle it now."

"Much obliged," Jenny said, smiling at Zeke.

Zeke tipped his hat, smiling back. "Any time."

Mac squinted at Jenny. Maybe she was more trouble than he'd thought. "You shouldn't impose," he said again. "Or people will talk."

She turned her back on him and climbed into the wagon.

May 18, 1847. Crossing the South Fork tomorrow. Need to tie everything down.

Reveille sounded at first light. The oxen pawed as Mac hitched them. "Nervous, boys?" he asked, slapping the lead ox's shoulder. He turned to Jenny. "Ready?"

She took a deep, shaky breath and nodded.

"I'll be in the river, driving teams along. Can you handle the wagon?"

She hesitated. "Where will Zeke be?"

"With me."

Jenny thrust her chin out. "I'll manage."

Mac mounted Valiente and headed toward the river. He glanced over his shoulder. Jenny sat on the bench, her mouth a thin line, her face white. He rode back. "You sure you can do this?"

"Just thinking about Mr. Purcell. I'll be fine."

"If you need help, send one of the Tanner or Pershing boys to find me."

She nodded.

The wagons lined up on the bank while men on horseback spread out across the water. "Keep your horses moving," Pershing yelled. "I ain't losing a single man nor beast today."

A man laughed. "I got a mule I could stand to lose. Won't do a damn thing I say."

Mac was stationed near the far side. He could see wagons moving into the water, but couldn't tell who was in them. He wouldn't know when Jenny headed into the river. He clucked at Valiente, and they traced a path back and forth in the muddy current. Once Valiente paused, then whinnied as he pulled a stuck hoof out of the sandy bottom.

Mac shouted and cracked his whip as the wagons passed. He aimed for the hindmost pair of each team, wanting to move them along but not scare them into stopping. He kept the whip away from the wagon so he wouldn't cut a driver.

Most of the wagons rolled smoothly, but occasionally a wheel mired. The mounted men shouted until that team lunged free of the mud that sucked their hooves. The Platte was too slow to push the wagons downstream like other rivers they'd crossed, but the quicksand lurking on the bottom was more treacherous than a fast current.

One of the last wagons stopped in midstream. Was it his? Mac hadn't seen Jenny yet. She must be hanging back, afraid. No, it was Tanner's—

the man's dark skin silhouetted against the white canvas cover. Mules pulled the vehicle, not Mac's oxen.

Men pushed the stalled wagon from behind. Others pulled on the frantic mules' bridles. Tanner cracked his whip on the rear animals' rumps. They screamed and strained forward, but the wagon remained trapped, sinking until the floorboard was submerged.

At a shout from Pershing, Mac joined the men rocking the wagon to dislodge it. "We have to lighten it," Pershing called. "Empty out everything you can."

Men pulled out barrels and sacks and handed them to others to carry to shore.

"Mama's cape!" Hatty Tanner cried, as a cloth floated downstream.

Mac reached for it, but missed. He wheeled Valiente and started to follow, glancing over his shoulder at the next vehicle in line. It was Jenny—her wagon sinking, too, stuck behind the Tanners. No one had noticed her in the frenzy.

Mac turned Valiente toward his wagon and Jenny. "Go around!" he yelled at her. "Don't stop!"

Captain Pershing and Zeke also splashed their horses toward Jenny. The oxen, bellowing in the frenzy, tried to back up.

"No, No!" Jenny cried, dropping her whip and covering her face.

Mac and Zeke reached the wagon at the same time. Zeke jumped on the bench and lunged for the whip. Mac grabbed the lead pair's yoke to pull them around Tanner. Mac's eight oxen quickly hauled the wagon out of the mud.

"Water's untested here," Zeke shouted. "Stay close to the team in case there's trouble."

Mac nodded and led the oxen step by step across the river.

Jenny clung to Zeke with one hand, cradling her belly with the other. Was she hurt? Mac wondered. He couldn't take time to ask.

The lead pair hit a hole in the bottom and plunged to their necks. They began swimming, straining to stay afloat.

"Stop!" Mac cried to Zeke. "Don't let the wagon into the pit." Mac dodged the lead pair's hooves and unfastened their yoke, swallowing muddy water in the process. Then he yelled for Daniel Abercrombie to herd the two loose oxen across.

Mac and Zeke steered the rest of the oxen around the drop-off. Mac walked Valiente back and forth searching for more holes ahead, until they maneuvered the wagon back to the tested ford.

"Anything lost?" he asked Jenny when at last he lifted her down from the bench.

She trembled and held his arms tightly as if she didn't trust her legs to support her. "No," she said.

"Scared?" Mac asked.

She nodded silently.

"Sit over yonder," Zeke said, gesturing to a hillock of grass. "We need to see to other wagons."

Mac half-carried Jenny until she reached the grass.

"I'll be fine," she said to Mac. "Thank you, Zeke," she called. "I wouldn't have made it across without you."

Mac followed Zeke, frowning back at Jenny. She sat on the grass, looking as forlorn as on the day she'd told him her story.

May 19, 1847. The Tanner wagon stalled crossing the Platte. They lost some food and cracked a wheel. My wagon almost followed suit, but we made it with nothing broken.

Chapter 14: Toward the North Platte

Wednesday, May 19th—I am still shaking after the dreadful crossing. If not for Zeke, I would have died. Hatty Tanner lost a cape— the only thing she had from her mother.

Jenny shivered as she wrote, remembering the treacherous Platte—calm on the surface, quicksand and sinkholes below.

Nearby, Mac and Tanner inspected their wagons. "I got two cracked wheel spokes," Tanner said.

"How do you make a wheel out here?" Mac asked.

"Don't need a whole wheel. Just new spokes. It'll take some doin', but it's a damn piece easier'n a new wheel."

"How long will it take?"

"Be done by late tomorrow. Can't move today."

Mac frowned at the broken spokes. "I'll tell Pershing." He walked off.

Hatty Tanner stirred her family's supper over the fire, her face tearstreaked.

"I'm sorry about your mama's cape," Jenny said.

"Ain't no help for it now," Hatty replied. "We all lose something along the way." Another tear trickled down her cheek.

The next morning a cold rain fell while Jenny made breakfast. Mac ate quietly. "Are you hunting today?" she asked.

He shrugged. "Need to help Tanner finish the wheel."

"Need anything washed? Thought I'd do laundry while we're still by the river. Though I don't know how it'll get dry."

"This shirt."

"Go change, and give me that one."

Mac headed for the wagon, unbuttoning his shirt as he went.

Esther wandered over, staring at Mac. "My, he's a fine man."

Jenny blinked and glanced at Mac. "I guess so." She seldom really looked at him. He was handsome—black hair, blue eyes, a pleasing smile. But so tall.

"Pa says we're laying by," Esther said. "Want to go look for prairie hen nests?"

"I'm doing laundry."

"Wouldn't fresh eggs taste good?"

"Maybe tomorrow. My clothes are so filthy they're stiff."

"They'll just get dirty again." Esther flounced off.

Jenny picked up the shirt Mac dropped on the ground and gathered clothes and towels. She filled a bucket and started scrubbing. She wasn't alone for very long. Mrs. Tuller carried over clothes in a tub. "Mind if I join you?" she asked.

Jenny smiled. "Glad to see someone friendly. Everyone seems out of sorts today."

"Maybe it's the rain. Or the crossing yesterday. "

Jenny shuddered. "I'll always be afraid of water. I was never so happy to see anyone as when Zeke jumped on the wagon seat with me."

"Mr. McDougall was there, too, wasn't he?"

"Yes, he grabbed the oxen."

Mrs. Tuller hesitated. "People are talking, you know."

"What do you mean?"

"About how friendly you've been with Zeke Pershing."

"He's very kind, helping me on the crossings and tending our wagon."

"People are talking."

"Oh." Jenny's cheeks flamed as she understood what Mrs. Tuller implied. "You mean I shouldn't let him help?"

"Best to rely on your husband."

They worked in silence as they washed and rinsed the laundry, then strung a rope between two wagons and hung the clothes in the rain for a final rinse. "Hope the sun comes out," Jenny said. "Maybe it was foolish to wash today, but I couldn't abide the dirt any longer."

"They'll dry sooner or later," Mrs. Tuller said, shaking out her damp sunbonnet.

Jenny didn't see Mac all morning, but he appeared at their campsite for dinner. "How's the Tanners' wagon?" Jenny asked.

"Almost done," Mac said. "Wish I'd gone with Pershing. He's scouting the route to the North Fork. Landmark is Windlass Hill, a day or two from here. With a resting place called Ash Hollow right past it." Mac wiped his sleeve across his forehead. He looked flushed.

"You all right?" Jenny asked. "Not chilled after being in the river yesterday?"

"Just tired."

The rain stopped after dinner. Jenny wrung out her laundry and hung it back up. By dusk the clothes were dry.

Thursday, May 20th—Slow day in camp. Mac looks weary or ill, and Mrs. Tuller scolded me.

The sun peeked out Friday morning with a promise of warmth. The emigrants bustled through chores, eager to get underway. Captain Pershing had found their next campsite on a small branch of the Platte, and they made their way there across a high plateau.

Jenny walked with Esther to make up for refusing the day before. The girls searched for eggs as they strolled through coarse, sparse grass.

"Ma says to wear sunbonnets," Esther said, "or our skin'll turn dark as an Indian's."

"My mama always told me the same thing," Jenny said.

"Don't you miss your ma?" Esther asked.

Jenny nodded. "But I had to leave."

"Well, of course—you got married. I'm going to marry Daniel and settle in Oregon near Ma and Pa."

"Life doesn't always work out like you plan." It surely did not, Jenny thought. Just a year ago Mama had married Mr. Peterson. Now Jenny was pregnant and following Caleb McDougall to Oregon. What would come next? And Mama? Must be close to time for her baby to be born.

"There's Daniel now." Esther ran toward him, leaving Jenny alone with her thoughts.

She lifted her head to the sun, not minding if it colored her skin, wanting the warmth on her face. A hawk soared overhead, then dove after a varmint. Or maybe a bird's nest. She searched again for eggs and edible plants, but it took all morning to find enough eggs for a meal.

They camped that night on a sandy creek. The hunting party had not returned, including Amos Jackson, who was scheduled to stand watch.

"Don't know why they went so far," Mac said, stabbing at his buffalo stew. "I'll have to take a double guard shift. Jackson will pay when he gets back."

"It's probably Mr. Abercrombie's doing," Jenny said.

"Jackson's accountable." Mac found his rifle and headed for his post.

He was so cranky, Jenny thought. Was he tired, or had he heard the same gossip Mrs. Tuller had?

Friday, May 21ˢᵗ—Pleasant traveling, but Mac is out of sorts. Some children have caught fever.

When Jenny awoke the next morning, Mac still slept beneath the wagon. She hauled water and started breakfast. He stirred when she dropped the eggs to sizzle in the greased skillet.

"What's that?" he asked.

"Eggs. Found them yesterday. It's a change from buffalo."

"Not hungry."

"You have to eat." His curtness made her short-tempered also.

Mac ate slowly.

"You feeling sick?" Jenny asked. "I can hitch up the team."

"I'll do it." Mac wiped his hand across his face and herded the oxen to the wagon. Jenny worried as she watched him. He did not look well.

"Homer!" a woman screamed across the wagon circle. "My baby!"

Jenny rushed toward the sound, Doc and Mrs. Tuller right ahead of her. "What is it?" Doc asked.

"My baby's dead!" Hatty Tanner sobbed. She cradled her son in her arms. "Had a fever yesterday. He's always sick with somethin'."

Doc Tuller felt the body. "Gone. Nothing I can do." He stalked off.

Tanner knelt next to his wife. Hatty keened, beating on her husband's chest, "You done this, Clarence! I tole you we shouldn't go west. Our baby's dead." Tanner's face was stone as he let his wife hit him until she collapsed at his feet.

Jenny put her arm around Otis, the older Tanner boy, whose eyes were wide with fright. Mrs. Pershing took charge of the grieving mother.

Mac walked over to Tanner. "Come on," he said, clapping a hand on the man's shoulder. "We'll dig a grave." Mac signaled Zeke and Joel to assist him.

While the men dug, the hunters returned, Abercrombie galloping in the lead. "Damn fool shot hisself!" he shouted when close enough to be heard. "Jackson's dead."

For the second time that morning, a woman's scream echoed through camp. Jackson's wife ran toward the riders. One man led a horse with a body across the saddle. He stopped beside Mrs. Jackson, who threw her arms around her husband's dangling head.

"Didn't even find any buffalo," Abercrombie said.

"Better dig another grave," Doc Tuller told Mac.

Jenny clutched Mrs. Tuller's arm. "Why is the doctor so gruff?"

"Hates it when he can't do anything for folks," Mrs. Tuller said, with a deep sigh. "Poor Mrs. Jackson. Alone with five children. At least her oldest is man enough to help."

Jenny shook her head. Elijah Jackson was only fourteen. Just like her.

Chapter 15: Windlass Hill

Mac rode Valiente beside the wagon, while Jenny sat on the bench. The travelers had spent most of the morning on burials and a graveside service. They didn't stop at noon but ate as they moved. The deaths of Amos Jackson and Homer Tanner cast a pall over the entire group. Not much could be done about a child's fever, Mac thought. But it was a damn shame when a man shot himself.

"His horse spooked and he dropped a cocked gun," Abercrombie had explained. "Good thing he didn't kill anyone but hisself. Stupid fool."

"Don't serve any purpose to call him names," Pershing said. "We got a bad day ahead. Windlass Hill. Steepest damn hill till we hit the Rockies."

"Can we avoid it?" Mac asked.

"Only by going miles out of our way," the captain replied.

Several in the company complained of fever and aches. The Tanner boy's death made them worry. Doc Tuller was busy all day.

"Is it cholera?" Pershing asked the doctor.

"Don't know."

They reached Windlass Hill in late afternoon. The drop was almost perpendicular.

"How we gonna git down that?" Abercrombie asked, spitting tobacco juice.

"Lower the wagons on ropes." Pershing rubbed his beard and squinted at the sun sinking in the west. "We'll wait till morning."

"Tomorrow's Sunday," Dempsey said.

"Ash Hollow's just past the hill. We'll rest there Monday."

"We'll make less'n a mile tomorrow," Abercrombie complained.

Pershing pointed at the slope. "Getting down this hill's a full day's work."

Mac frowned at the steep drop. River crossings didn't bother him, but the task ahead was daunting. He took off his hat and wiped the perspiration off his face with a handkerchief.

"Lighten the wagons," Pershing said. "Everything out, and carry it down." Every able-bodied member of the company hauled boxes and barrels down the hill. When it was too dark to move anything more, they posted a guard for the night.

On Sunday morning they lowered one wagon after another. Men tied ropes to the rear of each wagon and locked its wheels, leaving only one pair of draft animals hitched to the wagon, with a man to guide that pair. More teams and more men stood behind the wagon, pulling on ropes with all their weight to control the wagon's fall. Women and children repacked the wagons at the bottom of the hill.

Mac's muscles strained with the back-breaking work. Blood pounded in his head, and he felt dizzy.

"She's coming down!" a man shouted.

Mercer's wagon broke loose of its ropes and crashed down the last half of the hill. Mercer, who had been in front of his wagon, dove out of the way, but a wheel rolled over his foot. He yelled and crawled off the trail.

Doc Tuller inspected Mercer's leg. "Ankle's broke," he said. "I can splint it. Wagon's worse'n he is."

The wagon's front board had shattered. The oak wood of one wheel had cracked and its iron tire rolled off.

"Can we fix it?" Pershing asked Tanner.

Tanner, his dark eyes still sunken with grief over Homer's death, examined the wheel. He nodded. "Won't be like new. But I can splice it."

Another wagon tore loose of the ropes and ran over an ox, breaking its leg. Someone shot the ox, and they pulled it off the trail for the women to butcher.

From Windlass Hill they staggered toward Ash Hollow, travelers and teams exhausted. They reached camp as the sun set, leaving Mercer's wagon behind for the night. It was the prettiest spot Mac had seen since Alcove Springs in Kansas. Tall shady ash trees, a few cedar, and lots of green grass.

"Grass looks good," he said to Pershing.

The captain nodded. "Good water, too. Spring fed. We'll lay by tomorrow. See 'bout fixing that wagon. Tell your men."

Mac wanted to sleep, but he made his rounds to talk to his platoon. Finally, he sat by the campfire Jenny had started.

"Good thing we have the ox meat," Jenny said as she served Mac's supper. "I wouldn't have the strength to come up with anything else."

"Not hungry," Mac said, waving the plate aside.

"Eat. You worked hard today."

Mac shook his head.

"How about some broth? I could boil the meat."

"Sounds better," Mac said, wiping a hand across his sweaty face. He wrote as he smelled the broth simmering:

May 23, 1847. Made it down Windlass Hill, only one man injured. Lost an ox and damaged a wagon. The day took more out of me than I expected.

Cold rain splattered the camp Monday morning. Every muscle ached as Mac stumbled out of his sleeping roll. He sat by the wagon clutching his throbbing head.

"You sick?" Jenny asked.

He shrugged. "Worn out from yesterday."

Jenny touched his forehead. "You're burning up. I'll get Doc Tuller."

"It'll go away." He brushed her fingers away.

"Fevers that hot don't just go away," Jenny said, hands on her hips.

"Wait until after breakfast."

"If you aren't better after you eat, I'm getting Doc. How about ox meat?" She held out a plate with a thin steak on it.

Mac retched at the sight and smell. "Just coffee."

"You don't eat, I'm getting the doctor."

"Give me a minute."

Mac sipped the coffee. It burned his gut. He barely made it to the latrine before puking. When he returned, Jenny had Doc Tuller with her.

"See? He's sick," she said.

The doctor felt Mac's hot face and neck. "How long you been feverish?"

"Started this morning."

"Is it cholera?" Jenny's face was pale.

"Got the runs?" the doctor asked.

Mac frowned. He was embarrassed to talk about his bowels with Jenny there. "I'm fine." His legs wobbled and almost gave way.

"No, you ain't." Doc pulled Mac's arm. "Sit down."

"I don't have time."

"You got time to die?" The doctor pushed Mac to sit on an overturned bucket. "Three other cases of fever today. Another child about Homer Tanner's age, a man, and a woman. All different families. Got to assume it's cholera."

Jenny gasped. "How can you tell if it's cholera?"

"Puking, runny stools, high fever. It can kill folks in hours. No way to know for sure." Doc Tuller shook his head. "Lots of fevers look alike. Don't know what makes one man die and another pull through."

The doctor insisted Mac stay in camp when other men left to hunt. He felt worse as the morning progressed, his vomiting and diarrhea more frequent, even his bones hurting.

In early afternoon a woman shrieked. Jenny went to see what had happened and returned with a somber face. "Her sick child died," she said.

Mac tried to drink the water Jenny gave him, but he couldn't keep it down. By evening he was delirious.

Chapter 16: Cholera at Ash Hollow

Doc Tuller stopped by Jenny's wagon as night fell and examined Mac. He shook his head. "Need to get him to drink. I don't like his color. Try to force it down. Like this." The doctor demonstrated filling Mac's mouth with water, then holding his nose shut and his head back to make him swallow. Mac coughed and gagged, but didn't wake up. "You try."

"Gets more water on the blanket than down his throat," Jenny said, holding her hands behind her back.

"Go on, girl. You want him to live?"

Jenny dribbled even more water on Mac's bedding than the doctor had.

"Keep trying." The doctor left.

> *Monday, May 24th—Mac is sick. I can't get him to eat or drink. Another child died, and others are sickening. Their lives are in God's hands.*

Jenny sat by the smoking fire late into the night. She prayed for Mac, who lay under a tarp fashioned into a tent to shield him from the damp and cold. She wrapped Mac in her buffalo robe when he shivered, pulling her woolen cloak tight to keep herself warm. She spooned as much water into him as she could and worried about what would happen to her if Mac died.

Finally, she lay down beside Mac, who mumbled and tossed. She slept fitfully, waking often to check on Mac and force more water down his throat.

Tuesday morning she shook with the cold. Mac was soaked in sweat and tossed off the buffalo robe. She covered him and tried again to get him to drink, but had little success.

Then she looked after Valiente and their oxen. Zeke helped, but Jenny was careful when she thanked him—only a nod and a small smile.

Doc Tuller came over. "How is he?"

"No change. Will he live, Doctor?"

He shrugged. "Can't say. I've seen fever take bigger men than him."

Jenny choked back a sob. If Mac died, she would be like Mrs. Purcell and Mrs. Jackson, depending on the kindness of the company for survival.

"How are the others?" she asked.

Doc Tuller grimaced. "One man near death, worse'n McDougall here. Woman, too, with a baby two months old. Her milk's gone, so other women are caring for the babe. Mrs. Tuller's there now. Three new cases this morning, one of them's going down fast. Cholera moves quick."

"Can I help?"

"You care for your husband. He's got a chance. Skin not as pasty as the others. Get more water down him."

"I've tried. He won't take it." Jenny rubbed her forehead. "Isn't there anything else we can do?"

"Some doctors bleed folks. I don't. Seen too many killed by the bleeding. Keep him warm when he's cold, and wash him when he sweats."

"That's all I could do for Papa, too. He died." Her father's last illness had been dreadful. Jenny and Letitia had cared for him. Her mother said it was too much to bear. Jenny had watched his life seep away. "Take care of your mama" were his last words to her. She'd broken her promise when she left home.

Jenny sat by Mac all morning. His fever worsened, and he stopped thrashing. He was as still as if dead. She washed him when he soiled the clothes and blankets. She'd done the same for her father. Anything to keep him alive.

Mrs. Tuller came over at noon. "Here's some soup for you. And for Mr. McDougall, if he'll take any."

"Thank you." Jenny sighed. "But he can't even keep water down."

"Seven folks sick now," Mrs. Tuller reported. "One woman won't live more'n a few hours. She'll leave four children." Mrs. Tuller shook her head. "One an infant. Other nursing mothers will have to care for him."

Jenny sobbed, wiping her tears with her hand.

"Don't cry, child," Mrs. Tuller said. "Save your strength. You got a man near death to care for."

"Don't say that!" Jenny cried. "He'll pull through. I can't bear to go on, if he doesn't."

"You'd be surprised what you can bear when you must." Mrs. Tuller patted Jenny's arm. "Eat your soup. I'll be back later for the dishes."

In midafternoon Mrs. Tuller returned. "She's dead," she sighed. "Husband and older children are distraught. Poor baby don't even know his mother's gone."

"The others?"

"Still alive. Barely. But no new cases of fever since morning. How's Mr. McDougall?"

"No change." Jenny shook her head. "I don't know how long he can stay like this. He's still puking and worse. I can't get him to drink."

"You're doing fine, Jenny. As well as others twice your age. He's lucky to have you."

"Can you send the doctor?"

"He'll come when he can. Folks all over camp need him."

"What else is going on? I haven't been away from Mac all day."

"Tanner's fixing the Mercer wagon. Got a hot fire going to replace the tire iron. Mr. Abercrombie's raising a commotion over the delay. His family's not sick. He wants to move on."

"You won't leave us, will you?" Jenny panicked at that possibility.

Mrs. Tuller shook her head. "Captain Pershing says we'll stay together. At least for now."

Through the afternoon Jenny heard the usual bustle of camp, but she didn't leave Mac. The sound of hymns filled the air—probably a funeral for the dead woman. Such a sad place to leave a loved one behind.

Doc and Mrs. Tuller came to see her at twilight, bringing food again.

Doc looked at Mac. "Tonight will tell," he said. "If he makes it through the night, he should live."

Dread made Jenny's voice shrill. "What if he dies?"

"We're two wagons away," Mrs. Tuller said. "Come get us if he worsens."

"How can I leave him?"

Doc glared at her. "Your choice, girl. Deal with it alone, or come get me. Can't have it both ways." He stalked off, leaving Jenny with Mrs. Tuller.

Mrs. Tuller put an arm around Jenny. "Don't mind him. He's in a temper because he can't do nothing, and folks all think he should fix 'em."

"I'm sorry," Jenny said, trembling. "I don't know what to do."

"None of us do, child."

Jenny sat with Mac through the night. She wrote by the low light of the campfire:

> *Tuesday, May 25ᵗʰ—Mac is very ill. A woman died, leaving four children, one an infant. May God help me!*

She had no strength to write more.

During the night Mac's fever spiked higher. He tossed and moaned, mostly nonsense that Jenny couldn't understand. He talked about killing a man, shouting he'd had to do it. At one point, he called, "Bridget! Don't leave me, Bridget!"

"Who's Bridget?" she asked. He didn't answer.

The night air chilled Jenny. She worried Mac would catch cold, but his skin burned. She dampened his face and chest, trying to keep him from flinging off the blanket. He fought her, pushing her away. "Bridget!" he shouted.

Jenny didn't fear him, though his shoves hurt. He didn't know what he was doing.

When he called for Bridget again, she soothed him, "Be still." She put her hand on his forehead, and he pulled it to his cheek.

"Bridget."

"Shh," she said. "I'm here."

Mac calmed, and Jenny sat beside him for the rest of the night, her hand on his chest to make sure it rose and fell. Who's Bridget? she wondered.

Jenny didn't know how long she slept slumped beside Mac. Sounds of the camp stirring woke her at dawn. She felt Mac's forehead. He seemed cooler. His breath came deep and steady.

She struggled to her feet, muscles cramped and sore, and staggered out from under the tarp.

"Morning," Mrs. Tuller said, walking toward Jenny with a cup of coffee.

"Thank you." Jenny smiled as she took the cup. "You've been such a comfort."

"That's what friends do," the older woman said, wiping her hands on her apron. "How's Mr. McDougall?"

"Seems better. He slept some."

"How 'bout you?"

Jenny shrugged. "I'm all right."

"You need to take care of yourself, you know. Your baby needs you healthy."

"But the baby and I both need Mac well."

"There's truth in that," Mrs. Tuller said.

"What's happening?" Jenny asked, looking around at the bustling camp. "Looks like people are packing up."

Mrs. Tuller nodded. "Men met last night. Samuel Abercrombie is determined to move on. He got the men to vote, despite Captain Pershing saying we needed to stick together. Most families are moving out today."

"Mac can't travel!"

"Some are staying. Doc and me. The Tanners. Mercers—his wagon ain't finished. And the families with sick ones."

"Captain Pershing's going?" Jenny felt the blood drain from her face. "How will we get along without him?"

"He says he's got to stay with the main group. He's leaving Zeke and Joel with us. They'll help those who can't do for themselves. Zeke's caring for your oxen and horse now."

Jenny closed her eyes, head spinning with fatigue. She'd forgotten about the animals.

"You poor child," Mrs. Tuller said. "You're dead on your feet. You go freshen up, then come back and eat. I'll sit with Mr. McDougall."

Jenny washed her face and went in search of Zeke, who was moving Valiente to another patch of grass to graze. "I can't thank you enough for your help," she said.

89

"That's what neighbors do," he said smiling. "How's Mac?"

"Better, I think. Still sleeping."

"When he wakes up, you tell him not to worry. I'll take care of your team."

"You're staying behind when your family moves on?"

Zeke shrugged. "Someone's got to. Pa talked to Joel and me about the route. We follow the North Platte for fifty miles or so. We'll catch up."

Back at her wagon, Jenny found Doc Tuller examining Mac. "He tossed and shouted during the night," she told the doctor, "then slept."

"Keep at it, girl," Doc said. "I'll check back later.

Tears ran down Jenny's face as she struggled to make Mac drink. She heard wagons moving, but didn't leave the tent.

Esther Pershing stuck her head under the tarp. "It smells bad in here," she said, wrinkling her nose. "We're leaving. Pa says you'll catch up to us, but in case you don't, I wanted to say good-bye."

Jenny didn't even look up. She daubed at the water trickling down Mac's chin. "God be with you, Esther."

And with me, she thought.

Chapter 17: Leaving Ash Hollow

Doc told Jenny to continue making Mac drink, so she forced water down him, spoonful by painful spoonful. By noon she sat slumped beside Mac in the hot canvas tent, unable to hold herself upright. Mrs. Tuller and Hatty Tanner brought her food, but Jenny was so fatigued she could only eat a few bites.

"You need to rest," Mrs. Tuller said. "I'll sit with him a spell."

"No," Jenny insisted. "I can do it."

"You won't be any good to Mr. McDougall or your baby if you get sick. Get in the wagon and sleep."

Jenny staggered to the wagon. She tried to hoist herself up, but couldn't. She laid her cheek on the wheel, sobbing.

"Let me help." She heard Zeke through the fog in her head. He lifted her into the wagon. "Get some sleep."

Jenny awoke in the dark, startled and afraid. She clambered down and rushed to the tent. "How is he?" she asked Mrs. Tuller.

"Breathing better."

"Has he been awake?"

Mrs. Tuller shook her head. "Not a sound. But he's keeping water down."

Jenny ran a hand over Mac's forehead. "No fever?"

"No. That's passed, I think."

"How are the others?" Jenny asked.

"One man dead, the rest improving. Buried the man this afternoon." Mrs. Tuller sighed.

"I'm obliged to you," Jenny said. "I'll sit with him now."

"Eat first. Stew's on the fire."

After Jenny ate, Mrs. Tuller left, and Hatty Tanner sat with Jenny for a bit. "Seems like he'll pull through," Hatty said in a flat voice. "God willing."

Jenny nodded. Why should Mac live, when Hatty lost her little boy? She knew the question was on Hatty's mind.

Through the night Jenny gave Mac water and washed his face as he called for Bridget again. Toward dawn she dozed.

When Jenny awoke on Thursday morning, Mac was stirring, moaning softly. "Wake up," she said, shaking his shoulder.

He opened his eyes. "Where am I?"

"Ash Hollow. You've been sick."

He groaned, trying to sit. "You all right?"

She nodded. "Stay down. You need to rest. I'll get Doc."

Jenny found Doc and pulled him back with her. The doctor examined Mac. "No fever. Skin not so gray. How about some broth?"

Mac lifted himself on an elbow. "Might try it."

"Stay still," Jenny said. "I'll fix it." After Doc left, she put antelope meat in a pot over the fire to boil. When it was ready, she insisted on feeding Mac.

"I'm weak as a baby," he complained.

"You almost died," she said. "You'll feel puny for days."

"Anyone else sick?"

"Little Homer Tanner died. Then a woman, who left four children behind. And another man. Several others ill, but pulling through. Though I'm not certain—I haven't talked much with anyone since you've been sick."

"How long was I out?"

"Two days."

"Two days!" Mac lifted his head. "We were held up for two days?"

Jenny pushed him flat. "Most of the company went on. Tanners and Tullers and Zeke and Joel stayed with the sick folks."

"Captain Pershing left?"

"Mr. Abercrombie was determined. Most families wanted to go, too. Afraid of the fever, I suppose. Captain went with them. We'll have to catch up."

"How's our team?"

"All right, I think. Zeke's been taking care of them."

"Would you get him?"

Jenny sent Zeke to talk to Mac. Walking through camp, she saw Hatty at the Ash Hollow spring.

"Mornin', Miz McDougall. I heard your husband's better. I'm happy for you."

"Thank you." Again, Jenny couldn't think what to say to Hatty about her dead son.

"Hear we're pullin' out tomorrow."

"So soon?" Jenny asked. "Mac can't even stand yet."

"Can't fall too far behind. Zeke Pershing's stayin' with us. Joel's ridin' ahead to find the others."

Jenny hurried back to her wagon. "Is it true?" she asked Zeke. "Are we leaving?"

Zeke nodded. "Pa said to follow as quick as we could."

"But Mac can't—"

"I'll be fine," Mac interrupted. "We have to move on."

"I'll help you, Miz Jenny," Zeke said. "Don't worry. Before we leave, though, you might want to leave a letter in the log cabin by the spring. Next rider going east'll take whatever letters we leave behind."

There was nothing she could tell her mother, Jenny thought. But Mac decided to write his parents in Boston.

"You can hardly sit," Jenny said. "How're you going to write?" But Mac filled a page, addressed it, and sealed it.

As dusk approached Jenny stood by the spring. Ash Hollow was lovely, but all she would remember was her terror that Mac would die. She picked a wild rose growing under an ash tree and prayed silently for his recovery to continue.

Back at the wagon Jenny picked up her journal.

Thursday, May 27th—Mac is awake, but weak. I was so afraid of losing him. If it weren't for Zeke and the Tullers, I could not have managed. We must go on tomorrow.

In the morning Mac's legs shook when he stood. "Sit," Zeke said, gesturing at a barrel. "I'll hitch up your team."

Jenny watched Zeke move from wagon to wagon, assisting families with ailing travelers. Joel had left at first light to find the main company.

"Can you drive?" Zeke asked Jenny. "I can if you need me, but I'd rather ride horseback along the wagons."

"I'll drive," she said.

The small group pulled slowly away from Ash Hollow. Mac lay silently in the wagon. Around midmorning he said, "You saved my life."

"What?" She peered from the bench at Mac.

"Doc says you took care of me, made sure I drank."

Jenny shrugged. "I did what I had to."

"You know what the Chinese say?"

"The Chinese?"

"They say if someone saves your life, you're in their debt forever."

"Then I'm in your debt, too. For what happened in Arrow Rock."

"Maybe. But you would have done all right on your own."

Jenny glanced back again. "Why do you say that?"

"You're strong, Jenny. Stronger than you know."

Strong? She didn't think of herself as strong. "I get so scared."

"But you cope, even when you're scared."

Jenny smiled at his praise. Mac didn't say nice things very often.

Chapter 18: Back on the Trail

May 28, 1847. Two days lost. I have no memory from late Monday until yesterday morning. It took all my strength to write home—told Mother I'd been ill, but not how bad, nor that I had an angel watching over me.

Mac's hands shook, and the wagon jarred over rocks and clumps of Indian grass, so he stopped writing. Jenny had been an angel—a soft hand on his forehead, a gentle voice urging him to drink. She'd kept him alive.

"Your young wife took good care of you," Doc told him. "Better'n most of the older women. Now you take care of her and your child."

How could he care for Jenny when he would return to Boston in the spring? He couldn't take her with him. Not after what his mother had done to Bridget—his parents would never accept Jenny.

Jenny was strong, as he had said. But she needed someone to protect her. If Mac left, would Zeke marry her? The notion stuck in Mac's craw, but maybe it would be best. When he left her in Oregon, Mac decided, he should tell her to find a good husband. In the meantime, she needed to act like Mac's wife, not make eyes at Zeke.

The small caravan reached the North Fork of the Platte at midday noon and stopped to eat. "We follow this branch all the way to Laramie," Zeke said when he called the noon halt.

"Do we have to cross the river?" Jenny asked.

"Not now," Zeke said. "Pa said stay on the south side."

Mac struggled out of the wagon, managing to keep upright. He couldn't work, so sat on an upturned bucket until Jenny had dinner ready. Doc said he could eat solid food, but after a few bites of meat his stomach churned. He climbed back in the wagon, wondering if his dinner would stay down.

Mac tried to sleep as the wagon rocked through the afternoon. When they stopped, he looked out. The sun was still high. "What's the hold up?" he asked.

"Zeke called it a day," Jenny said. "Folks are feeling poorly. One man's vomiting again. Doc thinks we'd best stop."

Mac slept until evening. When he awoke, Jenny had soup ready. "Doc says to eat something easy. Or you might relapse, too."

He drank the soup slowly. It went down better than the meat at noon.

Jenny hovered over him. "I can make some mush," she said. "If you're still hungry."

"No, thank you. I'd best not."

Mac pulled out his journal and wrote:

May 28, 1847, evening. I have no strength. I'm no help to anyone. We're on the North Platte, stopped at Spring Creek. This branch of the Platte is cleaner, more sand than mud. How can we make up our lost time?

The next day, Saturday, the group got underway slowly. The few healthy men in the party were worn out—standing guard at night and doing heavy chores by day. Mac watched Zeke, Tanner, and Doc haul water and hitch wagons, while he sat, not even able to help Jenny cook.

He complained to Jenny, but she said, "You get better. That's your chore for today." Still, his patience grew thin, and he snapped when Jenny coddled him.

While they traveled, he dozed in the wagon. Jenny tried to make conversation. He grunted in response. After a while, she was silent.

Later, through his fuzzy brain he heard her say, "Who's Bridget?"

"Huh?"

"When you were fevered, you called for Bridget. Who is she?"

96

How much should he tell Jenny? "A girl I knew in Boston. She's dead now." The words hurt to say.

"Were you sweet on her?"

"I guess you could say so."

The wagon jerked along. Then Jenny asked, "How'd she die?"

"Fever, I think. That's what I heard."

"You aren't sure?"

"No."

"How'd you meet her?"

"She worked in my parents' home." He frowned. He didn't want to talk about Bridget.

"A governess?"

"A maid."

More silence. He could tell Jenny was trying to puzzle out what Bridget had meant to him. Bridget wasn't any of Jenny's concern, but maybe if he explained she would drop the subject. "My mother found out we were 'sweet' on each other, as you say, and dismissed her. I was away from home. I never saw her again. I later heard she died."

"Oh." Jenny paused. "I'm sorry. Sorry for your loss." Then she was quiet.

Mac slept. At noon he roused long enough to eat, then dozed again. In midafternoon the wagon stopped, and Zeke called, "We're halting."

Mac stuck his head out. "How far have we come?"

Zeke shrugged. "Far enough. It's a good place to camp. I got to hunt, if'n we're going to have meat."

"Damn. I feel so helpless. Let me get my rifle. I can at least stand guard while you're gone."

"Can you stay awake?" Zeke grinned.

"I'll manage," Mac said.

That evening Mac wrote:

> *May 29, 1847. Another short day. Still too weak to be much use. I could barely hold my rifle steady while healthier men hunted. They only shot small game— we're past the buffalo herds. I am determined to drive the wagon tomorrow. Jenny looks weary.*

But Sunday Mac shivered in the cool morning air. He forced himself to tote buckets to fill the water barrel, then had to rest.

"I'll be more help tomorrow," he promised Jenny.

"Don't push yourself," Jenny said, as she stirred porridge. "Won't do us any good if you relapse."

After breakfast Mac climbed on to the wagon seat and took the whip. Jenny frowned. "Can you drive?"

"For a while."

She clambered up beside him. "Tell me if you get tired."

He lasted about half the morning before his legs and back ached. "Think I'll lie down," he said. He napped the rest of the day.

In camp that night he wrote:

May 30, 1847. Can't seem to get enough sleep.

Chapter 19: Thunderstorm

Jenny found Mac yoking the team early Monday morning. "What are you doing?" she asked.

"What's it look like?"

"You feeling all right?" His dark hair hung lank against an ashen face.

"Better."

"You should eat." She hurried to boil coffee and make biscuits.

After he yoked the oxen, Mac sank down beside the fire and drank the coffee. "I'll drive," he said.

"You sure?"

Mac nodded. "Valiente needs a good ride. Take him out. He knows you now. Do you both good."

"I'll ask Zeke to stay close." She was afraid to leave Mac alone, but it would be a pleasure to ride. The warm sun promised a lovely day.

"Sure, Miz Jenny," Zeke said. "But stay within sight of the wagons."

Jenny saddled Valiente. The horse pranced and tossed his head as she walked him beside the wagon. "He wants to run," Mac said. "Go on."

She clucked at the stallion, and he sped across the high prairie. Dust rose in puffs as Valiente's hooves pounded the sparse grass. Jenny had paid little attention to the scenery in recent days. Now she saw mountains far to the west and odd rocks rising on the plateau.

She let the horse run, but kept the wagons in sight. When Valiente slowed, she turned him around and started back at a walk. How lonely and small their wagons looked in the distance. She would feel safer when they caught up with Captain Pershing and the others. Jenny missed Esther and even gruff Mrs. Pershing. She wondered whether Esther had enticed Daniel into proposing.

Mac said he'd been sweet on Bridget. He hadn't said much—he must have loved Bridget so deeply he couldn't speak of her death now.

Why had Mac left Boston? He said he wanted to see the West, but perhaps he was running away from losing Bridget. Jenny wondered if anyone would ever care about her so strongly. She felt so alone, friendless and unloved.

Her baby kicked and rolled in time with the horse's pace. But the baby was no companion, it was a worry. A tear trickled down her cheek.

Jenny dismounted when she approached the wagons and walked Valiente over to Mac. The horse nickered when he saw Mac.

"Have fun, boy?" Mac reached out to stroke Valiente's mane. "Did you go far?"

Jenny gestured. "To the top of the hills. There are some enormous rocks beyond. Big as buildings."

"Zeke said we'd be seeing stone formations." Mac stared at Jenny's face. "You been crying?"

She swallowed hard. "A little."

"Did you write your mother at Ash Hollow?"

"Nothing to say."

"Not even that you're doing well?"

Was she doing well? "I'll write when the baby comes."

Mac frowned. "Your decision."

They traveled slowly until midafternoon, when Zeke called the halt. Jenny was glad for the early stop—Mac's face looked ashen after driving all day. She fixed supper, then sat beside their wagon writing:

> *Monday, May 31st—We travel slowly. Mac tires quickly and barely eats. I hope he regains his strength. Silly of me to be sad today. No sense in fearing what lies ahead. I cannot change it.*

Tuesday morning was sunny and warm again. Summer would come soon, though the night on the high plains had been cold.

"How do you feel?" Jenny asked Mac. His face had better color today.

He smiled. "Almost like new."

She fixed bacon and biscuits. "Bacon's almost gone. No fresh meat left."

Mac took the plate she handed him. "Need to hunt soon."

"Shouldn't you wait until we've caught up with the others?"

"Need food now. I'll talk to Zeke." Mac walked off and returned shortly. "We'll stop early this afternoon again. Hunt before supper."

"Then rest this morning. Let me drive."

Mac scoffed, but she insisted. She smiled when she later heard him snoring in the warm wagon.

She stared ahead, imagining what the shapes in the distance might be. For days, there had been little on the horizon but grass-covered hills. The huge formations she'd seen yesterday now loomed beside them. The few healthy children in their group ran to climb the rocks. One stone was larger than a castle in a fairy tale, Jenny thought.

"That's Courthouse Rock," Zeke said, as he rode beside her wagon.

"I thought it was a castle." She pointed at the apex, laughing. "There's the turret, where the princess lives."

"Some folks call it Castle Rock." He smiled. "Guess you can call it what you want."

Zeke stopped them at Three Bluff Springs, and the hunting party set out, leaving Doc behind as a guard.

"Do you think Mac's all right?" Jenny asked Mrs. Tuller while they talked and sewed.

"He'll improve. Give it time."

"He thinks he's well now, but he tires so easily." Jenny shook her head.

Mrs. Tuller laughed. "Men think sickness ain't manly. But nature has a way of letting 'em know their limits."

When the hunters returned, Mac slid down Valiente's shoulder and staggered. "One antelope and six birds," he said. "Think I'll go sleep."

"What about supper?"

"Not now." He tottered toward the wagon.

After she ate, Jenny sat beside the fire and wrote:

Tuesday, June 1st—Hunting tuckered Mac out. He takes on too much and won't listen to reason.

The next morning heavy skies forecast rain by midday. And by the look of the clouds, maybe hail. "Best keep the wagon cover closed today," Jenny told Mac.

Mac grunted as he hitched the oxen. He didn't eat much breakfast, even though she urged him.

"I'll ride Valiente," he said. "You drive."

Jenny nodded. "Keep your coat with you. It's going to rain."

As she drove, Jenny watched Mac and Zeke ride along the wagons. Mac hadn't taken his coat, and she was sure it would rain. She feared his health would relapse.

The animals were restless through the humid morning. A terrier tethered in one wagon howled whenever the wind whistled through a loose flap of canvas. Jenny watched the clouds billow and churn, as dark as any she'd seen in Missouri. Black enough for a tornado.

They stopped at noon on the bank of a small creek. Jenny pulled pots and food out of the wagon. Just as she started a fire, huge raindrops splatted the ground. She stowed her provisions back in the wagon, then rushed to help Mrs. Tuller do the same.

"Coming down in buckets, ain't it?" Mrs. Tuller said.

"Yes, ma'am. Have you seen Mac? He doesn't have his coat."

Mrs. Tuller waved toward the other wagons. "Saw him not long ago."

Jenny retrieved Mac's coat and went in search of him. She found him at the Tanners' wagon. "Here," she said. "Put this on."

Mac was already soaked. "I need to tie this cover down," he said, but he shrugged his arms into the coat sleeves.

It started to hail. "Mac, come get in our wagon. It's too stormy."

"I have to finish. You go on. Take Valiente and tie him up."

"Mac, please." She pulled on his arm.

"Jenny, I can't. Take Valiente." He turned his back to her.

She ran with Valiente and tied him behind the wagon. The stallion whinnied when lightning forked to the ground. The oxen, still in their yokes, bellowed. Valiente stuck his head into the back of the wagon and flinched with every hailstone that struck his quivering hide.

Ice tore a hole in the wagon cover. Jenny spread her buffalo robe over their food. She cowered beneath the heavy skin as well, while thunder rumbled through the skies.

The hail didn't last long. Soon Mac returned, shivering in his wet shirt and sodden coat.

"What were you doing out there?" she asked, handing Mac a towel.

He stripped off his coat and shirt and dried himself while she found him another shirt. "Had to secure the camp. Zeke can't do it all. Sat in Tanner's wagon when it hailed, but I was already wet."

Jenny clucked over him and handed him dry trousers. "Here," she said, turning her back while he changed.

It poured all afternoon, forcing them to stay in the wagon. Mac shivered, though Jenny put her buffalo robe around him. "When it stops, I'll make soup," she said, as she stared into the gloom.

Mac tried to repair the gash in the wagon cover from the inside, but the water dripped on him faster than he could close the gap.

"Leave it," Jenny said. "We'll fix it when the rain stops."

As daylight faded, the rain slowed enough to prepare supper. Jenny used coals saved in a bucket and a few sticks kept dry in the wagon to start a smoky fire. Then she made a broth from antelope meat. Mac drank it slowly.

That night Jenny heard Mac groaning in the tent where he slept. When she went to check on him, his forehead burned with fever.

Chapter 20: Relapse and Reunion

By morning the storm had passed. Mac ached from his exertion the previous day. His head hurt, and he coughed uncontrollably.

"Mac, you're sick again!" Jenny said as soon as she saw him.

"Just a cold."

She touched his forehead. "You're burning up."

"I'll be fine." He tried to go hitch the oxen, but his head spun and he had to sit, cursing himself.

Jenny brought Doc to their wagon. "Look," she said, waving her hand at Mac. "He won't rest." She stood, hand on her belly, while the doctor examined Mac.

"It ain't cholera," Doc said when he was finished. "You got a chill, I expect."

"I'm driving today," Jenny announced, her chin stuck in the air.

Irritated by her interference, Mac glared. "All right, you hitch up. See how much you can do without me."

Doc Tuller chuckled as he left. "You two are married, for sure. Let her have her way, Mac. Won't hurt you to lose a spat."

Mac watched Jenny struggle to lift the heavy yokes onto the oxen's necks, then she smiled brightly when Zeke rushed to her aid.

Zeke frowned at him.

"She wouldn't let me help." Mac knew he sounded surly, but the sight of Zeke assisting Jenny made him furious.

Mac rode in the wagon that morning, not talking. Jenny stayed silent as well.

"Look!" she said much later, pointing out a tall spire of rock on the horizon. "What's that?"

104

He peered out. "Chimney Rock. Frémont wrote about it. Must be three hundred feet high." The tower's base was wide, but it rose above the plain to a thin shaft like the stone ruins of an ancient building.

Mac tried to watch the red clay tower grow closer. But his eyelids drooped, and he lay back on his pallet. The heat and dust lulled him into a stupor as the wagon bumped along.

When they stopped, Mac's head throbbed. Through a daze, he heard Jenny say, "I can't wake him up." He tried to sit, but a fit of coughing made him gasp.

Doc pushed him down. "Water and soup. Nothing more. Sweat the fever out of him." The doctor piled Jenny's buffalo robe on top of the blanket already covering Mac.

After slurping some soup, Mac slept again. In late afternoon he awoke soaked in sweat, but feeling better. He looked outside. They were now beside Chimney Rock.

"Are we stopping?" he asked when the wagon came to a halt.

"Yes," Jenny said. "Joel's here. He found Captain Pershing and came back. He and Zeke are talking now."

Shivering, Mac pulled himself out of the wagon and drew his coat close. His head still pulsed and his legs were unsteady, but he joined Doc and the Pershing brothers.

"What's going on?" he asked.

"The rest of the company is only a day ahead," Joel said. "They had sickness, too. Two children died. I stayed there two days to help out. They're waiting under Scott's Bluff." He pointed at a massive cliff barely visible in the distance.

"We'll push forward tomorrow," Zeke said. "Can you make it?" he asked Mac.

"I'll have to. We need to catch up."

Doc touched Mac's neck. "Fever's gone. You chilled?"

Mac pulled away. "I'm better than I was."

He wrote in a shaky hand before bed:

> *June 3, 1847. Sick again. Our company is a day away, and we must reach them. Wish I could ride Valiente on these curious plains. Rocks the size of castles. Chimney Rock like a stovepipe standing above burnt ruins.*

In the morning Mac's ribs and back hurt from coughing, but he rounded up the oxen and yoked them. One beast favored its front right leg.

"Jenny, how long has this ox's hoof been bad?"

Jenny looked up from cooking breakfast. "I hadn't noticed."

"Must be cracked. He can't pull today. I'll have to ride Valiente and herd the pair again."

"I can drive," Jenny said. "But can you ride?"

"I'll be all right." Despite the cool morning, fair skies offered a good day for travel. All he had to do was stay on Valiente's back.

His muscles ached with every step Valiente took. The loose oxen plodded ahead of him, staying close to the wagons all morning. Now that he could see the land they passed through, he understood why the ox had gone lame. The ground was alkaline powder—ready to grind itself into any crevice in a poor animal's hoof. Clouds of dust and grit billowed around the teams and wagons. Even the handkerchief over his face didn't cut the grimy taste in his mouth.

Chimney Rock still towered behind them, and other large formations rose on the plains to the south. They traveled through a wide valley with the silver ribbon of the North Platte to their right. The river was so calm he couldn't tell which way the current flowed, but he could see the ground rising gently to the west ahead of them.

By midafternoon Scott's Bluff loomed nearby, large as a fortress, a high steep crag with a few scraggly trees like sentries sitting on top.

"Why's it called Scott's Bluff?" Jenny asked. He now rode in the wagon beside her, trying not to cough, while Zeke herded the loose oxen.

"Man named Scott died there, I'm told. His companions deserted him. That's all I know."

The wagons rolled in shadows when the sun descended behind the massive cliff. Zeke raced ahead to find their company.

When they found the Pershing group under Scott's Bluff, Jenny jumped off the bench. "I'm going to find Esther," she called over her shoulder.

Head pounding, Mac clambered down. While he unhitched the team, Captain Pershing strolled over, thumbs tucked inside his suspenders. "Hear you're still sick."

"I'm not dead, so I guess I'm fortunate."

Pershing nodded. "Our group lost two children to cholera. Others sick, too. And no doctor." Mac freed his last yoke of oxen, and Pershing picked up the wagon tongue and chained it to the wagon in front of Mac's. "Guess we've all seen the elephant by now."

"Seen the elephant?" Mac hadn't heard that expression before.

"Seen how big a challenge we got ourselves up against. Sickness and death. Perilous storms and barren land. Ain't much a man can do against the elephant."

"Right now, I couldn't conquer a flea."

Pershing snorted. "Can you handle Abercrombie?"

"He still causing trouble?"

"He'll cause trouble till the day he dies. Kills more'n we need. Spouts off 'bout everything. Bellyaches about the pace. Thinks he knows more'n anybody else."

Mac shrugged. "He'll never change."

Pershing clapped him on the back. "You rest up, son. We're meeting tonight. Reorganizing our platoons, now we got fewer men. Make sure you're there."

The men met by Pershing's campfire that evening. A whiskey bottle passed from hand to hand. The alcohol flashed from Mac's gut to his head. At least it warmed his bones.

"Don't see no need to change," Abercrombie said, taking a swig when the bottle came to him.

"Some platoons are down two men. Others at full strength." Pershing's voice was mild, despite Abercrombie's belligerence. "We can come down a platoon. Put a wagon without a man in each group. Assign each a single man to help out."

"Who'll want to switch platoons this far in?" Abercrombie argued. "I ain't giving up mine."

"No one asked you to," Pershing said.

"I don't mind," Mercer said, leaning on the crutch he still used after breaking his ankle at Windlass Hill. "Divvy up my group. I'll go with McDougall, if no one cares."

Pershing assigned the families in Mercer's platoon to other sergeants, then raised his hat. "Don't leave yet," he said. "Need a young man without a wagon assigned to each platoon."

"Give 'em a choice," Doc Tuller said. "They're grown enough."

Zeke said, "I'll stay with McDougall. I been helping him already."

Daniel looked disappointed. The Pershing wagons were in Mac's platoon, and Mac thought Daniel probably wanted to spend time with Esther.

"Son, you're with me," Samuel Abercrombie announced.

Daniel shrugged.

Joel joined the Baker platoon, and another young man was assigned to Hewitt.

"How 'bout provisions?" Pershing asked. "Hear tell some folks are low on food."

"We're moving too slow," Abercrombie muttered. Others murmured in agreement.

"We're a week out from Laramie," Pershing said. "Maybe a day less if we push hard. Can we make it on what we got?"

"What if we can't?" Mercer asked.

"A man named Robidoux has a trading post nearby. But it's out of the way. We can press on to Laramie or go see Robidoux."

"Laramie," Abercrombie said. "I got enough for a week."

"Some families can't move that fast," Doc said. "We still got sick folks." He looked at Mac as he spoke.

"We can make it," Mac said.

"Or split up again." Abercrombie spat on the ground.

"We ain't splitting up again on my watch," Pershing said, frowning at Abercrombie. "We didn't move any faster. Caused worry we didn't need. My mistake. I won't make it again."

Abercrombie mumbled under his breath as he stalked toward his wagon.

Chapter 21: On to Fort Laramie

Saturday the reunited wagon train headed toward Fort Laramie. Esther wanted to walk with Jenny in the morning. "All right," Jenny said, "But I need to stay near our wagon." She wanted to keep an eye on Mac while he drove. Coughing fits still wracked his body.

Jenny, Esther, and the younger Pershings looked for berries as they walked, but few were ripe yet. When the children wandered off a bit, Esther clutched Jenny's arm and whispered, "He proposed!"

"Daniel?"

"Yes, silly. Who else? Near Chimney Rock. I said how splendid it was. He said it looked like a church spire. Like the one back home, where he always thought he'd get married. And he asked me!"

"What'd you say?"

"I said yes, of course."

"How do your parents feel?"

"Daniel hasn't talked to Pa yet. Pa's been too busy. You're the first person I've told, so don't let on till Daniel talks to Pa."

"I wish you both joy, Esther," Jenny said, smiling. Her own future seemed bleak, but she hoped her friend would be happy.

"What's it like?" Esther asked. "Being with a man."

Jenny tried to hide her shudder. "Ask your mama."

"I did." Esther sighed. "She just said to do my duty. Won't you tell me the truth?"

"It might not be the same for you as for me." Jenny hurried off toward the Pershing children. In her haste, she forgot to watch for thorns and ripped her skirt on a prickly pear.

Esther ran after her. "Well, at least tell me what it's like to have a baby

109

inside. Is it scary?"

"Sometimes. Nothing I can do about it."

Jenny drove in the afternoon while Mac rested in the wagon. She listened to him hacking and wheezing. When they stopped she asked Doc to recommend a poultice.

"Best thing is whiskey in his tea. And have him breathe steam over the kettle."

Jenny coaxed Mac to sit by the fire and breathe steam rising from a pot of boiling water, but he wouldn't stay. After two shots of whiskey, he went to bed.

Jenny sat by the campfire alone and wrote:

Saturday, June 5th—I cannot get Mac to treat his cough. Some in our company are short on food. Daniel proposed to Esther. I doubt they marry until they reach Oregon.

Mac coughed less on Sunday. "Maybe the whiskey helped," Jenny told him, feeling relieved.

He grunted and continued yoking the oxen in a pelting rain.

"Want me to drive?" Jenny asked. "You could stay in the wagon, out of the storm. Or ride Valiente, so you won't bump around so much."

"I'll drive."

Jenny sat under the wagon cover to stay dry. Mac hunched on the bench, hat low on his head and his coat collar pulled high. He coughed from deep in his chest. They didn't talk. He never talked much. She wanted to know more about his life in Boston, about Bridget, but she didn't know how to ask.

After the noon meal, Jenny insisted, "I'll drive now. You rest."

Mac looked at the sky, still spitting rain. He nodded wearily and climbed in back.

Jenny heard nothing from him all afternoon, except an occasional wracking cough.

That night Mac took another shot of whiskey and went to sleep early. Jenny wrote:

Sunday, June 6th—Rained until evening. Mac still coughing. Good progress toward Laramie.

The sun shone as the travelers pulled out of camp Monday morning. The rain had reduced the dust, and the sky sparkled. Jenny walked with Esther, and Mac stayed with the wagon.

"Daniel talked to Pa last night," Esther said when the girls were alone. "Pa came around. Ma don't like it."

"Why not? Daniel's a nice young man."

"She says he's too young." Esther sighed. "Pa likes Daniel, though he don't like Mr. Abercrombie. I can always get Pa to do what I want, so he said yes. There's land enough for everyone in Oregon. Once Daniel stakes his claim, he'll be able to provide for me."

"Your mama doesn't agree?"

Esther shook her head. "Says Daniel'll be stuck working for his pa. Says it'll be years before Daniel can afford a family."

"What now?"

"We're engaged," Esther said with a blissful smile. "But no wedding date set."

"That's something. You and Daniel can spend time together now. In the open."

"Yes." Esther nodded. "But Ma'll watch me twice as close, don't I know it."

Later Jenny told Mac Esther's news. He snorted.

"Don't you think it's a good match?" Jenny asked.

"Glad I'm not either one of them," Mac said. "Wouldn't want to be saddled with a silly girl like Esther. Couldn't abide Abercrombie for a father-in-law. Don't know which would be worse."

"But they love each other." Jenny didn't have any hope of romance for herself, but she could relish it in her friends.

Mac grimaced. "I doubt their love will even reach Oregon."

Jenny sighed as she wrote in her diary:

Monday, June 7th—Esther and Daniel have announced their engagement. Mac doesn't approve, but I hope they find happiness.

It took two more days of hard travel to reach Fort Laramie. Jenny was pleased that Mac coughed less each day and no longer wheezed.

They rode along the North Platte through meadows of wild grass. To the south, sand hills undulated, the only change in the scenery. To the north, the river shone in sunlight and darkened under clouds.

The wagons stopped at springs along the trail, avoiding the muddy Platte for drinking water whenever possible. Most of the families ran low on supplies as they traveled.

"Can I borrow some cornmeal?" Hatty Tanner asked Jenny apologetically on the last morning. "I ain't got none left."

Jenny smiled and filled Hatty's cup.

"Hope we can stock up," Mac said as they pulled into the campground outside the fort on Wednesday. "And that prices aren't high. Otherwise, many in our group will suffer."

Chapter 22: Fort Laramie

The next morning Mac rode Valiente into Fort Laramie with other men from their company. The trading post sat at the junction of the Laramie River and the Platte. Green willow boughs hung over the swift, snow-fed water. Wagons and tents surrounded the post, and people flowed in and out of stockade gates that stood in adobe walls fifteen feet high and six feet thick.

"American Fur Company's operated the fort since thirty-six. There's talk of the Army buying it," Pershing said as the group splashed across the Laramie to get to the fort. "But there's been talk for years. Be nice to have some troops stationed this far west, but having a place to get provisions is more important."

"How are the prices?" Mercer asked Pershing.

"Probably steep. Costs a lot to haul goods from Missouri or Santa Fe. The Indians 'round here ain't much at farming or milling."

"How long will we stay?" Mac asked.

Pershing shrugged. "A day or two. So get your trading done quick."

Mac wandered around the fort, perusing vendor stalls inside and outside the gates. The throng of human activity struck him as chaotic after the limited companionship of their small company. Laramie bustled with commerce of all types—blacksmiths, saddlers, and dry goods stores. A woman in a tight, low-cut dress lounged in an open doorway.

After he looked around on his own, Mac went back to camp to find Jenny. She and several other women were doing laundry.

"Want to see the fort?" he asked her.

Her face brightened in a smile, and she quickly finished her chore.

Mac hitched one pair of oxen to their wagon, drove into the post, and

113

left it outside the largest dry goods store.

"Land's sake, prices are high!" Jenny exclaimed, as she fingered a bolt of blue print fabric. "A dollar a yard for calico!"

"You need cloth?" Mac asked. "Seems you sew every night."

"My skirt is so ripped I can hardly mend it any more. I'll cut it up for baby clothes, if I can make a new one for myself."

"Put it in the pile," Mac said. "Flour and rice, too." He looked at a buckskin, wanting a new coat, but not sure how to turn the hide into a coat. He turned to Jenny. "Can you sew leather?"

"I can try. Hatty Tanner might know how."

Mac bought two buckskins, Jenny's calico, flour, rice, and a bottle of whiskey. He tried to dicker over prices, but the trader waved at other travelers browsing in the post. "If'n you won't pay what I'm asking, someone else will."

Mac took three twenty-dollar gold coins out of his pocket and put them on the counter.

The man looked at the money. "That more'n covers it, but I ain't got much currency. Will you take the change in goods?"

Mac nodded. "Add in more flour and lead."

Mac carried their purchases out to the wagon, then he and Jenny strolled through the fort. Emigrants sold furniture they didn't want to haul through the mountains. Jenny picked through the fancy belongings with a wistful smile.

Indians hawked furs and leather and dried meat they called "pemmican." One Indian was selling ponies. A young mare nickered at Jenny, and she patted its nose.

"What a sweet face she has," she said.

"Good mare," the native said. "You want?"

She shook her head. "I don't need a pony." She stroked the mare's mane and moved on.

Mac heard about an Indian pow-wow that evening. "Can we go?" he asked Pershing when he returned to camp.

"Anyone not on guard duty can go," Pershing said. "Just don't get into trouble. Oglalas ain't a problem, but watch out for the Cheyenne."

Doc, Mercer, and Tanner volunteered to stay in camp. The rest of the men were eager to go to the pow-wow. They took beads and trinkets for trade. At the Indian camp across the river, meat roasted on spits. The smell made Mac's mouth water.

"What are they cooking?" he asked Pershing.

"Dog."

Mac ate what was offered. The meat tasted as good as it smelled.

The Indians danced, and whiskey flowed between travelers and natives. "Go easy," Pershing told his men. "Indians get mean when they're drinking."

As the evening drew on, Samuel Abercrombie and his older son Douglass argued with a Cheyenne brave over a game of dice.

"You cheat," the Cheyenne said.

Abercrombie thrust his face into the Indian's. "You bet and you lost. Pay up." Abercrombie's hands curled into fists.

Another Cheyenne flashed a knife.

Fear churned in Mac's gut. A fight was coming.

Douglass Abercrombie pointed his pistol at the Cheyenne with the knife. "Let it go, Pa," he said.

"I ain't leaving till I get what I'm owed."

Indians gathered around the brave, and emigrants behind the Abercrombies.

"Damn it," Pershing said. "I said no trouble." He turned to the Cheyenne, his empty hands open in front of him. "We'll go now," he said. "No fight."

Mac worried whether Pershing's soothing tone was too late.

A gun fired, the brave fell, and bedlam erupted. In the brawl that followed, a Cheyenne slashed Samuel Abercrombie across his arm. Douglass and Mac dragged Samuel out of the Indian camp and back to their own.

"God damn it, Abercrombie, why'd you let this happen?" Pershing yelled.

"I ain't letting no savage cut me. He'll hang."

"Nobody's going to hang," Pershing said, as Doc Tuller inspected the wound.

"It ain't bad," the doctor said. "I can sew it up."

Abercrombie cursed as the stitches went through his skin.

The next morning, Mac wrote in his journal:

June 11, 1847. Abercrombie made a fool of himself at

*the Indian pow-wow last night. He was stabbed, an
Indian shot, and we all could have died. I've seen how
quickly guns can kill a man.*

After breakfast Mac walked to the fort. There were far fewer emigrants and Indians trading than the day before. Indians murmured together as Mac passed, none of them meeting his eye.

The Indian with the mare Jenny had admired had several ponies tied to a post right inside the gate. "You like mare for your woman?" he asked Mac.

Mac turned. The man's face showed no expression. Mac wondered whether the Indian was trying to provoke him or just make a sale. "Don't need a pony," Mac replied, but he patted the pretty mare on the nose.

"For you, fifty dollars." The Indian's eyes narrowed.

Mac shook his head. "Too much." He went into the trading post. With fewer customers, the man behind the counter had time to talk. "Why's everyone so tense today?" Mac asked.

"Indians say an emigrant cheated at dice last night, led to a fight. White folks are scared. Think the Indians want revenge. Indians are afraid of more shootings."

"What'll happen?"

The trader shrugged. "Depends on whether folks get more riled up. Wish people would stick to buying and selling. Whites and Indians don't mix."

"What's a fair price for an Indian pony?" Mac asked.

"Forty bucks. Thirty-five, if it's old."

Mac left the store and sauntered toward the gate.

"You want pony?" the Indian asked again.

Mac examined the mare's teeth and felt her legs. "She saddle trained?" he asked.

"Indian saddle and travois. I ride her. She ride good."

"Thirty-five dollars," Mac said.

"Forty-five."

"Forty."

The Indian nodded, and Mac gave him two gold coins. The Indian bit one, then handed the mare's rope to Mac.

Mac returned to the store, where he bought a saddle, bridle, and reins. He put them on the mare, then mounted. She danced a bit, but settled with a toss of her head.

He rode her back to camp, dismounted, and held out the reins to Jenny. "For you."

She looked up from her washing. "I don't need a pony." But her eyes lit up as she stood and nuzzled the horse's mane.

Her delight pleased him. "It'll get harder for you to walk. I bought her to make up for Abercrombie last night."

"You think he cheated?"

Mac shrugged. "I didn't see what happened. But confronting the Cheyenne in their camp was just plain foolish."

Pershing called the platoon leaders together that afternoon. "We're pulling out in the morning," he said. "Bad blood's brewing. Best if we leave before anything more happens."

"I ain't got restocked yet. And my horse needs shoeing," Lennox grumbled.

"Get it done today. We leave at first light."

Mac spent the afternoon writing a letter to his parents to leave at the trading post. He told them of his illness and recuperation, but still did not mention Jenny.

In his journal the next morning he wrote:

June 12, 1847. Leaving Laramie. A third of our journey done. The mountains lie ahead. Bought a pony for Jenny.

Chapter 23: Past Fort Laramie

Saturday morning the wagons set out across the narrow, dry plateau between the Laramie and North Platte rivers and resumed their trek along the south bank of the Platte. A high mountain range loomed to the southwest, capped by Laramie Peak.

Jenny rode her mare, which she named Poulette. "It means 'little chicken' in French," she told Mac. "That's what the groom called my pony in New Orleans, where I learned to ride."

Mac towered above her on Valiente. The warm sun shone on Jenny's back and a summer breeze teased her hair. She felt happy in a way she had not since before her father's death. "Thank you for the pony," she said, stroking the mare's neck. No matter how often she thanked Mac, it didn't seem like enough.

When the trail narrowed between sandstone cliffs to not much more than the wagon's width, Jenny urged Poulette ahead of the wagons. Mac stayed by the team.

"I don't suppose you'll walk with me much, now you have a horse to ride," Esther said, as Jenny passed by.

"Don't be silly," Jenny said, stopping. "Poulette can carry both of us for a while." She pulled Esther up behind her.

The mare snorted but plodded along.

"I bought cloth in Laramie. For a wedding dress," Esther said. "Light blue with pale yellow flowers. Ma says I can cut it out tonight."

"I thought you weren't getting married until Oregon."

"I ain't. But the print was so purty. And it may be the only trousseau I get."

Jenny laughed. "People leave lots of goods along the trail. You could

118

have a whole wagon of new things by the time we get to Oregon." They'd seen many heirlooms abandoned by earlier travelers.

"Did you have a trousseau?" Esther asked.

"Mac wanted to leave for Oregon right away," was all Jenny said in reply. She hoped Esther wouldn't count the months, as Mrs. Pershing had.

"I want all new things," Esther said, sighing. "Quilts and blankets and dishes. Won't happen, I know. I'll mostly get Ma's cast-offs. I still dream about it. My own home."

"Keeping house won't be easy," Jenny said.

"I know. I've watched Ma all these years. All that cooking and laundry while Pa was away." Esther sighed again. "My own family."

Jenny cradled her belly as the baby kicked. In three months she would have a child to care for. Where would she be when it was born?

They camped that night at Warm Springs, which bubbled tepid water onto sandy banks. Sagebrush and greasewood covered the dry plateau along the Laramie, but small trees and grass sprouted near the spring.

Jenny wrote:

Saturday, June 12th—Camped at Warm Springs. No need to heat the water for washing dishes. Rode Poulette. A fine day.

Jenny hummed as she fixed breakfast on Sunday. Every time she thought of Mac bringing her the pony she smiled. Silly how the thoughtful gift pleased her so much. Mac was no longer coughing, and she didn't worry about him any more.

Pershing held a brief prayer service, but no one mentioned laying by. They traveled up and down ravines cut into the highland. Many of the creek beds were dry, and none of them wet enough to be dangerous. Jenny's good mood remained despite the difficult, monotonous route, but others in the party grew cantankerous.

During the afternoon Jenny found herself walking beside Mrs. Pershing. The older woman panted as they climbed out of a ravine.

"Gracious," Mrs. Pershing said, "I can't hardly walk a step without losing my breath."

"How long until your confinement?" Jenny asked.

"'Bout a month. I seem to get bigger with every baby." She stopped and wheezed at the top of the gully.

"Are you anxious?" Jenny couldn't imagine getting used to being pregnant, even if it were her eighth time.

Mrs. Pershing laughed. "Anxious? That don't help none. Baby comes whether I worry or not." She looked at Jenny. "Are you scared, girl?"

Jenny nodded.

"Birthing's just part of being a woman. Not a thing you can do once it's planted." Mrs. Pershing patted Jenny's arm. "Don't you fret. I'll be there when your time comes. Mrs. Tuller, too. Lots of us to help."

Thinking about her child's birth dampened Jenny's mood.

"What you think about my Esther and young Abercrombie?"

"Esther seems to love him very much."

Mrs. Pershing snorted. "Love ain't important. It's whether a man and woman can work together. Daniel's a good boy, but I don't know if he's ready for a family, if he's strong enough to manage Esther. She ain't one who'll push a man to better himself. Some women do. Others just want a man to dote on 'em. I'm afraid Esther's in that last batch."

"She might surprise you, Mrs. Pershing." Jenny wanted to defend her friend, though Esther could be silly. "Maybe she thinks about dresses and such because she doesn't have much else to think about."

"You're steadier than Esther, Jenny, no matter what your past. She's got to learn to govern her own self. Won't always have me to keep her in line." Mrs. Pershing sighed and leaned on Jenny's shoulder as they walked.

Later Esther asked Jenny, "What were you and Ma talking about? Did she say anything 'bout me and Daniel?"

"She just wants to be sure you're ready for marriage."

Esther laughed. "I'm older'n you are. I'm ready."

"It's not me you have to convince," Jenny said. "It's your mama."

Jenny stared into the campfire that night, seeing her mother's face in the flames. She wrote:

Sunday, June 13th—Mama must have had her baby by now. Esther argues with her mother. How I wish I could see mine, no matter the terrible terms on which we parted.

With every passing day, the hills grew steeper and drier, with little grass for the teams. The emigrants found enough water and meat for themselves, but the oxen and mules on which they depended lost weight.

The Laramie Range rose to their south—snow-covered peaks, even in June. Jenny worried what terrors awaited them. Rivers crossings? Indians? More sickness and death?

"The mountains are so high," she said to Mac.

"This is only the beginning. Rockies lie past the Laramies. And more ranges after that."

"*Mon Dieu*! How will we ever get over them?"

"One step at a time," Mac said. "If the oxen make it. We're not even half way to Oregon, and they're weakening."

Through the night Jenny listened to the restless oxen lowing. Valiente and Poulette grazed during the day on brush when they could find it, but the oxen were trapped in their yokes as they pulled the wagon. At night they complained.

Finally, on the fifth day past Laramie, they came upon a creek with a large field of green grass. "Horsetail Creek," Captain Pershing said. "Full of them reedy plants. We'll lay by tomorrow and let the oxen feed. But don't let the horses get at it. Stuff poisons horses."

The emigrants made camp with a light heart. After supper fiddles came out, and the travelers sang and danced. Jenny sang ballads in both English and French for her companions, but shook her head at Mac's offer to dance.

The next morning Esther told Jenny, "Pa says there's a rock bridge nearby. Daniel and I want to see it, but Ma says we need a chaperone. Would you and Mr. McDougall please come? Pa'll let me take his horse."

Jenny asked Mac, who agreed, and they saddled their horses. The two couples rode up Horsetail Creek through a narrow gorge. About a mile away from camp, a bridge of red rock arched over the stream.

"Let's climb down," Esther said, swinging off her horse. She clasped Daniel's hand, and they headed down the slope to the rushing water beneath the natural span.

"You want to go?" Mac asked.

Jenny hesitated. "You go," she said. "I'm afraid I'll fall. I'm getting clumsy."

"I'll stay with you," Mac said, lifting her off Poulette.

Jenny watched Esther and Daniel laughing on the creek bank. When the courting couple returned to Jenny and Mac, Esther's skirt was wet to her knees.

"The water's cold," Esther said, giggling. "I don't know what Ma will say when she sees how wet I am."

"Then we'll wait till you're dry," Daniel said with a grin.

Jenny and Esther had packed food. The couples ate their dinner under the warm noon sun. Jenny smiled at the cloudless blue sky and was happy again. She might not be as nimble as before her pregnancy, but she could enjoy the beautiful day.

"We'd best be going," Mac said when they had finished eating. "I need to check on the oxen when I get back."

Jenny sighed as he helped her to her feet. That night she wrote:

Friday, June 18th—Warm today, very pleasant. We rode to a natural rock bridge—a wonder to behold. Mac is thankful the oxen's hooves are better.

Chapter 24: Toward Red Buttes

Mac rode last on the way back to camp from the rock bridge. Daniel picked out the route, Esther followed, then Jenny. Esther and Daniel flirted, while Mac and Jenny said little.

Jenny worked so hard that Mac forgot how young she was. Only fourteen—little more than a child, no matter what she had endured during her short life. Even so, Esther seemed less mature than Jenny. Jenny never flirted with him, though sometimes she seemed to with Zeke.

Back in camp, Mac examined his oxen's hooves. The day of rest and grass had helped, but he worried how the animals would survive the constant grit of the trail.

That evening he pulled out his journal:

> *June 18, 1847. Laid by. Oxen's hooves are some improved. Rode to a rock bridge, unlike anything I've seen before. This country is magnificent to behold.*

Saturday the wagons left Horsetail Creek and meandered on the rocky plateau along the Platte River. Mac checked his oxen frequently.

"Your beasts are in better health than most," Pershing told him.

Mac slapped the last ox on the rump. "We still have a long road ahead."

"Aye." Pershing scratched his beard. "I've been considering where to cross the Platte."

"What did the traders say at Laramie?" Mac asked.

"Land's bad both sides of the river. Don't know if it makes much difference where we cross. Mormons got a new ferry 'bout two days' ride from here. Or we can stay on the south bank till Red Buttes."

"You going to look at the ferry?"

"I'll take a few scouts tomorrow. Want to go?"

Mac nodded. "If Jenny can manage the wagon."

"Zeke's staying with ours. He can watch yours, too. It'll be you, me and Daniel. Talked Abercrombie into letting the boy go."

Mac grinned at the captain. "Checking him out as a son-in-law?"

Pershing snorted. "Need to see what he's made of afore he marries my girl."

Mac, Daniel, and the captain left at dawn on Sunday. The other travelers would take their Sabbath rest, then follow with the wagons on Monday.

The scouts reached the ferry at sunset, as the sky turned orange and gray. "We'll camp here. Talk to the Mormons in the morning," Pershing decided.

"I hear Mormons believe in angels and new Bibles," Daniel said.

Pershing nodded. "Mighty strange. But what matters is whether they got good boats and a fair price."

The next morning the three men approached the ferry operators. The landing bustled with wagons and animals—enough emigrants waiting to keep the ferry busy for the next two days. The ferry itself consisted of two dugout canoes about thirty feet long, covered with wooden planks to carry the wagons. The ferryman pulled the unwieldy contraption across the strong current with oars.

"Five dollars a wagon," a Captain Higbee told Pershing.

"Five dollars!" Captain Pershing exclaimed. "Ain't no one else charged that much."

"No other ferries on the North Platte," Higbee said, shrugging. "Ford the river on your own, if you don't like my price."

The scouts watched the ferry operation for an hour and talked to the emigrants in line. The makeshift boat could only handle one wagon at a time, which made for a long wait. "Never thought I'd pay five dollars for a rickety dugout," one man complained. "It's robbery."

"What's our alternative?" Mac asked.

Pershing rubbed his beard. "We could ride on to Red Buttes, but we won't get back to the wagons today, like we said."

"I could go back," Mac offered. "You and Daniel check the ford. We can meet the wagons here. After you see Red Buttes, we can decide which crossing to use."

"Hate for you to ride alone."

Mac shrugged. "Trail's marked. And I'll find our wagons by sunset." He leaned over to whisper with a wink, "Give you a chance to talk to Daniel."

Pershing agreed, and Mac turned Valiente back east toward their company. He relished the time alone, though he kept an eye on the hills, watching for Indians descending from the ridges. But all he saw was more wagons headed for the ferry.

Mac felt comfortable in this grand country, despite its dangers. He was free, unlike his constricted life in Boston. The work was hard, but if he did it well, other men respected him, as his father and brothers never had.

When the sun was low behind him, Mac found their group already camped for the night. Jenny looked up from cooking and smiled.

Esther was with her. "Where's Daniel? And Pa?"

"Still reconnoitering. We'll catch up tomorrow."

Mac called the other platoon leaders together and explained. "The ferry price is steep. Captain Pershing is scouting the ford at Red Buttes."

"How much?" Abercrombie asked.

"Five dollars a wagon."

"Christ Almighty!" Mercer said, stomping his crutch on the ground. "We oughta get rowed to heaven for that price."

Mac nodded. "If the ford's manageable, we should take it."

When the men left Mac's campsite, Jenny asked, "Is the ferry really too expensive?"

"I have the money," Mac said, "but a lot of families don't."

"Will the ford be safe?" Now he heard the worry in her voice.

"The ferry looked pretty rickety. Ford can't be any worse."

After supper, he wrote:

June 21, 1847. Mormon Ferry costs $5/wagon. Too much for some men, but Jenny fears the ford. Hope the current is not too swift.

The wagons reached the ferry Tuesday evening. Pershing and Daniel had staked out a campsite. "It's a day's travel to Red Buttes," Pershing said after the wagons circled. "Ford's deep. Won't be easy. We may have to build rafts ourselves. But we won't have to pay the Mormons."

For once Abercrombie didn't object to Pershing's decision.

Pershing had other news as well. "We rode this afternoon with men from Oregon. Going east to bring their families out next year. Oregon City'll be a boom town soon."

"Good thing we're ahead of the crowd," Abercrombie said. "Claim our land this fall and have our first crop harvested afore next year's wagons git there."

After the meeting ended, Mac couldn't resist teasing Pershing. "So how'd young Daniel do?"

"Boy's got a good head on his shoulders. Respectful, too." Pershing pushed his hat back on his head. "Too bad his father's such an ornery cuss."

Jenny was quiet as she and Mac made camp and ate supper. "How bad will the crossing be?" she asked when Mac brought her a bucket of water to wash the dishes.

"Pershing thinks it's better than the ferry. Maybe no easier, but it won't take any longer, and it's free."

Jenny sighed.

After supper Mac wrote:

June 22, 1847. We head for the Red Buttes ford tomorrow.

Chapter 25: Crossing the North Platte

Tuesday, June 22ⁿᵈ—The desolate Black Hills twist through ravines and around cliffs dotted with dark cedar and pine. Almost every day we see the grave of some poor soul whose journey West has ended.

Jenny looked up from her journal. Raucous laughter and music enlivened the ferry campsite, with so many companies waiting for their turn to cross. Mac said the ferry wasn't sturdy, but she dreaded fording the North Platte. She remembered Louis Papin and his Indian family—why couldn't every river have a strong ferry like theirs?

"It'll be strange to leave the Platte behind," Mac said as they left camp the next morning, walking together beside their wagon. "We've traveled beside it so long."

By afternoon Jenny was ready to ride Poulette. As her weight increased, she found it harder to walk in the heat. She struggled to lift the saddle onto the little mare.

Zeke Pershing came over. "Let me help."

She smiled in thanks, noticing that both Mac and Mrs. Pershing watched Zeke boost her onto Poulette.

They reached Red Buttes in midafternoon. Captain Pershing called a halt. "We'll cross tomorrow. Let the teams feed today. Not much grass north of the Platte."

They camped beneath the circle of high red cliffs that resembled a brick fortress. Grass covered the valley below, bright green where the buttes shaded it. And plenty of wood for fires.

Jenny wandered the edges of the glade where they camped. A trunk, a small armoire, and several chairs littered the valley—belongings earlier emigrants had jettisoned. Jenny and other women scavenged through the discards.

"A quilt," Jenny said, holding up a patchwork of blues and browns. "It's ripped, but I can mend it."

Hatty Tanner showed her husband drill bits and augers. He took a few small pieces, but shook his head at the rest. "Mules can't haul more weight."

Jenny made supper while Mac walked with Captain Pershing to the river. "What's wrong?" she asked when Mac returned frowning.

"River's deep and swift. Even though it hasn't rained recently."

"Can we cross?"

Mac nodded. "We need to decide whether to drive the wagons across or unload and build rafts. We'll test it in the morning."

Fiddles came out as the setting sun sharpened the shadows of the bluffs behind them, but Jenny didn't feel like singing. She remembered her wagon sinking in the quicksand of the South Platte.

She couldn't sleep and thrashed in her bedroll. In the middle of the night, Mac asked from below the wagon. "What's wrong, Jenny?"

"Just nervous." She was ashamed she'd awakened Mac, but it comforted her to hear his voice.

"We won't cross unless it's safe."

In the morning Mac and Zeke rode horseback across the Platte and back. "Teams'll need to swim," Mac told Captain Pershing. "Too deep to walk."

"Let's try pulling a wagon. Lot of work to unload 'em if we don't have to." One of the Abercrombie wagons was nearest the river. Pershing pointed to it. "Take that one."

Samuel Abercrombie climbed on the wagon bench, while Daniel rode beside the oxen and turned them into the water. Other men rode alongside, watching as the wagon sank into the swirling current. The wheels pitched over the rocky bottom, causing the wagon to sway.

"Stop!" Pershing shouted. "Wagon box is flooding."

"Well, I sure as hell can't back up," Abercrombie yelled in response.

Pershing ordered men to get everything perishable off the wagon floor.

They carried crates and sacks of flour to shore.

Abercrombie cracked his whip, and his team surged forward. Now lighter, the wagon lifted off the river bottom, and the oxen pulled it across.

Jenny couldn't hear the men on the far bank, but she could see Captain Pershing and Mr. Abercrombie arguing. Daniel stood next to them, his arms folded.

Mac returned on Valiente.

"What's wrong?" Jenny asked.

"Abercrombie's upset he had to go first. But someone had to. Now we know what the wagons'll do in the water."

"How bad is it?"

"Deeper than we thought. Need to lighten the wagons before they cross, and pull with ropes on the upstream side to keep them straight in the ford. Means two trips for each wagon, but it's safer."

Jenny and other women moved all their food off the wagon floors. When it was time for her to cross, Mac sat with her on the bench, leaving others to man the ropes. She clenched the seat as they started into the water. Her heart pounded as the wagon bounced over rocks. Then the jolting stopped as the current lifted them. She gasped when the wagon swung downstream, and again when it jerked as the ropes caught and men tugged it back into line.

"Whoa, there!" a man shouted. "Got her now." Slowly the oxen and ropes pulled them through the water until the wheels hit bottom on the far side. As they bumped up the riverbank, Jenny found herself clutching Mac with one arm and cradling her stomach with the other.

He grinned at her. "That wasn't so bad now, was it?"

Still trembling, Jenny let go of his arm. He had no fear, it seemed.

The crossing took all morning. Most wagons made two trips across the Platte to transport all the emigrants' belongings. Some food got wet, but no one lost anything else. They ate the noon meal on the north bank of the river, making biscuits to salvage as much damp flour as possible.

"Fill up your barrels," Captain Pershing said. "Not much water this side of the Platte. And watch what the animals drink. Lots of alkali in what water there is."

"How long until we find good water?" Mac asked.

"Three hard days ahead of us."

Mac hauled water while Jenny washed the noon dishes. Then the travelers headed away from the Platte into the high desert, through parched sagebrush and sparse grass shriveling in the summer sun. As they climbed out of the river valley, they approached high crests of stone with jagged peaks.

"Devil's Backbone," Mac said, pointing out the sandstone formations to Jenny. "Pershing says he chiseled his name into the rock there in forty-two."

Jenny shivered. "If it's the devil's backbone, I don't want any part of it."

That night they camped beneath the rock ridges, the only water a small stagnant stream filled with slimy moss. The trickle barely produced enough to drink, wash dishes, and refill their barrels.

Jenny felt the black peaks looming over her. She tried to think of the mountains as vigilant guards, but they looked more like monsters waiting to strike while she slept.

She wrote:

> *Thursday, June 24th—Crossed the North Platte. Now terrible dark rocks hang over us like evil goblins. There is only bitter water, and not much of that.*

Chapter 26: High Desert to the Sweetwater

June 25, 1847. The Platte is behind us. Now we cross the desert toward the Sweetwater, carrying what water we can. We can't bring enough for the animals. Oxen can survive on dew, but horses and mules need more.

The sand stung Mac's face as he rode Valiente beside his wagon on Friday. He pulled his neckerchief over his mouth and nose. A strong wind whistled through the canvas wagon covers and made the horses and mules skittish. Nothing bothered the placid oxen, although they lowered their heads toward the dry ground to escape the dust.

In midmorning the teams perked up and pulled faster. Valiente danced to run free. There must be water nearby.

Pershing trotted along the wagon train on horseback. "Don't let your animals loose," he shouted. "The water's poison."

Mac reined in Valiente and kept his oxen in line. He saw Jenny struggling with Poulette. "Can you hold her?" he called.

"I'm trying."

Zeke rode over to Jenny, grabbed her bridle, and walked Poulette over to the wagon. "Get in," Zeke told her. "I'll tie our horses behind and ride with you."

Mac wanted to object, but he had his hands full keeping Valiente under control and stopping the oxen so Jenny could climb in the wagon. "Much obliged," he said to Zeke.

"Pa calls this Poison Springs," Zeke said. "Full of alkali. Not drinkable, but the animals smell water and want at it."

In the distance a small basin of water sat surrounded by swamp. Mac's wagon passed it safely, but Josiah Baker's gelding bolted and drank at the spring.

"What'll happen to him?" Jenny asked.

Mac shrugged. "Depends on how much he drank. Could die. Could just get a bellyache."

"Better water 'bout five miles farther," Zeke said. "Pa says we'll stop there."

"Not a very long day," Mac said.

"Have to take the water where we find it."

Pershing called the halt at another sluggish creek. The emigrants cooked a quick supper and filled their barrels with slimy water—not pleasant, but safe for animals and people. Baker's gelding drooped, but was still alive the next morning.

Right before they set out, Mac jotted:

June 26, 1847. A miserable camp last night, but enough grass for the teams. Pershing hopes to get to Willow Springs tonight. Better water there.

The ride the next day was dry and rough, but a lighter wind kept the grit tolerable. They reached Willow Springs in midafternoon, where sparkling cold water turned the valley bright green with grasses and small willows. This time when the teams bellowed at the scent, the drivers let them go. Mac barely unyoked his oxen before they rushed for the stream. After they drank their fill, he yoked the lead pair back to the wagon to pull it into the circle for the night.

Wood and water were plentiful. That evening the travelers built a bonfire and filled the air with music. Pershing declared a Sabbath rest the next day, so no one rushed through chores.

A white powder resembling snow blanketed the ground around the spring. "Saleratus," Doc said, sniffing, then tasting the powder. "Same as soda."

Mac took a pouchful of the powder back to Jenny. "Doc says it'll make bread rise."

Jenny frowned. "You sure?"

"Try it. Worst that happens is we throw out the loaves."

Jenny shook her head, but took the powder. "I'll use it in the biscuits tomorrow."

The next morning she exclaimed, "It worked!" Soon he smelled freshly baked biscuits, though something smelled burned as well. Jenny brought him a biscuit dripping with honey. It was an off color, and he eyed it suspiciously.

"Saleratus made it green," Jenny said. "I don't have the hang of baking with it, and the bottoms burned. But they're soft in the middle."

Mac bit in. "Nice change from flapjacks," he said, nodding his thanks.

After the Sabbath service, Abercrombie organized a hunting party. Mac looked at Jenny. "You need me?" he asked.

She shook her head. "Go on."

Pershing led the hunters into the hills above the Willow Creek valley. "Might as well scout while we hunt," he said. The hills were arid, with trees only at the crests. The terrain spread ahead in waves of craggy cliffs and deep creek valleys. Pershing pointed out a valley in the distance. "Sweetwater's over there," he said. "We'll follow it to the summit."

"Deer!" Abercrombie shouted. The men had hunted together enough by now that they naturally split up to drive the small herd into a ravine. They picked off five animals and dismounted to dress the meat.

The men spent a few more hours hunting and shot some grouse. "Enough," Pershing said. "This'll feed us for a few days."

Back at Willow Springs, Mac found Jenny baking more biscuits. "I think I figured it out," she said, handing him one that was golden brown. "Didn't burn this batch." He ate and wrote:

June 27, 1847. Good hunting today. Next landmark is Independence Rock.

Monday morning a light rain fell. "Be easier to cross the desert in the rain," Pershing said. "Keep your barrels open to collect the water."

The terrain was too rough to permit the wagons to move quickly. Creek beds that began flat narrowed into steep ravines bordered by rocky ridges. Zeke and Joel rode ahead to find the easiest route. They switchbacked up hillsides, trying to avoid loose scree so the wagons wouldn't tip.

"Watch out!" Pershing shouted at one driver. "Your wheel's on the edge."

Just then, the rear wheel lost traction, and the wagon started to list. The driver cracked his whip, and his oxen quickened their pace, pulling the wagon back on to firm ground.

"Takin' us twice as long as it should," Abercrombie complained at the noon break.

"You want to scout?" Pershing asked.

Abercrombie spat. "That's young men's work."

"Then let the boys do it," Pershing said, slapping his hat on his head.

The rain had ended, and Mac walked with Jenny through the damp dirt beside the trail. She panted heavily. "We're in the mountains for sure now," Mac said, taking her hand and guiding her over a patch of rough rocks.

"Thank you," she said. "Will it get worse, do you suppose?"

"Probably. We're not to the summit yet. South Pass is still a couple weeks away."

"So far to travel." She sighed. "And what will we find in Oregon?"

Mac grinned. "Who knows? The fun is in the getting there."

Jenny stopped, hands on her hips. "Fun? You almost died, and you call it fun?"

"That's behind us now."

Jenny marched ahead.

"What's wrong?" Mac said, catching up to her. "This is a grand adventure. I've never seen so many wonders."

"Maybe it's an adventure for you," she said over her shoulder. "I have a baby to worry about."

The baby. Mac was silent. Once they reached Oregon, he'd have to decide what to do with not only Jenny, but her child as well. They would need a home.

The travelers camped that night strung out on a gravelly hill that had barely enough flat space for wagons and tents. A small creek ran below the camp, bordered by a little grass for the animals.

The next morning they started early under blue sky, eager to find their way out of the desert. They reached the Sweetwater, but the parched, barren terrain didn't change.

"We follow the Sweetwater toward South Pass," Pershing said. "Last river to the east. Once we pass the summit, rivers all head to the Pacific."

Reaching the Sweetwater didn't improve the emigrants' morale. Jenny and Esther squabbled over something—Mac didn't know what. Abercrombie couldn't speak a civil word to anyone. Even the docile oxen tossed their heads and snorted when Mac unyoked them.

Chapter 27: Wedding Plans

Tuesday, June 29ᵗʰ—Weather warm. Water scarce, except in small creeks. Esther wants me to ask her mother if she and Daniel can marry soon.

Jenny sighed as she wrote. Mrs. Pershing treated her more kindly, after Mrs. Tuller told everyone Jenny saved Mac from cholera. But Jenny didn't want to get between Mrs. Pershing and Esther.

Mrs. Pershing waddled over, wheezing as she sat down on a rock nearby. "Gracious, this mountain air is thin. Can't catch my breath to walk, and the wagon bruises my bones. I'll be glad when this baby finally comes. You've still got what, a couple months?"

Jenny nodded. "September. Early, I think."

Mrs. Pershing's eyes narrowed as she looked at Jenny. "Esther wants to marry the Abercrombie boy soon. You put that idea in her head?"

"No, ma'am."

"She has some romantic notion life'll be better after she's married. You tell her that?"

"No, ma'am."

"Well, what do you think?"

"Daniel's a nice man, Mrs. Pershing."

"You reckon they oughta marry now?"

"It's not for me to say, ma'am."

Mrs. Pershing sighed and stared out into the hills. "Soon as she's married, she's going to find herself like us. Swelling up with a baby. No idea what's in store for the child." She turned back to Jenny. "You want that for her?"

"Like I said, ma'am, it isn't mine to say."

"Captain's weakening. She always could wheedle him into anything. So I'm the one standing in her way." Mrs. Pershing sighed again. "I just want what's best for her. Don't know if Daniel's the one for her."

"You'll never persuade her otherwise. At least not unless there's another man she thinks better suited."

Mrs. Pershing squinted at Jenny. "That's the truth. She'll always want some man around." The older woman took a deep breath. "Captain says Oregon men are rough. I suppose Daniel's better than some she might find." Mrs. Pershing heaved herself to her feet and walked away, shaking her head.

The thin air blocked little of the summer sun, and Jenny made sure her sunbonnet was tied as the wagons set out the next day. She rode Poulette, Mac beside her on Valiente.

Esther ran over to Jenny. Her blond curls bounced free of the sunbonnet hanging down her back. "Rachel's minding the little ones. May I ride with you?"

Jenny lifted an eyebrow at Mac.

"Go whisper your secrets," he said. "I'll watch the wagon."

Esther scrambled up behind Jenny. "Ride away a bit. I want to talk."

When Poulette had trotted a short distance, Esther clutched Jenny's arm. "Thank you for speaking with Ma."

"I didn't do anything," Jenny said, slowing the mare to a walk.

"Well, she's agreed. Next preacher we see, I'm getting married."

Jenny couldn't help smiling. "I wish you and Daniel every happiness, Esther."

Esther chattered all morning about her wedding dress, now finished from the fabric purchased at Fort Laramie, and bedding and dishes her mother could spare.

"Which family will you ride with?" Jenny asked. "Yours or the Abercrombies?"

That silenced Esther. "Oh, it don't matter," she said after a moment.

"We'll work it out."

"Your mother might need you, with a new baby."

"I doubt we find a preacher before her time comes. I can help her."

They camped that evening at what Captain Pershing called Saleratus Lake. The white substance lay in chunks as large as teacups on the ground, and Jenny gathered it for use along the trail.

Word quickly spread through camp that Esther and Daniel would be married as soon as they found a preacher. "What do you think?" Jenny asked Mac.

Mac continued brushing the dust out of Valiente's coat. "They're a pair of damn fools."

"You don't think they should get married?"

"We'll have trouble enough making it to Oregon. Marriage only brings more trouble."

"Don't you want to get married some day?"

"Not until I'm good and ready. And not here."

"I probably won't ever marry." She couldn't imagine letting a man touch her. Not after being violated. Mac must still mourn Bridget, she concluded as she found her journal and wrote:

Wednesday, June 30th—Independence Rock tomorrow! Over two months on the trail and still not halfway to Oregon.

Jenny sensed excitement among her companions the next morning as they approached Independence Rock. By midmorning she saw the landmark on the horizon—it looked like an upside down bowl, or an egg half buried in the sand. A massive, treeless boulder rising alone in the middle of the desert.

"Why is it called Independence Rock?" she asked Mac.

"Some group celebrated Independence Day here several years ago. Now folks say if you get here by Independence Day, you'll beat the snows to Oregon."

Jenny could hardly remember snow, she was so hot. By afternoon the sun blazed with no mercy, and the dry wind blew. Dogs panted and tried to hide under wagons. Horses shook their heads and flicked their tails at flies that swarmed and buzzed endlessly.

Independence Rock loomed as they neared it, the only break in the flat horizon for miles around. They arrived around noon to find several other wagon companies already camped at its base.

The Pershing group made camp on the bank of the Sweetwater, just south of the rock. "We'll stay here a couple of days," Captain Pershing told them. "To hunt and rest."

Jenny unpacked as much as she could, leaving the heavy barrels for Mac. She wanted to sweep the dirt out of the wagon and launder their clothes. She raised her face to the sunshine, smiling at the prospect of two days without traveling.

Mac was away until supper. When he returned, he said he'd climbed to the top of the rock. "A wondrous view," he said. "You can see the Sweetwater almost to South Pass. And Devil's Gate to the west."

"That's nice." Jenny gripped her back as she stood from cooking. She ached after unpacking the wagon.

"I'll take you up tomorrow," Mac said. "If I get back from hunting in time."

"I have to wash clothes."

"It's windy at the top. Might have to weight you down," Mac said, grinning.

"Mmm." She didn't relish getting blown around, not even for a pretty view.

"There are dozens of names painted on the rock. Dating back to 1824. I aim to paint mine on it, too."

She didn't understand why he prattled on about a rock, when there was work to be done in camp. "That's nice."

"Shall I paint your name with mine?"

Anger flashed through her head. "And what name would you paint, Mac?" she asked. "Jenny Calhoun or Jenny McDougall?" What was she to him anyway?

Mac bit his lip, but did not respond.

Jenny shoved a tin plate of food in front of him. He ate.

After supper she washed the dishes with water she'd carried from the river. Mac left her. "Need to check on the team," he said over his shoulder.

She didn't see him again before she went to bed.

Chapter 28: At Independence Rock

*July 1, 1847. At Independence Rock. From the top I
could see for miles.*

Mac sat writing beside the dwindling campfire. He squinted in the poor light, but he wasn't ready to sleep. The splendid sights he'd seen swirled in his brain—the Sweetwater River stretching ahead until it became a tiny ribbon on the horizon, the narrow gap of Devil's Gate carved through the ages, and snowcapped mountains surrounding all sides of their route. He wanted to show Jenny these wonders, but she had snapped at him earlier. He had no idea what had set her off.

Pershing ambled over and sat beside Mac, then pulled a glowing twig from the fire and lit his pipe. "Thinking of staying here through the Fourth," the captain said. "You mind a few days' rest?"

"No. It'd be good for the teams."

"There's a rendezvous here on the Fourth," Pershing said. "Party of trappers from Oregon due in. Be a good chance to learn 'bout conditions in the West."

"Sounds fine." Mac frowned at the captain. "Why are you telling me now?"

"Abercrombie's going to raise a stink. He'll argue to leave sooner."

"He'll want to hunt tomorrow."

"Aye," Pershing said. "Then he'll be ready to move on."

"Surely we should hear what the trappers have to say."

Pershing nodded. "That's my thinking."

"I'll back you up," Mac said.

Mac went with the hunting party, leaving camp shortly after dawn. Abercrombie boasted he would shoot all his wagon could carry by noon. Through the morning they found sage hens and jackrabbits, but no larger game.

"Too damn many wagons and people," Abercrombie fumed. "Need to get away on our own to find the herds."

Toward midday the men came upon several sheep with large curling horns nestled in the hills near Devil's Gate. The sheep stared at the men without moving. "Bighorns," Pershing said. "Ain't seen 'em this far east before."

"Fire!" Abercrombie yelled. Shots sounded. Five of the strange beasts dropped.

Mac and two others rode back to camp to get a wagon to carry the meat. When he arrived, Jenny knelt beside a scrub board and a bucket, her face pale. "What are you doing?" Mac asked.

She frowned. "Washing." She pushed a stray lock of hair out of her face with a wet hand.

"Don't you want to get out of camp?"

"Everything's filthy from the dust."

"How much longer will the laundry take?"

She shrugged. "Half an hour. Still need to rinse and hang it up."

"I'll be back."

Mac strode over to the wagon being readied to haul the meat back to camp. "Can you do without me?" he asked. When the other men nodded, he returned to Jenny.

"We're climbing the rock," he told her.

"Mac, I don't—"

"Come on, Jenny, you need a pleasant day. Even a few hours." He lifted her by the elbow. She grabbed her sunbonnet as he led her toward the granite hill.

Mac grinned as he started to hike up the narrow path. It was a wonderful day, and he was glad to share a piece of it with Jenny. He turned to her. She wasn't following. "What's wrong?" he asked.

"It's too steep," she said, holding one arm under her belly.

"I'll help." Mac slid back down to Jenny and held her hand while she clambered over a boulder. They inched their way upward. Soon she returned his smiles and held out her hand for assistance over the larger stones.

The wind whipped Jenny's skirt around her legs, and Mac heard her puffing when they reached the top. But she had breath enough to gasp, "You can see forever!"

He pointed out Devil's Gate. "That's where we found sheep today. And see"—his boot tapped a bare spot on the rock—"here's where I aim to paint our names."

"I don't need my name painted, Mac."

"Don't you want to leave a record you were here?"

"I don't know what name to write."

Was that why she was mad? "Jenny. That's all."

She shook her head. "Do what you want."

When they arrived back in camp, Esther ran over to Jenny. "Where you been? There's a preacher here. I'm getting married tomorrow!" And Esther pulled Jenny over to the Pershing wagons.

The hunters didn't return to camp until after supper. Mac brought his share of the spoils to Jenny. "Fresh mutton tomorrow."

"That's nice." She hadn't said much since she returned from the Pershing campsite.

"What's wrong?" he asked.

"Nothing." She busied herself packing away the mutton.

Mac watched her. "So Esther and Daniel are getting married tomorrow," he said to make conversation.

"Mmm-hmm."

"What's her mother say?"

Jenny shrugged. "Now that it's decided, she thinks it was her idea."

"How do the Abercrombies feel?"

"Haven't heard."

"I thought you'd be happy for Esther and Daniel."

"I am." Jenny walked to the wagon. "Think I'll turn in now."

"I enjoyed the afternoon with you," Mac called after her.

She turned to him and smiled. "I did, too."

Grinning, Mac went looking for Pershing and found the captain sitting beside his wagons. "So you're letting Esther marry tomorrow?" Mac said.

"Seems so," Pershing said. "She and her ma are in a tizzy."

"What's Abercrombie say?"

"He's spouting off about moving on. Do this wedding some other time. But Daniel and Mrs. Abercrombie are holding firm."

"Mrs. Abercrombie doesn't say much."

"No, she don't." Pershing chuckled. "But when she does, seems like Samuel listens."

Mac laughed. "Good to know someone can get through to him. So we're staying through the Fourth?"

Pershing nodded. "Wedding tomorrow. Party tomorrow night, then another on the Fourth. Some goddamn fool brought a cannon here. Going to shoot it off at the top of the rock on the Fourth."

"How will they haul it up there?"

"Damned if I know. Bunch of foolishness."

Mac spent the next morning on top of Independence Rock using grease and gunpowder to paint "Caleb McDougall—July 3, 1847" in the spot he had chosen. He stepped back to admire his work, then added "and Jenny" underneath his name. The two words were inadequate to acknowledge all she had done on the journey, but they were all he could truthfully add.

Trappers from Oregon rode into camp around noon in a light rain. Mac joined men from several companies crowded under a tarp to hear their news.

"Still snow in the highest passes when we come through," a bearded man in buckskin said.

"How's the wagon trail?" Pershing asked.

Another trapper spat a stream of tobacco juice before answering. "Ain't paid no attention. My mules ain't wagons."

The first trapper responded, "Better'n last fall. Every wagon headed west tramples down another bush or two."

"So we can get our wagons through?" Abercrombie asked.

"Sure can," the man in buckskin replied.

"What about Indians?" a man from another company asked.

"Mostly scrawny no-count tribes along the way. Fight with each other, but don't bother us none." The mountain man spat again.

"Any skirmishes between Indians and settlers this year?"

"Ain't heard of none," the lead trapper said. "But stay on the main trail."

The discussion continued for an hour or more. When it was over, Mac went back to camp.

Jenny had put a lace collar on her loose blouse. "There's a clean shirt for you in the wagon," she said. "For the wedding."

Mac grunted and sat to write in his journal:

July 3, 1847. Trappers from Oregon say the road is good. No trouble with Indians. But perhaps their mules were not as tempting a target as the wagon trains, with our horses and women and food.

Chapter 29: Celebration

Jenny fussed over her appearance as she dressed for Esther's wedding. She'd made a collar from the lace Mrs. Jenkins gave her in Independence, but she didn't have any nice clothes. All she had were drawstring skirts and baggy shirtwaists that hung over her bulging stomach. But then, no one cared how she looked.

She braided her hair and pinned it up. She thought it was still pretty, though she didn't have a mirror to check.

It was almost time for the ceremony, and Mac wasn't ready. "You are going, aren't you?" she asked as he sat writing.

"Give me a minute." He shut his journal and climbed in the wagon. Jenny found a jar of honey to take with the cornbread she'd baked for the wedding feast. "Ready," Mac said, stepping down from the wagon. "Let's go." He took the cornbread dish from her.

His clean blue shirt matched his eyes, and black slicked-down hair touched the collar. He'd shaved recently. She rarely noticed how handsome he was—it didn't matter to her. He would make some girl a good husband. He was responsible and easy to look at. She hoped he'd find someone to replace Bridget in his heart.

Across the camp several tarps draped between wagons formed a covered pavilion. A rough table of boards laid across barrels was already laden with pots and dishes.

Children ran around under the canvas shouting. Mrs. Pershing bustled about, wheezing for breath. She ordered Mac to set the cornbread on the table.

Esther wore her pale blue frock with the yellow flowers and a blue ribbon braided through her golden curls. "See what Mrs. Tuller gave me,"

145

she said to Jenny, touching the ribbon. "Something new and blue. Like my dress. And Mrs. Tuller made me a quilt, too. And Ma gave me this old bit of lace. It was her ma's before her. And I borrowed Rachel's locket."

"You look beautiful, Esther," Jenny said, hugging her friend.

The Abercrombies stood apart from the crowd. Mrs. Abercrombie smiled, and Jenny went over to the small, meek woman. "Congratulations," she said with a little curtsy. "I hope Daniel and Esther will be very happy."

Samuel Abercrombie snorted, as his wife thanked Jenny.

The preacher arrived and began, "Dearly beloved, . . . " A beaming Esther and stammering Daniel said their vows.

What a wonderful wedding, Jenny thought, even in this wilderness. Esther had what she always wanted—a man to love her. Jenny sobbed as she wondered whether she would ever marry—ever want to marry—and whether any man would ever love her. Mac's arm came gently around her shoulder. She tensed, then leaned into his comfort.

After the vows, they feasted. Fiddles and harmonicas played, and as dusk approached dancing began. The rain ended, and a soft sunset filled the fresh evening air.

Jenny sat on a log watching the merriment. Esther danced with Daniel, with her father, then with a parade of other men, young and old. She waved at Jenny each time she whirled by.

Mac came and stood over Jenny. "Let's dance," he said.

"I've told you, I don't know how."

"It's expected. This is a wedding." He pulled her to her feet. "Relax," he said, smiling. "I'll lead. Listen to the music. Move with it."

The lively jig did make her want to dance. So she did—better than the last time she'd tried.

The next tune was a waltz. Many of the older couples sat down. Mrs. Pershing shook her head and muttered, "Indecent."

Jenny turned to leave. "I don't know how to waltz."

"It's easy," Mac said. "I waltzed in Boston for years."

Mrs. Pershing stood off to the side with her lips pursed. Then Jenny saw Mrs. Tuller leading the doctor out to dance. "All right," she said.

Mac placed his hand on her waist and pulled her closer, until her stomach almost touched his. She smiled up at him. Their eyes met, and she glanced away, afraid she was blushing.

"You don't even reach my chin," he said as they swirled. "Are you ever going to grow?"

Jenny stiffened and missed a step. "I'm tall enough."

"I suppose."

After the waltz Jenny claimed she was tired and sat. She watched Mac skip by with Esther, then with Rachel and other women. He even took a turn with Mrs. Tuller.

Later Zeke asked her to dance. "No, thank you," she said. "I've had enough." Zeke sat with her until the shivaree began.

"What's a shivaree?" Mac asked.

Jenny laughed. "We had them in New Orleans. And Missouri, too. We serenade the newlyweds. No shivarees in Boston?"

He shook his head.

"Grab a pot and make some noise."

Zeke and Joel pulled Mac along with them. The young men banged pots and pans and shot a rifle into the air while they escorted the newly married couple to a wagon pulled just outside the main camp. Esther hid her face in Daniel's shoulder when he lifted her into the wagon.

After watching, Jenny excused herself and went back to her wagon. By light from an oil lamp, she wrote:

Saturday, July 3rd—Esther and Daniel are married. I hope they remain as happy as they are today. I waltzed with Mac.

A loud boom awakened Jenny in the morning. She dressed hurriedly and climbed out of the wagon. "What was that?" she asked.

Mac stood staring at the top of Independence Rock. "A cannon."

"Cannon?"

"Soldiers from Laramie are here on patrol. Brought a cannon with them."

"They pulled a cannon all the way from Fort Laramie?"

"No worse than some of the thingamajigs the emigrants bring. At least a cannon provides protection. But they hauled it to the top of the rock." He sounded amused.

"Heavens!" was all Jenny could say as the cannon boomed again.

"It's the Fourth of July," Mac said. "How did you celebrate back home?"

She shrugged. "Mama didn't pay much attention. Papa liked a good parade."

"In Boston there's always a big parade." Mac grinned. "Children waving flags. Old soldiers marching. One old man was a drummer in the Revolutionary War."

"There's another big dinner at noon," Jenny said. "May I ride Poulette this morning?"

"I'll saddle both horses," Mac said. "We'll ride along the Sweetwater."

As they left, Esther and Daniel, hand in hand, returned to the main campsite. Jenny waved, and the newlyweds waved back.

Mac led her along the Sweetwater to Devil's Gate. "We hunted here two days ago." He pointed at the narrow gap in the granite crags. "Pershing told me the Indian legend. They say the Great Spirit told them to hunt a huge beast. But the beast carved that gap with its tusks to escape. It disappeared through the gap and was never seen again. What a strange notion."

Jenny smiled. "No stranger than our tales of dragons. Like Saint George."

"No one believes those fairy tales," Mac scoffed.

"You'd be surprised what people believe in New Orleans. Voodoo and magic."

Mac pointed at a cliff above them. "We saw Indian graves all through the bluffs when we hunted. There's one."

Jenny winced. "I don't like being around the dead. Indian or white."

They returned to camp, splashing through the river bed. "The wagons will have to cross the Sweetwater several times," Mac said. "But you can see—it's not deep like the Kaw, nor as wide as the Platte."

Jenny worried nevertheless. The Sweetwater here was green and lovely—would it remain so as they climbed the mountains?

Esther ran over to Jenny when they reached their wagon. "Come help me get ready for dinner," she said.

"I need to make my own dish," Jenny said.

"It'll just take a minute," Esther pleaded, pulling Jenny's arm.

"I'll see to the horses," Mac said. "Go on."

Esther linked her arm with Jenny's. "Why didn't you tell me?"

"Tell you what?"

"How wonderful being with a man is."

Jenny stared at Esther. "It isn't all wonderful," Jenny finally said, shaken that Esther had found pleasure in what she had felt as violation.

She returned to her campsite and fried mutton with wild onions and sage. The sage along the route was more bitter than that in the garden at home, but it did flavor the meat. She didn't have any pretty plates like some women did. The frying pan would have to do.

After the emigrants feasted again, children banged pots like drums, and soldiers set off the cannon once more.

"We'll head out early tomorrow," Pershing told his company.

They spent the evening packing. When she finished, Jenny eased herself down on an overturned bucket to write:

Sunday, July 4th—We have rested for three days and celebrated. Tomorrow we return to the trail. More rivers to cross.

On Monday they broke camp after a quick breakfast in light rain. Jenny found herself walking beside Mrs. Pershing and some of her brood.

"Where's Esther?" Jenny asked.

"With the Abercrombies." Mrs. Pershing sighed. "I miss her already. She was a help with meals and young 'uns. Rachel can't do it all. Ruthie's too young."

"Esther's still here," Jenny said.

"It ain't the same. She'll have her own doings now."

"She seems happy with Daniel."

Mrs. Pershing nodded. "That she does. And I'm pleased to have her settled."

Chapter 30: Trouble on the Sweetwater

Mac rode Valiente as they detoured around Devil's Gate. "Can't take the wagons through the canyon," Pershing had said. "Riverbank is narrow and full of rocks." So they crossed the Sweetwater for the first time, drove south of the cliffs and back to the river on the far side of the gap. From there the trail followed the flat, grassy banks of the Sweetwater.

Shortly after they passed Devil's Gate they came across a fresh grave. "Frederick Richard Fulkerson. July 1, 1847," Mac read from the board marking the grave. "Just four days ago. He died the day we arrived at Independence Rock."

Pershing pointed out a notch in a mountain peak ahead of them. "Split Rock," he said. "We head straight for it. Leads to the pass."

"Looks like a gun sight," Hewitt said.

Despite the jagged crests around them, the path toward Split Rock was gentle. They camped near a pool in the Sweetwater created by an old beaver dam.

"Beaver are mostly hunted out," Pershing said. "Trappers been in these mountains over forty years. Have to go a lot farther west to find 'em now."

Before turning in that night, Mac sat by the blazing fire and wrote:

July 5, 1847. On the Sweetwater beyond Devil's Gate.
Good grass. Travel along the river is easy.

In the morning Mac told Jenny, "We cross the Sweetwater again today. We'll cross back and forth all the way to the summit."

"Wouldn't it be easier to stay on the same side?"

"It would add days," Mac said. "River twists through the valley. Better to keep to a straight path."

Jenny saddled Poulette. "I'll ride this morning," she said. "Esther's with her mama. She spent last night with the Abercrombies, so she's taking care of her brothers and sisters today. I may help her this afternoon."

Mac kept quiet. He'd told Jenny there'd be problems between the Pershings and Abercrombies, and they were starting already.

The wagons rolled along the south bank of the Sweetwater until they were even with Split Rock. That evening, Split Rock behind them, the men discussed the next day's route.

"Tomorrow's the hard day," Pershing said. "Three river crossings in two miles."

"Can we avoid any of them?" Mac asked, knowing Jenny would be nervous all day.

Pershing pushed his hat back on his forehead. "We could swing wide south. But then we're in deep sand. Harder on the teams."

"We should stay near the water," Abercrombie said. "Better hunting, I reckon."

Mac didn't say any more. He would deal with Jenny.

Back at their wagon, he told her, "Pack everything tight. Three crossings tomorrow."

Her eyes widened. "Three!"

"The Sweetwater twists. No way around it." No need for her to know about the sandy route. The men had decided.

In the morning he helped her wrap food in oilcloth and tie perishable goods on top of other belongings. "You want to ride in the wagon or on Poulette?" he asked.

"Poulette. At least to start with."

The sun removed the chill from the early morning air, and riding was pleasant. They reached the first crossing midmorning.

"Stay here while I get the wagon across," Mac told Jenny. I'll come back for you."

The Sweetwater was shallow enough to drive the wagons across, but the snow-fed stream was cold. On horseback, Mac led the oxen to the far side. He sucked in his breath when the icy water splashed him.

"Come on," he said to Jenny when he returned to her, "You'll do fine.

I'll ride downstream of you."

Jenny's knuckles on the reins and pommel were white. She was silent until her legs hit the cold water. Then she shrieked.

"You can do it," Mac said, urging Poulette along. Mac kept Valiente beside Poulette until her hooves were on dry ground.

"Go dry off," he told Jenny. "I'm going back to help others."

When all the company had crossed the Sweetwater, they rode on briefly, then repeated the crossing two more times that day. They halted after the third crossing.

"Might as well dry out here," Pershing said.

Mac hadn't changed clothes between crossings. When the sun dropped below the mountains ahead of them, he felt the bite of cold evening air. He shivered, and Jenny brought him a dry shirt and towel.

"I've warmed leftover stew for supper," she said. "Soda bread, too."

July 7, 1847. Made it through Three Crossing Canyon. Mercer lost a barrel of cornmeal. Teams are exhausted after pulling the wagons through water. I suppose sand would be worse.

As he wrote, Mac heard a shout from across the camp. It sounded like Abercrombie. Mac walked over to investigate.

"God damn it! We ain't stopping!" Abercrombie yelled at Pershing. "I aim to get my family over the mountains afore snowfall."

"Now look, Abercrombie," Pershing said, his bearded jaw jutting forward. "We got to keep the company together. Folks is tired. Oxen 'bout dead on their feet."

"Leave 'em behind, if they can't keep up, I say," Abercrombie bellowed, fists clenched. "I'm able. And I'm going on."

Behind the two men, Esther stood gripping Daniel's arm. Tears ran down her face. "Stop them, Daniel," she said.

"Pa—" Daniel said.

"Don't you 'Pa' me," Abercrombie snarled at his son. "Your new wife needs to learn her place. She'll go where I say."

"Pa!" Daniel said again.

"We're laying by tomorrow, and that's that." Pershing stalked toward his campfire.

Esther sobbed into Daniel's chest. Men argued, some supporting Pershing, some Abercrombie. Mac didn't want any part of it and headed back to his wagon.

"What's all the commotion?" Jenny asked.

"Spat between Pershing and Abercrombie," Mac said. "Pershing says we're laying by. Abercrombie wants to move on."

Jenny sighed. "Poor Esther." She climbed into the wagon.

Doc Tuller wandered over and sat beside Mac. "Got to do something about them two," he said. He lit his pipe. "Ain't healthy, them pissing on each other."

"Pershing's in charge," Mac said.

"Only as long as the rest of us let him be." The doctor puffed on his pipe. "My money's on Pershing, but some folks agree with Abercrombie."

"I'm with Pershing. He knows these mountains." Mac was still glad to be traveling with a man who'd been west with Frémont.

"Abercrombie's no fool. He'd probably get us through."

"But at what cost to our teams and families?" Mac shook his head. "We need to stick with Pershing."

Chapter 31: More Trouble in Camp

Jenny awoke Thursday morning to Esther's whisper. "Jenny, I need to talk to you."

Jenny stuck her head out of the wagon. "What's wrong?"

"Hurry! I only got a minute."

Jenny dressed and clambered out of the wagon. She didn't see Mac. "What is it?"

Esther clutched Jenny's arm. "Did you hear the fight?"

Jenny shook her head. "Mac said there was a spat, but that's all he said."

"It was more'n a spat. Pa and Mr. Abercrombie almost came to blows."

"Whatever for?"

"Because Pa's laying by today. I tried to get Daniel to stop them, but he couldn't." Esther sniffled. "Afterward I had to listen to Mr. Abercrombie yelling. At his wife, at Daniel, at everyone. Even his granddaughters."

"He'll get over it." Jenny put an arm around Esther.

"Now I need to help Ma. She's feeling poorly. Rachel came to get me. Mr. Abercrombie shouted when I left. But Ma needs me." Tears streamed down Esther's face.

"Hush, now. You go help your mama. I'll come over as soon as I have Mac fed."

Esther sighed. "You're so lucky—only you and Mac. No family to worry about."

Lucky, thought Jenny. Was she lucky not to have any family? Then why did she feel so lonely? And soon she'd have a child to worry about.

She had finished frying flapjacks and meat when Mac returned to their wagon. "I hear Captain Pershing and Mr. Abercrombie fought last night," she said handing him a plate heaped with food. "Won't they ever get along?"

"I doubt it."

She looked at Mac. "Esther's trapped in the middle."

Mac was silent.

"Can't you do anything?" Jenny asked.

"Not much."

Jenny put her hands on her hips. "Well, I'm going to help Mrs. Pershing. Take some of the load off Esther."

"Suit yourself," Mac said. "I'm hunting today."

"Will both Captain Pershing and Mr. Abercrombie be going?"

"Probably."

"Be careful." She didn't want Mac caught between the two other men.

Jenny cleaned up after the meal and walked over to the Pershing camp. Esther's arms were in dishwater to her elbows. "Thank goodness you're here," she said. "Ma's in bed, and I can't stay. Mrs. Abercrombie's looking for me."

"Rachel and I can manage," Jenny said, linking arms with the younger girl. "You go on. Come back when you can."

Esther lugged the bucket of dirty water outside the wagon circle and dumped it. "Thank you," she said. She dried her arms on her apron and headed toward the Abercrombie camp.

"Rachel, can you watch the children while I see to your mama?" Jenny asked.

Rachel nodded. "I'll take 'em to play by the river."

"Don't let them fall in." Jenny quaked at the thought. Then she peeked in the wagon at Mrs. Pershing. "Can I get you anything, ma'am?" she asked. "A cup of tea or a biscuit?"

Mrs. Pershing lifted her head. "Why, Jenny. Where's Esther?"

"She couldn't stay."

"Where are the other children?"

"Rachel's got them."

Mrs. Pershing lay back on her pallet. "I'm sorry to be a bother, child. My back hurts bad today. Baby's pushing all the time. Be here soon, I think."

"It's a good thing we're laying by today. You can rest."

"I told the captain not to halt on account of me. He says others needed to rest, too, but I think he did it for me. He ain't used to seeing me just before the baby comes."

"The men are glad to be hunting. We can use the meat. I fried up our last bit this morning." Jenny squeezed in next to Mrs. Pershing and plumped up her pillows. "Now, how about some tea?"

"Thank you. Tea would be nice."

Jenny busied herself at the Pershing campsite through the morning. Around noon Esther returned, carrying a pot of soup in a heavy Dutch oven. "I made this for Ma," she said. "Meat broth and wild onions. Mrs. Abercrombie knows, but I'll need to bring back some of our provisions to replace what I took. So her husband don't complain."

"I'll fix enough supper for your family," Jenny said. "Mac won't care."

"I'm up," Jenny heard Mrs. Pershing say behind her. "Can't stay in bed all day." The older woman sat with a wheeze on an overturned bucket by the fire. Mrs. Pershing ate her soup while Esther combed out her mother's hair and braided it.

Esther left the Pershing wagons in midafternoon, taking some of the Pershings' flour and vegetables back to the Abercrombie wagons.

Mrs. Tuller visited with Mrs. Pershing. When the doctor's wife was ready to leave, Jenny pulled her aside and whispered, "Is Mrs. Pershing all right?" Jenny had worried all day about the older woman, and about her own baby as well. Would she feel this poorly when her time was near?

Mrs. Tuller smiled and patted Jenny's arm. "It's always hard right before the birthing." Mrs. Tuller was trying to comfort her, but Jenny still felt uneasy.

Jenny stayed with the Pershings until the hunters returned in late afternoon.

"Shot some pronghorn antelope and a couple of deer," Mac said as he dismounted.

"And saw grizzly tracks," Captain Pershing said. "Don't anyone leave camp without a gun."

Jenny shivered. She'd never seen a bear and didn't want to.

"I'll fry some meat, Captain," she said. "Enough for your family, too."

"Where's Esther?" he asked. "Thought she was with her ma today."

"She was here," Jenny said. "But had to get back."

Captain Pershing scowled, but was quiet.

Jenny was cooking when she heard shouts from the Pershing wagons

She lifted the skillet off the fire and ran to see what was happening.

"Who gave your girl leave to feed your family with my food?" Mr. Abercrombie bellowed at Captain Pershing. "You think 'cause you're captain you can take what you want? It's thievery."

Esther pulled at her father-in-law's arm. "I asked Mrs. Abercrombie," she said, tears running down her face. "I brought back some of Ma and Pa's food. I didn't steal."

Samuel Abercrombie shook her off. "Stay out of this, girl. Your goddamn pa put you up to it, I know he did."

Captain Pershing pulled Esther behind him. "Don't touch my girl, Abercrombie. This has gone far enough. You keep a civil tongue in your head, or we'll leave you behind."

Abercrombie looked at the crowd that had gathered. "You hear?" he said. "Pershing's threatening me."

Jenny couldn't keep quiet. "I was there today, Mr. Abercrombie," she said. "Esther's telling the truth. She borrowed some food, then paid you back."

"You keep out of it, missy," Abercrombie shouted, spittle forming in the corners of his mouth as he spun toward Jenny.

Mac stepped in front of Jenny. Doc Tuller pulled Captain Pershing away from Abercrombie, while Daniel put a hand on his father's back.

"Back off, both of you," Mac said. "Jenny saw what happened. Esther borrowed from you, Abercrombie. We've all done that along the way."

"Pershing had no call to take from me," Abercrombie insisted.

"You and Pershing are practically kin now, Abercrombie," Doc said. "Esther and Daniel need to assist her folks. You'd expect the same of Esther if it were your wife sick."

When the crowd nodded, Abercrombie shook his finger in the captain's face. "This ain't the end, Pershing." He strode toward his wagon. Daniel and Esther followed, Esther with a glance back at her father.

Jenny fed the Pershings and Mac, washed up, then sat by her own campfire writing:

> *Thursday, July 8th—Laid by and helped Mrs. Pershing. How will Captain Pershing and Mr. Abercrombie travel together all the way to Oregon? Poor Esther.*

Chapter 32: Grizzly Bear

July 9, 1847. The land along the Sweetwater alternates between sand and swamp, both hard on the animals. Pershing and Abercrombie quarrel daily.

Mac scribbled in his journal, then went to hitch his team.

"Want some help?" Zeke asked.

"Much obliged." Mac handed Zeke one yoke bow.

"I had to get away from our camp," Zeke said. "Pa's fretting about Ma. Complaining about Abercrombie."

Mac shook his head. "Don't know what to do. Both your father and Abercrombie are bullheaded, but your father's our captain."

"Joel, Daniel, and I've been talking," Zeke said. "We need to keep them apart. Can you help?"

Mac nodded. "I'll do what I can. And I'll talk to Doc."

When the wagons set out, Mac pulled into line behind the Tullers and gave his whip to Jenny. "You drive. I need to see Doc."

Mac strode ahead to the Tuller wagon where Doc walked beside his team. "Mind if we chat?" Mac asked.

Doc grunted.

"Pershing and Abercrombie," Mac said. "One of them will kill the other if we don't do something."

"They ain't getting along, that's for sure."

"What can we do?"

Doc rubbed his chin. "Sometimes there ain't much a man can do. 'Cept let other folks work out their differences." He winked at Mac. "And keep 'em away from guns. I don't have a liking for digging bullets out of flesh."

Doc didn't seem worried, though Mac still chafed to do something.

He went back to his own wagon and saddled Valiente. "Think I'll ride today," he told Jenny.

In the afternoon the travelers reached the fifth crossing of the Sweetwater. "We'll camp on the far side," Pershing announced. "Tomorrow we go overland across a bend in the river. Try to reach the Sweetwater again by dusk."

The crossing was easy, and camp beside the river peaceful. No arguments disrupted the evening. Fiddles and banjos entertained them until late. In the morning they followed a small tributary of the Sweetwater. The narrow, hilly valley and sandy soil made for slow travel. Masses of treeless granite rose high above the valley.

In late morning Joel, who was scouting, rode back to the wagons. "Ice," he shouted. "There's an ice field ahead."

"Ice Slough," Pershing said. "I heard tell of it, but ain't never seen it. Stays cold enough underground to keep the water frozen."

A short time later the wagons reached a grassy swamp. Children dug in the mud with Zeke and Joel, all of them laughing. They found a large sheet of ice just inches under the grass. Zeke chopped it into pieces the children could carry. The Pershing twins and Otis Tanner shrieked at the cold until Hatty Tanner gave them a bucket to put the ice in.

"What strange country," Jenny said to Mac. "Not like New Orleans."

The clumpy sedge grass on top of the ice field was difficult to traverse, but the ice was such a welcome treat that no one complained. Mac even saw Abercrombie smiling at Esther as she helped Mrs. Abercrombie churn chipped ice and sugar into a frosty treat.

After the midday meal they filled buckets with ice to enjoy through the afternoon. Their route went through dry, cracked land, broken occasionally by small streams. But the novelty of the frozen field kept their spirits high. In the early evening they saw the Sweetwater in the distance. They ate a quick, cold supper and kept going until they reached the river.

"We'll cross in the morning," Captain Pershing said. "Then take a Sabbath rest."

Mac wrote before bed:

July 10, 1847. Nooned at Ice Slough. A curious place—ice underground in the middle of summer. Tomorrow we cross the Sweetwater again, then lay by. Perhaps I can take Abercrombie away to hunt.

The mountain air was cool during the morning crossing, despite bright sunshine. After they set up camp on the far side, Mac left Jenny hanging a tarp to dry and went hunting. Pershing stayed in camp with his wife.

Mac rode with Zeke and Joel, letting Abercrombie steer the group into the mountains. Mac grinned at an eagle that soared above.

Toward noon they found fresh grizzly tracks. Abercrombie found more spore and led them after the bear.

Mac had never seen a grizzly. "How big is it?" he asked Abercrombie.

"Bear's a bear," Abercrombie said. "Seen 'em in Tennessee."

"Them's black bear," Zeke said. "Grizzlies are bigger. Much bigger."

Abercrombie's dog, a pointer mix, ran ahead of the riders. Soon the men heard the dog baying, followed by a roar.

"He found it!" Abercrombie yelled and spurred his horse over a crest.

Mac followed as the commotion grew louder. The dog barked and snarled, and the bear roared. Valiente shied nervously.

When Mac rode over the hill, he saw a huge animal standing on its hind legs, taller than Valiente's head. The pointer had the grizzly cornered against a rock face. The dog darted and danced, baying all the while.

Abercrombie lifted his rifle. "Mine," he called, and shot, hitting the beast's shoulder.

The grizzly howled, but didn't fall. It swiped at the dog with its uninjured paw. The dog sprang away. The bear dropped to all fours, bawled when its injured leg hit the ground, surged forward, and caught the dog in its massive jaws. The pointer squealed once and went limp.

"Goddamn bear!" Abercrombie fired again.

The enraged beast charged the hunters. Mac and several others had their guns aimed by then, and a volley struck the bear. It slowed, turned once, staggered, and fell.

"Is it dead?" Daniel asked, dismounting.

"Stay back!" Zeke shouted. He reloaded his rifle and shot the grizzly in the head. It didn't move. He got off his horse and kicked the bear. "Dead."

"You ruined the head," Abercrombie said. "Bastard kills my dog, I should at least get a good rug out of it."

"Christ, Abercrombie," Zeke said. "You coulda got us all killed, not just your dog. Bear this size can take down a whole posse."

"Yeah? Well, at least I found meat. I want the heart and the skin, since it cost me my dog." Abercrombie spat.

Zeke shook his head. "Come on," he said to the others. "Let's get it butchered."

The men cut up what they could carry, and Mac wrapped a haunch in oilskin. Valiente whinnied nervously when Mac tied the messy bundle behind his saddle. Abercrombie loaded the bearskin on his horse and gave Daniel as much meat as his horse could carry.

"You want the dog, Pa?" Daniel asked.

"Nah," Abercrombie said. "Leave it for the birds." Vultures watched from rocks above.

Mac eyed Abercrombie as they rode back to camp. Now that the horror of the bear attack was over, Mac was furious. This trek to Oregon may have started an adventure, but Mac had no desire to risk his life for another man's whim. Nor to leave Jenny alone on the trail.

Jenny greeted Mac when he returned. "How was the hunt?"

Mac dismounted. "Abercrombie went after a bear." He didn't tell her how close they had come to disaster.

They fried the bear meat for supper. "Buffalo tastes better," Jenny said.

"Don't tell Abercrombie," Mac said. "He'd think you were criticizing him."

That night Mac wrote:

July 10, 1847. Killed a grizzly. Abercrombie's dog died. We would have been better off hunting sheep.

Mac looked across the campsite and saw Abercrombie talking to Tanner. The raw bearskin was on the ground between them. Mac hoped Tanner could cure the skin well enough to suit Abercrombie, or there'd be another feud in the camp.

Chapter 33: Reaching South Pass

Frost covered the ground when Jenny woke up. Mac said they were near the summit. After breakfast she wrote:

Monday, July 12th—Greasy bear meat for supper and again for breakfast. Something happened with Mr. Abercrombie on the hunt, but Mac won't tell me what. Wood is scarce.

When the company got underway, she walked beside the wagon to stay warm. Rachel and the Pershing twins joined her.

"Where's Esther?" Jenny asked.

Rachel shook her head. "Ain't seen her today. Nor last night neither."

"We'll find her at noon," Jenny said.

One of the twins limped, complaining of a cut on his bare foot.

"What happened to your shoes?" Rachel asked.

"Don't fit no more," the boy said. "Took 'em off."

Rachel glared at him. "Where'd you leave 'em?"

He gestured behind them.

Rachel pulled him back toward their last camp. "Someone else can wear them, if you can't." They left Jenny to walk alone.

After another meal of bear meat at noon, Mac helped Jenny saddle Poulette. She couldn't catch her breath in the thin mountain air. "I'm sorry," she said. "I should be able to do this myself."

Mac smiled and lifted her onto Poulette. "No reason for you to when I'm here."

"How far to the pass?" she asked.

"A day. Maybe two."

They climbed through the afternoon through monotonous terrain. Same dry soil and stark granite hills. Same sun beating down as they trudged higher in the mountains. Similar crossings of the Sweetwater as it twisted through the heights.

At day's end they camped where the river joined another small creek. Esther stopped by while Jenny washed dishes.

"I can't stay," Esther said. "I just finished helping Ma with supper."

"Can I do something for your mama?" Jenny asked.

Esther shook her head. "She's settled now. Maybe tomorrow we can walk together. Mrs. Abercrombie says she don't need me tomorrow. I told Rachel I'd take the children and let her stay with Ma."

Jenny wrote before she went to bed:

July 12th, evening—One of the Pershing boys lost his shoes. I wonder if my child will cause me such trouble.

Tuesday morning Esther hurried over to where Jenny rode Poulette. A band of children—the Pershings, Otis Tanner, and others—frolicked along, the boys teasing the girls with sticks and insects.

"Do you want to ride?" Jenny asked Esther. "I'd walk, but it's so hard to breathe in the mountains."

"That's what Ma says. I'll ride a spell."

Jenny guided Poulette next to a stone, and Esther climbed up behind. The little mare took the added weight without a sound.

"Ma don't leave the wagon no more'n she has to. I don't remember her being so poorly with the other babies."

"The journey's hard on all of us. Even Mac stops to catch his breath sometimes," Jenny said. "Ever since he was sick."

"I'm hoping Ma'll be better after her confinement."

"How are you doing?" Jenny asked.

She felt Esther shrug behind her. "Mrs. Abercrombie's kind enough, but she don't stand up to her husband. Daniel tries. He tells me I can help Ma, then backs down when his pa complains. It'll be better when Ma don't need me so much. Rachel does what she can."

"Rachel's a good girl."

Esther laughed. "She pestered me something fierce when we were little. Now she's good with the young'uns and can cook. But I've always been the one Ma turned to most."

Through the morning they rode up a long wide valley, barren except for bitter smelling sagebrush. The children ran from bush to bush until they were sunburned and wind-chafed.

Jenny's lips were parched. She went to the wagon to get a drink. Mac rode Valiente nearby. "It's right around here," he said. "South Pass."

"How can you tell?"

"Frémont map says it is."

Jenny gazed around. It all looked the same—snowcapped mountains on every side of the valley, wind blowing without end. "What's Captain Pershing say?" she asked.

"Zeke's scouting today. Captain's driving his wagons."

"Does Zeke know where we're going?"

"We follow this valley," Mac said. "Can't get lost."

Soon Zeke galloped back to the wagons, hollering, "South Pass! We've crossed it."

"How do you know?" Mac asked.

"Water's flowing west. We're over the summit."

Captain Pershing saddled his horse and rode ahead with Zeke. When they returned, the captain confirmed, "Spring up ahead. Pacific Spring, it's called. Water runs to the Pacific from here. We'll rest there this afternoon and head on tomorrow."

They camped when they reached the spring on the western slope of the mountains. The terrain hadn't changed—still barren and windblown. But the travelers were jubilant, perched as they were on top of the world.

"Halfway to Oregon," Mac said grinning.

Jenny smiled back, wishing the entire trip was behind them.

The festive mood continued through the evening. They sang and danced to mark their crossing into Oregon Territory, but Jenny didn't feel a part of the merriment. What did it matter if they were through the pass? More months of arduous travel lay ahead. Childbirth. And an uncertain future at the end of the road.

As she watched the dancing, she wrote:

Tuesday, July 13th—Went through South Pass. Half the journey yet to come. "To the far, far off Pacific sea," the song says. Oregon still feels far away. And so far from home.

Chapter 34: Greenwood Cutoff

July 13, 1847. Crossed South Pass, now in Oregon Territory, halfway through our grand adventure.

The men passed a bottle of whiskey around as the company celebrated. Mac wondered where the spirits had come from. Whenever the fiddles and banjos came out, whiskey did as well. He drank his share.

The next morning Mac thought about the distance still to travel. Hard as it was to imagine in the heat of summer, they would not reach Oregon City until near winter.

That night they camped beside Dry Sandy Creek. The men dug in the creek bed to eke out enough water for people and animals. The water was so alkaline Mac could smell it from their campsite.

"Ice Slough seems far behind us now," Jenny said as she fixed supper.

Mac nodded. "Last night I was eager for the rest of the journey. Today it feels like a long grind. And for what? Adventure?"

Maybe he should have stayed in Boston. He could have done quite well in his brother's law practice, as his father expected him to do. But staying would have felt like acquiescing in how his parents—and he—had treated Bridget. He had blamed them—and himself—and needed to escape.

And Jenny would be in Arrow Rock, still threatened by her stepfather and the Johnsons. Rescuing Jenny had provided partial absolution for his guilt over Bridget.

Pershing gathered the men and said, "We have a decision to make. We can go south to Fort Bridger, along the Sandy and Green Rivers. Or cut across the desert, like the Greenwood party did. Desert route saves a week's travel, but there's no water for forty miles, from the Little Sandy to the Green. And not much forage."

"We can make forty miles," Abercrombie said.

"My team's wore out," Mercer objected. "I'd rather stay with the rivers. If I lose another ox, I'll be down to two yoke."

"I'm plumb near out of flour," Hewitt said. "If we don't stop at Bridger, where's the next place for provisions?"

"Fort Hall," Pershing said. "Two weeks past the Green."

Mac scratched his jaw. "We can share food," he said. "I'm worried about the teams. How many sick oxen and mules do we have?"

Others chimed in, arguing over which route to take, until Abercrombie announced. "I'm taking the cutoff."

Pershing's face reddened. Mac put a hand on the captain's arm. "We'll vote," Mac said, eyeing Abercrombie. "But I'm staying with Captain Pershing."

"I don't mind the desert," the captain said. "But y'all need to know what you're in for."

"Let's vote," Doc said.

The majority voted for the cutoff. A few men grumbled about their teams. "We'll stick together," Pershing said. "Won't leave anyone behind."

"When do we start?" Abercrombie asked.

"We'll travel to the Big Sandy tomorrow. It's a short day," Pershing said.

"Why can't we go farther?"

Pershing ignored Abercrombie. "We'll lay by the next day, then head out at night. Travel all night and through the day until we reach the Green. So rest your teams good at the Sandy. Horses, too."

Back at their wagon, Mac told Jenny the plan.

"More desert!" she said. "We've been parched for weeks."

"We'll take it easy until the long haul Thursday night."

July 14, 1847. We have decided on Greenwood Cutoff through the desert. This land fights us at every step.

The travelers arrived at the Big Sandy at noon Wednesday. They let their animals drink and forage, though water and grass were sparse.

"It's all they'll get till we reach the Green," Pershing warned. "Don't tax 'em today or tomorrow."

Abercrombie said, "Me'n my sons are going hunting. Our horses are fit. Anyone else coming?"

No one else wanted to go.

The Abercrombies were gone all afternoon. Esther came to sit with Jenny. Mac heard her say, "Daniel didn't want to go. But he didn't want his pa to be mad."

"I hope they don't get too tired," Jenny said.

The Abercrombie men returned shortly before supper, an antelope slung across each saddle. "We'll eat well tonight," Samuel boasted to Pershing.

"Hope you're not eating your horse Thursday night when its legs give out," Pershing muttered.

July 15, 1847. Abercrombie defied Pershing and went hunting. I for one was happy to rest. A hard night tomorrow.

On Thursday everyone stayed in camp. They filled every container they had with water, and the women baked biscuits and fried meat.

"We won't stop from dusk tonight until we reach the Green," Pershing said. "Straight shot west. Follow the wagon ruts baked in the ground."

They broke camp when the sun dipped in the west. Sagebrush undulated in the heat waves rising from the dirt.

Jenny rode Poulette, while Mac rode Valiente and guided the oxen. "Ride until you and Poulette are worn out," he told her. "It'll save the team not to carry you in the wagon."

"Riding is pleasant," she said. "The evening air is fresher than the heat of the wagon."

They marched forward, hour after hour. Dark descended and the brilliant stars appeared, too many to count in the vast sky. Mac plodded on Valiente, step after step.

Around midnight he noticed Jenny swaying in her saddle. He helped her off Poulette and into the wagon and tied the mare behind. They trudged on.

Before dawn Mac heard a shout and rode ahead.

"Goddamn ox fell," Mercer said. "Won't get up."

"Get it out of its yoke," Pershing said. "We can't stop."

Mercer unhitched the fallen ox and its yokemate and moved his wagon out of line. Mac and Pershing worked with Mercer to get the ox to stand. It heaved to its feet, fell down, moaned, and died.

"Tie its mate to your wagon," Pershing said. "We're moving on."

Mercer led the surviving ox forward, looking back once. "Sure wish I could have butchered it," he said. "Hate to lose the meat."

Abercrombie seemed none the worse after his hunting escapade. His horse ambled along as if the large man were no burden. Daniel's horse stumbled once or twice, but all the mounts were weary when the sun rose behind them.

On and on they went, dry land surrounding them like a desolate sea. When the sun had risen fully, Jenny handed Mac a biscuit with a slice of meat tucked inside. He ate as he rode.

She mounted Poulette again. "Too hot in the wagon."

Poulette walked beside Valiente, the mare's short legs struggling to keep up with the stallion. But the Indian pony's endurance lasted longer than Jenny's. Toward noon she gave up riding. "My back's too stiff to keep my balance," she said and returned to the wagon.

In midafternoon Poulette broke her tether to the wagon and stampeded ahead. It was all Mac could do to keep Valiente from racing after her.

Just then, Zeke hallooed the company. "Green River straight ahead!"

The oxen bawled and started to run, pulling the wagon faster. From his prancing mount's back, Mac cracked a whip over the team, but they didn't slow. Inside the careening wagon, Jenny screamed.

"Hold on, Jenny," he yelled. "They'll stop at the river."

The animals milled into the water, the ones behind pushing the first arrivals deeper. Many of the emigrants ran into the river also, splashing and laughing.

Chapter 35: Green River

Saturday, July 17ᵗʰ—Traveled all night and all day. Poulette and our oxen stampeded at the Green River. I was stuck in the wagon in midstream until they drank their fill and Mac pulled us all out of the water.

As dusk fell Jenny wrote in her journal, sitting by the river with her feet cooling in the snow-fed current. Deep emerald water rushed past her. Tall trees along the banks rustled in the cool breeze. Across the river to the west, red bluffs turned black in shadow as the sun set beyond them.

"Captain says we'll keep the Sabbath here tomorrow, then cross the Green on Monday," Mac said. "The teams need to rest, and we need to hunt. Lots of game nearby."

"Another river crossing." Jenny sighed. The river was delightful to sit beside, but she hated the water when it rose around the wagons.

"There's a ferry south," Mac said. "But it's out of our way, and there'd likely be a wait. Zeke will go take a look. But I think we'll cross here, unless Zeke finds a better ford downstream."

"Why Zeke? Why not the captain?"

Mac shrugged. "I don't think Pershing wants to leave his wife."

Mac was gone when Jenny got up Sunday. Mrs. Tuller called from the next wagon over, "He went hunting, dear."

Those left in camp held a prayer service by the river after breakfast. Jenny's voice wavered as she sang the third verse of "How Firm a Foundation,"

When through the deep waters I call thee to go,
The rivers of sorrow shall not overflow;
For I will be with thee thy trouble to bless,
And sanctify to thee thy deepest distress.

Each time they crossed the deep waters, Jenny feared she would die. The song said God would be with her, but she hadn't always felt the Lord's presence. Not in Missouri, and not on the trail.

After the singing, Esther asked Jenny to walk. "Let's look for eggs," Esther pleaded. "I want to get away from camp." They took their baskets and walked through the sagebrush in the hills above the river. Quail and sage hens ran out from under the brush every few yards. Nests were plentiful.

As they walked and gathered eggs, Esther talked. "Ma's poorly. I've told Daniel I need to stay near her. I can walk with you now 'cause Pa's there. It's got to be Pa or me with her till her baby comes. Or the Tullers."

"What do you know about birthing babies?" Jenny asked.

Esther shrugged. "Not much. Only birth I've seen was Noah four years ago, though I cared for Ruthie when she was newborn. I was seven then. But I told Pa I'd stay with Ma while Rachel cares for the other children."

"What's Mr. Abercrombie say?"

"I ain't asked, and I ain't going to. She's my ma."

"And Daniel?"

Esther stuck her chin out. "He'll let me do what I want. He ain't said anything different, anyhow."

Esther was probably right. Daniel was far less bossy than Mac. Must be what being in love did for a man, Jenny decided.

It took until the sun was high to fill their baskets with the tiny eggs. Then the girls returned to camp to prepare dinner. The eggs were a treat, and Rachel took the twins and Ruth to look for more in the afternoon.

Jenny and Esther sat with Mrs. Pershing and Noah. Mrs. Tuller joined them, bringing a sweater she was unraveling. "Doc tore the sleeve so bad I can't darn it. I can reuse the yarn for baby sweaters. One for each of you,"

171

she said, nodding at Mrs. Pershing and Jenny.

"That's right nice of you," Mrs. Pershing said, "to give this baby something to call its own. I've been cutting down clothes for so long, we don't have nothing that ain't been worn by at least three of us."

Mrs. Tuller smiled. "Doc was the only one wore this, so it's almost like new."

While the women chatted, Tanner fished in the river with Otis beside him. Some of the other boys wandered over, and Tanner strung lines for them as well. The boys shrieked each time they landed a fish, and they soon had a string of trout in a puddle on the bank. Captain Pershing rode his horse back and forth across the river looking for a good crossing.

In the hottest hour of the afternoon, the hunting party returned. Most of the men had an antelope slung behind their saddle.

The women decided to make supper a communal meal and began frying meat and gathering side dishes. With a potluck, they wouldn't have to listen to Mr. Abercrombie complain about feeding the Pershings again, Jenny thought. None of the Pershing men had hunted, so they had no fresh meat.

While the travelers ate, Zeke and Joel returned from the ferry.

"What's it look like, boys?" their father asked.

"Ferry's four or five miles south. Not far," Zeke said, "But there's a three day wait."

"Ain't waiting three days to cross the damn river," Abercrombie said, spitting a stream of tobacco juice.

"Hear the boys out," Pershing said.

Zeke pushed his hat back on his head and wiped his brow. "Could cross at Names Hill. Two miles south of here. Almost as many names written there as at Independence Rock. Even Jim Bridger wrote his, clear as day. But best place is right here, if we don't want the ferry." Zeke drew in the dirt. "River valley's wider on the other side. Be more room for the wagons and teams once we cross."

"Water's deep here," Pershing said. "Current's fast. But we can do it if we're careful."

Jenny's heart sank. If Captain Pershing said to be careful, she knew she would find the crossing fearsome.

"We'll need rafts," Pershing said. "Let's fell some trees."

All evening the men chopped down trees along the riverbank and lashed them together. By dark, they had built two rafts. While the men made the rafts, the women unloaded the wagons to lighten them.

Just after sunup Jenny watched Captain Pershing direct the men in loading the first wagon on to a raft and floating it across the swift Green River. Even with two yoke of oxen swimming the raft across, it was swept far downstream before it reached the west bank.

"Need to rig some ropes to guide it," the captain said.

Mac swam Valiente across the river carrying a heavy line with him. He tied the rope to a large tree on the far side. The next wagon fared better, though the water threatened to lap over the raft.

"We should lighten the loads more, or we'll lose our provisions," Mac suggested to Captain Pershing.

Jenny watched the men work with her heart in her throat. Soon she would have to cross. She left the riverbank and sat beside Mrs. Pershing.

"How will you get across?" she asked the older woman, who sat on a log rubbing her lower back.

"Captain will tell me when the time comes."

Some women rode horseback, and a few intrepid souls sat on the rafts with their wagons. Those who crossed early reloaded wagons on the other side. Jenny and Esther stayed with Mrs. Pershing.

While she fixed a bite for the women to eat, Jenny heard a shout. "Man overboard!"

She ran to the shore. One raft had broken loose from its ropes, tumbling a load of boxes and barrels into the river. Two men steering the raft had fallen in the water. They tried to swim but were swept around a bend in the swift current. Mac and Zeke lunged after them on horseback.

Jenny heard another shout from men across the river. "Safe! They got across." But the raft and its load were lost.

With only one raft remaining, it took until midafternoon to get most of the belongings and people across. A soaked Mac rode over to the three women. He pulled Poulette behind him. "Two men almost drowned. You'll be safer on Valiente with me," he said to Jenny.

"How will Poulette get across?"

"I'll tie her to my saddle horn."

"What about Mrs. Pershing?" Jenny asked.

"Zeke and his father will take her in their wagon. It's the last one we need to get across. And Daniel's coming for Esther."

Jenny couldn't delay any longer. Mac pulled her up behind him. "Hang on," he said, and Jenny grasped his waist. Mac wrapped Poulette's reins around his saddle horn. "Here we go."

They waded into the river. Jenny buried her face in Mac's back as her feet touched the frigid mountain water. Poulette whinnied when her belly got wet. The little mare started swimming well before Valiente, and Poulette's reins tightened as she floated downstream. Valiente neighed when the mare's weight pulled on him. Poulette squealed and went under.

"She'll have to make it on her own," Mac said and cut the mare loose. Poulette drifted away, struggling against the current.

Mac urged Valiente onward until the stallion swam, too.

"Hold on, Ma!" Zeke shouted from behind them. "We're in the current."

"Come on, boy," Mac yelled at Valiente. Finally, the Andalusian's hooves caught on the slippery rocks of the far shore.

Poulette had made it to the bank downriver and neighed as she picked her way back to the wagons.

"We'll camp here," Captain Pershing said. "Need to dry out."

After they reloaded their wagon and ate supper, Jenny wrote,

> *Monday, July 19th—Another horrible river crossing. Poulette almost drowned. One family lost half their belongings. Mrs. Pershing seems dreadfully uncomfortable.*

Chapter 36: Birth

Monday evening after they crossed the Green, Pershing called the platoon leaders together. "Rough stretch ahead," he said. "Once we pass Names Hill we head into the mountains to find the Bear River."

"For how long?" Mercer asked.

The captain pushed his hat back, baring his forehead. "'Bout a week. Need to send scouts ahead. Otherwise, we could get trapped in a canyon."

"Don't you know the way?" Abercrombie asked, thumbs in his suspenders.

"Trail ain't marked," Pershing said. "Greenwood Cutoff is new. Don't know the best way through the mountains."

"I'll go," Zeke volunteered.

Pershing nodded. "You'll be in charge. But we need enough scouts to relay with the main company."

"Hold on," Abercrombie said. "You're putting a boy in charge?"

Pershing squinted at Abercrombie. "Zeke led the folks left at Ash Hollow till they caught up with us."

"Why ain't you leading the scouts?" Abercrombie demanded. "If it's so all-fired important."

"I'm staying with the wagons."

"Wouldn't be because your wife's near her time, would it?" Abercrombie asked. "Putting her ahead of your command, maybe?"

Pershing ignored him. "Who else'll go with Zeke?" he asked. "Daniel?"

Before Daniel could speak, Abercrombie said, "I'll decide where my son goes. You want to go, son?"

"Fine with me." Daniel's voice was low.

After more discussion, they decided that platoon sergeant Josiah Baker and another farmer from Missouri would accompany Zeke and Joel Pershing and Daniel.

"You didn't want to scout?" Doc asked Mac as they returned to their wagons.

Mac shook his head. "I don't like to leave Jenny."

"She's getting purty large for such a little woman," Doc said.

Mac had noticed Jenny's bulk as she rode behind him on the Green River crossing.

"Young, too," Doc continued. "Babies come easiest when a woman's a little older . . ." his voice trailed off. "But younger'n Miz Pershing."

Mac wrote that evening:

> *July 19, 1847. Difficult crossing of the Green. Abercrombie still taunting Pershing, whose wife's confinement is drawing nigh.*

The scouts left at dawn. The wagons made their way slowly along the Green River, pausing beneath Names Hill. As Zeke had said, many explorers before them had carved or painted their names on the granite bluff, Jim Bridger among them. Mac wanted to leave his own name in the rock, but Pershing wouldn't delay. The captain was tense, barking his orders.

At Names Hill they filled their water barrels, then left the Green and edged up a slope above a muddy, trickling creek. They followed piles of rocks the scouts had left to mark the trail, the sun burning them from above and dust choking from below.

Mac rode Valiente beside his oxen, a damp neckerchief over his nose and mouth. He sent Jenny ahead on Poulette to spare her the worst of the grit. Mac's wagon was near the front of the train. Emigrants in wagons farther back suffered more.

When the heat was at its worst, Mac heard a shout from behind. The wagons halted, and he rode back to find out what was happening. Pershing rode toward him, circling his hat in the air.

"Need to halt as soon as we get to flat ground," Pershing said.

"What is it?" Mac asked.

"Baby. We'll wait until it's born."

"Wait?" Abercrombie bellowed. "Ain't no place we can wait in these goddamn hills. Women been having babies since before Moses. We didn't stop for the Dempsey baby."

"Doc's with her now. Something ain't right." Pershing's voice quavered. "We'll stop soon as we can."

An hour later the land leveled where another muddy stream joined the one they had followed. Mac heard a woman groaning as he unhitched the oxen. Jenny flinched at every sound as she bustled about their campsite.

When a moan rose into a scream, Jenny dropped a tin plate. "I'll see if I can help," she said. "There's biscuits and jerky in the wagon."

Mac ate his cold supper. The wailing grew more frequent.

When it grew dark, Jenny returned.

"How is she?" Mac asked.

"Doc says it's breech," Jenny said. "I sat with her while Esther and the Tullers ate. They're with her now. I'm going to bed."

Mac wrote:

July 20, 1847. Hot, dry day through the mountains. More of the same tomorrow.

He sat by the fire with nothing to do but listen. How did women bear it? How would Jenny bear it? Finally, he made up his pallet under the wagon and tried to sleep.

Mac woke to silence. He put away his bedroll and walked to the Pershing wagons. Esther sat beside the fire rocking a bundle.

"Baby come?" Mac asked.

Esther beamed. "Another boy. Ma's mad about that."

"Is your mother all right?"

"Worn out. Pa, too."

"I'll send Jenny over when she gets up."

Esther nodded.

Jenny poked her head out of the wagon when he returned. "How's Mrs. Pershing?"

"Had a boy."

"What's his name?" Jenny asked as she climbed down.

"Didn't ask. I told Esther you'd go see her."

Jenny smiled and started toward the Pershing camp. "I'll get your breakfast when I'm back."

"No rush. I'll put coffee on." All they had left was a bitter root sold at Fort Laramie. But it warmed the soul on cool mountain mornings. How could the days be so hot, Mac wondered, when the night air chilled them through?

Jenny returned shortly shaking her head.

"What's wrong?" Mac asked.

"Baby's awful quiet. Name's Jonah, by the way. I don't know much about babies, but I thought they cried a lot. This one's been sleeping since he was born, Esther says."

"Mrs. Pershing's probably glad," Mac said.

"I suppose, but it doesn't seem natural."

After breakfast Captain Pershing announced they would lay by that day.

"Lay by!" Abercrombie exploded. "We're stuck in the middle of the mountains in a God-awful valley, mosquitoes big as hornets. Gone soft, have you, Pershing?"

"Say what you want, Abercrombie. We're laying by."

Abercrombie stalked to his wagon and came back with his gun. "Might as well make use of the time. McDougall, you coming? Ain't no other able-bodied men left with a good horse."

Mac raised an eyebrow at Captain Pershing.

"Go ahead," Pershing said.

Mac saddled Valiente and followed Abercrombie out of camp and into the hills.

Chapter 37: Resting

Jenny sat with Esther through the morning. "Took most of the night," Esther said, smiling at baby Jonah as she rocked him in Mrs. Tuller's rocking chair. "Breech babies come slowly." She shuddered. "I hope I never have one."

Around noon Doc and Mrs. Tuller came over. "You go rest a spell," Mrs. Tuller told Esther. "Mrs. Abercrombie's got soup ready for you, then you sleep. We'll sit with your ma."

"Will Mrs. Pershing be all right?" Jenny asked.

"She's birthed enough babies, she'll be fine," Doc said. "If the fever stays away."

"Now, doctor," Mrs. Tuller said, "Don't scare the child. Fever can hit any woman. No special reason to worry now."

"Don't know why it happens," Doc said. "Sometimes the baby comes easy enough, then the mother dies of fever."

Jenny's face must have shown her horror. Mrs. Tuller patted her arm and said, "Don't fret, Jenny. You'll be fine when your time comes."

Jenny did more than fret. She feared never knowing what had happened to her mother, and she dreaded her own childbirth ahead.

In late afternoon Jenny took a heavy pot of stew over to the Pershings' campfire. Esther sat with Mrs. Abercrombie and Douglass's wife Louisa.

"Thank you," Esther said. "I haven't had time to cook."

"How is your mama?" Jenny asked.

"She was up, but she's napping again. Jonah's asleep, too. He's a quiet baby."

"Well-mannered from the start," Mrs. Abercrombie said.

"A good sign," Louisa added.

Jenny looked around. No sight or sound of the younger Pershings. "Where are the others?"

"Rachel took 'em to the creek," Esther said. "Expect they'll come back muddy and hungry."

"I'll go look for them," Jenny offered.

"Tell 'em to be quiet. Don't want to wake Mrs. Pershing," Mrs. Abercrombie said.

Jenny headed for the creek, her hand bracing her back. Seemed she waddled more than she walked these days. She heard the children before she saw them. A whole passel of boys and girls shouted and laughed as they waded to their knees in the muddy swamp where the two creeks met.

"Dinner time," she said. "Back to camp. Be quiet, though,"

Otis Tanner giggled as he launched a frog at her.

She yelped softly. "How can there be frogs so high in the mountains?"

The dark-skinned boy flashed a grin. "Got me a whole string of little croakers. Ma'll fry 'em up tonight."

"I got a new brother," four-year-old Noah Pershing said, taking Jenny's hand.

"I saw him," she said. "He's mighty little, isn't he?"

Noah nodded. "My ma's sick."

Jenny ran a hand over the boy's hair. "She'll get better."

"That's what Esther says," Noah said, skipping beside her.

The hunters returned in early evening. Mac slid off Valiente when he neared their wagon and lifted a large bundle from behind his saddle.

"Antelope everywhere," he said, dropping the carcass on the ground.

"Did you see the trail the scouts marked?"

Mac nodded. "We tracked it a ways. Follows one of these creeks into the hills."

"Is it bad?" Jenny asked. "Mrs. Pershing's still poorly."

Mac grimaced. "Bouncing around in the wagon will be hard on her."

After supper Jenny heard Mr. Abercrombie yelling at Captain Pershing. "We need to move on. Can't wait for your wife to stop swooning."

"Hold on, Abercrombie," Doc said. "It ain't Pershing's fault the baby came now."

"Let him and his family stay behind twiddling their thumbs." Abercrombie shouted, loud enough for the whole camp to hear. "That's all he ever does."

Captain Pershing lunged at Abercrombie. Mac and Doc held the captain back.

"Leave him be," Mac told Abercrombie. "We'll talk to him."

Abercrombie strode toward his wagons. "Come on, girl," he said to Esther, who followed him with a glance back at her father.

"Is my wife fit to travel?" Pershing asked the doctor.

Doc shrugged. "Won't be easy. But no different than Mrs. Dempsey earlier."

Pershing nodded with a sigh. "Then we'll head out tomorrow."

After supper Jenny sat with Mrs. Pershing. "We moving on?" Mrs. Pershing whispered as she nursed the baby.

"That's what the captain says," Jenny replied.

Jenny stayed with the older woman late into the night. While Mrs. Pershing dozed, Jenny wrote:

> *Wednesday, July 21st—Mrs. Pershing was delivered of a baby boy during the night, named him Jonah. Wednesday's child is full of woe—I hope it will not prove true. Tomorrow we climb into the mountains.*

Chapter 38: Fever in the Mountains

Mac woke Thursday as the sun peeked over the ridges to their east. Mountains surrounded the creek bank where they camped. The barren hills held no vegetation bigger than sagebrush. Mac didn't think they were above the tree line—there simply was not enough water to support trees.

Mac hoped the scouts knew what they were doing. He wished Pershing were scouting, but the captain wouldn't leave his wife.

Mac heard the thin cry of a newborn. Jonah was awake.

Jenny heaved her awkward bulk out of the wagon. She was no longer the scrawny girl he'd met in Arrow Rock. In two months she would give birth. Anxiety stabbed Mac's gut. He didn't want her to suffer, and childbirth was always a risk. Nothing he could do about it.

"Did the baby wake you?"

She nodded, arching and clutching her back as if it hurt. "I should see to the Pershings."

"I'll get breakfast." He made coffee and fried an antelope steak. At least they had fresh meat. Flour and cornmeal were low, and Fort Hall was a good two weeks off, according to Pershing.

"Mrs. Pershing's better," Jenny told him when she returned. "But she says she was up cooking by this point after her other births. Traveling must have sapped her strength."

The wagons climbed out of the creek valley through dry, rough terrain, switchbacking up sage-spotted hillsides. Mac and Abercrombie rode in front watching for stones the scouts had piled. At first it was easy, because they had seen the trail the day before while hunting. By midmorning, however, they passed into new territory.

The company nooned in a saddle between two hills. There was no water, and the teams shifted restlessly in their yokes and harnesses.

"Damn trail's turning south," Abercrombie fumed when they resumed their trek. "Don't those damn scouts know where they're going? I have half a mind to head north. I would, if Daniel weren't one of the scouts. I raised him to know what he's doing."

Thank heaven for small favors, Mac thought. He didn't want another argument between Abercrombie and Pershing. With Zeke, Joel, and Daniel gone, he had only Doc to back him if a confrontation arose.

"They'd come tell us if the route weren't passable," Mac said.

Abercrombie snorted.

Pershing called a halt at another small creek. They had detoured far south around a high ridge that rose two hundred feet above them. "There's water here. We'll stop," he said.

"It can't be much past three o'clock," Abercrombie argued. "We can go another couple of hours."

"Don't know where the next water might be," Pershing said. "We'd best stop."

Mac rode Valiente to his wagon. While he unyoked the oxen, Jenny headed toward the Pershing wagons. As he finished, she returned looking frightened.

"Mrs. Pershing has a fever," she said. "Esther sat with her all day." Jenny wiped a hand across her eyes. "The wagon bounces her poor mama around. It's hot and miserable, even with the sides open. And the dust. How can she get better if we don't stop?"

"We have to keep moving," Mac said. "Everyone's low on provisions. All some folks have is the meat we can kill."

Daniel rode into camp at dusk. Esther ran into his arms sobbing, "Ma's bad off."

"Why we heading so far south, son?" Abercrombie yelled.

"Trail goes west up this creek valley a ways. It's purty flat," Daniel said. "Then there's another detour south around a high ridge. Then mostly west again. We've tried not to go out of our way, but the land's wretched. Little water. Mostly bare rock, or loose dirt and sage. We need to get through it as quick as we can."

"But Ma!" Esther said.

"Ain't no help for it, honey," Daniel said. "We can't stop."

Jenny, Mrs. Tuller and Hatty Tanner arranged to relieve Esther through the night with Mrs. Pershing. "You take the first shift, Jenny," Mrs. Tuller said. "Then you can get some sleep yourself. We put Jonah with Mrs. Dempsey again."

After Jenny left, Mac sat beside his campfire and wrote

July 22, 1847. Another hot day through dry land. Teams are skittish on the sparse grazing. Scouts report the trail ahead is rougher yet.

Mac roused when Jenny returned to the wagon around midnight. "How's Mrs. Pershing?" he asked.

"Very ill." Jenny sounded weary. "Fever's high. As bad as yours with cholera."

Before dawn Mac awoke again to find Daniel saddling a horse. Esther stood beside him weeping.

"How's your mother?" Mac asked.

Esther shook her head, her lips pursed.

"I'm going to find Zeke and Joel, send them back," Daniel said. He galloped up the valley.

The Pershing wagons led the company through the morning, so Mrs. Pershing would be spared as much dust as possible. The captain drove, while Mrs. Tuller sat in back with his wife.

Mac rode Valiente next to Pershing as they left camp. "You need anything, Captain?" Mac asked.

"You ride with Abercrombie," Pershing said. "We'll be fine."

As Daniel had said, the initial path up the creek bed was not hard. Red cliffs rose all around them, but the valley was wide and not too steep. They splashed back and forth across a shallow, narrow stream.

After the noon break the trail left the creek and climbed south along a rocky crest. Jenny checked on Mrs. Pershing and reported to Mac, "Her fever's still high. Can you stay with our wagon? I want to sit with her a spell."

Mac nodded. "Abercrombie can watch for the scouts' markers. What's Doc say?"

Jenny shrugged. "He just shakes his head."

Mac's wagon jerked along behind the Pershing wagons. Around three o'clock, the captain jumped off the wagon bench, waved his hat, and shouted, "Hold up! We're stopping."

Mac slowed his wagon to a halt and walked over to the captain. "What's wrong?"

"She's having a seizure." Pershing called for Doc to come.

Doc raced over and climbed into the wagon.

Abercrombie rode back. "What the hell's going on?" he asked.

"Seizure," Mac said.

Abercrombie swore, but didn't say anything more.

After a short while, Doc climbed out of the Pershing wagon and walked back to Mac. "Seizure stopped. Cooled her down with water." He looked at the harsh landscape around them. "We can't camp here, so let's go on. But we should halt as soon as we find a place."

Jenny followed Doc out of the Pershing wagon, her face ashen. Mac convinced her to drive their wagon. "I'll ride with Abercrombie."

As they rode off, Abercrombie asked, "Is she bad off?"

"Sounds like it," Mac said.

The two men rode in silence. "Man depends on his wife, don't he?" Abercrombie said sometime later.

Mac wasn't sure if Abercrombie was talking about Captain Pershing or himself or men in general. "That's right," he said.

"We come off this ridge in a little bit to another creek. We can stop there." Abercrombie cleared his throat and was silent again until they reached the creek.

Chapter 39: Blessed Sleep

Friday, July 23rd—Mrs. Pershing died this evening, leaving her family speechless with grief. Esther tries to be strong for the younger children.

Tears clouded Jenny's eyes, and she couldn't write any more. Mrs. Pershing had been a good woman. The older woman had promised to be there when Jenny gave birth—now she wouldn't be.

As dark fell, Zeke and Joel rode into camp. "Where's Ma?" Zeke asked. "Daniel said she was poorly."

At the wagon next to Jenny's, Esther broke down sobbing and clung to Zeke, who looked over her head at Captain Pershing. The captain shook his head and walked away. Joel strode after his father, while Zeke stood holding Esther.

Jenny went to the Pershing wagons. Hatty Tanner cared for the younger children, while Mrs. Tuller was in the wagon washing the body.

"What can I do?" Jenny asked Hatty.

"Can you take young Noah for the night?" Hatty said, wiping a hand across her brow. "The baby will stay with Mrs. Dempsey to nurse, and the older children are all right. But poor Noah don't understand. He shouldn't see his ma's body."

Jenny led the sleepy toddler back to her wagon. After she climbed up, Mac lifted Noah into her arms.

"Need anything?" Mac asked.

"No." She hugged the boy to her, and they went to sleep.

In the morning as Jenny lifted Noah out of the wagon, he asked, "Where's Ma?"

"Gone." Jenny gave him a quick hug.

"Gone where?"

"Heaven. She has to live there now," was all Jenny could think to say.

"I'll help Zeke and Joel dig the grave," Mac whispered.

While she prepared breakfast, Jenny snuck glances at the men shoveling a hole outside the wagon circle. Tanner piled stones nearby.

After their morning chores, the somber travelers assembled around the fresh grave. The body was wrapped in the quilt the Tullers had given Esther as a wedding present. "She needs it more'n I do," Esther whispered.

Esther held baby Jonah in one arm and clung to her father with the other. Zeke and Joel lowered their mother's body into the grave. Hatty kept Noah away near the wagons.

Captain Pershing opened his mouth to speak, but no words came out. Doc stepped forward and led the group in prayer. Jenny sang "Asleep in Jesus! Blessed Sleep." Her voice trembled on the last verse,

> *Asleep in Jesus! Far from thee*
> *Thy kindred and their graves may be;*
> *But there is still a blessed sleep,*
> *From which none ever wakes to weep.*

How far Mrs. Pershing's grave was from any of her kin, how isolated in these desolate mountains! Jenny's voice broke off in a sob. Surely this trip was not worth the price the Pershing family had paid.

Each emigrant dropped a rock in the grave. Then Mac and Tanner rolled heavy stones on top to keep the animals away. Mac wrote Mrs. Pershing's name and the date in tar on the largest rock.

"Will anyone passing after us stop to pray for poor Cordelia Pershing?" Mrs. Tuller whispered to Jenny as they watched Mac. "She's all alone in the mountains."

After hugging their father and younger siblings, Zeke and Joel left to join the other scouts. Abercrombie waved his hat, and the wagons followed him away from the grave.

Jenny sat on the bench while Mac drove. "Do you want to ride Poulette ahead of the dust?" he asked.

She shook her head.

"How about sitting with Esther? She's with her father."

Jenny shook her head again.

"Are you all right?" Mac asked.

"Yes." But she wasn't all right—she was afraid. Afraid of the mountains. Of death. Of Oregon. She didn't want to be in this God-forsaken land where women died in childbirth, their bodies buried under rocks.

It was all an adventure to Mac. But how could he be excited about a journey that killed good people like Mrs. Pershing, a journey that had almost killed him? Maybe she would have been better off in Missouri, Jenny thought. Now she was trapped in these mountains, nowhere to go but forward. A sob escaped her throat.

Mac touched her hand. "I didn't think you liked Mrs. Pershing. She wasn't always kind to you."

"She was only protecting her family," Jenny said. "She was a good woman."

"Anyone who thought you were a threat couldn't have been all good." Mac's voice was grim. "Women shouldn't judge others so harshly. Women can be very cruel."

"What do you mean?" Jenny asked.

"My mother," Mac said. "She judged Bridget."

"Bridget worked for her. Your mother had to judge her work."

"Her work wasn't why Mother let her go."

"Then why?"

"Bridget was carrying my child."

Jenny gasped.

"I didn't know about the child," Mac said. "I didn't know until after Bridget was dead."

"I'm sorry," Jenny said, forcing the words out. "You must have grieved for them both." Mac's revelation took all thought of Mrs. Pershing out of her head. How could Mac have behaved so carelessly? It must have been carelessness—she couldn't imagine Mac cruelly forcing Bridget as Jenny had been forced. It must have been love.

Then it dawned on her—Mac had brought her on this wild journey to Oregon out of guilt for not saving his own child. He didn't care about her and her child.

Jenny couldn't stay with him. She jumped off the wagon bench while the wheels still turned. She stumbled until she got her footing on the ground.

"Jenny, watch out!" Mac shouted, vaulting down beside her.

"I think I'll ride after all." She spun around to get Poulette.

Mac grabbed her saddle as she tried to wrestle it out of the wagon. "Let me do it."

Jenny tried not to cry while Mac saddled the mare. She shook her head at his offer of a boost onto Poulette's back and hauled herself up. She trotted ahead of the wagons, but stayed behind Mr. Abercrombie. She didn't want to talk to anyone.

Chapter 40: Leadership in Dispute

Only as he spoke to Jenny did Mac realize how much the purpose of his journey was to escape his guilt over Bridget and the baby. Adventure was part of it. Avoiding—or at least delaying—the path his father expected of him was part of it. But mostly he had fled his shame over causing Bridget's death.

He'd graduated from Harvard in 1846 and planned a summer tour of Europe—a last lark before practicing law. Before he left, Bridget offered herself freely. He'd given no thought to conceiving a child.

When Mac returned home from Europe in late autumn, Bridget was gone. No one mentioned her. Finally, he asked his mother where Bridget was.

Mother looked at him severely. "Why should you care, Caleb?"

He mumbled something. He couldn't tell her about his intimacy with Bridget.

"She was with child," his mother said. "I dismissed her."

Shocked into confession, Mac started to tell her the baby was his.

Mother held up her hand. "Don't say a word. I did what I had to. Her morals were a scandal to the other help."

"Where is she now?" he asked.

"I don't know. I gave her some money and told her to leave."

Mac asked Cook where Bridget was. "Dead," Cook said. "Typhus. Died about a month after she left here."

"Her baby?" Mac asked.

Cook grimaced. "She died before it was birthed."

That was all Mac knew. He hadn't loved Bridget. But he had owed her and his child a chance at a better life. A chance they never had.

He couldn't bear to stay in Boston, to live in his parents' house. So, when he saw John Frémont's report on Oregon, he decided on another adventure—this time heading west.

Now Mac watched Jenny race ahead of the wagons on Poulette. He'd brought her along out of guilt and to convince Pershing to let him join the company.

They'd done well together on the trail. Why was she so upset now? Was it grief over Mrs. Pershing's death? Or learning of his shameful behavior with Bridget?

During the noon halt Jenny silently prepared their meal.

"You up to driving?" Mac asked after they ate. "I want to ride with Abercrombie."

She nodded.

Mac saddled Valiente and rode to the head of the train.

"Where's Pershing?" Abercrombie asked.

Mac shrugged. "Haven't seen him since morning. Probably with his family."

"He won't be no good no more," Abercrombie said. "Man loses his wife, takes a while to get over it."

Mac frowned at Abercrombie.

"Lost my first wife in childbirth. Couldn't think straight for a year." Abercrombie cleared his throat. "So I'm taking over."

"What?"

"Ain't no one else here with the gumption to get us through."

"Give Pershing a chance," Mac urged. "And we need to vote on any new captain."

"No one'll vote against Pershing. They're all sorry for him. But he ain't no good. Taking his sweet time about getting us to Oregon. Snow could start in September. I'll captain."

"We'll put it to a vote tonight," Mac said.

Mac went to find Doc. "Abercrombie says he's taking over as captain. Says Pershing's not fit to lead."

"The man's wife just died," Doc said. "He's not focused on the company now, but he'll heal in time."

191

"Abercrombie won't give him time. Doesn't even want to vote. I told him we have to. Can you get Pershing ready to talk to the men tonight?"

The doctor nodded, his bushy eyebrows coming together in a frown.

All afternoon they struggled through rugged hills. At last the wagons swayed down a steep slope into a wide valley covered in lush grass. The emigrants set up camp, and their animals grazed contentedly.

Word of the conflict spread through the company. There was little laughter as the travelers did their chores. Perhaps they were still disheartened by the funeral that morning, but Mac thought it was more than that. Small groups murmured in shadows beyond the campfires.

No one called a meeting, but the men showed up at Pershing's campsite after supper. "What's this about?" Pershing asked, though his grim face indicated he knew.

An uncomfortable silence. Then Abercrombie spoke. "It's about getting to Oregon, Pershing. Don't want to burden you no more, so I'm taking over."

"Before there's any change," Mac said, "we have to vote."

Pershing looked at Mac. "You with Abercrombie?"

"No, sir," Mac said. "I joined this company because of you. But we need to follow the majority."

Pershing grunted, then walked away. After a few steps, he halted and looked back. "I'm the only man here who's been to Oregon. I'll captain if you want. But I'll be damned if I'm going to beg. Take your vote, and let me know." He stalked out of the wagon circle.

"You heard him," Mac said. "He's still willing to lead. He's had a terrible loss, but I think he's the best man for the job. Let's vote."

"Now hold on, city boy," Abercrombie said. "I git to have my say. We're moving too slow. I'm sorry as the next man for Pershing's loss. But can he git us to Oregon afore winter?" He shrugged. "I'll keep us moving, you can count on that."

"All right, men," Doc said. "Those for Pershing step right. Those for Abercrombie go left. I'll count."

Mac and Doc moved with Pershing's followers. Mac did a quick count. It was close.

"Pershing wins by two men," Doc said. "He's still captain. I'll tell him."

Mac exhaled slowly. He thought backing Pershing was the right thing. Pershing had made mistakes, but not as many as Abercrombie. And he'd rather follow Pershing than Abercrombie.

"We'll be hip-deep in snow by October." Abercrombie strode off to his campsite.

Mac sighed when he returned to his wagon. It had been a long day, starting with Mrs. Pershing's funeral, a difficult trek down the mountains, and Abercrombie's attempt to take control. And Jenny—he still didn't know why she was upset.

He pulled out his journal and sat by the fire:

July 24, 1847. Mrs. Pershing was buried this morning. We reached Ham's Fork, a tributary of the Bear River. Pershing barely retains control of our company.

Chapter 41: Across a Barren Land

Sunday, July 25th—We buried Mrs. Pershing yesterday in a lonely grave in the mountains. Esther cares for Jonah, while the Captain hides in his wagon.

Jenny wrote beside the fire after breakfast. She could write about the Pershing family's loss, but not about Mac and Bridget. She was still numb after Mac's revelation, fearing she was only an obligation and atonement to him.

"Captain says we'll lay by," Mac told her.

"All right," she said. "I'll visit Esther, if there's no need to pack up."

Esther paced around the Pershing campsite, holding a screaming Jonah. "How can such a little mite make so much noise?"

Jenny held out her arms. "Let me take him." She rocked the baby while Esther collapsed on a stone by the fire.

"I'm dead beat," Esther said. "Up all night. Rachel can't make him happy either. He needs milk. Mrs. Dempsey don't have enough for her daughter and Jonah both. I tried broth, but he don't take it."

"Where's your papa?" Jenny asked.

Esther glanced around, then whispered, "He was drinking last night. Ain't up yet."

"Mac said we're laying by."

"He came to talk to Pa. I heard Pa moaning."

Doc joined the girls. "Where's Pershing? Mac said I should see to him."

"Asleep," Esther said.

The doctor climbed into the wagon. A minute later Abercrombie stormed over. "What's this about laying by? Didn't that damned fool hear anything I said?"

Mac was right behind Abercrombie. "Captain isn't well this morning. We're laying by."

"I ain't." Abercrombie spat a long stream of tobacco juice on the ground, then said to Esther. "Girl, git back to camp and help Mrs. Abercrombie pack up. We're heading out."

"But, Mr. Abercrombie, I got to see to Jonah," Esther said, taking her brother back from Jenny.

"You're my kin now."

Esther buried her face in Jonah's blanket.

"Go on, girl."

"Let her be, Abercrombie," Mac said. "Pershing isn't well enough to move today."

Doc clambered down from the Pershing wagon. "He can travel. Just an upset stomach." The doctor scowled at Esther. "Go on with Abercrombie. Mrs. Tuller and Jenny will see to the baby."

Esther handed Jonah to Jenny and scurried off, Abercrombie striding behind her.

"He's hung over," Doc said to Mac after Abercrombie left.

Mac grimaced. "I wanted to let him sober up today."

Doc shook his head. "Better to make him work. We can't let him crawl into the bottle."

As Jenny turned to take Jonah back to her wagon, Doc stopped her. "You keep quiet about this, Jenny. No need to upset other folks."

She nodded, knowing he meant Mr. Abercrombie. As she walked past the Tuller wagon, Mrs. Tuller said, "Why don't you let me have that sweet baby? I'll take him today."

"He's awfully fussy," Jenny said. "Hungry, Esther says."

"I'll see what Mrs. Dempsey can do," Mrs. Tuller said. "Or get some thin porridge in him."

The wagons climbed out of the Ham's Fork valley and into another rocky range. Because of the late start, they were only halfway up the mountain when dusk came. They camped on a narrow ridge, where the wagons couldn't circle, with no water except what they carried in barrels. The men posted double guards to keep the animals from wandering.

"I hope those fool scouts know what they're doing," Abercrombie said. "Marks they left show us going south again tomorrow."

After supper Esther came by to see Jonah. Mrs. Tuller had coaxed him to eat a bit, and he slept peacefully for the moment.

"How's Pa?" Esther asked.

"Better than this morning, I think. Mac talked to him at noon."

"I need to see him," Esther said. "And make sure the young'uns are all right. How's Rachel doing?"

Jenny smiled. "Chasing after the twins and Ruth. Mrs. Tuller fixed them supper."

Esther shook her head. "I should be there. If only Mr. Abercrombie would let me."

"Have you asked Mrs. Abercrombie?"

"She's nice enough, but won't do anything without him nodding his head first. Says a woman oughta listen to her husband."

"You need Daniel here," Jenny said, embracing her friend.

Esther's eyes watered. "If he would stand up to his pa."

Jenny was relieved Mac was gone the next morning—she still didn't know what to say to him. She fixed enough breakfast to take some to the Pershings and left a plate for Mac.

"Pa's hung over again," Esther whispered, when Jenny brought the food to the Pershing wagons. "Don't let the young'uns know."

Jenny sighed. Mr. Abercrombie wouldn't let drunkenness pass if he found out. "How's Jonah?" she asked.

Esther shook her head. "He needs more milk, but Mrs. Tuller thinks he's all right. She's spooning what broth she can down him."

Jenny went back to her own camp, where Mac was finishing his biscuits. "Captain's been drinking again."

Mac nodded. "I checked on him before I went to bed last night. Took his bottle away, but he must have had another. I hope we find Zeke and Joel soon. Maybe they can handle him."

Pershing slumped in his saddle through the morning, while the caravan plodded south skirting hillsides and ravines. The emigrants nooned at a sluggish creek, which the animals drank to a trickle.

Finally, in late afternoon, the trail turned west again, ascending another mountain slope. The scouts met the wagons as they switchbacked up a massive hillside.

"There's a flat meadow atop this ridge," Zeke said. "We'll camp there."

Jenny wobbled wearily as she slid off Poulette's back. She looked around. A meadow? This wasn't a meadow. It was flat, but grassless. No water. Room for the wagons, but the wind whipped down from the peaks and across the desolate plateau.

"There ain't no other place to camp for miles," Zeke said. "We'll have to haul water."

Jenny started cooking. Esther stopped by to tell her, ""Don't you worry 'bout us tonight. Mrs. Abercrombie said I could spend the evening with Daniel and my brothers. I'll fix our supper." Esther smiled for the first time since her mother had died.

Jenny wasn't sure she could have helped the Pershings if she'd had to. She was so exhausted she could barely manage meat and cornbread for Mac and herself.

"We're running low on food," she told Mac while he ate.

"Can't stop until we find a place to rest the teams. They need good grazing."

"Why couldn't we have laid by yesterday?" she asked. She didn't want to whine, but she was dead tired.

"Abercrombie refused."

Jenny sighed. "I suppose he won't change until we get to Oregon."

"Doubt he will even then." Mac stretched and rose. "I'll go get water so you can wash."

After Jenny washed the dishes, she pulled out her journal:

Monday, July 26th—A terrible climb from one dry camp to another. The scouts are back.

197

Chapter 42: Arrival at Bear River

July 26, 1847. The scouts say we are through the worst of the mountains and should reach Bear River tomorrow. For days, we have had little water or grass.

Mac exhaled when he finished writing. He needed to talk to Zeke and Joel. As the camp quieted for the night, Mac joined the Pershing brothers.

"Where's the captain?" Mac asked.

"Bed," Joel said, tossing a piece of sage on the fire.

"With a bottle?" Mac asked.

Zeke looked up sharply. "What do you mean by that?"

"He's been drinking. Hung over in the mornings."

"Maybe he needs the comfort." Zeke sighed. "Ma's only been gone three days."

"Maybe," Mac said. "But it won't be a comfort if Abercrombie finds out. You know he tried to take over?"

Zeke nodded. "First thing folks told us. Thanks for backing Pa."

"If Abercrombie hears about the drinking, he'll take another shot. We have to keep your father sober."

Joel snorted. "He does this sometimes."

"Does what?" Mac asked.

"Goes on a bender. Used to happen when he came home from a campaign," Zeke said.

"Ma's passing set him off this time," Joel added.

"There's not a man here who doesn't sympathize with him," Mac said. "Even Abercrombie. But he can't lead us if he's drunk."

Zeke climbed in the wagon where his father lay. When Zeke didn't return, Mac shrugged at Joel and headed for his own wagon.

In the morning Pershing sauntered over to where Mac was yoking his oxen. "Hear you talked to my boys 'bout me last night," the captain said, pushing his hat back on his head.

"Yes, sir."

"I can take care of myself. And my family, too." Pershing stomped off.

"Yes, sir," Mac said to the captain's back. He had made his point with Zeke and Joel, he didn't need to confront the captain.

Jenny still seemed tightlipped. Mac worried she was thinking about Bridget. Bridget wasn't any concern of hers. "You want to drive or ride Poulette?" he asked her.

"I'll ride," she said, so he saddled Poulette.

From their camp on the mountain plateau, they descended a steep hill, slowing the wagons with ropes. They nooned at the bottom of the hill, then rode along the valley and up another range.

"Last mountain before the Bear," Joel said, riding alongside Mac's wagon. "The descent is horrendous."

"Do we have time to get down this afternoon?" Mac asked, squinting at the sun ahead of them.

"No place to stop, so we got to," Joel said. "It'll be a long day, but then we're in the Bear valley."

As Joel had said, the descent was difficult. Mac estimated they took the wagons down five hundred feet of altitude in the space of a mile, using ropes again to brake the wagons. Some men hitched all but one yoke of oxen behind their wagons to slow their descent.

The Dempseys' wagon broke loose of the oxen, spilling boxes and barrels as it tumbled down the slope. "My china!" Mrs. Dempsey screamed, as a box split open and spewed plates and cups across the ravine. She thrust her baby into Jenny's arms and plunged down the hill after her precious dishes.

"Smashed beyond repair," she said when she returned. "Only one cup whole." She cradled that cup in her hands.

The men sweated and groaned with the effort to control the wagons and teams. Finally, all the wagons reached the bottom. Mac's chest heaved as he took a break. Dusk spread over the valley. "How far to the river?" he asked Zeke.

"Another two or three miles."

"We can't make it before dark."

"There's a small creek closer. Pa says to camp there. Move to the river tomorrow."

Mac nodded, his breath still coming too fast. He was glad Pershing had issued the halt. Or had Zeke decided without consulting his father?

After supper the men gathered at Pershing's campfire.

"I need to hunt tomorrow," one man said. "Out of food."

Others nodded.

"We got to get the wagons to the Bear first," Captain Pershing said.

"With the scouts back, we got enough men for both," Abercrombie declared.

The men agreed the hunters would leave early in the morning, while the rest of the company drove the wagons to the Bear and set up camp.

Mac returned to his wagon and asked Jenny, "Can you drive tomorrow? If so, I'll hunt."

She nodded. "We need meat. I can manage. What about the Dempseys' wagon?"

"Tanner's staying with the wagons. He'll fix it once we reach the Bear. Good thing the axle didn't break."

Mac left with the hunting party before Jenny was up the next morning. Captain Pershing stayed in camp, but Zeke and Joel joined the hunters.

Mac was happy to be out of the mountains and riding through an easy valley. No rain since Independence Rock. He wondered if the summers were always so dry in the mountains. How could horses and cattle survive on the grassless land?

The men rode toward the Bear River. Mac was surprised to find their camp had been several miles and a small ridge of hills away from the river. "Will there be any trouble moving the wagons so far?" he asked Zeke.

Zeke shook his head. "It's an easy route."

"I worry about Jenny," Mac said. "She tires easily now." An eagle screeched above, and Mac looked up to see the bird dive. "Eagle sees prey nearby."

Zeke nodded. "We saw birds when we blazed the trail. Bigger game, too. Antelope, mule deer, and elk."

The men splashed across the Bear, then found a herd of antelope grazing on the bank of a nearby stream. They shot several, and Mac strapped a carcass behind his saddle. "That's enough for today," he said to the others.

"I seen elk spoor," Abercrombie said. "Aim to track 'em down."

"The meat will spoil before we eat it all," Mac said, shaking his head. He turned back and rode across the Bear. The wagons had camped on the south fork of the river.

"Shot an antelope," he told Jenny. She sat by the Pershing wagons with Esther and Mrs. Tuller. To his surprise, Mrs. Abercrombie and Douglass's wife were there also.

Jenny stood, stretching her back. "I'll help," she said. She walked beside Valiente over to their wagon.

Mac lifted the meat off his horse, and he and Jenny cut it up. The rest of the hunters returned about supper time, and the company celebrated their safe arrival at the Bear.

Chapter 43: Women Talk

Jenny enjoyed the day without Mac. When he was around, all she thought about was Bridget. She was convinced Mac had brought her on the journey out of guilt, which was a horrid reason to have dragged her so far from home.

Travel to the Bear River wasn't difficult, not compared to the mountains they'd traversed since crossing the Green. By noon they were camped beside the Bear.

The women made the noon meal together. Even Mrs. Abercrombie and Douglass's wife Louisa, who usually kept to themselves, joined them.

Tanner and the other men in camp busied themselves with fixing the Dempsey wagon, leaving the women to wash and sew and talk. "How's Jonah?" Esther asked Mrs. Dempsey. "Is he eating enough?"

"He's fine," Mrs. Dempsey said, hugging her infant daughter. "I give him what I can."

"He's all I have left of Ma," Esther sighed. "I can't let anything happen to him."

"You have your father and your other brothers and sisters," Mrs. Tuller said softly, touching Esther's hand.

"But I'm all Jonah has," Esther said. "Pa and the others don't know what to do with a baby. If I don't care for him, he'll die."

"You'll have your own children someday," Mrs. Tuller said.

Mrs. Abercrombie nodded. "Mr. Abercrombie wants a grandson to carry on his name. So far, he only has granddaughters." She gave an apologetic glance at Louisa.

"I got to care for Jonah as Ma would."

"You'll have to let God care for him," Mrs. Dempsey said. "Seeing as

202

how you can't feed him."

"Maybe I can find a milk cow at Fort Hall," Esther said. "Others in the company could use milk, too. Maybe we can buy a cow together."

"Don't set your hopes too high," Mrs. Tuller said with a sigh, reminding Jenny that Mrs. Tuller had lost all her own children.

"And how are you, Jenny?" Mrs. Dempsey asked. "Don't you fret none about Mrs. Pershing's death. I'm sure you'll be fine when your time comes." Jenny wished Mrs. Dempsey hadn't reminded her—she thought about poor Mrs. Pershing enough as it was.

The talk shifted from children to husbands. The other women teased Esther gently about Daniel. "Don't mean to speak unkindly of your son," Mrs. Dempsey said to Mrs. Abercrombie.

"Daniel's my stepson," she replied. "I married Mr. Abercrombie because he needed a wife to care for the children he already had. I've never been blessed with a child of my own."

"You were fortunate in your stepchildren," Mrs. Tuller said.

"That I was. Douglass and Daniel are good men," Mrs. Abercrombie said, nodding. "And I'm blessed with who they married, too." She smiled at Louisa and patted Esther's hand.

"Thank you, Mrs. Abercrombie," Esther said, burying her face against Jonah's back.

"Mr. Abercrombie's first wife was my sister," Mrs. Abercrombie said. "She died at Daniel's birth."

"You'd think Mr. Abercrombie would be more civil to Captain Pershing," Mrs. Tuller said. "Seeing how they both lost wives in childbirth."

"Mr. Abercrombie's never been one to cotton to weakness," his wife said. "Not in himself, and not in anyone else. Not many know how hard he took my sister's death."

After a while Mrs. Tuller said she would sit with Jonah if Jenny and Esther wanted to walk with the other Pershing children. Esther pulled Jenny away from camp.

"I couldn't abide that Mrs. Dempsey," Esther said. "Talking 'bout how she was doing the best she could for Jonah, when I know she's favoring her daughter. And worrying you 'bout your baby."

"She couldn't make me more nervous than I already am," Jenny said.

"Well, she's a silly goose." Esther crossed her arms. "I hate to let her have anything to do with Jonah, but I ain't got a choice." Esther leaned over to Jenny and whispered, "I might be in the family way, too. I missed my monthly last week."

"Heavens," Jenny said. "That was fast."

"No faster than you," Esther said.

Jenny was silent. One dreadful day had caused her misfortune.

"I'm waiting to tell Daniel when I miss another. So don't you say anything." Esther spun around. "Oh, I wish Ma were here. I want to talk to her so much. I don't know what I'll do with two babies."

Jenny linked arms with Esther. "I wish I could talk to my mama, too." They had parted badly, but Jenny still wanted her mama.

When the hunters returned, Jenny helped Mac butcher the antelope he'd killed, then fried steaks for supper. That night, with her stomach full of fresh meat and her baby kicking inside, she sang to the accompaniment of the fiddles and banjos. When couples started dancing, she returned to her campfire and wrote:

> *Wednesday, July 28th—Bear River Valley. A quiet afternoon in camp. Mac shot an antelope, and we ate well. If Mrs. Pershing were here, it would have been a happy day.*

Chapter 44: Men Talk

When Mac returned from hunting, he thought Jenny seemed happier. Maybe her earlier mood was grief over Mrs. Pershing's death, not brooding over Bridget.

Thursday morning the travelers crossed a branch of the Bear, the water cold and fast. Mac and Zeke rode ahead on horseback to steer the wagons away from deep water. "Pa says we follow the Bear to Fort Hall," Zeke said as they splashed through the stream.

Pershing kept close to his wagons and younger children. Zeke had become his voice to the company. Mac didn't think the captain was drinking, but he wasn't sure. Pershing was courteous, but curt, when Mac saw him in camp.

Bare granite mountains rose above the river basin, though clusters of evergreens softened the valley itself, and clumps of willows grew along the banks. Ducks, geese, and grebes lifted into flight from the water as the caravan rolled by. They trekked north along the Bear all day through marshy soil, splashing back and forth across the meandering stream. After days in the rugged mountains, the valley seemed full of life and promise.

In midafternoon the emigrants reached the north end of the valley. Zeke conferred with his father, then Pershing called the men together. "Good camp here," he said. "Grass, wood, and water. We'll stop."

"Still lots of light," Abercrombie said. "Weather's good. Why not keep going?"

"River turns south here." Pershing pointed at the bend. "If we go west, we're back in the mountains for another hard day tomorrow. If we follow the river, we go south out of our way, but the trail stays easy. Need to scout the route tonight."

"Should have scouted today," Abercrombie muttered, as Pershing walked away.

Mac offered to go with Zeke and the captain. He wanted to see how Pershing fared. The three men rode in silence past the bend in the river, trotting through deepening shadows.

"How far we going, Pa?" Zeke asked. "It's getting dark."

Pershing pointed at the peaks to the west. "Past that ridge. Need to see where the river goes."

They reached the ridge and saw another crest about a mile farther. "Let's keep going," the captain said.

"We won't get back before dark," Mac said.

The captain shrugged. "We'll camp out."

At the second ridge, the Bear curved north through a gap in the mountains. Pershing nodded. "Like I thought. Ain't much out of our way. We'll follow the Bear." He squinted at the setting sun. "We'll stop here. Go back at first light."

"Jenny will worry," Mac said.

Pershing got off his horse. "She'll be fine."

"Your family will worry about you and Zeke, too," Mac said.

Pershing frowned as he unfastened his saddle. "Quit bellyaching. Let's make camp."

The men started a small fire and ate a quick meal of jerky and hardtack. Mac was fidgety, concerned about leaving Jenny alone. Otherwise, he would have enjoyed the evening with Pershing and Zeke.

Then Pershing pulled a flask of whiskey out of his pocket, took a swig, and passed it around. Mac took a swallow and wondered how the captain had kept a supply.

"Not too much, Pa," Zeke said. "We need to be up early."

"Don't be a pantywaist, son. Many a time in the Army I had a hard night and was up before the bugle."

"Yeah? Well, I'm turning in." Zeke rolled himself up in a blanket and faced away from his father. Soon he was snoring.

Mac sat while Pershing drank. "Drinking won't help," Mac said.

"What do you know?" The captain's voice was harsh in the quiet night.

"I've lost someone. A woman."

"Bet it weren't your fault she died." The captain took another swallow.

But Bridget's death *was* his fault, Mac thought. He shrugged.

The captain peered at him over the flickering fire. "That what you running from?"

"Running?"

"Something ain't right. With you and Miz McDougall. If that's who she is."

"What do you mean?"

"When we first talked, you wasn't married. Then you was. Then she's showing a big belly damn quick."

"Don't say anything about Jenny." Mac would put up with a lot from the captain. He respected the man, despite the drinking. But he had to defend Jenny.

"Just seems to me—"

"Don't turn this on me or Jenny," Mac said, angering. "You're upset your wife died. Rightly so. But don't let us down because of it."

The captain took a long chug, saying nothing.

After sitting awhile in silence, Mac said, "Think I'll call it a day, too."

Mac lay down by the fire and put his hat over his face. As he settled, the captain said, "Cordelia didn't want to come."

"What?" Mac said.

"My wife didn't want to make this trip. She wanted to live in Tennessee. Near her family. I wanted freedom after all my years in the Army." Pershing took another swallow. "Now she's dead, and the baby'll likely die, too. It'll be on my conscience for the rest of my days."

"Your other children depend on you," Mac said. "As do we all."

"That's why I haven't put a bullet through my head yet."

Mac sat up. "Put the bottle down and get some sleep. Better yet, give it to me." Mac took the flask from the captain, stuck it inside his shirt, and returned to his bedroll.

Mac awoke to chirping birds. The stars were still out, though the silhouette of the surrounding mountains was faintly visible. Mac poked Zeke with his boot. "Get up. We need to be moving," he whispered.

Zeke groaned and lifted himself on one elbow. "It ain't even light." Zeke squinted at his father, who snored, then looked up at Mac. "I heard him last night."

"It was probably the whiskey talking," Mac said.

Zeke sighed. "He's been crying in his cups ever since Ma died. Don't know what to do."

"We'll watch him. Keep him from drinking." Mac remembered the captain's words about Jenny. "What else did you hear?"

"Just that Ma didn't want to come. Ain't that enough?"

Mac hoped Zeke hadn't heard the captain's suspicions about Jenny. He leaned over and shook Pershing's shoulder. "Time to get up, sir. First light."

Pershing clutched his head when he stood, then saddled his horse in silence. The three men rode back toward the wagons. They spotted a herd of deer grazing along the Bear in the dawn mist. Mac and Zeke each shot one. The captain sat on his horse while the younger men gutted and packed the carcasses.

When they arrived at the wagons, the company was finishing breakfast. Pershing staggered as he dismounted. "We'll head south," he announced. "River turns back north in a few miles."

"God damn," Abercrombie said. "How far south?"

Pershing slammed his hat on his head. "I ain't arguing, Abercrombie. We're going south."

Abercrombie shook his head and grumbled.

Jenny handed Mac a plate of fried meat. "Where were you last night?" she asked.

"We rode until dark. Camped out."

Jenny sighed.

"Miss me?" Mac said with a grin.

"I worried."

"I told Captain you would. He said you'd be fine. You were, weren't you?" Mac stabbed a bite of meat with his fork.

"Yes. It was you I was anxious about."

Mac shrugged. "I couldn't avoid it."

Jenny grabbed Mac's plate and turned to wash the dishes.

"I'm sorry, Jenny," he said. "But we have bigger problems than you fretting. Captain's still drinking."

"What'll we do?" Her eyes widened.

"Just keep it quiet. I'll talk to Doc."

Doc Tuller was packing his wagon. "Let me help," Mac said, lifting a sack of flour into the wagon bed.

"Thank you, son."

"We have a problem with Pershing," Mac said.

"Drunk again," the doctor said, grunting as he heaved another sack into the wagon.

"You know?"

"Don't take much to see. Not when you been doctoring as long as I have."

"We need him sober to lead us."

"That we do." Doc stared Mac in the eye. "But if a man wants to drink, he'll find a way. Unless we get rid of all the whiskey in camp, and that ain't likely."

"So we make excuses for him?"

"Ain't what I said. Man's got to live with the consequences of what he does."

Mac sighed. Doc didn't have the answer. With help from Zeke and Joel, Mac would have to cover for Pershing where he could and step in when the captain failed.

Chapter 45: Along the Bear River

Friday, July 30ᵗʰ—Mac was away all night.
Mrs. Tuller and I struggled to feed Jonah
broth. He has outlived his mother by a week,
but how long can he last without milk?

Jenny packed away her journal and climbed on the wagon seat when Mac said, "Time to get underway." The weather remained pleasant—warm sun and clear skies. But even in the bright morning light, Jenny's head drooped as she sat beside Mac.

"What's wrong?" he asked when she shook her head to stay awake.

"Mrs. Tuller and I had Jonah all night."

"Don't you need more sleep?"

"I didn't want to be alone, and Mrs. Tuller had the baby."

"Where was Esther?"

"She and Mrs. Tuller are trading off keeping Jonah for the night."

"You shouldn't have to worry about him. You'll have your own soon enough."

The baby pushed on Jenny's lung, and a stab of panic shot through her. She groaned. Less than two months until it came.

"What's wrong?" Mac asked. His voice rose, mirroring her fear.

"Baby kicked. That's all."

Mac glanced at her belly, then looked away, his face flushing.

"Mac?" She had to talk to him. She had no one else.

"Hmm?"

"If I die, will you take care of my baby?"

Mac stared ahead, his jaw tight. "You're not going to die."

"Mrs. Pershing did."

"She was older." He tapped his whip on the lead ox's back, and the team stepped faster.

"If I do die," Jenny's voice caught, "will you keep my baby?" Perhaps his guilt over the loss of Bridget's child would make him take hers. It was the only hold she had over him.

"Jenny, I wouldn't know what to do with an infant," Mac said. "Lots of women here. Someone will take your baby. What about Esther?"

"Esther has Jonah. And soon—" Jenny remembered to keep Esther's secret. "Someday she'll have her own." She grasped Mac's arm. "Just say you will."

"How about this? I'll make sure your baby is well cared for."

Jenny didn't think she'd get a stronger commitment from Mac, so she nodded.

"Here's where we camped last night," Mac said when they halted for the noon meal. The Bear River curled through a broad basin of green grass and shrubs. Cottonwood and willows grew in clumps along the banks. The water was swift and shallow, the bottom covered with smooth rocks. Whitewater churned around the few large boulders.

"Where's the trail from here?" Jenny asked.

Mac pointed north. "Through that gap in the hills."

After the emigrants ate, the wagons rolled alongside the river, except when cutting across oxbows. Jenny succumbed to her fatigue and rested in the wagon. The warm air lulled her to sleep, despite the jostling. She woke in late afternoon and peeked out.

"Mac?" she called.

"Here," he said. He vaulted onto the bench. "I was talking to Zeke."

"I worry when you jump in the wagon while it's moving. Remember Mr. Mercer's ankle at Windlass Hill." Jenny shivered.

"I'm careful."

Jenny climbed forward and sat beside Mac. "I feel better now. I can drive. You go talk to Zeke."

"We were talking about his father."

"How is he?" Jenny asked.

"He's been on horseback this afternoon. Doesn't seem bothered by last night. Hope he stays sober tonight."

They followed the Bear through the gap Mac had pointed out. Then the river curved for two miles into another broad valley. "We'll stop here," Pershing said, waving his hat as he cantered beside the wagons. The emigrants were festive that evening after the pleasant day of travel. Jenny felt rested enough to sing while the fiddles and banjos played.

Next morning the company continued north along the Bear, still in the verdant valley surrounded by rugged pine-covered peaks. Their wagons mired in marshy creek beds hidden by tall grasses. Mosquitos swarmed when disturbed, biting people and beasts alike. But with a little care, they made decent time.

At noon they found another company of emigrants camped beneath a huge hill, reloading their wagons. Mac went with Captain Pershing and Zeke to talk with the other company, while Jenny started cooking.

Mac rode back. "They just came over that hill," he said, pointing. "Said it was the steepest hill they'd seen so far."

"Steeper than Windlass Hill?" Jenny asked. Nothing could be worse than that.

"They had to unload everything and lower the wagons on ropes," Mac said. "They lost two of them. Smashed."

"*Mon Dieu!*" Jenny said. "Good thing our scouts didn't lead us that way."

"They're reloading their belongings now. Pershing told them we'd make their noon meal and help with repairs. They have some meat and deerskins they'll trade."

"I'll bake extra biscuits," Jenny said. "But our flour's running low."

"We're less than a week from Fort Hall. We should make it."

Jenny fixed extra portions of stew and lugged a Dutch oven toward the other camp, holding the pot out away from her large stomach. She stumbled in the rough grass.

Zeke hurried to her side. "Let me carry that," he said.

"Thank you," Jenny said, smiling.

Zeke set the Dutch oven down beside a campfire and headed off to join the men. Jenny stayed with the women, trading stories about their journeys, illnesses and deaths. One woman had lost a husband to fever, another had a baby die at birth. Jenny told them about the cholera in their group, Mrs. Pershing's death, and poor Jonah who needed milk.

"I have a milk cow," one of the women said. "Her calf died two days ago. She's still fresh. I'd hoped to get her to Oregon, but when the calf died I decided to sell her at Fort Hall."

"Would you sell her to me?" Jenny asked. She didn't have money, and she didn't know if Mac would buy the cow. "Or trade her? For a horse?" She loved Poulette, but she could give up the mare.

The woman nodded.

"Let me find . . . my husband," Jenny said, stuttering as she hefted herself to her feet. "I'll be back."

She found Mac among the men. "They have a milk cow," she said.

Mac looked puzzled.

"Please buy it. For Jonah. He'll die without milk."

"Why are you asking me?"

"Would you please buy the cow? If you won't, I'll trade them Poulette. Jonah needs the milk."

"Have you talked to Pershing? Or Esther? Jonah's their responsibility."

Jenny shook her head. "I came to you first." She turned away. "I'll go get Poulette."

Mac grabbed her arm. "For God's sake, Jenny, don't trade your pony. I'll buy the cow if Pershing won't. But you're interfering with his family. Let me talk to him." Mac strode off.

Jenny hurried back to the woman with the cow. "We'll buy your cow." Taking the now empty Dutch oven, she rushed off to the Pershing camp to find Esther and Jonah. Then she and Esther washed the noontime dishes, while Jonah fussed nearby.

Soon Mac returned to their wagon leading the cow on a rope. "Here's she is," Mac said. "I bought her. Captain will pay me back. Milk her and feed the baby."

Esther stammered her appreciation to Mac and embraced Jenny. Her friend's beaming face more than made up for Jenny's discomfort at begging Mac to buy the cow. "Thank you," Jenny whispered to Mac over Esther's shoulder.

"Pack up," he said. "We're moving on. Tanner says the other company has the tools they need to mend their wagons. Don't need our help."

Jenny rode beside Mac that afternoon, feeling almost as delighted as when Mac had bought Poulette. "Now you can take care of my baby."

Mac stared at her.

"The cow," she said. "We have the cow. Now will you take my baby if I die?"

Mac shook his head. He didn't say anything for a moment. "Jenny, you do beat all." It sounded like he was choking. "If I didn't take your baby, you'd come back to haunt me, wouldn't you?"

That evening, camped again along the Bear River, Jenny wrote:

Saturday, July 31st—We shared our noon meal with another company facing their own hardships on the trail. Mac bought a cow. Jonah relishes the milk.

Chapter 46: Beer Springs to the Port Neuf

July 31, 1847. Met a company at noon that lost two wagons. They face days of repairs. Bought a cow.

Mac looked across the campfire at Jenny, also writing in her journal. She smiled as she wrote. She'd been smiling since he'd bought the cow and agreed to take her baby if she died. He couldn't care for an infant. He had enough on his hands. But she wouldn't die. She was healthy.

When Mac had talked to Pershing about the cow, the captain cleared his throat before responding, "I don't have much silver." The older man looked at Mac. "I could trade an ox."

"I have money, sir," Mac said. "I'll buy the cow. Your child needs milk."

"I wouldn't take charity if it weren't for the babe," Pershing said. "I'll make it up to you."

"I'm counting on it," Mac said, clapping the captain on the back.

What else could he have done? Mac wondered. He couldn't let the infant starve. But now the captain was beholden to him, and the older man didn't like it.

Pershing was still drinking. Zeke had found him with a bottle after supper and taken it away.

"I don't know where he's getting it," Zeke said to Mac and Joel. "But if Abercrombie finds out, he'll take over."

"Not if we make decisions in your father's name," Mac said.

"How?" Joel asked.

"You two have to be his voice. I'll read Frémont's maps. Between the three of us, we'll handle the scouting. Daniel's a good man, but if we bring him into it, he'd let it slip to his father. It needs to be the three of us."

"Won't Doc know Pa's drinking?" Zeke asked.

"Maybe," Mac said. "But he'll keep his mouth shut."

The next day Zeke got the travelers underway. Mac rode Valiente at the front of the wagons, comparing the Frémont map to the terrain. Pershing remained in his wagon all morning. They should be approaching Beer Spring, Mac thought, but he wasn't sure. If he read the map correctly, they would reach the spring about noon. Mac beckoned to Joel.

"Ride ahead and see if there's a spring," Mac said, showing Joel the map. "Don't know why it's called 'Beer Spring', but that's what this says."

Joel trotted off, and Zeke joined Mac. "Where'd Joel go?"

"I sent him to find a spring."

"Pa thinks it's at the north end of this valley."

"That's what the map shows," Mac said. "Let's try to get there by noon."

In late morning Joel returned. "Found it," he said. "No more'n another hour."

Mac nodded. "All right. We'll noon there."

Joel shook his head. "This country's mighty curious. Water tastes like beer, all right. Animals might not like it."

The spring water bubbled from the ground like a boiling cauldron. Crusty mounds of white powder surrounded the geyser. Soda, Doc said. And the ground was white clay, dazzling in the sun.

Mac sipped the water. It did taste like beer, but with a bitter sting.

"This whole area used to be a volcano," Pershing said. He seemed recovered from his dissipation of the night before. "Leastways, that's what Frémont told me."

The women collected soda for baking bread. "We're almost out of flour," Jenny told Mac. "I hope we can buy more at Fort Hall."

Children played in the gushing spouts from the spring. One of the Pershing twins sat on the geyser, laughing when the water hit him. The thrust was so strong he couldn't balance on the spray.

Some emigrants wanted to stop for the day, but Pershing refused. "Folks are short on food, and it's still several days to Fort Hall. Indians 'round here ain't as friendly as the plains tribes."

The company continued along the Bear, though the path now followed a ridge above the river. The wagons could not descend the rocky cliffs that dropped to the water, so they stopped at creeks for the animals to drink. On the far side of the Bear, high hills rose, covered with pine and cedar. The summer heat became more oppressive as they traveled out of the mountains.

They passed more strange springs and geysers through the afternoon. Anyone not tending a wagon frolicked along the way. Mac saddled Poulette for Jenny and took her to see one geyser. They washed their feet and drank fizzy water that prickled their tongues.

The company stopped for the night at a point of rock where the Bear River curved south. "Indians call it Sheep Rock," Pershing said. "Don't know why, but that's what we heard in forty-two. Lots of wars between tribes around here. Skirmishes with the mountain men, too."

Mac wrote:

August 1, 1847. Three and a half months on the trail, but still far from Oregon. The country grows stranger. Springs that taste of bitter ale. Rocks where tribes fought vicious battles. Jenny worries Indians will attack.

In the morning Pershing was alert and rode ahead of the wagons. Zeke and Joel must have kept him away from his whiskey.

They headed west, away from the Bear, across a dry basin dotted with sagebrush. The hills on the far side of the valley beckoned with green grass, but they found little water in the August heat. Once over the first range of hills, they came upon a creek and let the animals drink.

"This'll take us to the Port Neuf River," Pershing said. "Then to Fort Hall and the Snake River."

The travelers moved slowly through the hills in the afternoon and arrived at the Port Neuf late in the day. After the wagons circled, Pershing called a meeting. "It's about three days to Fort Hall," he said. "Maybe two if we push it. Do we have enough provisions to make it?"

Some men shook their heads. "Out of flour," one said. "Only a little dried meat left."

"I say press on," Abercrombie said. "Get there in two days."

"We could send some men ahead to buy food," Pershing said. "Bring supplies back to the wagons."

"No need, if we can get there in two days," Abercrombie argued.

"We can share," Mac said. "Let's keep going."

"Be hard on the teams," the captain said.

Abercrombie spat his vile tobacco juice. "Don't you want to get to Oregon, Pershing?"

"I want it, Abercrombie, same as you. But I want us all to get there." Pershing took off his hat and wiped a hand across his brow, muttering, "Those of us the Lord don't see fit to take."

"We can make it, Captain," Mac said. "How many still have flour or cornmeal?"

About half the men raised their hands.

"How many have meat?"

Fewer men raised their hands.

"Some of us can hunt in the morning, while the wagons keep moving." Mac realized he sounded like he was taking command. "Will that work, Captain?" he added.

Pershing nodded.

Some men grumbled, but no one dissented aloud.

After supper a shout arose, "Hot springs!" One of the children had found a spring not far from camp. Many travelers rushed to soak their tired feet in the warm water.

Mac chose to rest in camp.

August 2, 1847. Reached the Port Neuf. Provisions are low. Can Pershing keep control of the company?

Chapter 47: Trail to Fort Hall

Monday, August 2ⁿᵈ—Jonah thrives on cow's milk. Esther also churned butter—enough for the Pershings, Abercrombies, and Mac and me. We used our last flour for soda biscuits tonight. Two days to Fort Hall.

Jenny smiled at the children playing in the hot springs near camp, their shrieks louder than the crickets chirping in nearby sage. The Port Neuf babbled as it danced over rocks and tree snags. The creeks and rivers they passed now were fast and shallow, with rapids where the water fell many feet in short spans. Captain Pershing said there were terrible cascades on the Snake.

The Snake—Jenny shivered at the name. What horrors gave the river such a fearsome name? She would soon see.

First they had to get to Fort Hall. Their cornmeal was gone, and now their flour was also. They had a little dried meat and whatever game Mac could shoot, and not much else. In the morning Jenny gave the remaining pemmican to Mac when he left to hunt, along with leftover biscuits. She kept just one biscuit for her noon meal.

Esther brought Jenny the milk Jonah hadn't drunk during the night. "It'll go bad if you don't drink it," Esther said. "I got fresh milk for him today."

"What about the other children?"

"I made flapjacks for them with the last of our cornmeal. Drink it. For your baby."

Jenny drank. The milk was rich and sweet.

Joel helped Jenny hitch up her team. "Where's Zeke?" she asked.

"Hunting. I'm staying with the wagons." Joel said as he yoked the lead oxen.

"Thank you," Jenny said. "How's your papa?" she whispered.

"Seems fine." Joel nodded and walked off.

Joel wasn't as friendly as Zeke. Or maybe he didn't know how to talk to girls.

The company set out, following the Port Neuf. They stayed mostly to the north of the river, skirting hillside after hillside that rose steeply above the banks. Occasionally there was not enough room for the wagons on the north side, so they splashed across to the south. Jenny didn't fear the shallow Port Neuf, but she watched the fast current with each crossing to be sure no belongings were swept downstream.

By midmorning the valley widened and the trail turned north between hills of porous black rock. At noon Jenny ate the last biscuit and some berries Rachel had gathered. When they resumed travel after eating, the ground slowly shifted from dry sage to marsh. Birds rose from the wetlands as they rode along the valley. Tanner and Doc each shot a duck, and the doctor later downed a turkey.

"We'll have fowl tonight, no matter what the hunters find," Mrs. Tuller said with a smile.

Jenny was glad for the birds, but the marsh also brought swarms of biting mosquitoes. The oxen's tails twitched but could not reach their faces. The lead oxen suffered most, with no way to shield their eyes and noses from the buzzing insects.

Poulette was tied behind the wagon and nickered at the stinging pests. When Jenny saw Jonathan and David, the Pershing twins, loping alongside the wagons, she called. "Come here, boys." They ran over to her wagon.

"Would one of you sit on Poulette and brush away the flies for her?"

"What'll we use?" one asked.

"A branch of sage will do," she said. "Anything. See how the mosquitoes bother her?"

"Can we both ride her?"

They weren't that big. "Yes, you may."

"Can we let her loose of the wagon?"

"No. I can't watch you while I'm driving."

"Aww, it's no fun to ride behind the wagon," one boy argued.

"Later," Jenny said. "This evening. When Esther or I can watch you."

With that, the boys agreed. Jenny stopped the wagon, and they clambered on Poulette's back. Both lads had switches, and she heard giggles and shouts behind her. They were probably beating each other as much as the mosquitoes, but Poulette no longer complained.

When Captain Pershing called the halt at the north end of the valley, Jenny shooed the twins off Poulette and sent them back to Esther. The wagons moved away from the river to avoid the worst of the bugs. A gap in the cliffs ahead pointed the way for tomorrow's journey.

Jenny and Mrs. Tuller fried pieces of turkey and duck. "Be better to roast the birds," Mrs. Tuller said, "But we don't have time." At least they had sage to season the meat.

Tanner put his fishing line out as soon as the wagons were in place. He quickly caught fresh trout to add to the fowl for supper. Children collected berries in baskets and aprons. There was no flour for cobbler or biscuits, but the berries were tasty eaten plain or boiled with a little sugar.

Jenny heard Valiente neigh before she saw Mac. He carried a gutted deer across his saddlebags. "Had some luck," he said as he dismounted. "But the country's rugged. Sage taller than Valiente's withers. And scrub pine. Huge boulders we had to work our way around."

Jenny served Mac fowl, fish, and berries. "It's all we have," she said.

"Tomorrow we'll reach Fort Hall. Buy flour and cornmeal then." Mac seemed to relish the food they had, but Jenny craved vegetables and bread.

Jenny helped Mac pack the venison, then watched the Pershing twins ride Poulette. The setting sun silhouetted black bluffs against an orange sky streaked with purple clouds. She took out her journal and wrote:

Tuesday, August 3rd—Desolate country, mosquitoes big as birds. We will not starve, but I look forward to a more varied diet when we reach Fort Hall.

In the morning, after fried venison for breakfast, Jenny rode Poulette ahead of the wagons. She enjoyed the fresh morning air before the heat of the day. After they passed through the gap in the bleak hills above the Port Neuf, Jenny glimpsed more mountains in the distance, snow on their peaks, even in August. Would they have to cross that range as well?

Soon the river valley widened again. They nooned in the flat basin. Mountains loomed ahead. "We could travel due west to the Snake," Mac told Jenny. "But Fort Hall is north, and we need supplies."

Again they ate fried meat. All afternoon Jenny's stomach churned, sickened by the monotonous diet. The emigrants finally spotted Fort Hall as the sun lowered behind hills to the west, and everyone cheered. They made camp outside the fort. Jenny couldn't see much of the buildings in the dim light.

Despite the late hour, Mac and others rode into the fort. He came back with a small bag of flour. "Prices are high," he said shaking his head. "This cost me a dollar."

"That's barely enough for a loaf of bread," Jenny said.

"Make do tonight. We'll get more tomorrow."

Chapter 48: Fort Hall

August 5, 1847. At Fort Hall, a shoddy cluster of whitewashed adobe brick. Hudson's Bay Company owns it now—the Bostonian who built it could not make a profit. Prices are steep.

Mac wrote early in the morning as the camp began to bustle with activity. The weary travelers had been excited to reach Fort Hall the evening before, but the morning light revealed how primitive the structure was.

After breakfast Mac asked Jenny if she wanted to see the fort.

She nodded. "I need to do the washing, but Captain says we're laying by. Let's get fresh food."

They walked past the splintered palisade and into the fort. "It's not nearly as nice as Fort Laramie," Jenny said.

A small cannon sat in the courtyard. "Pershing said Frémont's company brought the cannon in forty-two," Mac told Jenny. "I can't see why they dragged it over the mountains. Not much here to defend."

The fort's store teemed with emigrants. "Why do you charge so much?" Mac asked the man behind the counter.

"Everything we got was raised in this valley or hauled from Astoria," the man said. "Sugar and flour packed in by mule. But I got good prices on dry goods. Better'n Laramie."

"We need more flour than you bought yesterday," Jenny whispered.

Mac tried to negotiate, but the proprietor wouldn't budge. "More people through here every day. If you won't pay, someone else will."

Mac bought a sack of flour and a sack of rice. He saw Jenny fingering a bolt of calico, and he added that and a piece of shirting to his stack. "Make me a shirt?" he asked.

"Of course," she said.

After making their purchases, they walked back to camp, Jenny carrying the fabric and Mac with a sack on each shoulder. "Shall we ride through the valley?" he asked. "Save the washing for tomorrow."

Jenny smiled. "All right."

Mac saddled their horses, and they rode north. The Port Neuf hugged the west side of the valley. Its tributaries ran out of the eastern hills and across the lowland.

A few miles north of Fort Hall a large butte rose four hundred feet above the valley. They urged the horses up the hill. At the top Jenny gasped. A wide, silver river cascaded beneath the north side of the butte. "What's that?" she asked.

"Must be the Snake. Runs to the Columbia."

Jenny shuddered. "What a loathsome name."

"We'll follow it for weeks."

"Will we have to cross?"

"At some point. But way downstream." Even this far upstream the Snake was wide and furious, tumbling over rocks as big as chairs. Pershing had said the river dropped a hundred feet or more in places. "We'll manage," Mac said to soothe Jenny. "Others have crossed before us."

They rode back to camp, and Jenny made soda bread for supper. Esther churned butter, which she shared. Jenny ate three slices of the fresh bread lavishly spread with butter. "Did you leave me any?" Mac asked with a grin.

Jenny blushed. "It tastes so good."

"Flour won't last long at this rate," Mac teased.

Jenny sighed. "I know. I won't eat so much tomorrow."

"It's all right. We have rice, too."

After the evening meal the companies sang and danced. Fiddles, banjos, and voices sounded through the camp. They had survived the highest mountains. Only the Snake and Columbia rivers remained before they reached Oregon.

In the morning Jenny started laundry, and Mac wandered back to the fort. Abercrombie had gone hunting, but Mac didn't feel like joining him. At the fort, Mac found Pershing and Zeke talking with a Hudson's Bay Company agent. "Leave your wagons here. Switch to pack mules," the agent said.

"Why's that?" Pershing asked.

"Can't get the wagons through."

"Folks been hauling wagons for years now," the captain argued. "Ever since Whitman. I was with Frémont in forty-two."

"Look at all the wagons left here," the agent said. "Best to take mules."

Pershing snorted and shook his head. "We'll keep our wagons."

"Indians on the Snake," the agent said. "I tell folks to go to California."

"We're headed for Oregon," Mac said.

"Oughta at least consider California." The agent thrust his thumbs through his suspenders. "Route's easier."

"Why do you want folks to go to California?" Pershing asked. "Hudson's Bay Company ain't got no one there."

"Maybe he wants fewer Americans in Oregon," Mac said, grinning.

"Suit yourself," the agent said, shrugging.

Pershing stalked off. Mac followed. "You hit it, son," Pershing said. "They don't want Americans claiming land in Oregon. Big argument between the States and England over boundaries. Until that's settled, the British want to keep us Yankees out."

"Should we ask the men if anyone wants to go to California?"

"You want to split up the company?" Pershing asked, eyeing Mac.

"No," Mac said. "I'm for Oregon. But what if others hear what this man has to say?"

"We can meet tonight." Pershing scratched his head and chuckled. "Maybe Abercrombie'll choose California."

"What if Esther leaves with him?" Mac asked.

The captain sighed. "Guess I'm stuck with Abercrombie for life."

Pershing called the men together after supper. "Hudson's Bay agent says we should go to California. Also says to leave our wagons here and pack our belongings on mules." He snorted. "Seems foolish to me."

"I ain't leaving my wagons," Abercrombie said. "Got furniture no mule could carry."

"Finally something we agree on, Abercrombie," Pershing said, then spoke to the group again. "The wagons can make it. Won't be easy. More mountains ahead. But we can do it."

"Why not California?" one man asked. "Hear tell it's warm all year round. Crops grow themselves."

"Got all them Papist Spaniards," Dempsey said. "At least I can understand the British."

"What route we taking, Captain?" Doc asked.

"Down the Snake, then down the Columbia," Pershing replied. "Why?"

"Man here mentioned a mission near Fort Walla Walla run by a doctor. Will we stop there?"

"Marcus Whitman." Pershing nodded. "Met him at Walla Walla in forty-two. There's a more direct route now that bypasses his station. It'll depend on whether we need provisions. Supposed to be converting Indians, but I don't reckon he's had much success at that. Making a profit on emigrants instead."

"I ain't going out of the way to see no doctor when we got one of our own," Abercrombie said.

Later Mac wrote by his campfire:

August 6, 1847. Despite the urgings of the Hudson's Bay Company agent, we will keep our wagons and stick with Oregon. The road ahead will be hard.

Chapter 49: American Falls

Friday, August 6th —We leave Fort Hall this morning, an ugly place with little to recommend it. The Snake lies ahead.

Jenny packed up the wagon, and Mac helped her onto Poulette. They headed southwest across the Port Neuf valley toward the Snake, splashing through several swampy streams. Where the land wasn't marshy, it was dry as a bone and covered with sage.

Jenny rode her mare beside one of the Pershing wagons. Esther spent the days with her younger siblings and evenings with the Abercrombies. Today Esther drove a Pershing wagon, cow tied behind it, while Jonah napped in the back.

"How's the baby this morning?" Jenny asked.

"Bigger every day." Esther smiled. "The milk cow is a blessing."

"Where's Daniel?" Jenny hadn't seen him since they left Fort Hall.

"Scouting with Pa and Zeke," Esther said.

"What's Mr. Abercrombie say about that?"

"I didn't hear nothing from him this morning." Esther shrugged. "Daniel's his own man."

"Have you told Daniel you're expecting?"

Esther nodded. "I couldn't wait."

"How'd he take it?" Jenny wondered how a man would react to becoming a father.

Esther grinned. "Busting his buttons. Wanted to tell everyone. I had to forbid him to say anything." Esther frowned at Jenny. "You haven't told, have you?"

"Not a soul," Jenny said.

"You don't tell your husband everything?"

Jenny shook her head. "You said I shouldn't."

The heat became oppressive as the day wore on, until Jenny felt like she was roasting on a spit. The dry air hurt to breathe. As the sun lowered ahead of them, dust dulled the sky and shimmered above the ground.

"Huge falls!" Zeke trotted along the chain of wagons with the news. "On the Snake. Pa says we'll camp just beyond."

The trail stayed well back from the cliffs above the river, but Mac took Jenny to see the falls. "*Mon Dieu!*" she gasped when she saw the furious water tumble down gigantic rock steps, throwing spray across the sky.

"River must drop fifty feet," Mac said.

"Look," Jenny pointed. "A rainbow." A band of colors shone through the mist.

"Pershing says a boat of American trappers went over the falls many years ago. So everyone calls it American Falls."

"How could anyone live after going over that falls?" Jenny asked.

"Most didn't. Only one man survived."

After supper Mac went with other men to bathe in the falls while Jenny washed dishes. Esther came over carrying a towel. "I'm going to wash my hair. Do you want to come?"

Jenny was tempted. A bath would feel wonderful, but she feared the rushing water. "The men are there," she said.

"We'll find another spot. Mrs. Tuller's coming. And Mrs. Abercrombie and Louisa and her girls. And Rachel and Ruthie. It'll be fine."

"Who's watching Jonah?"

"We'll take him with us."

"I can't swim."

"Don't worry. I can't either."

Jenny found a towel and followed Esther. At the bank, she took off her clothes, except for her shift, and waded in. The water was frigid. Her skin turned to gooseflesh and her teeth chattered. But the cold felt heavenly after the heat of the day. She even ducked under to wash her hair.

That night Jenny listened to the falls as she wrote:

Saturday, August 7ᵗʰ—American Falls is a

beauteous place in this terrible country. The heat and dust are dreadful, and the black rocks hide more horrors. I hope Oregon is not so hot. No stop for the Sabbath tomorrow.

Then she went to bed in the stifling wagon, with the constant rush of the river lulling her to sleep.

The next day the travelers rode along the south side of the Snake, over arid plateaus above the black cliffs. Sometimes Jenny saw the river far below, which foamed into white froth between its rocky banks. Sometimes the trail left the river to meander through steep ravines cleft by dry tributaries of the Snake.

She rode Poulette, trying to stay away from the worst of the dirt. A hot wind blew, adding to the grit stirred up by wheels and hooves. It had done little good to bathe the evening before. By midmorning her clothes were full of dust and grime. She kept her hair braided and coiled under her sunbonnet, but the wind pulled strands loose that whipped at her face as she rode. She had never seen a more alien land.

The Snake was often visible, but unreachable because of the lava walls. The tantalizing ribbon of silver water made Jenny feel the heat of the beating sun all the more. She drank often from the bucket on the wagon and pitied the poor oxen with their faces in the dust all day. Poulette took the steep path through the ravines with relative ease, but the men had to brake the wagons with ropes on the descents and hitch extra oxen or mules to pull on the ascents.

The company stopped for the night at one of the few places with easy access to the river. The cliffs abated for a narrow stretch along the Snake, and the wagons circled for the night on a slope covered with dry grass and sagebrush. The riverbank was full of boulders, but the travelers could clamber down to the water. Jenny wondered how water could move such enormous rocks, many of them larger than the emigrants' wagons.

"Devil's Gate Pass," Mac reported their location as they made camp.

"Why does everything have wicked names?" Jenny asked. Though the name fit the land. "Are there Indians around?"

Mac shrugged. "They were at Fort Hall. We've seen their tracks today, so they must travel this route. Pershing says Shoshone have fishing grounds nearby."

Jenny opened her journal and wrote:

Sunday, August 8th—Even the ink bottle has sand in it. I feel I shall never be clean again.

Chapter 50: Along the Snake

The monotonous travel along the Snake bored Mac. The wagons creaked down a ravine and up the far side, then repeated the process at the next ravine. The parched land held little water and no relief from the August sun. He sweated beneath his hat, but kept his kerchief over his face to avoid swallowing dirt.

By midday Jenny leaned in her saddle, as if she might fall off Poulette. He took her a dipper of water. "Drink this."

She gulped the whole dipperful without a word.

"Why don't you rest in the wagon?"

Jenny shook her head. "It's worse there. I can't breathe for the heat."

"Can you stay on the mare?"

"I'll be all right."

They reached a high ridge above the river. Pershing rode over to Mac in midafternoon. "We should stop here. Fall Creek, according to Frémont's map."

"We haven't gone very far today," Mac said.

"Next camp is Raft River. A couple of steep gulches between here and there. We're too tired to make it by evening."

Mac looked at Jenny slumped on Poulette. He nodded at Pershing. They pulled into a shallow gully near the Snake. There was grass for the animals, but the wagons could not circle in the tight space.

"Guards need stay mounted to corral stray animals," Pershing ordered.

"Any chance of Indians?" Abercrombie asked.

"Always a chance," Pershing replied. "But not many signs of 'em today."

"Hope we don't lose more horses to savages," Abercrombie said.

"Stand guard yourself if you're worried." Captain Pershing stomped off.

Jenny went to bed right after supper. Mac wandered over to the Pershing wagons where the captain, Zeke, and Joel sat around their fire. "How much longer to Oregon City?" he asked.

"Two months, more or less," Pershing replied.

"Jenny only has a few weeks until her time." Mac didn't know how to talk about the coming birth, but it troubled him. She didn't seem well. "Where will we be in a month?"

"Maybe Grande Ronde."

Mac had never heard of it. "What's there?"

"Old fur trading stop. Nothing much now."

"Can we rest there?" Mac asked.

"Nope. Still got the Blues, then the Columbia. Abercrombie won't stand for delay. Don't like the idea myself. Could snow in early September in these parts."

"What are the Blues?" Zeke asked his father.

"Damnedest mountains yet." Pershing shook his head. "Not as high as what we been through, but just as steep. No, we can't stop." The captain stood and went to his tent.

"Any sign he's drinking?" Mac whispered to Zeke and Joel.

"Don't think so," Zeke said. "But he moves purty slow in the mornings."

Mac returned to his campsite and wrote by the fire as the dusty sky flamed into a magnificent golden sunset.

August 9, 1847. The gullies and dry land we pass through are hard on man and beast alike. More mountains ahead, and then the Columbia—the mightiest river of them all, Pershing says.

The next morning the trail started along the Snake, but by noon the emigrants had turned away to avoid a steep ravine. Then they rolled on to the Raft River. They crossed and camped. The Raft valley was cramped, and the only place for the wagons to camp was right on the banks.

Mac joined other men fishing. He didn't much like fishing, but the trout were plentiful.

"What's your precious map say 'bout the Snake crossing?" Abercrombie asked.

"Frémont crossed about a week's journey downstream from here," Mac said. "Past the Shoshone fishing grounds."

"Shoshone." Abercrombie spat on the ground. "Damn savages."

When Mac had a string of fish, he took it to Jenny. She pushed herself up from the crate where she sat in the shade of the wagon. "How will we ever eat so many fish?"

Mac shrugged. "We'll be eating them three meals a day. Pershing says there are deer and moose around, but the trout are easy—they practically jump onto the hook."

After supper Mac and Pershing rode upriver to greet another group of emigrants camped not far away.

"We're headed for California," their captain said. "Following the Raft to the Humboldt."

"Why didn't you turn south to California sooner?" Pershing asked.

"Didn't decide until we reached Fort Hall. Man there convinced us to forget Oregon. Too hard to get through the Blues, he said. Scared my wife silly to hear about more mountains."

"Mountains between here and California, too," Pershing said.

"Hudson's Bay man said Sierras ain't as bad as the Blues. Gave us a map of a new route. Aim to try it." The other captain showed Pershing a piece of brown paper with a pencil drawing.

"Good luck." Pershing said. Later he shook his head at Mac as they returned to their camp. "Damn fools. Following a map scribbled on scrap paper."

Mac settled himself beside his campfire and took out his journal. Jenny was already asleep.

August 10, 1847. A short day through ravines along the Snake. Good fishing. Other companies still splitting off for California. Will the Blues be as bad as men say?

A soft cry woke Mac in the middle of the night. "Jenny?" he called.

"I'm all right," she said from the ground next to his bedroll under the wagon.

"What happened?" he asked, throwing off his blanket.

"I slipped getting out of the wagon."

"Why were you getting out?"

"You know," she said.

"No, I don't. Why?"

"I needed to relieve myself," she whispered.

"Oh." Her cheeks would be pink if Mac could see her. "Do you need help?"

"No."

"Let me walk with you."

"Leave me be," she said.

Mac lay awake waiting for Jenny to return. He usually slept deeply, weary after the day's journey and his shifts at guard duty. He hadn't heard Jenny up in the night before.

A soft squeak of the wagon wheel told Mac she was back. "Are you up most nights?" he asked.

"Yes. Go back to sleep."

"I can't have you falling out of the wagon."

"Don't worry about me."

But he did worry. How was he going to keep her safe until the baby came? And what then? Jenny's predicament was becoming more and more real with every day. He was now realizing the commitment he had taken on when he brought her along.

Chapter 51: Injury and Heat

Jenny's left wrist throbbed the next morning and was swollen and stiff. She must have sprained it when she fell in the night. She was so tired of being pregnant—heavy and clumsy. No wonder Mama said women took to their beds in New Orleans when they were "enceinte".

She carefully maneuvered herself out of the wagon and started breakfast. More fish and flapjacks. She was already tiring of the tender trout. She was hungry all the time, but nothing tasted good. Jenny held the heavy iron skillet in her right hand and tried to turn the fish with her left, but her left wrist wouldn't bend.

"What are you doing?" Mac asked, as she hefted the skillet off the fire with one hand.

"Turning the fish," she said.

"What's wrong with your arm?" he asked, taking hold of her left hand.

She winced and pulled away.

"You hurt it last night?"

She nodded.

"I'll get Doc." Mac walked off.

Jenny had the fish fried when he returned with Doc.

"Let's see," the doctor said. He confirmed her wrist was sprained, rubbed a smelly, greasy ointment on it, and wrapped it up. "Don't use it," he said, then left.

"Why didn't you tell me you were hurt?" Mac asked. "Aren't we in this together?"

"Are we?" She was angry all of a sudden. "I didn't want this trip. I don't want to be here. I want my home—and Mama and Letitia." She burst into tears, and the display of weakness infuriated her even more.

235

"Jenny, you told me in Arrow Rock not to take you home. You said it again in Independence."

"But I didn't want to go to Oregon!" she wailed.

"Well, it's too late now," Mac shouted. He stomped off a few steps, then turned back. "I'll wash the dishes. Go sit in the wagon."

She didn't want to follow his orders, but she couldn't work. And she couldn't get herself into the wagon with one arm.

"Here," Mac said behind her. "Let me help." His voice was gentle now. He lifted her into the wagon.

Jenny sat crying softly. Nothing was the way it should be. She shouldn't be in this God-forsaken land. She shouldn't be having this baby. She shouldn't be living with Mac in this wagon. Mrs. Pershing shouldn't have died. No one could help her, no one understood her dreadful life. She wished she had someone to talk to.

Mrs. Tuller poked her face into the wagon. "Heard you hurt yourself. Can I help?"

"Mac's washing the dishes," Jenny said, wiping her eyes.

"Kind of weepy today, are you?" Mrs. Tuller climbed into the wagon, sat on a box, and put her arm around Jenny.

Jenny nodded. "I don't know why. My wrist doesn't hurt that much."

"Women have crying spells when they're expecting." Mrs. Tuller laughed. "Why I remember one time I was so mad at the doctor, just because he killed the wrong chicken for dinner. Didn't really matter—there'd be another neck to wring the next week. But I sobbed all day."

"I miss my mama. And Mrs. Pershing."

Mrs. Tuller's expression grew somber. "We all miss our loved ones back home. And we were all felled by Mrs. Pershing's death. Feels wrong when a woman dies after giving birth—a loss in the midst of joy." She turned Jenny to face her. "We'll have to be family for each other."

Jenny sniffled.

"I'll stay with you today." Mrs. Tuller leaned out and called to Mac. "Mr. McDougall, you tell the doctor I'm riding with Jenny."

"Yes, ma'am."

Jenny and Mrs. Tuller talked through the morning while the wagons rolled west across a scorched plateau, so dry even the sagebrush looked thirsty. The Snake curved north, but they didn't follow the river.

"Captain says we'll get back to the Snake by nightfall," Mac rode up to tell the women. "I think we have enough water, but drink sparingly."

At noon Mrs. Tuller cooked for Jenny and Mac as well as for herself and the doctor. Jenny walked around camp after dinner, her back aching from the constant jostling.

"Would you please saddle Poulette?" she asked Mac. "I can't bear to sit in the wagon any longer."

He shook his head. "With only one good hand, you might not stop her if she bolted."

"I guess I'll walk then," Jenny said. "It's flat enough."

"Won't you get worn out?" Mac asked.

"I haven't done anything else today."

But by midafternoon, after trudging under the hot sun, shaded only by her sunbonnet, Jenny was exhausted. Dust rose with every step, filling her shoes. The children complained of the hot sand burning their bare feet.

"Please may I ride Poulette?" she begged Mac.

"Jenny, you can't control her if she spooks. Ride with me on Valiente."

"I'm too big to fit on Valiente with you now." She marched off with her chin in the air.

By the time Pershing called the halt at a stagnant creek, Jenny felt flushed. She couldn't catch her breath and slumped to the ground beside the wagon as soon as Mac pulled it into place. Her pulse beat rapidly, and the horizon spun around her.

"Gracious, girl," Mrs. Tuller said. "You're plum tuckered out. Let's get you something to drink."

"I'm so dizzy," Jenny said.

Mrs. Tuller handed her a dipper of water from the barrel on the wagon. Jenny gulped it down. The warm water turned her stomach, and she leaned against the wagon wheel.

"What's wrong?" Mac said. His worried expression brought Jenny some satisfaction.

"Heat got to her, most likely," Mrs. Tuller said.

"What do we do?" Mac asked.

"Keep her face and neck damp to cool her off. She'll be all right."

Jenny heard Mac say something about "silly chit," as he reached into the wagon to get a towel. He dipped it in the water barrel and handed it to her. "Here," he said. "Do what Mrs. Tuller says."

By the time Mrs. Tuller had supper ready—more fish and rice flavored with sage—Jenny felt well enough to eat. Mrs. Tuller and Mac both pressed her to drink. She knew she'd regret it in the middle of the night when the baby kicked her bladder.

At dusk Mac said, "You have two choices, Jenny. Stay in the wagon all night with a chamber pot, or sleep on the ground with me. You can't climb out in the dark with one hand."

Jenny blushed. She shouldn't be talking with a man about chamber pots, even a man she'd nursed through cholera.

"Look, Jenny, I don't bite."

"I know," she said.

"I'm not like those men who hurt you. I'm trying to take care of you."

"I don't want anyone to take care of me."

"You need help."

She knew she did, but she didn't like being reminded of it.

"It's cooler on the ground," Mac said.

She sighed. "All right."

Mac rigged a tent beside the wagon and put her buffalo hide and bedroll beside his.

Jenny plopped to the ground clumsily. The shaggy skin was surprisingly cool in the warm evening. She wrote:

> *Wednesday, August 11ᵗʰ—The heat overcame me today. I foolishly hurt my arm and am of little use to anyone.*

Chapter 52: Goose Creek to Cauldron Linn

August 11, 1847. Today we traveled over desolate land along the Snake. Camped now at Swamp Creek in a wet valley. Mountains to our south, but none visible ahead.

Early the next morning Tanner brought fresh trout through the camp. Mac took two as long as his forearm.

"More fish?" Jenny asked. "All we've eaten for two days is fish."

"Would you rather have jerky?" Mac responded. "Trout are fresh."

Jenny sighed and struggled to get out of her bedroll using just one arm.

"How's your wrist?" Mac asked.

"Still hurts. Not as bad. I'll cook, if you clean them."

"I'll fry the fish." Mac held out his hand and helped Jenny to her feet. By the time she returned from the latrine, the fish were almost done.

Jenny put leftover biscuits from Hatty on two plates, and Mac added the fish.

"What a morning," Mac said. The sky was clear, the dust settled from the day before. "Hope the wind stays calm."

After breakfast Jenny picked up Poulette's saddle. "I'm riding today," she told Mac.

"Give me that." Mac took the saddle, lifted it onto the mare, and boosted Jenny into the saddle. He didn't care if she heard him mutter, "Stubborn miss." She was the most hardheaded woman he'd ever known. "Stay near the wagons."

Mac hitched the oxen and saddled Valiente. On horseback beside the wagon, he could keep an eye on Jenny and ride after her if she lost control of Poulette. But Jenny didn't seem to have any trouble holding the mare to a slow walk. She stayed close by, as he had ordered, but far enough away that they didn't have to talk.

In midmorning Zeke rode up to Mac.

"Where's Captain Pershing?" Mac asked.

"Scouting." Zeke wiped his hand across his brow. "Though what there is to scout in this damn country, I don't know. It's flat as far as the eye can see."

They had ridden south from the Snake to avoid ravines and through the morning had crossed only a few small gullies.

"Pa wants to know if folks need meat," Zeke said. "Goose Creek's coming up. Good camp, though it makes for a short day. We can hunt this afternoon."

Mac nodded. "Jenny's complaining about eating fish all the time. I wouldn't mind stopping early."

"Then we'll stop at the creek," Zeke said, and rode along the wagons to spread the word.

After the wagons were circled and they'd eaten the noon meal, the hunting party set out. One group rode west, and the other south toward the hills. Mac joined the southbound group.

"Don't know what we'll scare up in this heat," Abercrombie said. "Too hot for any self-respecting deer."

"I seen some quail," Pershing said.

They rode all the way to the southern hills through low sagebrush and sand.

"Ho!" one of the hunters called as a deer bounded away.

"Got it!" Abercrombie yelled. He shot, but the deer kept running.

"Damn it, Abercrombie. I was closer," Dempsey shouted.

"There's more where that one came from," Abercrombie said with a shrug. "Probably a whole herd of 'em down in the ravine."

But the hunters didn't see any more deer all afternoon. A bevy of quail rose from under the sage, and the men shot several birds. "Not even enough for dinner," Dempsey grumbled. "Wish I'd had a shot at the deer."

"Better head back," Pershing said.

The riders returned to camp about supper time. Jenny looked up hopefully at Mac. "One quail is all," he told her.

Her face fell, but she said. "We still have Tanner's fish. I'll fry it and roast the bird. At least we have plenty of sage and rice to stuff it with."

As Jenny settled into her bedroll on the ground, Mac wrote:

August 12, 1847. Hunted in the hills south of Goose Creek. We must scavenge for food until we reach Fort Boise.

In the morning the company started early to make up for the short distance traveled the day before. They trekked across more desert, again skirting the worst of the ravines by staying away from the Snake.

"We'll camp near the river tonight," Pershing said. "Some of the purtiest falls are along this stretch."

"Is it out of our way?" Abercrombie asked.

"Not far," Pershing replied. "Snake curves south at Cauldron Linn."

"What kind of name is that?" Zeke asked his father.

"Scottish," Pershing said. "Linn means waterfall. Some Scot trapper said the water under the fall churned more'n a witch's cauldron."

The travelers camped on the plateau above the falls. "No water here," Pershing said, "But plenty in the river below."

The men took buckets down to the Snake to haul water to refill their barrels. When he reached the riverbank, Mac looked downstream at the top of the falls. Where he stood, the river was a wide pool of water. At the end of the pool, high bluffs squeezed the current into a narrow chute.

"Don't let it fool you, son," Pershing said, as Mac stepped out on a rock in the pool. "Water's fast, even here. If'n you slip, you can't escape the cauldron."

Mac left his buckets and worked his way along the shore and down the steep hill to the bottom of the falls. There he could see the river rushing in a two-tiered cascade down a thirty-foot drop that ended in boiling froth at the bottom. From this angle, it did look like a witch's pot.

He retrieved his buckets, then carried them up to camp. After filling the water barrel, he asked Jenny, "Want to see the falls? I found a path down."

She stood, bracing her back with her hand. "How far is it?"

"Not far. It's steep, but I'll help you."

"I may have to stop," she warned, but headed toward the river with him. Near the edge she stared down at the water and gasped. "*Mon Dieu!* How did you get down?"

Mac pointed out the path he'd taken.

She peered down, hands on her hips. "You think I can make it?"

"If you get tired, we'll turn around," Mac assured her.

Mac led and Jenny followed. He held his hand out, and she grabbed it at the steeper points in the descent. By the time they reached the water, the late afternoon sun colored the cliffs behind them orange and black and the water a pale gray.

At the bottom Jenny stared at the falls. "It's so beautiful. And frightening," she said. "I'm glad we don't cross the river here."

"We have about a week more on the Snake before we cross."

She shuddered.

On the climb back to camp, Jenny led, with Mac behind to break her fall if she slipped. They went slowly, stopping frequently for Jenny to catch her breath. "I made it," she said, smiling at the top of the bluffs. Her face shone in the glow of the setting sun.

She was a very attractive girl, Mac thought. The kind of girl a man could fall in love with, if he were so inclined. Which he wasn't, he told himself. Besides, Jenny had no interest in marriage, and neither did he.

He reached out and tucked a strand of hair behind her ear.

Chapter 53: Indians at Shoshone Falls

Friday, August 13ᵗʰ—Camped at Cauldron Linn. Mac took me to the falls, which are splendid. The dry air chaps my skin.

On Saturday they rode west, leaving the Snake as it curved north. They arrived at Rock Creek while the sun was still high, and Captain Pershing called the halt.

"What's that roar?" Jenny asked Mac as they made camp.

"Shoshone Falls. Pershing says it's bigger than Cauldron Linn. Higher than Niagara," Mac said, "That's the biggest falls I've ever seen."

Cauldron Linn had been huge—Jenny couldn't imagine anything larger. "Where's Niagara?"

"Western New York. I saw it two years ago on a summer trip." Mac smiled. "Magnificent."

Zeke stopped by their wagon. "Pa says we're taking a rest day tomorrow. Folks need more meat. Those who want can ride to Shoshone Falls."

"Would you like to go?" Mac asked Jenny.

"We need meat," Jenny said. She did want to see the falls, but she didn't want to take Mac away from what he should be doing. And she was so sick of eating fish.

"I'll hunt this afternoon. If I shoot something, we'll ride there tomorrow. Maybe Esther and Daniel will come, too."

"All right." She smiled up at him.

Mac set off with the other hunters after the noon meal. Jenny found

Esther at the Pershing wagons with Jonah and Rachel.

"Where are the other children?" Jenny asked.

"Fishing with Tanner and his boy. I hope they catch something."

"I'm tired of fish," Rachel complained.

"Me, too," Jenny said. "First, all we had was buffalo, now it's fish. What I'd dearly relish is some boiled greens."

Esther shrugged. "Probably greens around, if we knew what to use."

"Sage. That's all there is." Rachel sighed. "Sage and more sage."

Jonah let out a wail.

"How's he doing?" Jenny leaned over to touch the baby's cheek. Would her child be as sweet as Jonah?

Esther laughed. "He's getting fat. Cow's milk surely agrees with him. I don't bother Mrs. Dempsey at all now, and I even gave her little girl a cup of milk yesterday. I hope the cow stays fresh."

"How are you feeling?" Jenny asked. If Jenny had counted the weeks right, Esther was far enough long in her pregnancy to start feeling queasy.

Esther gestured at Rachel and shook her head. "I'm fine," she said.

So Esther had not told Rachel about her pregnancy yet. "Would you and Daniel like to ride to Shoshone Falls tomorrow?" Jenny asked.

Esther grimaced. "Depends on Mrs. Abercrombie. I said I'd help her tomorrow, if I could spend today with Jonah and the others."

"If she'll let you go, I'll watch Jonah," Rachel offered. "I don't mind."

Esther hugged her sister. "Rachel's such a help, now she's not afraid of the baby."

"He was so little at first. And cried all the time," Rachel said.

"Now he's got milk, he's the happiest baby." Esther smiled at her brother, then looked up. "I swear he smiled back."

"You're like his mama to him," Jenny said.

Tanner and the children soon returned with a string of fish. "Catfish!" Jenny exclaimed. "Just like in Missouri."

"Yep. Also trout. Take your pick," Tanner said.

Jenny and Esther chose what they wanted.

"You ladies be careful," Tanner said. "Saw Indians fishin' on the creek nearby."

"Indians?" Jenny looked up in alarm. "What'd they do?"

"Didn't bother us none," Tanner said. "But stay near camp."

"I won't leave the wagon, if there's Indians around," Rachel said.

The hunters returned at sunset. Mac carried a gutted deer carcass slung across the back of his saddle. "This'll feed us for a while," he said as he dismounted. "We found a small herd. Shot several. Whole camp will eat well tonight."

"And Tanner brought us catfish," Jenny said. "I'll smoke the fish tonight to eat tomorrow."

They ate a quick supper. Later, while the fish smoked, Jenny sat beside the fire and wrote:

Saturday, August 14th—Camped at Rock Creek. Indians nearby. Fresh venison tonight. Tomorrow we ride to Shoshone Falls.

On Sunday morning Jenny made breakfast of smoked catfish on biscuits, then packed a picnic for their ride. After their Sunday prayers, Mac saddled the horses.

Esther and Daniel joined them, along with Zeke and Joel. As the six rode out of camp, Captain Pershing said, "Watch out for Indians. Doubt they trouble you, but don't let yourselves be surprised."

Shoshone Falls was an easy five-mile ride north of camp across the high sage-covered plateau. As they rode, Jenny heard the roar. "Must be close."

Mac shook his head. "Still more than a mile away."

"The water is that loud?" she asked.

Zeke laughed. "Pa says you can't hear yourself talk when you're right at the falls."

They reached the black lava bluffs above the river and looked over the edge. "My heavens!" Jenny cried.

"Must be a thousand feet wide," Mac said. "And two hundred feet down."

The water fell like a veil over cliffs in the river. Several veils really, Jenny thought, gazing from one gushing torrent to the next.

"Shall we ride down?" Zeke asked.

"How?" Esther said.

"I see a way to the top of the falls." Zeke pointed with his hat. "Not sure how to get down farther."

"Let's take our picnic to the top," Daniel said.

They rode down the hill, their horses stepping solidly on steep switchbacks, until they stood by the water cascading into a crashing pool below.

The men tethered their mounts to sage bushes, while Jenny and Esther laid out biscuits, venison, and dried fish. They ate, but talked little, deafened by the roar of the falls.

Zeke pointed to a pool at the bottom. "Indians."

Jenny grabbed Mac's arm. "They have spears."

"Fishing," Joel said. "Fish can't get any farther upriver, 'cause of the falls. Bet that pool is teeming with trout."

"Shall we go see?" Zeke asked, jumping to his feet.

"I'm not going down there," Jenny said.

"Me neither," Esther said.

"I'll stay with the women," Daniel said. "You all go on."

Mac stood. "You all right here?" he asked, looking down at Jenny.

"As long as you come back," she said. She worried, but he should be safe with Zeke and Joel.

Mac grinned. "I'll be back." He and the Pershings saddled their horses and picked their way down the steep bank to the bottom.

Jenny saw when the Indians noticed the men approaching. Several braves stood up, facing the white men, spears no longer pointing at the water, but held ready to attack. Zeke raised his hand to the Indians. Jenny couldn't hear, but saw gestures between Zeke and the natives. Mac took something out of his saddlebag and handed it to one of the braves. The brave nodded and handed Mac a parcel. The three white men waved and started back to the top of the falls.

When the men returned, Esther asked, "What did they want?"

Zeke laughed. "We bought fish from them. And told them we'd take all the dried fish they could bring us in camp tonight."

"Was that wise?" Daniel asked. "How many will come?"

"Oh, I don't think we have anything to worry about," Zeke said. "I didn't see any guns."

"We'd better get back to camp before they do," Mac said. "So the rest of our company isn't surprised."

As the group rode back, Jenny asked Mac, "What did you give the Indians?"

"A button," Mac said. "Came off my shirt yesterday. Bought a fresh trout for a button." He held out the parcel he'd received from the Indian brave.

More fish, Jenny thought.

That evening as the travelers fixed supper, ten Indian braves rode their horses to the edge of camp. Even though Jenny expected them, fear rose in her throat. Would the Indians trade and leave? Or would they bother the company?

Captain Pershing walked over to the Indians and raised his hand in greeting. Zeke and Mac joined him. Jenny watched as the men bartered with gestures and offerings of blankets and other goods to exchange for the fish.

Mac brought back an armload of dried salmon. "What'd you have to give for them?" Jenny asked.

"Your buffalo robe," Mac said.

Jenny swallowed hard. The robe had been such a comfort on the trail. She started for the wagon to get it.

"Stop," Mac said. "I was joking. I traded the rest of our venison for the salmon."

"Why?" Jenny asked, almost as perturbed about losing the venison as the buffalo skin. "We had fish from Tanner. And more from the Indians at the falls. The deer was the first real meat we've had since Fort Hall."

"Indians know how to keep the salmon from spoiling. We can eat it for days." Mac piled the fish on a barrel. "I thought you'd be pleased."

"I don't like eating fish all the time." Jenny knew she sounded petulant, but that's how she felt. She didn't want to eat the same thing every day. She didn't want to be in this hot, dry land. She didn't want to be with these people any longer. And she hated Indian food.

"Just find someplace to store it." Mac slammed his hat on his head. "And pack up the wagon. We're starting out at first light." He turned to leave.

"Where are you going?"

"Peace pipe with the Indians. I'll be back late."

Jenny did as Mac ordered, but got angrier as she worked. What right did he have to tell her what to do?

She threw the last of the fish in the wagon, then took out her journal.

Sunday, August 15th—Indians at Shoshone Falls today. Mac traded fresh venison for dried salmon. I am so sick of fish. When will this journey end? The wonders we have seen do not make up for loss of comforts and home.

Chapter 54: Toward the Snake River Crossing

August 15, 1847. Traded with Shoshone. They spear fish with elk horn points tied to thin tree branches. They said to cross the Snake where three islands make the river shallow. Frémont's map is vague, so we will follow the Indian advice.

As he wrote, Mac remembered the Shoshones' unkempt appearance. They had dressed in odd assortments of Indian and white clothing—one man had worn a woman's cotton shirtwaist over his leather pants, another a black armband as his sole garment above a breechclout. Many wore pierced pennies and buttons on leather thongs around their necks.

Communication was difficult. One Indian knew a little English, learned from trappers, he said. Another spoke a little Pawnee, as did Pershing. Pershing and the braves drew maps in the sand. The Indians indicated the best river crossing was a few days west.

The next morning Jenny fixed breakfast in silence, slapping a plate of dried salmon and flapjacks in front of Mac.

"Thank you," he said.

She walked off. In a snit again, Mac thought.

He wondered why he'd brought her. Surely he could have convinced Pershing to take him, even without a wife. But he couldn't have left Jenny alone in Independence, though now he didn't know what he'd do with her and her child in Oregon. They were his responsibility.

Pershing ambled over and sat on a stone while Mac ate. "Shoshone said we can hug the Snake or cut across the desert to get to Three Island

Crossing. Desert might save a day, but maybe not. Might be some purty steep canyons to get through."

"Which way we going?" Mac asked, swallowing the last bite of flapjack.

Pershing shrugged. "What do Shoshone know about wagons? Fishing's better along the Snake—that's all they care about."

Jenny had nearly collapsed from the heat on their last spell in the desert. "I vote for the river," Mac said. "But Abercrombie won't."

Pershing nodded. "I'm with you. We'll head for Salmon Falls tonight. No need to tell Abercrombie there's another option. He wouldn't put store in what a Shoshone said anyway."

They crossed Rock Creek and headed northwest. Pershing rotated Zeke and Joel as scouts through the day. "Indians say the Snake turns north afore Salmon Falls," Pershing said. "But there's rough land between here and there. Keep us south of the ravines."

Joel returned to the wagons at the noon halt. "There's a terrible patch north of here," he said, as Mac and other men watered the teams. "We can get to the river, but I ain't sure we can move along the shore once we're there."

"Then where to?" Pershing asked.

Joel drank a dipperful of water. "Zeke's looking for a path to the south."

"Need another scout?" Mac asked. "I'd enjoy it." Jenny was still upset.

Pershing nodded. "Go with Joel. Send Zeke back. He can lead the company around the rough land ahead."

Mac and Joel rode northwest over another arid plateau. "Wagons can get by here," Joel said. "But look yonder," he gestured to the north. A rock-strewn slope creased with gullies spread for miles toward the river. The Snake was just a narrow band of silver glinting in the distance.

They skirted the stony slope, and Joel pointed to the west ahead of them. "Another gorge."

Mac couldn't see the ravine until they reached its crest. They peered over the sheer volcanic cliffs at the small blue creek below. Mac whistled. "Must be four hundred feet deep. How do we get across?"

"Can't. Got to travel the canyon lip till it hits the Snake," Joel said. "Indians told Pa the bluffs flatten out at the river. Zeke should be up ahead."

Mac heard a yell and peered ahead. Zeke trotted toward them.

"You find the way?" Joel asked.

Zeke nodded and wiped his brow with a handkerchief. "I didn't go all the way to the Snake, but I seen a path."

"Pa says to go back. Bring the wagons here," Joel told his brother.

"We'll mark the way down to the river," Mac said. "Watch out for Jenny, if you would, please."

Zeke grinned, saluted, and trotted off. Mac and Joel picked their way toward the Snake, marking the route with piles of stones. After they staked out a campsite, Mac suggested they ride up the valley. Within a mile, the black walls of the gorge rose above them, though it was cool and green in the valley.

"What a sight," Mac said, gazing at the looming cliffs. An eagle soared and swooped high above the creek, but still below the crest of the ravine.

Joel shuddered. "I don't like feeling hemmed in by walls," he said. "I'd ruther be in open land any day."

They surprised a small herd of mule deer drinking at the stream. Mac fired, and one deer dropped. They packed up the carcass and returned to camp. "Jenny'll be pleased," Mac said. "She's tired of fish."

While waiting for the wagons to arrive, Mac wrote:

August 16, 1847. Reached Salmon Falls Creek. Rode up a deep canyon, walls steeper than I've ever seen. Good camp tonight with plenty of grass. Should reach the Snake crossing tomorrow.

The wagons arrived in early evening. Jenny exclaimed over the deer, and Mac fried venison steaks while she made biscuits. "Is this all it takes to make you happy?" he asked with a grin.

She smiled and shook her head. "I'm sorry I've been so ill-tempered. I'm just worn out."

Mac touched her arm gently. "It'll all be over soon."

"Yes," she said, her face turning sober.

The next day the travelers picked their way through a narrow path along the Snake below towering lava cliffs. The route was strewn with rocks and rough grasses, making the teams strain with their loads.

In midmorning Jenny pointed at a wall of water pouring out of the bluffs on the opposite bank. "Look! Falls dropping from the middle of rocks."

"Must be an underground stream," Mac said. As they got closer, he saw a series of thin cascades, trickling like lacy threads from the lava walls, so numerous they covered the rocks.

"Hundreds of falls coming straight out of the cliff," Joel said. "What a sight."

When they left the wonder behind, the wagons clung to the slope of the hill above the Snake. Even along the river, the soil was barren except for scraggly sage bushes, so faded they were more gray than green.

"Too bad there ain't no grass," Zeke said. "There ain't nothing along this God-awful river."

Some places they had to climb the hills above the Snake. The slopes were too steep for switchbacking—the wagons would have tipped over. They skirted an enormous gulch, much like the one they had circumvented the day before. When they stopped for the noon meal, there was no grass or water for the animals.

Only the children enjoyed the halt on the hot, dry plateau. Jonathan and David ran up to Mac and Jenny. "See," one boy said. "A bone."

"Looks like a horse's leg bone," Mac said, after inspecting it. "Where did you find it?"

The boys gestured toward the river. "We been climbing down the rocks. Looking for Indians," one said.

"Didn't find no Indians," the other boy said. "Just bones."

"Maybe the Indians ate the horse," Mac said, winking at Jenny. She looked appalled, but the boys giggled.

Zeke, who had been scouting, came galloping back to the wagons. "We can't keep to the river," he reported to his father while Mac listened. "Gets worse'n this." He waved at the ravine they were detouring at the moment. "I don't know what the damn Indians were thinking, sending us this way."

"What's the alternative?" Pershing asked.

"The desert," Zeke said. "I seen a couple of gullies ahead. Both have water and grass. We can camp there. But we got to stay back from the Snake. Hills are too steep."

Pershing squinted, then nodded. "Lead on, son." He called for the wagons to head out.

Abercrombie rode over to Pershing. "What the devil you doing?" he asked. "Why are we moving away from the river?"

"Zeke says we can't make it."

"Then why the hell was he taking us that way?"

"Leave him be, Abercrombie."

"We could've been crossing the desert in the cool of the morning." Abercrombie spat tobacco juice and wiped his mouth on his sleeve.

"No help for it now," Pershing said. "We got bad advice."

"What advice?"

"From the Shoshone."

"You listened to those savages?" Abercrombie's face turned darker than brick. "Them heathen sent us here on purpose. Probably murder us in our sleep tonight."

"They don't know how to pull a wagon," Pershing replied. He waved his hat for the company to proceed.

Abercrombie rode beside Mac. "Can you believe him? Following the trail of a bunch of savages."

Mac grunted in reply.

"What's that fool Frémont's map say?" Usually Abercrombie paid about as much attention to Frémont as to Indians.

"Not enough detail," Mac said. "Places where Frémont stayed by the river, and places where he cut across the river bends. Don't know exactly where we are."

Abercrombie griped further, but rode off when Mac didn't argue back. Soon Mac saw him complaining to men in his platoon.

They reached a thin stream in late afternoon. As Zeke had said, there was plenty of grass and water for the teams.

August 17, 1847. Camped on a creek in the high desert. Impossible to follow the Snake. Grass enough for the oxen.

Chapter 55: Three Island Crossing

Tuesday, August 17ᵗʰ—I have never felt such heat. Not a whisper of a breeze. We cannot escape the sun either on horseback or in the wagon.

Jenny fanned herself with a sage branch as she wrote. Despite the darkening sky, heat still radiated from the ground, as intense as the campfire. Venison did not appeal to her appetite. Even the water was tepid after sloshing in barrels all day. She could ask Mac to haul a fresh bucket, but she hated to bother him.

Sleep eluded her that night. She slept on the ground now beside Mac. It was too much effort to climb into the wagon, knowing she'd be up two or three times in the night. Only a few more weeks until the baby came. She was afraid of the birth, but weary of feeling bloated and heavy.

Nothing seemed to bother Mac. He didn't stir when Jenny pushed herself awkwardly to her feet at dawn.

After breakfast the travelers headed west across the desert, the terrain unchanged from the days before. The wagons careened down the descents, and the teams strained to haul the loads up the hills. Jenny rode Poulette, but even the mare's easy gait made her back knot in pain.

"We'll hit the Snake by nightfall," Mac said. "Cross tomorrow." Of all her fears, she dreaded crossing the wild river most of all.

At noon they rested beside a gaping canyon. "Two hundred feet down, maybe," Mac told Jenny. "Not as deep as the gorge Joel and I explored."

It was steep enough for Jenny. "How will we get across?" she asked.

Mac shrugged. "Zeke must have found a way. He's marked this as the route."

When they resumed their travel, the bluffs flattened and formed a small valley between them and distant mounds to the west. They descended into the valley, crossed it, then climbed the far hills. From the summit they could see the Snake.

Zeke waited near the river and gestured at the three islands. "Here's the crossing. Like the Shoshone said."

Jenny's heart sank. Between each island water rushed as wide as many of the rivers they had crossed on the plains. And here they had to move from island to island. It was four crossings really, not one.

"How?" she whispered.

"I rode across," Zeke said. "It's fast, but I think we can float the wagons."

"You ain't trying it with mine," Abercrombie said. "Did that last time."

"We'll test it in the morning," Pershing said. "Decide what to do." He squinted at the river. "Won't be easy. Heard men died here a couple years ago."

Jenny wrote that evening:

Wednesday, August 18th—Reached the Snake Crossing. The water is fearfully swift. I shall not sleep a wink tonight.

At dawn the men started planning the crossing. They pulled ropes behind them to measure distances and called out when they hit holes in the bottom of the river. "Watch it here." "Need to shift west." "Give me more rope." Jenny heard them shouting until midmorning.

Mac returned to the wagon wet to his thighs. "Did you fall in?" she asked.

He grinned. "Valiente stepped in a hole. We ended up swimming."

"Is it too deep to ford?"

Mac shook his head. "We have a path. We'll take it slowly. Move to the first island, then the next and the next, until we get across. A few wagons at a time."

"Will I ride Poulette or in the wagon?" Jenny asked.

"Which would you rather?"

"The wagon. I'd feel safer."

"I'll ride with you when it's time," Mac said, touching her shoulder. "You'll be fine."

But men had died here, Captain Pershing had said. Like poor Mr. Purcell back in Kansas Territory, leaving his wife widowed.

The men guided a few wagons to the first island, then to the second, then to the third. "Lash 'em together," Pershing shouted. "Make it harder for the current to grab 'em."

The teams pulled the wagons to the far bank, more than half a mile from where Jenny stood. The current was so fast the men clung to the oxen's yokes or the wagon sides to stay upright as they walked the teams across. Those watching from the shore cheered when the first wagons bumped up the north riverbank.

Over and over the process repeated. "Will we all get across today?" Jenny asked Mac when he returned to their wagon for a quick meal.

Mac took his plate. "Captain says we'll try. We've seen Indians lurking in the cliffs."

That left Jenny with a new worry. She glanced at the crags above her.

After eating, Mac left for the river. He returned in midafternoon. "You're next," he said. He lifted Jenny into the wagon.

They were in the last group of wagons to ford. The men must know what they were doing. But Jenny was still frightened as Mac steered into the rushing river.

"Hang on to the bench," he said. "Don't grab my arm. I may need to jump in to guide the oxen."

Zeke rode beside the wagon. "Don't worry, Miz Jenny. I'll be here, too."

She clutched the wagon seat. The oxen lowed as the water caught their bellies. But they forged ahead.

Jenny remembered the wagon sinking on the North Platte. She had to ask, "Is there quicksand here?" Her voice quavered.

Mac laughed. "Quicksand? Water's too fast. No quicksand, only holes. We know where the worst of them are. We think."

The wagon swayed as the wheels bumped over the rocky bottom. She'd been through this before. They passed the first island, then the second, and headed out from the last island toward the far shore.

Upstream a man shouted. "Mule under!" Jenny couldn't see around the wagons beside her.

Zeke splashed off. "Cut it loose!" he yelled. "Cut the harness!"

An animal screamed—was it the mule? "What's happening?" Jenny cried, grasping Mac's arm.

Mac pulled away. "Let go, Jenny. I need to manage the team."

"What's happening?"

"Mule went under. Cutting it loose."

"Where?" A mule swam by, heading downstream. A man on the far side rode into the current. He reached for the mule's mane, missed, and fell off his horse.

"He's down!" someone yelled.

Other men splashed into the water, but the first man did not surface. Jenny craned her neck looking for the man and mule. Another mule's body floated downstream behind the first.

They reached the far shore, and Mac drove up the bank, the wagon jostling over the stony ground. Mac handed Jenny his whip and jumped off the wagon seat. "Going to help." His face was grim.

Daniel guided Jenny's team away from the river and into the camp the earlier arrivals had started. Doc strode toward the shore with a deep frown. Daniel lifted Jenny off the wagon seat, then ran to join the other men at the water's edge.

Jenny hugged Esther as they stared. "Did you see it?" Jenny asked.

Esther nodded. "Mule got caught in his harness. Went under. The driver got into the water. He cut the mule and its partner free. Mules were swept away. Someone went after them. I'm afeared he drowned."

"Who?"

"Couldn't tell. Who crossed with you?"

Jenny shook her head. "I wasn't looking. I was too scared."

They named the families using mules and looked around camp to see who was there. But so many men were in the water, they didn't know who was missing.

After an hour, as the sun fell behind the western hills, Mac trudged up from the bank, his clothes soaked, Daniel right behind him.

"Who was it?" Jenny asked.

"Didn't find the body. Everyone's accounted for but Horace Mercer."

"Mr. Mercer didn't drive mules. He had oxen," Esther said.

Mac took the towel Jenny gave him. "Mercer went after Scott's mules. Scott is safe. But no sign of Mercer. His leg was still weak."

"One mule drowned, too," Daniel said. "Other one made it, but ended up two miles downstream."

The camp was somber that evening, Mrs. Mercer and many other women sobbing. "He was a kindly man," Mrs. Tuller said.

"We'll lay by tomorrow," Pershing said. "Let the teams rest. Maybe we'll find Mercer."

Later Jenny wrote through tears:

Thursday, August 19th—We crossed the Snake, but lost a man. Horace Mercer leaves a wife and children. All to save a mule.

Throughout the next day, the men searched both banks of the Snake for Mercer. At dusk, when Pershing led the men into camp, he had a load strapped behind his saddle.

Mrs. Mercer ran up to Pershing. "Horace!" she wailed.

"No, ma'am," the captain said. "It's a deer. No sign of your husband."

Mrs. Mercer fell to her knees.

"You didn't find anything?" Jenny whispered when Mac returned to their wagon.

He shook his head wearily. "Not a trace. No clothes, not even a hat. Nothing of him or the mule."

In the morning while she fixed breakfast, Jenny heard Mrs. Mercer plead with the captain, "We can't leave. What if Horace made it out of the water and he's hurt? We got to search again."

Pershing's face was drawn. Jenny wondered if he'd slept at all. "Ma'am, his body could be anywhere," he said. "Might not come up for months. We can't wait."

The Mercer children's eyes were huge. Tears streamed down the oldest girl's face, but she didn't make a sound, even as her mother wept and pulled at the captain's arm.

Mrs. Tuller packed up the Mercers' belongings and guided Mrs. Mercer to the wagon seat. "I'll ride with you today," she said to the grieving widow.

As the first wagons pulled out of camp, Mrs. Mercer screamed. "Horace!"

Three Indians walked into the emigrants' camp. One carried a body, and laid it on the ground—Horace Mercer, his body battered and clothes ripped from the force of the river.

Captain Pershing went over to the braves. One spoke a little English. "Down river," the Indian said. "Found body at sunrise."

The company delayed its departure to bury Mr. Mercer, and finally left camp in late morning. Dark lava bluffs rose above the north bank of the Snake, no different than on the south bank. The travelers skirted the bases of the cliffs, sometimes with room to drive the wagons side by side, sometimes in single file where the rocks came close to the water's edge.

Saturday, August 21ˢᵗ—Indians found Mr. Mercer's body. We buried him and left Three Island Crossing behind. How much more grief will this journey bring?

Chapter 56: Hot Springs and Horse Thieves

August 21, 1847. Crossed the Snake, now heading to Boise. Mercer drowned attempting to save Scott's mule. The Scotts are now short a team, and Mrs. Mercer is a widow. Late start today. No Sunday rest tomorrow.

They camped beneath a low ridge of black rock. Water and grass were more plentiful on the north side of the Snake, but Mac worried about the company's morale. The adults moved mechanically about their chores, and children laughed and shouted less than usual. He wondered if Pershing was drunk—the captain had been morose and taciturn all evening, only speaking when asked a direct question.

Mac went to search for Zeke. "How's your father?" Mac asked.

Zeke squinted. "What do you mean?"

Mac raised an eyebrow.

"You mean, is he drinking?" Zeke scuffed the ground with the toe of his boot. "Don't know where he could be getting it."

"You don't smell it on him?"

"He don't let me get close enough."

Mac wiped his forehead. "Abercrombie's still looking for a chance to take over."

Zeke nodded. "I'll watch Pa."

Sunday morning the wagons began on level ground but soon climbed away from the Snake through rocky cliffs eroded by water and wind. The plateau above held no vegetation except thin grass and sage. In spots the dirt was red, elsewhere gray sand. Everywhere it was dry and gritty, rising in clouds of dust that choked both teams and travelers.

As he rode Valiente beside the wagon, Mac yearned for a rainstorm like they'd seen on the plains. Even hail would be welcome.

Jenny rode Poulette away from the wagons. She sagged in her saddle. It was a few weeks at most until her baby arrived—how would she fare?

"Hot spring at the base of that wall," Pershing said, pointing at a high bluff ahead. "We'll camp there tonight."

The crag seemed rougher and more rugged as they approached, its columns of black lava and red quartz looming above them. Two creeks flowed from the bottom of the cliff with grass along their banks.

When they made camp, Mac checked the team's hooves for wear, while Jenny fixed supper. He hoped the oxen would survive to Oregon—or at least until Fort Boise.

As Mac finished with the oxen, one of the Pershing twins ran into camp. "Pa! Esther! Come quick! Jonathan boiled his finger."

Pershing hurried to his son. "What is it, David?"

"Water's hot. Jonathan got hurt." Jonathan trailed behind his twin holding his hand in the air and crying.

"I put my hand in," Jonathan sobbed. "It burned."

Pershing inspected the hand. "Not too bad. Go get Esther to put some salve on it."

The twins ran off.

"I recollect the water's hot enough to cook in," the captain said. "Shall we try?"

Mac went with Jenny to the spring. They put their salmon in a small pot to simmer. "Too hot for doing dishes," Jenny said. The fish poached in less than ten minutes. They ate, and Mac hauled a bucket of hot water back to camp to cool so Jenny could wash.

He wrote by firelight:

August 22, 1847. Cooked supper in a hot spring. Still several days to Boise. No relief from the heat or dust.

The next day the wagons headed north beneath hills covered with bunch grass. Boulders the size of houses had fallen from the granite columns onto grassy knolls below. Pershing called the noon halt at a creek that barely trickled, though the grass on its banks was green. "The oxen'll do all right," he said. "Horses and mules need more water."

That night they camped on another small creek. As they circled the wagons, Pershing told the platoon leaders, "Post extra guards. I seen Indians in the hills. In forty-two they tried to steal our horses near here."

"I'll be on duty tonight," Mac told Jenny. "Might be horse thieves."

"Indians?" Her voice quavered.

He nodded. "Get Mrs. Tuller to stay with you tonight. And sleep in the wagon. It'd be safer."

Mrs. Tuller arrived as Mac saddled Valiente to take his guard shift. "I'm sure you'll both be pleased as Punch when your baby comes," the older woman said with a smile.

Mac nodded with a thin grin, and mounted Valiente. As he circled the camp, he worried again about what to do with Jenny. She needed someone to take care of her. Should he stay? But he had to leave.

Again, Zeke seemed like the answer. Maybe Zeke would marry her once Mac was gone.

In the middle of the night, Joel relieved Mac. He crawled under the wagon, listening to Mrs. Tuller's snores above him. The wagon creaked as Jenny climbed out. Mac got up to help her down the wheel. "What's wrong?" he asked.

"Just need the latrine," she mumbled.

"I'll wait for you."

"You don't have to," she said. He waited anyway. She could barely heft herself into the wagon now.

Before dawn Mac awakened to a shout. "Indians!" a man yelled. Shots rang out and a horse whinnied.

Mac rolled out of his blanket, grabbed his rifle as he stood, and ran toward the noise. "What is it?" he asked Zeke.

"Horse thieves. I think they got a couple."

Mac searched for Valiente in the churning herd. It took Mac a moment to find the black stallion against the night sky. He looked for Poulette, but didn't see the little mare.

"Animals are stampeding," Joel said, riding up to Mac and Zeke. "Don't think the Indians got many. But they may try to round up the loose horses before we can. Saddle up. Let's go."

Mac saddled Valiente and rode out. They worked the rest of the night to find the missing animals. Poulette had run off, but Mac found her munching grass in a hollow.

The sun was well up before all the men returned. "How many'd we lose?" Pershing asked.

"Two horses and an ox," Zeke reported.

Abercrombie spat on the ground. "Won't never see those horses again. And the ox is stew by now."

"Whose were they?" the captain asked.

"Douglass Abercrombie and James Hancock each lost a horse," Zeke said. "Don't know whose ox yet."

"God damn it," Samuel said. "Doug's horse is a good one. Oughta shoot those thieving savages. We need to search longer."

"You just said we'd never see 'em again. We can't stop," Pershing said. "You wouldn't if it were someone else's. We'll head on to Boise. Buy another mount there, if you've a mind to."

"Fine one you are," Abercrombie sneered. "Lollygagging for months, and now you want to hurry."

Pershing slapped his hat on his head. "You can come or you can stay, but we're heading out."

Mac led Poulette back to his wagon, glad he'd found the mare. Jenny and Mrs. Tuller had breakfast ready. Jenny handed him a plate of biscuits and venison. "What's Mr. Abercrombie mad about?" Jenny asked, after she exclaimed over Poulette.

"Stolen horse. You'd think it was one of his granddaughters." Mac was hungry and ate quickly.

"You must be tired," Jenny said. "I can drive. Why don't you rest?"

Mac shook his head. "Too keyed up to sleep."

He dashed off a note in his journal before they moved on:

August 24, 1847. Indians stole two horses and an ox. One horse was Abercrombie's. I found Poulette.

Chapter 57: Toward Fort Boise

Tuesday, August 24th—Last night I heard the Indians whooping as they stole our horses, then our men gave chase. Poulette ran away, but Mac found her. All day I worried the Indians would return.

Jenny glanced behind her as she drove the wagon along the hilly side of the valley. The huge granite rocks above threatened, and a squeaking wheel on the wagon behind her sounded like the Indians' cries as they fled with the horses the night before. The baby pushed hard against her lungs these days, and she couldn't catch her breath. She worried she would die like Mrs. Pershing—her only solace that Mac had promised to care for her child.

The emigrants took their noon break at a small rivulet of muddy water trickling out of the hills. There was little forage for the animals.

Jenny invited Esther and Jonah to ride with her through the afternoon. Mac scouted with Daniel and Joel, and Zeke minded the Pershing wagons.

Esther sighed as she plopped on the wagon bench beside Jenny. "I'm so tired of the Abercrombies. And of Pa and the children as well."

"How is your papa holding up?" Jenny asked.

Esther lifted one shoulder, Jonah cradled on the other. "Quiet. Brooding. Sometimes he's curt with the young'uns. It's just been a month since Ma left us."

"How about you?" Jenny asked.

"Some sickness. And you?"

"I don't know if I want this baby to come tomorrow or never." Jenny sighed. "I just want it done with."

Esther sniffed her baby brother's neck. "Babies smell so precious. Sweet and sour at the same time. Like porridge with molasses."

Jenny swallowed a lump in her throat. "I never thought it would be so hard."

The girls took turns holding Jonah and guiding the oxen, and the afternoon passed quickly. The sun was low enough to shine under Jenny's sunbonnet brim when Mac rode over. He had two dead grouse tied to his saddle horn.

"Captain says we'll stop soon. Some water and grass up ahead, but not much." Mac handed her the birds.

"Did others get any game?" she asked.

He nodded. "More birds. We saw some deer. Abercrombie's still searching for Douglass's horse. Took Daniel with him."

Esther gasped. "They went after the Indians?"

"Don't worry," Mac said. "Indians and horses are long gone."

He rode off, and Esther peered behind the wagon. "I wonder when Daniel and his pa will be back."

After they made camp, Mac brought Jenny two buckets of water. "That's all we can have now," he said. "Need to let the teams drink."

Jenny plucked the grouse and stuffed them with sage. Horses galloped into camp—Abercrombie and Daniel had returned.

"Any sign of the Indians?" Mac asked.

Abercrombie swung off his gelding. The horse's coat was lathered in sweat. "Nope. Shot a deer, but no Indians."

Daniel rode over to Esther. He lifted the gutted deer off his saddle and laid it on the ground. Esther ran for the bushes, retching.

"What's up with her?" Abercrombie asked Daniel.

Daniel grinned. "Guess I'll be butchering the deer tonight."

Jenny skewered the birds and sat beside the fire rotating the spit every few minutes. The air was stifling, and the flames made her cheeks burn. She undid the top button on her blouse and ran a dry cloth over her neck. There wasn't enough water to wash, and she felt so dirty. They hadn't seen rain in weeks. She pulled out her notebook:

August 24th, evening—A long hot day, made

better by Esther's company. Mac shot two birds for supper, but I shall be as cooked as they are after turning them on the fire.

In the morning a light wind blew down the valley, but the ground still radiated heat. "We should reach the Boise River today," Mac said. "It's past that ridge." He pointed north. "Then we'll have plenty of water and grass."

When they reached the top of the ridge, Jenny saw a river several miles ahead. It spilled out of black bluffs in the east and wound west across the valley below. The travelers trudged through arid land all afternoon before reaching the Boise. Cottonwoods and willows lined the river's shores. A cool breeze wafted above the gurgling current, offering relief from the dust and grit of the trail.

Smiles and laughter replaced the grim faces Jenny had seen for so long. Animals waded into the stream and drank their fill. Children splashed water on each other, giggling until their mothers reminded them of chores.

Mac helped Jenny down from the wagon. Her back was stiff and sore after sitting all day.

"Two days to Fort Boise," Mac said with a grin. "Back to civilization."

"Do we have to cross the river?" Jenny asked, stretching her back and shoulders.

"The Boise's not bad." Mac gestured at the pretty stream. "We'll be fine."

Zeke joined them. "Going hunting. Want to come?"

Mac raised an eyebrow at Jenny.

She smiled. "Bring me another bird to eat, and I'll be happy."

Mac swung into his saddle and set off with Zeke.

Jenny ate with the Tullers. Doc eyed her as he chewed. "When's that baby's coming?" he asked.

"First part of September," Jenny said.

The doctor grunted. "September starts in another week."

"Do you have what you need? Enough diapers laid by and shirts?" Mrs. Tuller asked.

"Yes, ma'am." She had everything prepared, but she wasn't ready to care for a baby. She still worried she wouldn't love a child conceived in such horror.

While the women washed dishes, Tanner brought over a string of salmon. "They practically jump onto the hook," he said. "Keep 'em for breakfast."

Jenny took two fish. "Thank you. Mac'll appreciate it."

She stowed the fish in oilcloth for the night. Mac returned as she finished the task.

"Get anything?" she asked.

"Zeke killed a deer, but I missed my shot."

"Tanner brought us fish. Shall I fry you one?"

Mac shook his head. "I'm beat. Think I'll turn in."

"Nothing to eat first?" She wondered if Mac might be getting ill again.

"No. I'll wait for breakfast."

"You all right?" What would she do if he were sick, so close to her time?

"I'm fine," Mac said. He found his bedroll and curled up under the wagon.

Nothing she could do but let him rest. Jenny was sore from the wagon, but not sleepy. She took out her diary:

Wednesday, August 25th—Reached the Boise River. The trees on its banks are a relief from the dreary sage. I can hear the stream babbling and fish jumping.

"Indians!" A woman's scream cut through the quiet evening.

Painted men on horseback rode through camp and around the fires where emigrants sat. One Indian galloped so close to Jenny his horse's tail brushed her neck. She shrieked in terror, "Mac!"

And he was beside her, rifle in hand. She grasped his arm and buried her face in his chest.

"Jenny, let go." Mac shrugged her off and aimed his gun.

A shot sounded from across the camp. Jenny didn't know who fired. She collapsed on the ground and covered her head with her hands, sobbing.

The Indians slowed and halted in the middle of the wagon circle. One gestured at the others, who dismounted and started pawing through the pioneers' belongings.

"What do you want?" Pershing asked the mounted leader. Jenny peeked between her fingers and saw the captain confronting the braves, hand hovering above his holstered pistol. Other men, Mac included, stood beside him, rifles ready.

"Trade," the chief said. "Got food. Need hooks, beads."

"No trade tonight," the captain said. "Morning."

"Now."

"Morning."

Another rifle shot cracked, and a bullet zinged near an Indian who had grabbed a sack of flour.

"Take the grain and go," Pershing said. "Come back tomorrow when the sun is over the mountains."

The chief nodded at his men. The Indians remounted and left the camp as quickly as they had entered, uttering shrill cries as they rode off.

"Who fired?" Pershing demanded, when the Indians had left.

"I did," Abercrombie said, stepping forward. "No savage going to scare my women. Thieving varmints. Would have stripped us bare, if we let 'em."

"No need to fight if we can talk 'em down." Pershing strode toward his wagons. Then he turned back, saying to the men as a group. "Double guards. And be ready to trade at sunup."

Mac knelt by Jenny. "You all right?"

She nodded. "Just scared." Mac pulled her to her feet. A pain lanced through her side, and she groaned. "My baby!"

"Doc!" Mac yelled.

They lifted Jenny into the wagon, where the doctor poked and prodded. "Can't see nothing wrong," he said. "I'll check on you in the morning."

Chapter 58: Indian Traders and Hudson's Bay Traders

Mac stood his watch, though he could barely stay upright in his saddle. He woke Zeke after midnight to take his place and fell into his bedroll.

The camp began to stir at first light. Mac groaned as he got to his feet, his head pounding. Maybe he was getting sick again, like Jenny said. He didn't have time to be sick—he had to help Pershing with the Indians and he had to take care of Jenny.

He looked in the wagon. "How are you?" he asked.

"Fine."

"Stay still. I'm getting the doctor."

Mac found Doc eating a biscuit. "Be right over," the doctor said. "How's she doing?"

"She says fine."

"We'll see." Doc accompanied Mac back. Jenny stood beside their campfire.

"I told you to stay in the wagon," Mac said.

Jenny lifted her chin and looked at the doctor. "I'm fine," she said.

"Sit down, girl." Doc felt Jenny's stomach and back. "Any pains?" he asked.

Jenny shook her head.

"No squeezing or cramping?"

Jenny blushed and shook her head again.

The doctor looked at Mac. "No sign the baby's coming." Doc turned to Jenny. "Take it easy, you hear?"

She nodded. "Mac's sick," she said.

"Just tired, Doc."

Doc frowned. "Let me know if you're feverish." Then he left, and Jenny picked up the skillet.

"What are you doing?" Mac asked.

"Getting breakfast."

"Didn't you hear the doctor say to take it easy?"

"No time for that, is there?" Jenny unwrapped the fish and put them in the skillet. "You find our trade goods for the Indians."

Mac frowned, but did as she said. Then he stalked off to find Pershing.

"Keep your rifles close, men," the captain said. "No shooting unless the Indians start it." He looked at Abercrombie as he spoke. "They'll have food to trade. Maybe furs. You can give 'em anything except spirits, weapons, and ammunition."

Before the captain finished speaking, about twenty Indians rode silently into camp, mostly men and young boys, but a few women. The white women and children shrank back against the wagons, and the men stood with rifles in hand.

The Indian chief and two braves dismounted. The chief signaled, and a brave handed Pershing a parcel. The captain unwrapped it to find a smoked salmon. He nodded at the chief.

"Joel," the captain said, "Bring me some sugar. In a leather pouch."

When Joel returned from the wagon, Pershing gestured toward the chief. Joel handed the pouch to the Indian leader.

The chief tasted a pinch and nodded at Pershing. Then he raised his hand, and the rest of the Indians dismounted.

For the next hour Indians milled around the camp. They poked their noses into the wagons and pointed at what they wanted. Their women laid out food and leather clothing on the ground for display. A few white women crept forward to examine the Indian offerings. One Indian girl demonstrated how to pound a root into powder, and Jenny traded buttons for the roots.

Mac had his hands full keeping a young brave from climbing into their wagon. The Indian wanted gunpowder and offered a deer skin. Mac convinced him to take a pouch of glass beads instead of the powder.

When the trading slowed, Pershing raised his hand to the Indian chief. "You go now," he said. "We leave for Fort Boise."

The chief signaled to the Indians, and they rode away silently.

"Pack up," Pershing said. "We're leaving in fifteen minutes."

They traveled west through the Boise River valley all day, with only a brief noon stop, then camped that night on the river's bank. "We'll cross tomorrow," Pershing said. "Fort's on the north side. 'Bout a day's journey."

Mac tried to assist Jenny with supper, but she brushed him off. "I'm making camas bread," she said. "Indian girl showed me how."

"Aren't you tired?" Mac asked. He was weary from lack of sleep the night before.

"I'm all right," she said, as she always did.

While Jenny's flat loaves of bread baked on a stone set in a slow fire, Mac wrote:

August 26, 1847. We'll reach Fort Boise tomorrow, after crossing the river. Traded with Indians today. Bought food, which we needed. Abercrombie managed not to shoot anyone. Extra guards again tonight.

Mac awoke refreshed after sleeping all night. Although Pershing had ordered extra guards, others in Mac's platoon had taken the watches. He devoured the sweet camas bread along with dried salmon.

"I hope we can buy beef when we stop at Boise," he told Jenny.

"How bad will the crossing be?" she asked.

"Zeke and Joel marked it," Mac said. "We have to dodge tree snags, but it's not deep. Current's not swift either."

The crossing took most of the morning. Then the emigrants plodded along the north bank of the river. In late afternoon Joel returned to the wagons. "Good campsite in two miles," he said. "Just this side of the fort. Zeke's there now."

Pershing nodded. "We'll camp there. Lay by tomorrow at the fort."

The low adobe buildings of Fort Boise were visible from their campsite. Beyond the fort the wide Snake River shone silver in the setting sun.

Mac sat after supper, listening to a banjo strum.

August 26, 1847. Outside Fort Boise. Good grazing.

We'll buy supplies tomorrow.

In the morning Mac rode into Fort Boise with Pershing and most of the men in their company. "It's another Hudson's Bay Company post," Pershing said. "British built here when the Americans built Fort Hall. Got to hand it to the British—they know how to trade. Don't expect any bargains."

Inside the trading post Mac heard his companions mutter.

"Highest prices yet. Sugar fifty cents a pint. And they ain't got no coffee."

"Beef seven cents a pound. Hell, I'll shoot my own meat for that. Just sell me lead and powder."

"What'd'ya expect when they haul the goods in from Oregon City?"

The Indian offerings—more camas roots, salmon, and pumpkin—were cheaper. Mac bought from the Indians, figuring Jenny would know what to do with the food, but he added a pint of sugar as a treat.

"How's the Snake crossing?" Pershing asked the agent at the fort.

"It's just west of here. Ford goes to the tip of the island, then bears left. It's purty deep, but the current ain't fast."

"How does it compare to Three Island Crossing?" Mac asked.

"Deeper. But the water's slower." The man shrugged. "Usually not as dangerous. But we lost a man on horseback earlier this year. Horse reared, he fell off."

Mac hoped Jenny didn't hear that story. It was too similar to how Horace Mercer died. He wouldn't let her ride Poulette.

"Where's the trail go on the other side?" Pershing asked. "In forty-two, we went west to the Malheur, then north. Hear tell there's a route along the Malheur now."

The agent shook his head. "Can't recommend it. Meek took a party that way in forty-five. Kept 'em out of the Blues, but there's no grass. Rocks cut the animals' hooves. They got lost. More'n fifty people died."

"Don't sound good," Pershing agreed. "What about getting down the Columbia? Rafts? Ferry?"

Leaning his elbows on the store counter, the agent said, "There's a toll road at The Dalles now. Don't know much about it. Head for Whitman's place. He'll know whether it amounts to anything."

Pershing shrugged. "Whitman's as bad as any of you traders. Charging whatever you can get away with. I got a man always after taking the shortest route. Don't know I can convince my company to detour to Whitman's."

"Whitman might have an agent at Grande Ronde," the Hudson's Bay man said. "Look for him."

Mac followed Pershing out of the store. "Why would Dr. Whitman send an agent to Grande Ronde?" he asked.

"Whitman and his wife came out in thirty-six. He has a mission for the Cayuse near Walla Walla. He also sells supplies to the emigrants. He may say he's converting Indians, but he's also making money for himself."

Surely it would be safer for Jenny to have the baby at the mission than on the trail. "How far are we?" Mac asked.

Pershing shrugged. "Couple hundred miles. Maybe three weeks."

Three weeks. Would the baby wait three weeks?

Chapter 59: Trouble at Fort Boise

Saturday, August 28th—I have been distressed since the Indians invaded our camp three nights ago. Truth be told, I have felt this way since Mrs. Pershing died. My fate feels so uncertain.

Jenny sat in camp outside Fort Boise. A breeze wafted a strand of hair across her face. The air held a hint of autumn. She needed to do laundry, but she relished the moment of stillness. She had so little time to herself, and she was exhausted. Even first thing in the morning her bones ached, and it took effort to lift her swollen body, let alone an armload of wet clothes.

Jenny sighed, picked up a bucket, and headed to the nearby stream. As she filled the bucket, Doc walked by.

"What are you doing, girl?" he asked.

"Getting water."

"Where's McDougall?"

"At the fort."

"Let me get that." The doctor took the bucket. "What's the water for, anyway?"

"Washing."

"Were you planning to fill a whole tub?"

Jenny nodded.

"Didn't I tell you to take it easy?"

"The clothes won't wash themselves." He was no better than Mac. She had chores to do. It didn't matter how she felt.

Doc sighed. "I'll fill your tub. And I'll send Mrs. Tuller over. She can help you."

Jenny gathered soiled shirts and socks while the doctor filled her washtub. Mrs. Tuller carried over a pile of clothes and knelt beside Jenny. "You sit, child," the older woman said. "I'll scrub, and you wring."

While they worked. Esther and Mrs. Abercrombie lugged over a tub, filled it, and washed as well. Rachel sat with Jonah on a blanket nearby, while Ruth ran errands for the women.

"Where are the boys?" Mrs. Tuller asked Esther.

"Playing in the fields. The twins are minding Noah, though I can't rightly see them keeping him out of trouble." Esther sighed. "Rachel and Ruth, can you go look after them?"

After the girls left, Mrs. Abercrombie whispered to Esther, "Do they know your news?"

Esther's face reddened. "Jenny does." She turned to Mrs. Tuller. "I'm expecting."

"I wondered," Mrs. Tuller said. "My, you are blessed."

"Seems like just yesterday I was praying Daniel would look at me." Esther sighed. "Now Ma's gone, and I got Jonah and the other young'uns to mind, and my own on the way."

Mrs. Tuller patted Esther's wet hand with her own soapy one. "The good Lord will provide."

"I surely hope so, ma'am."

"You and Mr. Abercrombie must be pleased," Mrs. Tuller said to Mrs. Abercrombie.

"Oh, yes. Mr. Abercrombie thinks it'll be a boy."

After hanging the wet clothes on ropes strung between wagons, Jenny started dinner. She hoped Mac would bring back provisions from the fort. They only had a little meat and flour left. She made a stew from the meat and camas roots, seasoning it with the ever-present sage and a few wild onions.

"Will you and the doctor eat with us?" she asked Mrs. Tuller. "I want to thank him for hauling my water this morning."

"That'd be right nice, Jenny," Mrs. Tuller said. "Let me find him."

Mac returned from the fort about noon. He brought sacks of sugar and cornmeal, and some Indian foods. "Wasn't much to be found," he told her.

"Sugar's nice," she said. "But we're low on flour again. And the meat's gone."

"Have to make do with camas and cornmeal instead," he said. "Indians only had fish to sell. I'll hunt this afternoon."

"May I visit the fort?" Jenny asked.

"If I'm hunting, I can't take you. Go with Mrs. Tuller. Or Esther. It should be safe enough, if you're together." Mac reached in his pocket and gave her a silver coin. "Here's a dollar, if you see something you want."

After Jenny had washed the dishes, she found Esther at the Abercrombie wagons. "Would you like to go to the fort?"

Esther asked Mrs. Abercrombie, "May I go? Or would you like to go with us?"

Mrs. Abercrombie nodded. "Let's all go. I'll get Louisa and her daughters, and you can bring your brothers and sisters."

"Is that all right?" Esther asked Jenny.

Jenny smiled. "We'll make it a party. I'll find Mrs. Tuller, too."

The women and children walked to the fort. It was smaller than Fort Hall, but seemed cleaner to Jenny. The group roamed the store, the Pershing twins and Abercrombie granddaughters giggling at Indian toddlers who peeked from behind their mothers' buckskin skirts.

Jenny filled a sack with fifty cents worth of flour and put salt in another bag, saving a few pennies out of Mac's dollar for the children to spend on candy.

When the women finished shopping, they started back toward camp. A man staggered out of a building.

"Pa!" Esther shouted and rushed over to her father.

Captain Pershing fell to his knees and vomited in the dirt.

"Oh, Pa," Esther said.

Mrs. Tuller turned to Jenny. "Take the children back to camp. I'll help Esther." She pushed Jenny gently, and Jenny hurried off with the other women and children.

Jenny kept the younger Pershings at her wagon until Esther came to see her an hour later.

"He drank most of a bottle," Esther said. "Mrs. Tuller and I barely got him back to camp. Doc's there now." Esther wiped her face with her apron. "It'll be all around camp tonight. Mr. Abercrombie won't let it go."

"It's not your fault, Esther," Jenny said. "He's just grieving the loss of your mama."

"Well, I'm grieving, too, but I ain't drinking." Esther's voice was bitter. "I'm raising Jonah and the others and dealing with the Abercrombies, too. 'Cause that's what Ma would want me to do. I wish we'd never taken this journey."

"I sometimes wish the same thing," Jenny said. "Then I remember what it was like back home."

Esther sighed. "Zeke and Joel don't help. Not with the children. They're always out scouting or hunting. Like now."

"They're doing men's work. That's important, too."

Esther sniffed and smoothed out her apron. "I got to start supper. The young'uns won't wait for me to finish crying." She called, "Let's go, children," then left, followed by her younger brothers and sisters. Rachel cast a backward glance at Jenny.

Jenny ate supper alone and pulled out her journal.

Saturday, August 28th—Our pleasant afternoon at Fort Boise was spoiled by Captain Pershing. Why do men drink when troubled? Esther manages the best she can.

Mac returned as the shadows from the mountains lengthened across the Boise valley. He slid off Valiente, then lifted a gutted deer off his saddle.

"Venison!" Jenny exclaimed. She handed him a plate. "I saved you salmon and camas cakes. But tomorrow we'll have meat."

Mac smiled as he took his supper. "Thank you."

"You're late getting back."

"Didn't see any game until sunset," he said, his mouth full.

"We'll eat well for a few days, anyway," Jenny said. "I'll get to butchering it."

"You can hardly get down on the ground now," Mac said. "I'll do it after I eat."

"Did you hear about the captain?" Jenny asked.

Mac nodded. "The Pershing twins ran out to greet us. Told us their pa had been drunk."

"It was awful. The Tullers had to help Esther handle him."

"Abercrombie's all swaggers. He's calling for a vote on who'll captain us the rest of the way."

"What'll happen?"

"Don't know. Expect we'll vote tomorrow." Mac handed her his plate and found his knife to butcher the deer.

The next morning Jenny awoke to shouts. "We'll vote, God damn it," Abercrombie bellowed. "You're a scandal, Pershing. I won't stand by and let you kill us all."

"I'm twice the man you are, Abercrombie. Even drunk. Shall we settle this for good?" The captain's voice wasn't loud, but menacing nonetheless.

Men, women, and children thronged toward the fight. Jenny saw Mac and pushed her way through the crowd to stand beside him. Pershing and Abercrombie both had their fists raised, circling each other.

People opened space around the two men. Esther sobbed into her brother Zeke's chest. Joel had his hands balled into fists. Daniel stood staring at his father and father-in-law, hands hanging limply.

"Now, hold on," Mac said, stepping into the circle.

"Ain't your fight, McDougall," Abercrombie said. "Stand back."

Doc moved beside Mac, between Pershing and Abercrombie. "Brawling won't help. This argument concerns all of us."

"That's right," Dempsey said. "We signed on for Pershing as captain. You made a play before, Abercrombie. It didn't take."

"I ain't following no drunk," Hewitt said. "Time for someone new."

"We'll do this proper," Doc said. "Take a vote."

Mac raised his hand. "Tempers are short. Breakfast first. We'll vote after we eat, before we break camp. Come back in an hour."

Chapter 60: Another Vote

Mac took a deep breath and turned away from the crowd surrounding Pershing and Abercrombie. Jenny stood nearby. "Come on," he said to her. "Let's eat."

"What's going to happen?" she asked as they walked to their wagon.

Mac shrugged. "Don't know. It's gone so far, I'm not sure they can stay in the same company, no matter who's leading."

Mac wondered if their group would split up. If it did, he wasn't sure what he would do. He despised Abercrombie, but he had to stay with the Tullers—Jenny would need their assistance during childbirth. What would Doc do?

Mac and Jenny ate in silence. When they finished, he sought Doc out.

"Let's take a walk," Doc said, leading Mac out of camp. "Do you have a sense of how the vote will go?" the doctor asked.

"Nope. You?"

Doc shook his head. "Folks don't like Abercrombie. But they're not happy with Pershing either. He wanted a company for families, but he ain't setting a good example."

"Man's had a hard time of it," Mac said. He stooped and picked up a small stick that he twirled idly in his fingers.

"Yes, he has." Doc nodded. "Folks know he's grieving. But his drunkenness puts them in harm's way."

Mac glanced at Doc. "Who you voting for?"

"You."

The stick snapped in Mac's hands. "Me?"

"You're the best man to keep our group together. This company'll split apart if either Pershing or Abercrombie wins." Doc Tuller put a hand on

Mac's arm and stared him in the eye. "If I nominate you, will you do it?"

"Why not you?" Mac asked.

The doctor shook his head. "I'm too old. Not a good hunter or scout. You've earned their respect as a man. You're smart, too."

"I never looked to lead this group."

"That's why you can do it." Doc's hand tightened on Mac's arm. "Folks need a way to get rid of Pershing, but not vote for Abercrombie. Dempsey and Hewitt will both back you."

"You talked to them already?" Mac was shocked

Doc nodded. "They want a secret ballot. But they'll back you. It's our best way out of this mess."

Mac couldn't believe he even contemplated becoming captain. "What about Pershing and Abercrombie?" he asked. "What'll they do?"

"Abercrombie won't be happy if he ain't chosen. But if you're elected, he can't do anything, unless he wants to leave. Pershing?" Doc shrugged. "He likes you. His pride'll be hurt. But what's he going to do? I don't think we'll lose him."

"It would hurt the company if Pershing left," Mac said.

"He'd have to leave if Abercrombie wins. Think what that'd do to Esther, the choice she'd have to make—staying with her husband or going with her father and the younger children."

Mac stared at the ground. Could he do this?

"My one concern," Doc continued, "is your wife. She's about to give birth, and she'll need you close. She's awful young. It's your call, son. But you're the only man who can hold this company together."

Mac took a deep breath. Jenny wouldn't distract him. He could take her confinement in stride. He only worried because he was responsible for her. It wasn't as if he was in love with her.

Mac looked Doc Tuller in the eye. "If you nominate me and I win, I'll get us to Oregon," he pledged. "Somehow."

The men gathered in the wagon circle to vote. Pershing and Abercrombie stood in the middle of the group.

"Wait." Dempsey raised his hand. "Before we vote, are there any candidates besides Pershing and Abercrombie?"

Doc stepped forward. "I nominate Caleb McDougall."

Mac heard a woman in the crowd gasp. Was it Jenny?

"Now hold on!" Abercrombie yelled.

Dempsey ignored Abercrombie and frowned at Mac. "You willing?"

Mac saw Jenny in the crowd. She stared at him, a hand over her mouth. "If Doc thinks I should be a candidate, I'll do it," he said.

"Anyone else?" Dempsey looked around.

"I want a secret ballot." Hewitt moved beside Dempsey waving slips of paper. "Every man eighteen or over can vote. No need for speeches. Let's get on with it."

"Some men can't write," Abercrombie said.

Hewitt passed out the paper. "If you can't write a man's name, it's one X for Pershing, two for Abercrombie, three for McDougall." He handed out pencils. "Doc and I'll count."

The balloting took several minutes. Then the counting. Mac's stomach churned—was he worried that he'd win or that he'd lose?

Three piles of paper rose in front of Doc and Hewitt. One was smaller than the others, but that's all Mac could tell.

"New captain's McDougall," Hewitt proclaimed.

A cheer rose from the men.

"Let me see," Abercrombie said, snatching the ballots. He sifted through them, then threw the papers on the ground and stalked toward his wagon.

Pershing sat, silent. Zeke and Joel stood beside him looking stunned. Zeke squinted as Mac walked toward them.

Mac held his hand out to Pershing. "I need your support, sir," he said. "You have the experience. Will you back me?"

Pershing pushed himself to his feet and looked at Mac. He shook Mac's hand without saying a word, then walked to his wagon, stooped like an old man.

Mac looked at Zeke. "Zeke, I want you to take over my platoon. I'll understand if you won't, but I'd like you backing me, too."

Zeke nodded. "I'll say this to you, though not to anyone else—Pa brought it on himself. It's not us you got to worry about. It's Abercrombie."

Mac returned to his wagon. Jenny had packed up and was ready to head out. "So you're captain now?" she asked.

"Guess so."

"You can do it."

"I'll have to." Mac leaned against the wagon wheel. "How'd I get myself into this?" He didn't know if he was talking to himself or to Jenny.

"What do you mean?" she asked.

"All I wanted was adventure." He sighed. "Then I took you on. Now a whole wagon train."

"Don't worry about me," she said, lifting her chin.

Mac saddled Valiente, mounted, and waved his hat. "All right, folks. There's a river to cross. Follow me." He led the way to the Snake crossing just downstream from Fort Boise.

The crossing took longer than Mac thought it should. Were the men slow to follow his orders? Some men glanced at Pershing as if to confirm what Mac told them. Pershing and his sons moved their wagons into line, right where Mac directed them. Surely Pershing would say something if Mac steered the group wrong. He relaxed a little.

Abercrombie hung back at the ford, like he was waiting for something to go wrong. At last, only the Abercrombie wagons and Mac's were left to cross. Mac gestured at Abercrombie to proceed.

"No, you first." Abercrombie bowed low to Mac, scraping his hat almost to the ground.

Mac glanced at Jenny on the wagon bench. Her face was white. One hand gripped the bench and the other clasped the whip tightly. He should ride with her. But a captain waited until last, so he'd have to ride back after he took her across.

Zeke stepped over beside Mac. "I'll take your wagon, Captain. You ride behind Abercrombie." Zeke jumped up beside Jenny.

Mac watched Zeke drive the wagon with Jenny into deep water, then he gestured again at Abercrombie. The older man cracked his whip, and the Abercrombie wagons followed Zeke into the river. Mac brought up the rear on Valiente.

The sun was high when they completed the crossing, so Mac called the noon halt. After they ate, they headed north along the Snake.

Mac sent Joel ahead to scout. "We won't make the Malheur River by dark," Mac told him. "Find us a campsite."

"At least we don't have to cross the Snake again," Jenny said as Mac boosted her onto the wagon bench.

"No. But the Columbia's coming up. Biggest river since we left Missouri. The best way to Oregon City is to float down on rafts."

Late that evening, after Mac had organized the camp and discussed the next day's travel with the men, he wrote:

August 29, 1847. Elected captain. Crossed the Snake and camped by a small creek. Tomorrow we reach the Malheur. I never intended for this journey to lead to so much responsibility. Grandfather would be proud. I wonder about Father.

Chapter 61: Malheur

Jenny felt a lump in her throat as she climbed into the wagon Monday. Mac had spent the early morning wandering the camp and talking to other men. She prepared breakfast and packed their belongings by herself. Mac paused just long enough to eat with her and to yoke the oxen. After breakfast he saddled Valiente and rode off, saying barely a word. She didn't know if he was angry or preoccupied.

They had camped on a small creek beneath dry bluffs on the west side of the Snake River valley. The creek trickled out of a ravine between two cliffs into the broad valley. Soon they would climb through more hills—if not today, then tomorrow.

Mac returned to their wagon. "Stay close to the Tullers today," he said. "I need to talk with the scouts about getting to the Malheur. Can you drive?"

Jenny nodded. She had no choice. Mac wasn't hers any longer. He never had been. He assumed his new authority easily. Already his voice sounded more commanding.

The morning was pleasant, not yet hot. A slight breeze scented with sage blew from the hills. Poulette, tied behind the wagon, nickered. Jenny longed to ride the mare to the banks of the Snake. The river looked placid in the distance, no longer a cauldron of spray and cataracts like at Shoshone Falls.

Esther walked over carrying Jonah. "May we join you?"

Jenny halted the oxen and took the baby while Esther climbed up. "How's your papa?" Jenny asked as she cracked her whip to get the oxen moving.

Esther shrugged. "He ain't said much. He's driving today. Zeke and Joel went off with Mac. Daniel, too."

"What's Daniel say about all this?" It was rude to ask, but Jenny was curious.

"He ain't said a word. Just nods at his pa. Mr. Abercrombie's bellyaching. Says we're doomed."

"Doomed?" Jenny was surprised at the harsh word. "Mac will get us through."

"I'm just repeating what Mr. Abercrombie said." Esther bounced Jonah on her lap.

The young women chatted through the morning. When Mac stopped the wagons at noon, Esther rushed off. "Got to get dinner going."

Jenny wandered over to the Tuller wagon to avoid being alone. "Why don't you eat with us?" Mrs. Tuller asked. "Got enough for Captain McDougall when he's ready, too."

Captain McDougall—it sounded strange. But it suited him, Jenny decided, watching Mac move about camp talking with the platoon leaders. Joel rode over to Mac, and the two men talked and gestured. Mac pulled out a piece of paper, probably the Frémont map.

Jenny helped Mrs. Tuller prepare the meal. Mac stopped by. "Joel found a path to the Malheur," he said. "Should reach it by evening."

All afternoon Jenny drove the wagon again. Her back knotted and her bones ached by the time Mac stopped the company for the night. He came to their wagon and lifted her off the bench before she could climb down.

"Thank you," she said, clutching his arm to keep her balance.

"Can you set up camp?" he asked. "I need to talk to the men about the Malheur crossing." He touched her shoulder. "I'll be back when I can."

Jenny arched her back, hands on her hips, and looked around. The Malheur River was small, burbling, with bright green grass along the banks. Beyond the river to the north were more buttes and barren hills—more of what they had traveled for so long.

Mac appeared when supper was ready. He ate quickly, then stood. "Have to go."

"What's wrong?" she asked.

"Argument over the route. Some want to go to Grande Ronde, others to follow the Malheur."

"What's Captain Pershing say?" Jenny asked.

Mac frowned. "He's not the captain."

"I'm sorry," Jenny stammered. "I didn't mean to offend you. It's just habit. What's he say?"

"Wants to go to Grande Ronde. Like the Hudson's Bay man said."

"Is it Mr. Abercrombie who wants the Malheur?"

"Of course," Mac said. "Contrary as always."

"What do you think we should do?"

"Damned if I know." He slammed his hat on his head and strode away.

Jenny cleaned the dishes, then sat by the fire. She could go listen to the men, but she'd find out soon enough what they decided. The setting sun glowed brighter than the campfire as she wrote:

Monday, August 30th—Camped beside the Malheur. The name means misfortune. I pray Mac can hold our company together.

Jenny didn't hear Mac get in the tent beside her that night, and he must have had guard duty, because he wasn't there when she went to the latrine. The next morning his bedroll was folded neatly, and he was already gone. She made breakfast and ate it, leaving a plate of food out for Mac. Then she washed the dishes and packed the wagon.

Mac rushed into camp as the sun peeked above the eastern hills. "Get ready to cross the river," he said.

"Don't you want breakfast?"

He shook his head. "Ate a bite with the Dempseys."

"I wish you'd tell me whether to fix you anything."

Mac shrugged as if throwing away food didn't matter.

"We don't have much food left. Shouldn't waste anything." She worried about their provisions, even if Mac didn't.

"We'll probably stop at Whitman's place. We'll get by until then."

"So we're crossing the Malheur?" she asked.

Mac nodded. "Abercrombie backed down. Enough men heard the talk at Fort Boise. About the Malheur valley being too dry. But he's grumbling. We'll have more trouble."

Jenny hoisted herself onto the wagon bench.

"I'll have Zeke or Joel help you today," he said. "This crossing won't be bad, but I don't want you to worry."

The Malheur wasn't deep, so Jenny wasn't worried. Not about the crossing. What troubled her was whether she could count on Mac, now that he had the whole company to care for. She could stick close to the Tullers, but she wanted Mac, too.

She should be happy Mac was captain. He was a good and brave man who deserved a chance to lead. Captain Pershing—she couldn't stop thinking of Esther's father as the captain—had let them all down by drinking.

At least Mr. Abercrombie wasn't captain. Jenny didn't think the blustery braggart would deliberately hurt anyone, but he reminded her too much of Sheriff Johnson—a big man with a loud voice. It was a good thing Daniel wasn't like his father, or Esther would be in for a hard time.

Zeke swung up beside Jenny. "Morning, Miz Jenny," he said, tipping his hat at her. "Let's get this wagon across." Zeke urged the team into line.

"How's your family?" Jenny asked, not wanting to sit in silence waiting for their turn.

"Doing fine."

"Is the captain all right?"

"You mean Pa?"

Jenny nodded, blushing. She'd made the mistake again. "I'm going to call him Captain Pershing all the way to Oregon, I'm afraid. He'll always be the captain to me."

Zeke smiled. "He'd like to know you think kindly of him."

"Your papa's a good man. He has troubles like the rest of us, but a good man."

Zeke's smile widened. "Yes, he is. I'll tell him you said so." He snapped a whip to get the oxen moving and pulled into the water.

Chapter 62: Responsibility

Mac rode along the wagons on the north side of the Malheur. The crossing had gone well—the men had followed his orders better than on the Snake crossing outside Boise. Had they decided he knew what he was doing? No matter, he was doing his best.

The trail past the Malheur was rough. They climbed into desolate hills with only a few tufts of grass and the ever-present sagebrush. White alkali patches burned the animals' hooves and the feet of any emigrants so poor or so foolish they didn't wear shoes. Mac wondered whether the cutoff along the Malheur would have been worse. He called the noon halt near a small alkali spring. Some children refused to drink the bitter water, but the animals took their fill.

"How much farther in the hills?" Mac asked Joel, who had returned from scouting to report.

Joel shook his head. "All afternoon. 'Bout ten miles to the next valley."

"We'll camp there." Mac waved his hat, and wagons rolled on, Joel leading.

Mac hadn't spent much time with Jenny, other than to eat the dinner she prepared. Zeke or Mrs. Tuller or Esther rode with her, so she was safe. But Mac missed talking to her. Or just sitting with her. Often, they rode or walked in comfortable silence. No need to bother her with his thoughts, but if he wanted an opinion, she gave it.

He wanted to talk to Jenny about his election as captain. But he didn't have time—too many people and problems to worry about. Jenny had expressed confidence in him after the vote, but how was she adjusting to his new responsibilities?

Mac rode over to his wagon. Zeke drove it alone.

"Where's Jenny?" Mac asked.

"With Esther."

Mac found the Pershing wagons, Franklin Pershing walking alongside his lead oxen. "Where's Jenny?" Mac asked.

"She and Esther went off to the Abercrombie wagons."

Mac brought Valiente in step with Pershing's horse. "Joel says we're in these hills all day." Mac gazed at a lava cliff looming above. "This land's worse than anything we've seen so far."

Pershing snorted. "Dryer, maybe. Ain't as steep as what we'll find in the Blues."

Mac made more small talk, but Pershing's responses were curt. So Mac left to find the Abercrombies.

Jenny and Esther rode in one of the Abercrombie wagons. Esther drove while Jenny held Jonah. Mac greeted them.

"Hello, Mac," Esther said, then beamed. "Or must I call you Captain?"

"Call me whatever you like," Mac said, smiling back at Esther.

"It's surely hot enough, isn't it?" Esther fanned herself, arching her neck and batting her eyelashes from under her sunbonnet.

Jenny's mouth grew thin. "No hotter than other days," she said.

Mac grinned. Esther didn't mean anything by flirting. She was happy with Daniel and had her hands full dealing with both the Pershings and Abercrombies. But Jenny's reaction amused him.

"McDougall." Abercrombie trotted toward Mac.

Mac stopped Valiente and raised an eyebrow.

"We ain't moving fast enough," Abercrombie said.

"Moving as fast as we can. I don't want to harm the teams in this dry soil."

"Just like Pershing. Coddling the animals." Abercrombie spat on the ground. "It's September tomorrow."

"I'm aware of the date."

"Snow could come any time."

Mac squinted at the searing cloudless sky. "Don't look like snow today."

"Don't use your college wit on me, boy," Abercrombie snarled. "I was farming afore you started wearing long pants. I seen the weather turn often enough once it's September."

"No sense traveling any faster than the slowest wagon," Mac said. "Need to stick together."

Abercrombie lowered his voice to a growl. "If you favor your wife over the rest of us, McDougall, I'll call you on it. That's what Pershing did, and it cost us. We're running out of time." He galloped off.

The trail kept to the hills until the sun had almost set. Then the travelers trudged into a valley not much wider than a ravine. "One more ridge," Joel said, "There's a better camp in the next valley. Or we can stay here."

Mac looked around. "Barely room here."

Joel nodded. "It's tight. But the creek's spring fed. Good water. Should be enough grass for the teams."

Mac sighed. He knew he'd hear more from Abercrombie. "All right. We'll stop." He waved his hat to signal the halt.

Sure enough, down the line of wagons, Mac heard Abercrombie yelling at Jenny. "Why's that damn husband of yours stopping now? Cosseting you, is he?"

Mac kneed Valiente and trotted back to his wagon. "You have something to say, Abercrombie, say it to me. Leave Jenny alone."

"I told you we needed to move on."

Mac raised his chin. "And I told you we'd stay together. We're stopping."

Abercrombie pushed his horse against Valiente's withers. "You won't be captain for long, boy. Not if you bollix it up."

Valiente shied, but Mac held him and stared at Abercrombie. The older man swore, wheeled his horse, and rode off.

"Don't worry about me, Mac," Jenny said. But her face was pale.

"If he bothers you again, you tell me." Mac went to talk to the platoon leaders.

Late that evening Mac sat beside his wagon. The stars were brilliant in the dark sky. He wrote in the glow of the campfire:

August 31, 1847. I had hoped Abercrombie's antagonism would lessen without Pershing as captain, but it has not. I would ignore the scoundrel, but he threatened Jenny.

In the morning Mac suggested a hunting party and put Abercrombie in charge. He sent Zeke and Joel out with them. Zeke had volunteered to stay with Jenny, but Mac shook his head. "I will."

Before the hunters left, Mac and Joel discussed the route. "Just over the next hill is Birch Creek. Follow it east to the Snake," Joel said. "Pa says we stay by the Snake briefly, then follow the Burnt River." He pointed out the route on the Frémont map.

"What's your pa got to do with this?" Abercrombie sneered at Joel.

Mac glared at Abercrombie. "He's still the one man here who's been on this trail before."

Once the hunters left, the mood in camp relaxed. The travelers packed their wagons and headed over the chalky hills to Birch Creek. Children raced ahead of the wagons to the stream. Mac wondered how the youngsters had so much energy—the adults drooped with the hardships and monotony of the journey.

It was no longer an adventure. Still another month to endure, including Jenny's confinement.

And he had to get them all safely to Oregon City.

Chapter 63: From Farewell Bend to the Burnt River

The confrontation with Abercrombie shook Jenny more than she admitted to Mac. She sat alone on the wagon seat, bumping up the hills, then down. They rounded a curve, and a green valley spread out ahead. They reached Birch Creek in late morning and followed its narrow basin east toward the Snake.

Mac checked on Jenny every hour or so. She was embarrassed that he took time to look after her, though it pleased her as well. Valiente's coat was more streaked with sweat and dust each time Mac rode by.

"You all right?" he asked. "Not too hot?"

"No worse than it's been."

Once he caught her clutching her belly. "What's wrong?" he asked.

Jenny shook her head. "Baby kicked. I'm fine."

"It hurts?" His voice cracked, and he looked alarmed. "I'll get Doc."

She chuckled. "Don't bother. It happens all the time."

"Can't Doc stop it?"

"Not unless you want the baby to come right now."

She laughed again at Mac's startled expression. She fretted about the birth, and it was nice to know he worried, too.

They halted for the noon meal, then continued along Birch Creek. The air in the valley was stifling, but it was less dusty than in the hills. The trail narrowed as they approached the Snake.

On one of Mac's rides by the wagon, Joel cantered over, back from scouting. "Snake's around the next hill," Joel said. "We follow it for a couple of miles, then reach a broad campsite this side of the river."

"What next?" Mac asked.

"Up into the hills again. This is the last we see of the Snake. Farewell Bend, it's called."

Farewell Bend. Jenny sighed. Such a depressing name. Another segment of the trail left behind. Farther and farther from home.

That evening in camp, the mood was gay. The company they had met on the Bear River before Fort Hall caught up, and the two groups of settlers reunited like long-lost friends.

Jenny embraced the woman who had sold them the milk cow, and the woman exclaimed over how large Jenny had become.

"Your baby's due any time, isn't it?" the woman asked.

Jenny nodded.

Esther showed off how healthy Jonah was on his diet of rich cow's milk. At six weeks, Jonah's arms and legs were rolls of fat.

While Jenny cooked, Mr. Abercrombie stalked over and asked Mac, "How'd they catch up to us? Never seen 'em at the forts. They must be making more'n twenty miles a day."

"Their travel isn't my concern," Mac replied. "My focus is on getting our company to Oregon."

"We ain't laying by tomorrow, are we?" Abercrombie demanded.

"I wasn't planning to," Mac said. "You think we should?" he added with a straight face.

"Hell, no! We'd best leave first thing. Get ahead of them others, so's we get good grazing." Abercrombie stormed off.

Jenny smiled at Mac. "You shouldn't taunt him."

Mac grinned. "What makes you think I was taunting?"

"You don't have any intention of laying by tomorrow."

"Isn't that what I told him?"

Jenny giggled, glad that Mac took the time to joke with her. "I'd best be getting supper."

After supper the two companies sang and danced until stars filled the sky. The half moon provided enough light to pick their way to the bonfire on the banks of the Snake.

The rushing rapids of the broad, swift river roared in the distance as Jenny sat by the fire. She sang along with the fiddles and accordion, "To the far, far off Pacific sea." That song always made her melancholy. Now the Pacific was not so far—now it was home that was distant.

After the singing Jenny snuck away to her wagon and pulled out her journal:

Wednesday, September 1ˢᵗ—Farewell Bend. Tomorrow we leave the Snake. In a month we'll be in Oregon. So far from home. I can barely remember the farm.

Mac woke Jenny early Thursday. "I thought the other company was laying by," she said. "Why do we need to rush?"

"It's not them," Mac said. "I'd just as soon sit here until noon, if only to spite Abercrombie. But we should start out early, before the heat."

The emigrants traveled away from the Snake and up another crest of bleak hills. It took most of the day to ascend and descend this ridge, but by late afternoon they reached the Burnt River.

"Why is it called the Burnt?" Jenny asked.

"Smell," Mac said. "Fires burn here all the time, the grass is so dry." He pointed at a distant hill. "See how black. Burned off earlier this year."

A new worry. "Will we see fires?"

"Hope not," Mac said. "Journey is hard enough without fighting fires."

Jenny wrote before bed:

Thursday, September 2ⁿᵈ—Camped on the Burnt with signs of fire all around. I smell smoke, and wonder if it is only our campfire, or if the hills above will burst into flames.

Again on Friday they traversed steep hillsides, down and up gorges along the Burnt, rougher land than any since the windswept mountains where Mrs. Pershing had died. The river and springs in the hills provided plenty of water, but little grass for the animals. Most families had run low on everything but meat.

Mac sent out a hunting party, again placing Abercrombie in charge.

Jenny wondered if Mr. Abercrombie realized Mac sent him to hunt merely to keep him away from the wagons. Regardless, his skill kept the emigrants alive.

Jenny's stomach rebelled at venison almost as badly as in the early months of her pregnancy. They ate venison in some form—fried, stewed, dried—at every meal. If they were fortunate, they found camas roots and onions to go with it. Occasionally, they saw berries, but most of the berries were picked over by birds and bear and deer.

They traveled on a narrow strip of green land bordering the Burnt, sometimes only the width of a wagon or two. Mac ordered men to drive the loose animals ahead to graze, before the wagons and yoked teams trampled the grass. Those travelers with extra oxen or mules switched them out every two hours to let all the animals get a chance to forage.

The day passed slowly. They splashed through the shallow Burnt again and again. Jenny drove the wagon, though Mac spent much of the day by her side.

By late afternoon Jenny's throat swelled in the parched air, and she wheezed to get a breath. She groaned at the aches running from neck to shoulders, down her back to her legs. They worsened with every jolt from the wheels. Each rock, each stump of brush punished her.

She swayed on the wagon seat. Mac vaulted from Valiente's back onto the bench beside her as she pitched forward in a daze. "Get in the wagon," he said.

With his assistance, she crawled into the back and laid down in the stifling heat. "I'm sorry," she mumbled.

"My fault," Mac said. "I should have seen how tired you were."

The motion was no less bruising under the wagon cover. She lay on top of wooden boxes and barrels, still panting to get breath.

"Zeke," Mac called. "Find Mrs. Tuller. And grab Valiente before he wanders off."

The wagon slowed to a stop, and Mrs. Tuller climbed in. "Here's a wet rag for your face, dear. Let's get you cooled off."

Chapter 64: Along the Burnt River

September 3, 1847. Camped above the Burnt, with three more days of desert until we reach the Powder. Jenny suffers dreadfully in the heat.

Mac wrote late Friday night, while his fellow travelers slept. The dim, flickering light of the fire suited his mood. One moment he was confident he could lead the company through the wilderness, the next he despaired of surviving one more day in the unforgiving land.

Abercrombie's hunting party had only shot one deer and a few birds. The company had food for maybe two days. And it was three days to the Powder River valley.

Mac slept little that night, unable to shake his doubts. In the morning, tired and tense, he wished they had real coffee or tea, instead of the bitter mountain grape they brewed as a substitute.

Jenny looked better. But another day of riding on the hot wagon seat or under the stifling canvas cover could bring on more illness from the heat.

"Would you like to ride Poulette?" he asked.

She sighed. "Horseback wearies me, too."

"Try it. Get away from the dust of the trail."

Jenny gazed at the hills. "I wish there were a breeze."

Mac saddled the mare and helped Jenny step from a barrel onto Poulette's back. "Don't try to dismount by yourself. Get someone to help."

Mac strode off to line up the wagons. He would have to stay near his team while Jenny rode ahead. Maybe Abercrombie would lead the wagons, though he tended to ride too far in front.

"Will you lead today?" he asked Abercrombie, who was mounted and ready to go.

"Was thinking I'd hunt some more." Abercrombie pressed his hat down on his head. "My family's scraping the bottom of our barrels."

"We all are," Mac said. "What if Daniel leads?"

"Taking him with me."

"Douglass?" Mac knew Abercrombie's older son usually drove their wagons.

"Him, too."

"Then I'll get Pershing." Mac turned on his heel.

"Wait a minute." Abercrombie wheeled his horse beside Mac. "If you need me, I'll lead."

"Need you to stay close, help those behind you. If you can't, I'll get Pershing."

Abercrombie spat. "I'll stay. Douglass and Daniel can hunt by themselves."

"Thank you," Mac said through his teeth. "Watch for the women and children out riding. Don't let them get too far ahead."

"Well, which is it?" Abercrombie asked. "Do I watch those ahead, or those behind?"

"Just keep us all together, not strung out in these hills."

"Where'll you be?"

"I'll be here," Mac said. "I'm tending our wagon today. Jenny needs a break."

"Feeling poorly, is she?"

Mac couldn't tell if Abercrombie's question was solicitous or sneering. "Her confinement's close." With that, Mac left Abercrombie, got the wagons moving, and returned to his own at the rear of the train.

Several times during the morning they stopped to double up teams to climb a difficult hill. It took a minimum of eight oxen to pull a wagon. The descents proved equally challenging. They hitched three yoke of oxen behind to prevent runaways, with only one pair in front to steer.

Most animals were weak from the months of hard labor and sparse grass. The oxen fared better than the mules, but all the beasts were thin. Many had sores where harnesses and yokes chafed, and some had split hooves. But they could not rest in this harsh land.

In addition to climbing hills, the travelers twisted through ravines and splashed through muddy creeks. Though the damp was welcome, the mud was no easier for the teams to traverse.

At noon Mac halted the company and found Jenny. They were high in the mountains, with jagged peaks all around. Trees were few, mostly juniper. They had ascended far enough to leave the sagebrush behind— only a little dry grass clung between the rocks.

Mac guided Poulette next to a stone so Jenny could dismount. "How are you?" he asked.

Jenny's face was flushed, with white patches around her lips. "Fine," she said.

"Tired?"

"A little."

"You'd best spend the afternoon in the wagon."

She sighed, but nodded. "I'll get dinner ready."

"What do we have?"

Jenny wrinkled her nose. "Just venison. Unless anyone shot something else today."

"Not yet."

No sign of the hunting party. Abercrombie boasted his sons must have found a bear.

Franklin Pershing sat at his wagons with Noah and Jonah, while Rachel fried venison hash. "How's the family, Rachel?" Mac asked.

The girl nodded. "Fine, sir."

Rachel was a good girl, Mac thought, but young to handle the whole Pershing brood. They needed Esther. Maybe he shouldn't rely on Zeke and Joel for scouting so much. Maybe he should send their father—make use of the former Army man's talents and let Zeke or Joel help with the children. "Need me to keep Zeke or Joel here tomorrow?" he asked, not sure if he was asking Pershing or Rachel.

Rachel shook her head. "No, Mr. McDougall." She reddened and glanced at her father. "I mean, Captain McDougall."

Mac ignored the girl's confusion, said goodbye, and continued his rounds. At the doctor's wagon, Mrs. Tuller offered him two biscuits. "Take one to Jenny," she said. "She needs to keep her strength up, and she says venison don't sit well with her."

Doc harrumphed. "Girl's going to have a hard time," he said.

Mac's stomach spasmed. "What do you mean?"

"Don't scare the young man, Doctor," Mrs. Tuller said.

"Hips aren't ready for childbirth," the doctor said. "What is she— fourteen, maybe fifteen? Wish you young fools would wait to marry."

"Now, Doctor," said his wife. "You go on, Captain McDougall. You tell Jenny I'll ride with her this afternoon."

Mac smiled. "Thank you, Mrs. Tuller. If you stay with Jenny, I'll go find the scouts. Haven't seen Zeke or Joel since dawn." Maybe they had lost the trail. Or run into a band of Indians.

Mac took the biscuits to Jenny. "Here," he said, handing both to her. "From Mrs. Tuller. She'll ride with you this afternoon."

"Don't you want one?"

"Ate one earlier," he lied.

Jenny ate, they rinsed off the dishes, and Mac helped her onto the wagon bench. "Don't you think you should lie down?" he asked.

"I'll try sitting for a while. Talk with Mrs. Tuller."

Mac frowned, but left when Mrs. Tuller arrived. He took Valiente ahead of the wagons, stopping to tell Abercrombie he was looking for the scouts.

"Trail's marked, so those fool Pershing lads have been here," Abercrombie said. "But I ain't seen hide nor hair of 'em all day."

"I won't go more than a few miles ahead," Mac said. "If I lose the trail, I'll be back."

Abercrombie snorted. "May be back soon."

"Any sign of your sons?" Mac asked, ignoring the snide remark.

"Naw," Abercrombie said. "Probably found a herd of deer. Or a bear. Takes time to butcher and pack a large carcass. We'll eat well tonight."

"Hope so," Mac said, and rode on ahead.

Jagged peaks loomed over the valley. After about a mile, Mac saw fresh signs along the trail. Dirt pitted where rocks had been dug out for trail markers. A ring of blackened stones, still warm. He rode Valiente to the crest of a hill and shouted. He might draw Indians, but more likely Zeke or Joel was nearby.

"Halloo!" His shout was returned.

After a couple more shouts back and forth, Zeke appeared.

"What'd you find?" Mac asked.

"Trail's rough," Zeke said. "You'd think following the Burnt would be easy, but sometimes we have to stay in the valley, sometimes move to the hills above the water."

"Want to trade duty tomorrow?" Mac grinned. "You can deal with Abercrombie instead."

Zeke laughed. "We got one more ridge to get over, then the valley widens. We can camp there tonight."

Mac returned to the wagons to pass along Zeke's report.

"How's Jenny?" he asked Mrs. Tuller.

"Sleeping, I think. She got in back an hour ago."

"I'm awake," Jenny said, poking her head forward over the wagon bench.

"We're almost to our camp for the night," Mac said. "Another hour or so."

"Can't hardly think for the bumping and squeaking," Jenny said. "Someone's axle."

"The Baker wagon," Mrs. Tuller said. "Been like that all afternoon."

"I'll see to it," Mac said. He found Josiah Baker, whose wagon screeched with every turn of the wheels.

"Front axle needs grease," Baker said, pulling on his mustache. "But worse'n that, look at the rim. Near to falling off."

Mac inspected the wheel. The iron tire was separating from the wooden wheel, which had dried and cracked. "Can you work with Tanner tonight to fix it?"

Baker nodded. "If we stop early enough. Got to unload the wagon to take the wheel off."

Mac sought out Tanner and told him about the Baker wagon.

"Hope it don't need no iron work," Tanner said. "Can't build a hot fire, less'n we lay by a day."

Mac shook his head. "Can't stop. See if you can patch it, make it last until we reach the Powder. Pershing says there's a nice valley there. But it's another couple days."

They descended a hill, and Zeke rode to meet them. "Camp's straight ahead," he said.

That evening Mac was bone tired. But after supper, he roamed the camp and talked to Baker and Tanner. They'd greased Baker's axle.

"Have to hope the tire stays on," Tanner said, shaking his head. "Don't hit no rocks, Mr. Baker."

The hunters returned. Contrary to Abercrombie's predictions, his sons had found little game. A single deer to feed the entire camp. It might have to make do until they reached the Powder.

As the twilight darkened, Mac discussed the route to the Powder with Pershing. "Should make it in two days, if we don't have any problems," Pershing said.

Finally, Mac could return to his own wagon. Jenny was already asleep. He pulled out his journal and wrote:

September 4, 1847. Hard day along the Burnt. Wagons and teams are weakening.

Chapter 65: Reaching the Powder

Sunday, September 5ᵗʰ—No rest this Sabbath.
I am so weary, each day harder than the last.
How I miss Mama!

Jenny awoke early Sunday and wrote in the quiet dawn before she even climbed out of the wagon. Mac would chastise her if she didn't call him to help her down.

As she wrote, tears came to her eyes. She was so alone. She wanted her mother and her nurse Letitia. Mama had been furious when Jenny told her about the baby. Then Mama sent Mr. Peterson to Independence to bring Jenny back, which showed Mama did love her. It had seemed impossible to go home at the time. But now Jenny wished she were there.

She was just a burden to Mac. He would be glad to leave her in Oregon. If she made it. What would she do alone with a child? What would she do without Mac?

"Are you up?" Mac's face appeared in the back of the wagon.

"Ready," she said.

He lifted her down, catching her when she stumbled.

The morning started easily, the wagons following the Burnt River valley. Soon they were in the hills again. At Mac's request, Hatty Tanner rode with Jenny. Her boy Otis ran beside the wagon laughing with the Pershing twins.

After a few miles Jenny heard a shout from the front of the line. "Whoa!"

"What is it?" she asked Hatty.

"Can't see. Otis, you run along, see what's happ'nin'."

The boy ran off, then came back grinning. "Wheel come off."

"Whose wheel?" his mother asked.

He shrugged.

Hatty sighed and handed the whip to Jenny. "I'll go find out."

Jenny sat in the bright sunshine, sweating under her sunbonnet.

Hatty returned. "Mr. Baker's wagon. Rim come off. Here in the mountains, of all places."

"What'll we do?" Jenny asked.

"Ain't no room to git around. They's movin' the busted wagon. Folks unloadin' it now."

It grew hotter and hotter as the sun rose to its apex.

"Might as well eat," Jenny said. "Though all I have is venison."

By the time they'd eaten, the men had moved the Baker wagon, and it sat listing beside the trail in the junipers. They pulled Tanner's wagon with its tools beside the maimed wagon also.

"Best go on," Mac said. "Tanner and I'll stay here with the Bakers. Abercrombie will get you to the night's camp."

"Why's Mr. Abercrombie leading?" Jenny asked.

"Keeps him out of trouble," Mac said. "I'm putting you right behind him. Shout if he goes too fast for you."

After they filed down the hillside, Hatty drove Jenny's wagon into line behind Abercrombie's horse. Jenny heard him mutter, "Fool McDougall wants to take it easy on his little woman." But Abercrombie kept a slow, steady pace all afternoon.

They camped where a small creek entered the Burnt River. The ground was wet, but the animals had grass. Hatty gathered plants from the swampy creek banks and boiled them.

"I'm glad for something other than venison," Jenny said. "Seems all I've had has been venison or fish for weeks."

"Mmm-hmm. Since we ran out of buffalo." Hatty smiled. "I got plum tired of buffalo."

"Thank you for sitting with me today."

"Captain would have my hide if I left you alone. You feelin' all right, Miz McDougall?"

"I wish I was home again," Jenny said.

Hatty got a far-away look in her eyes. "Don't we all, ma'am. Don't we all."

Hatty looked so sad. "Are you thinking of your little boy?" Jenny whispered.

"Yes'm."

"I'm so sorry you lost him."

"Lots of folk gone. My baby Homer. Others with cholera. Mr. Purcell. Miz Pershing. Mr. Mercer. I surely hope Oregon is worth our pain."

Mac did not return that evening. When night fell, Jenny hefted herself into the wagon to sleep, while Hatty and Otis slept underneath.

In the morning Jenny heard Otis giggling while his mother fixed breakfast. "Sorry I wasn't up earlier," she said after climbing out of the wagon.

"Now why didn't you call me to help you?" Hatty said, hands on her hips. "You want the captain mad at me?"

Jenny smiled and shook her head. "We don't have to tell him."

After breakfast Mr. Abercrombie ordered them to hitch the teams. "Shouldn't we send someone back to see about the wagon repairs?" Jenny asked.

"Don't tell me what to do, girl. You ain't in charge. I am."

"But—"

"Just git in line."

Zeke helped Hatty yoke the oxen. "I'll ride back to find the Bakers, Miz Jenny," he said. "Joel's scouting with Pa. I'll let you know when I return."

Jenny smiled her thanks as Zeke boosted her onto the bench.

"Take care now, and do what Hatty says," he said, tipping his hat at Jenny with a grin.

They meandered through the hills above the Burnt River all morning. Mr. Abercrombie kept Jenny's wagon right behind him, though he said nothing to her. She watched him ride along the wagons from time to time, but he didn't talk with the platoon leaders the way Captain Pershing and Mac did. Of course, with Zeke and Mr. Baker away, the only other sergeant was Mr. Hewitt. Mac said Abercrombie hadn't spoken much to either Hewitt or Dempsey since the last vote.

Esther came over to Jenny's wagon at the noon stop. "You and Hatty eat with us," Esther said. "I'm fixing the children's dinner. Mr. Abercrombie can just fret about it."

"Zeke's not back?" Jenny asked.

"Ain't seen him."

Esther grimaced as she fried the meat. "Why didn't someone tell me morning sickness lasts all day?"

Hatty laughed. "Everyone's different," she said. "Each woman, each child. It'll pass."

"Sickness'll pass, maybe," Jenny said. "But then you get huge."

Esther and Hatty cooked, while Jenny sat with Jonah on her lap, breathing in his milky baby scent. Her child would smell the same.

They had barely eaten when Abercrombie called them into line again. On they traveled through the desolate hills dotted with sage and a few scrubby pines.

In midafternoon they met Joel. "Camp's about a mile ahead," he said. "Nice big valley. Pa's waiting there."

Jenny glanced at the threatening hills above. "There's a valley?" she asked Joel when he passed her wagon.

He nodded. "We've reached the Powder. Meets the Burnt here."

They found Pershing, settled in, and started supper. As Jenny cooked, Mac rode Valiente into camp.

"Mac!" Jenny almost dropped her skillet into the fire. "I didn't think you'd be back tonight."

"Left Tanner and Zeke with the Bakers," he said as he dismounted. "Iron tire needs to cool overnight. They'll start out in the morning. How are you?"

"Hatty's taking good care of me."

"Abercrombie been moving too fast?"

Jenny shook her head. "We're fine." She looked beyond the wagons. "It's a lovely valley, don't you think? I'm glad to be out of the mountains." And to have Mac back.

Mac snorted and waved to the north. "The Blues are ahead. Pershing says they're fierce."

Jenny sighed. "Must you spoil it?"

"What do you mean?"

"There's so little to be glad of. I simply wanted to be happy for a moment."

Mac tied Valiente to the wagon with a jerk of the reins. "I don't have time to be glad about anything. Need to talk to the men about tomorrow." He strode away.

Tears came to Jenny's eyes. Mac didn't care a fig for her feelings. Well, his supper could burn.

She took out her notebook and wrote:

> Monday, September 6th—Mac returned, talking only of the hard road ahead. Tonight we are camped in a pretty valley. There are more mountains ahead, I know, but this evening is sweet. Tomorrow's troubles can wait.

Chapter 66: Powder River to Grande Ronde

What did Jenny expect? Mac asked himself as he went to find the platoon leaders. He'd left the Bakers sooner than he should have to make sure she was all right. And all she did was complain he made her unhappy. Well, he wouldn't bother her again tonight.

Mac spoke tersely as he asked Pershing about the Blue Mountains.

"Need to come at 'em gradual," Pershing said. Frémont's map lay on a crate in the wagon circle, and men crowded around. "Stay on the east side of the valley. Head for that notch." Pershing gestured toward the mountains at the north end of the Powder River basin. "From there we head to Grande Ronde."

"How far?" Mac asked.

Pershing shrugged. "Two days maybe."

"That's not so bad," someone said.

"That ain't the worst of the Blues." Pershing squinted at the mountains. "Past Grande Ronde we got several days of steep, hellacious country. Worse'n the Rockies."

"God damn it, Pershing," Abercrombie sneered. "Ain't no wonder women are scared to death, if that's what you tell 'em."

Pershing raised an eyebrow. "Only telling facts. You don't like it, you can leave."

"Stop it," Mac said. "We need to know what's ahead."

"Fancy maps don't matter. We got to plow ahead," Abercrombie said.

Dempsey scratched his head. "Teams are plum worn out. Don't know if my oxen can take more mountains. Maybe we oughta rest a few days. Plenty of grass here."

"Should we go on?" Mac asked the group. "Or lay by and wait for

Baker?"

The men argued, but couldn't agree. Mac would have to decide. This wouldn't be a bad place for Jenny to have the baby, though only God knew when it would come. They couldn't wait long. "Any place else to rest farther on?" he asked Pershing.

"Grande Ronde. Then nothing till past the Blues."

"We'll keep going," Mac declared. He hoped the baby would hold off at least the two days to Grande Ronde.

"We'll have to decide about Walla Walla," Pershing said.

"What about it?" Mac asked.

"Do we go to the fort or not? And Whitman's place is near there, too."

"Let's take it one step at a time," Mac said, weary of planning beyond what he had to.

He returned to his wagon. Jenny slept inside, with Hatty and Otis curled up underneath.

Mac took his bedroll to the fire. By the flickering light, he wrote:

September 6, 1847. Rejoined the company on the Powder, leaving the Bakers with Tanner and Zeke. Tomorrow we head north.

In the morning the company trundled up the wide, grassy valley. Mac ordered families with plenty of oxen or mules to let half their animals graze through the day. "Don't know when we'll see more good feed," he said.

The mountains to the west were covered in pine and other evergreens, a welcome sight after weeks of sage and scrub. After seeing signs of deer in the valley, Mac sent Abercrombie and other men hunting.

"Bring back as much as you can shoot and carry," Mac said. "We're all low on food."

In late morning a small band of Indians riding large spotted horses approached the wagons.

"Nez Perce," Pershing told Mac. "Probably camped in a summer lodge nearby."

The Indians had dried meat and vegetables to trade. Mac called the noon halt early. He exchanged fish hooks for the Indians' camas roots, potatoes, dried salmon, and red chokecherries. Jenny smiled when he took her the food. Apparently, she was over her hurt feelings.

He grinned. "Think you can make something to eat from these?"

"Between Hatty and me, we'll manage."

The Indians told Mac a party from Dr. Whitman's mission was waiting in Grande Ronde. "Doctor want wagons come Waiilatpu," one Indian said. "Trade. Stay winter."

"Stay the winter?" Mac was surprised.

Pershing nodded. "Some folks hole up with Whitman for the winter. Go to Oregon City in early spring to claim land and start farming."

"Waiilatpu—is that Whitman's place?" Mac asked.

Pershing nodded.

"Should we winter there?"

Pershing shrugged. "If we get that close, I'd rather stake my claim this fall."

After the long halt at noon, the travelers only reached the north end of the Powder valley that afternoon. "We'll camp here," Mac said.

Abercrombie's hunting party found them in early evening. The hunters all had meat slung across their saddlebags.

"Why'd you stop so soon?" Abercrombie asked before he even dismounted.

"Spent time trading with Indians," Mac said.

Abercrombie spat on the ground. "Why'd you trade when we was out hunting?"

"They had vegetables and fish as well as meat." Mac squinted at Abercrombie, sick of the man's pugnaciousness. "No need to question everything."

"Just asking."

The emigrants unloaded the carcasses and butchered the meat. The work took time, but the prospect of heading into the mountains with fresh food lifted everyone's spirits. Some women sang as they worked.

"Wish Clarence was here," Mac heard Hatty Tanner sigh to Jenny. He wondered where the Baker wagon was. Had they made it into the Powder valley yet? But the missing wagons did not appear by dark.

Mac wrote that night:

September 7, 1847. Traded with Nez Perce. No sign

of Baker's wagon.

In the morning Mac rose before the sun. He asked Joel and Daniel to scout. "Find a place for the noon halt. Then one of you ride back to guide us, the other ride on to find a night camp."

"Should someone go back for the Bakers?" Joel asked.

Mac thought a moment. "Would your father go?" he asked Daniel.

Daniel grinned. "Keep him out of trouble?"

Mac shrugged, but grinned back.

"Ask him," Daniel said.

Mac sought out Samuel Abercrombie. "Need someone who isn't afraid of Indians to ride back and guide the Bakers."

Abercrombie puffed out his chest. "No reason to fear a few savages."

"If you see any Indians, don't start anything. The Nez Perce are harmless traders." Mac wondered whether it was a good idea to send Abercrombie by himself. "Want someone to ride with you?"

"What's Daniel doing?"

"Scouting with Joel."

"Send someone else. I'll take Daniel."

Mac didn't want to get between Daniel and his father. He ordered Hewitt to scout.

Through the morning Mac rode ahead of the wagons, watching for the piled stones Joel and Hewitt left to mark the route. Hatty stayed with Jenny, which put Mac's mind at ease.

As the trail climbed, the hills were at first as infertile as those around the Burnt River. Soon, however, pine trees studded the tops of the cliffs above the trail. The travelers picked their way up the mountain range, following the scouts' marks.

Hewitt met the wagons in late morning. "Route widens out in another two miles," he said. "Marked the noon stop there. Joel's ridden on ahead."

Mac nodded. "You want to scout this afternoon, or should I send Dempsey?"

"I'll do it. Let me get a meal with my missus, then I'll ride on."

The wagons lumbered up the hills to the noon camp. The trail widened, as Hewitt had said, but barely. They ate and rested between rock walls that towered four hundred feet on either side of them, then resumed the trek.

The trail narrowed again on the descent in the afternoon. Soon they were in a canyon hardly wide enough for a single file of wagons. Cliffs now rose one thousand feet above the gorge where they traveled. Pine trees dotted crevices in the rock faces wherever their roots could cling.

The sun dipped behind the western bluffs in midafternoon, though the sky overhead remained bright blue. After another hour of travel, the canyon opened out. The steep cliffs halted abruptly, and a wide, grassy basin spread before them.

Mac rode Valiente back to his wagon to check on Jenny.

"What a beautiful valley!" she exclaimed. "Even nicer than the Powder."

"Grande Ronde," Pershing said, halting his wagon next to Mac.

A horse and rider galloped toward them. "Ho!" Joel Pershing cried, reining his mount to a stop. "Party from Waiilatpu is here. Camped a mile ahead. Three Indians and a white man. They'll guide us to Whitman's."

"Should we go?" Mac asked Pershing.

"You're captain," Pershing said. "When I was here in forty-two, heard tell Whitman had scratched a fine place out of the wilderness. Wouldn't mind seeing it. But it's out of our way, and we got fresh food. And don't expect 'em to give you any charity in their trades."

"Let's see what they have to say." Mac waved his hat, and the wagons rolled into the valley.

As they finished making camp, Samuel and Daniel Abercrombie returned.

"Where are the Bakers?" Mac asked.

"Past the summit," Abercrombie said. "Thought you'd want to know, so we come on ahead."

Mac looked at the sky. "It'll be dark by the time they get here."

"Most likely."

Mac sighed. "I'll send a couple men out to guide them in."

"Zeke and Tanner are there."

"It didn't occur to you to let those two come back first? They've been away from their families for days."

"Zeke's single. And it's just Tanner."

Mac turned away, not wanting to confront Abercrombie's prejudice. Over his shoulder he said, "Meeting tonight. Agents from Waiilatpu."

Abercrombie followed him. "What do they want?"

"Want us to detour to their mission."

"Another goddamn delay? We got provisions now."

"We'll hear them out. Then vote." Mac kept walking. He sent Hewitt and Daniel to guide the Baker wagon in.

Night had fallen when the Baker wagon arrived, the new moon providing little light to aid the stars.

"Grab a bite," Mac said to the arrivals, clapping Zeke on the back. "Then join us. Talking to men from Whitman's place in Waiilatpu."

The men listened to Marcus Whitman's representatives extol the wonders of their mission on the banks of the Walla Walla River. "Good farm. Blacksmith shop. Fresh oxen to trade for your worn teams. Plenty of space for folks to winter," the white man said.

One of the Nez Perce spoke English. "We take you. Not far. Then you stay, or make easy trip to Columbia and Oregon City."

"We need to talk among ourselves," Mac said, and the men from Waiilatpu retreated.

"What do you think?" Mac asked his group.

"No more delays," Samuel Abercrombie said. "Head straight for Oregon City."

"I'd like to see the mission," Doc Tuller said.

"Teams are spent," Hewitt said. "I got one ox with hooves split to the quick. Another with neck sores from the yoke."

"Prices at Whitman's won't be cheap," Pershing warned. "But it's a purty place for anyone who wants to wait till spring to finish the journey."

"Maybe the widows might want to keep their families at the mission," Dempsey said. "We been carrying 'em a long time—Purcell family since Kansas. Sounds like Waiilatpu's civilized, despite its heathen name."

Mac was torn. He wanted this journey to be over, his quest for adventure long gone. But he wanted Jenny safe. Perhaps she and her baby could stay at Waiilatpu—Mrs. Whitman could care for her.

The discussion continued until Abercrombie announced, "I ain't going to Waiilatpu. And that's final."

"Need to vote, Abercrombie," Doc said.

"Take your goddamn vote. I ain't going."

"Show of hands," Mac said, waving his hat. "Who wants to go to Waiilatpu?"

Two-thirds of the men raised their hands.

"Opposed?" Mac asked, but the outcome was clear. He made a show of counting hands opposed, then said, "Waiilatpu it is."

He beckoned the Whitman agents back. "We'll go with you," he said, though they had probably overheard the company's argument.

"Route's the same till after you're through the Blues," the white man told them. "You can change your mind till then."

Why hadn't the guides told them that before Abercrombie declared himself? Mac wondered.

Chapter 67: In the Blue Mountains

Wednesday, September 8ᵗʰ—Mac decided we'll go to Waiilatpu. It will lengthen the journey, but I would like to meet a white woman living in this wilderness. Every day is harder.

Jenny slept fitfully. In the morning she stumbled about her chores. Hatty had returned to her own wagon now that her husband was back.

The company traveled up the Grande Ronde River into the Blue Mountains. Dark green pines and blue spruce covered the hillsides. More mountains rose beyond the far end of the canyon.

As the wagons rounded a bend in the gorge, Jenny gasped. A massive hill ahead blocked their way. The trail traced around the hill until they reached another curve, when another huge tree-covered mound loomed beyond.

Cliffs rose hundreds of feet above the trail. The dense vegetation seemed more ominous than the barren rocks of the Snake desert. Or perhaps, Jenny thought, she was more fearful as childbirth approached.

Shortly after the noon halt, the trail became steeper. The emigrants struggled up the middle of a draw, oxen pulling the wagon so slowly Jenny felt every rock beneath the wheels.

They traveled just a few miles before she heard one of the Indian guides tell Mac, "Stop now. Rest. Many more mountains tomorrow."

"We can go farther than this!" Samuel Abercrombie bellowed.

"Look at your team," Mac said. "Your oxen are lathered in sweat. So's your horse."

Abercrombie spat. "I'll be leaving you behind soon enough."

That night Jenny wrote:

Thursday, September 9th—Climbing through the Blues. Dank pines hide the sun, though their scent is fresh and sharp. I have never seen forests so thick, not even in the bayous of Louisiana.

The next morning they picked their way through the forest. Earlier emigrants had cleared most of the logs off the trail, but on occasion the men had to hitch a yoke of oxen to a gigantic tree trunk and drag it out of the way. In other places, they hacked at the dense underbrush to widen the trail so the wagons could get through.

At noon Mac returned to the wagon, mopping sweat off his brow. "Slow going today," he said, slumping to the ground beside Jenny as she cooked.

A chill breeze blew through their camp, causing the tall trees around them to creak and sway. Jenny looked up at the narrow band of gray sky overhead. "Could storm."

Mac snorted. "Now that we're shaded from the sun, it rains. Where was it when we needed water on the Snake plateau?"

"Will it snow?" Jenny asked.

Mac shrugged. "Abercrombie thinks so. But he doesn't know any more than I do."

Jenny shook her head. "Snow in September. I can't believe it."

"Anything is possible in this strange land." Mac took the plate Jenny handed him with a nod. "Get Rachel or Hatty to gather berries for you this afternoon. We've seen lots of black haws."

"I can do it."

"You should ride Poulette. Or stay in the wagon. The hills are too much for you."

Jenny didn't respond. She wouldn't let Mac pamper her. "How's Abercrombie taking the decision to go to Dr. Whitman's mission?"

Mac shook his head. "Still says he's leaving when we're past the summit. If he does, the rest of his platoon might go with him."

"Captain Pershing said we shouldn't split up."

"We shouldn't. But I've made up my mind. I'm taking the company to Whitman's. Abercrombie can do what he wants." Mac handed his plate back to her and got up. "Need to get moving. Make time before the weather turns."

Jenny rode in the wagon until Mac went ahead to assist with clearing the trail. Then she found Rachel Pershing. They walked through the bushes along the route gleaning berries, staying close so they could be sure the oxen didn't stray. But the oxen couldn't leave the trail—there was nowhere else to pull the wagon.

The girls had filled their baskets with berries when Mrs. Tuller joined them. "You should rest, Jenny," the older woman said.

"I suppose. The hills do wear me out." Jenny sighed. "But I am so sick of bouncing in the wagon."

Mrs. Tuller patted Jenny's arm. "When we stop, I'll help you boil those black haws for supper."

"Plenty of wood, that's for sure," Rachel said. "I'm glad the buffalo chips are behind us."

They camped in a small glade surrounded by forest. "Water's down a steep ravine," Mac told Jenny. "I'll haul it for you, as soon as I see to the team."

While Mac unyoked the oxen, Zeke brought Jenny a bucket of water. "Mrs. Tuller said you'd need this for your berries," he said.

"Much obliged," Jenny said. "Come by later and I'll give you some."

"Rachel picked plenty for us," Zeke said, tipping his hat as he left.

"I said I'd get the water," Mac said.

"Zeke was kind enough to bring it," Jenny replied. She dumped the berries into a Dutch oven, covered them with water, and set the pot to boil. "Be better with sugar. They'll be mighty tart without it." Then she straightened and stretched.

"You all right?" Mac asked.

"Asking doesn't do any good," she said, annoyed at his frequent inquiries. "My back hurts, but it's hurt for weeks now."

"Let me fry the meat," Mac said.

"You have the company to see to. I can do it."

"I'm only trying to help."

"I can do it."

"Damn it, Jenny. Don't be stubborn. I said I'd help."

"And I said I could do it. I don't want to be a bother."

"You're not a bother. But you'll be a bother if you bring your baby on before we get to the mission."

Jenny stared at him, her heart sinking. "Is that why we're going? Because of me?"

Mac poked at the coals under the Dutch oven. "One reason."

"I don't want you making decisions because of me. That's why folks were upset with Captain Pershing."

"I think it's best if you have this baby at Whitman's."

Jenny threw up her hands. "This baby's coming when it wants to, not when you tell it to. You can't control everything."

"We're going to Waiilatpu. We all need supplies. It's best for everyone. I'll get more water." Mac picked up two buckets and headed toward the creek.

Jenny sat by the fire stirring the berries until they cooked to a dark, pulpy mass. She served them over johnny cakes with meat and greens. The berries made the mouth pucker, but the tart, earthy flavor was a welcome change in diet. She shared her compote with the Tullers and Tanners.

The rain held off until evening. After she washed dishes under dripping trees, Jenny wrote:

Friday, September 10th—Gathered black haws. Mac is going to Whitman Mission for my sake. He must be as fearful as I am about the baby.

The skies cleared by morning, though the heavy evergreen boughs above them dripped as if the rain continued. The Whitman guides led them higher into the mountains, and they wended their way through forest and glades, up hills and down ravines. In places the route was so steep they had to double-team the oxen to haul the wagons uphill. On the descents they braked the wagons with ropes and chains looped around trees.

Jenny rode Poulette. "It's dangerous in the wagon," Mac said. The mare picked her way along the trail. Sometimes Jenny closed her eyes, afraid to watch Poulette's hooves on the steep hillsides. The sound of scree sliding downhill was fearsome enough.

They made camp by a mountain spring nestled under tall evergreens. The animals grazed in a meadow nearby, guards posted to keep them corralled.

"Stay alert," Jenny heard Mac tell the guards. "There are panthers and wolves around. Did you hear them last night?"

Jenny had not heard any wild beasts the night before, but she'd listen for them tonight. After supper she stayed near the fire with her journal:

Saturday, September 11th—Camped at a spring. Summer is dying, and night comes early now.

In the middle of the night, Jenny woke to the scream of a wildcat. She needed to use the latrine, but wouldn't leave the wagon. She tossed and turned and finally dozed. At dawn she awoke, tired and uncomfortable.

It was Sunday, but no one mentioned resting. The travelers went silently about their morning chores, awaiting Mac's signal to set out.

Mr. Hewitt joined them as they ate. "Lost an ox last night," he told Mac. "Wild animal?" Mac asked.

Hewitt shrugged. "Guards heard cats, but no sign of a struggle. Could have wandered off."

Mac called the Whitman guides over. "Should we search for the ox?" he asked.

"Can't hurt," the white agent said. "Might find it." The man sent one of the Indian guides off with Hewitt to search for his lost animal.

The rest of the emigrants pulled their wagons into line and headed up the mountain. The road became increasingly steep and stony as it switch-backed up to the pass. Progress was slow—most of the oxen and mules were worn out, barely able to pull the heavy wagons up the hills.

"It's too much for them," Jenny heard Captain Pershing say to Mac. "We oughta slow down."

"No place to rest," Mac said. "And half the company would revolt if I lay by for even a day."

"Going to lose Abercrombie anyway."

"You don't think he'll change his mind?" Mac asked.

Captain Pershing shrugged. "No great loss if he leaves."

But Mr. Abercrombie would take Esther, Jenny thought. Esther would have to go with Daniel. Captain Pershing would have to care for his family all alone, with only Rachel to cook and mind the children. What would happen to poor Jonah without Esther?

Late that afternoon they reached the summit. Mr. Hewitt and the Indian guide met the wagons there. "No sign of the ox," Mr. Hewitt said. "Not dead or alive."

"It'll be dead soon, if not already," Mr. Abercrombie said. "Ox can't fight wolves or wildcats."

After supper Jenny sought out Esther at the Pershings' campsite. Esther looked haggard, her face ashen and her dress loose at the waist. She hadn't gained any weight in her pregnancy yet.

"Tired?" Jenny asked her friend.

"Don't you know it. I helped Mrs. Abercrombie with supper, then rushed over here to help Rachel."

"You ought to drink some of the cow's milk yourself. Keep up your strength."

"Still can't keep much down," Esther said. "It'll pass in a few weeks, I hope."

"You can't help anyone if you get sick. Here," Jenny said, taking the wooden spoon from Esther. "I'll stir the stew. You sit and feed Jonah."

"Ain't you tired yourself?" Esther asked.

"Yes, but I only have Mac and myself to worry about."

Esther spooned milk into Jonah's eager mouth. "I can't wait till he can drink from a cup. We spill as much milk as gets into him."

Jenny watched the two of them with a pang. "Is Mr. Abercrombie going to leave the company?"

"That's what he says." Esther pursed her lips into a thin line.

"I'll miss you."

"Miss me?" Esther looked up, her eyebrows raised. "I ain't leaving."

"Won't you go with Daniel?"

"I'm staying with Pa," Esther said. "I can't leave him with the young'uns. I've told Daniel what I'm doing. What he does is up to him."

"You'd leave your husband?" Jenny asked.

"I don't want to." Esther's voice broke. "I love Daniel. But my family needs me."

"What will happen to you and your baby without your husband?"

"I'll find out, won't I?" Esther said with a sigh.

Chapter 68: Out of the Blues

Mac walked out of camp at the Blue Mountain summit as the sun set. To the west a vast valley spread beyond the mountains. Past the valley rose snowcapped peaks. The Cascades, the last mountain range to pass, though they would avoid those peaks by rafting down the Columbia. He couldn't imagine climbing the huge mountain that rose above the others—Mount Hood, it was called.

Would Abercrombie really leave? It didn't bother Mac to lose the man—he'd been a scoundrel since they left Independence. But if Abercrombie took his family and the rest of his platoon—maybe more families as well—could the remainder of the company survive?

Who could he count on to stay? The Tullers. The Pershings. If the Captain, Zeke and Joel all stayed, Mac would have good support. The Tanners, most likely—and Clarence and Hatty were good workers.

Could they get to Whitman's before Jenny's baby was born? Doc Tuller could deliver the baby on the trail, but Mac wanted a safer place for Jenny when the baby arrived.

Mac hoped to persuade her to stay at Whitman's mission. As captain, he had to take the company on to Oregon City. But Jenny could have her baby at the mission and maybe stay to live with the Whitmans. Mac could check on her next spring on his way back to Boston.

He wouldn't worry as much, if he knew where they could winter in Oregon City. Maybe he'd find a place for Jenny there, but maybe not. It would be best if Jenny spent the winter at Waiilatpu with Mrs. Whitman. Mac didn't want to chance not finding a place for Jenny and her child.

He decided—Jenny would stay at the mission.

Daniel Abercrombie joined Mac at the overlook. "Pa's bound and determined to leave when we get out of the mountains."

"I can't force him to stay with us," Mac said.

"Esther wants to remain with her family."

"Puts you in a bind, doesn't it?" Mac squinted at Daniel. He seemed too young to be married.

"It surely does."

"Well, you think on it." Mac clapped Daniel on the back and returned to camp.

Rain poured Monday morning. Not quite freezing, but cold enough to make morning chores miserable. Despite the abundance of wood, the logs were too damp to burn. Most travelers settled for a cold breakfast.

Mac hunched into his hat and coat, turning his back to the driving wind. No sight of Mount Hood this morning. He nodded at the Whitman guide who tramped over to the wagon. "Can we travel through this muck?" Mac asked.

The man rubbed his moccasin on the grass underfoot. "Wheels'll slip in the mud. But ain't no reason to stay here."

"Then let's go," Mac said.

The wagons headed down the steep mountain on slick grass. Mac put Jenny on Poulette again. "That Indian pony won't lose her footing," he assured her.

"I can't bear looking down the mountain," Jenny said, shivering. "And it's cold."

"It'd be warmer in the wagon," Mac agreed. "But safer on horseback."

Shortly after they started out, one wagon slid twenty feet off the trail before banging into a spruce tree. Mac ordered the rest of the wagons to pass, then spent two hours with Zeke and Tanner helping to unload the wagon, pull it back to the trail, and reload the family's possessions.

"Lucky just one board splintered," Tanner said. "We can fix that later."

The wagons navigated along the hillsides, headed ever downward. By late morning the rain slowed, but trees still dripped. Everyone was soaked to the skin. Jenny's lips were blue as she huddled under the buffalo robe on Poulette. She looked wretched, but Mac wouldn't risk her life in the wagon.

At a wide clearing in the hills, he called the midday halt.

"Why are we stopping?" Abercrombie demanded. "Still early."

"Need to warm up," Mac said. "I've seen folks stumbling. Don't want anyone following a wagon off the trail."

Mac started a dank, smoky fire and settled Jenny beside it. "Warm your hands," he said. "Do you have any dry clothes?"

She nodded.

"Go change while I boil water." He boosted her into the wagon.

Across the campsite Abercrombie gathered his platoon together. Abercrombie waved his arms, but his voice was too low for Mac to hear. Mac thought about wandering over to see what the man was gabbing about, but Jenny called for assistance getting out of the wagon. Abercrombie would make his plans known soon enough.

The travelers took time to heat a meal and fill their bellies. They had meat and camas roots, though not much else in the way of provisions.

They faced a cold wind all afternoon, but the descent became less steep. Through gaps in the forest, Mac could see a broad grassy plateau stretching out to the north and west.

"Columbia Plateau," their white guide said. "Dry land. Lots of horses."

"Indians?" Mac asked.

"Cayuse and Nez Perce. Mostly friendly."

They were not quite out of the mountains when they stopped for the evening, but the next day's travel would get them to the open plateau. The company was somber as they went about their chores. Glances from one man to another signaled something, but Mac didn't know what.

After supper Abercrombie stalked over to Mac's campfire. "I'm leaving in the morning," he announced. "Heading due west. Taking my platoon and some others with me."

"Any room for discussion?" Mac asked.

"Nope. We're leaving."

Mac stood and called the men together. The whole camp, men and women alike, gathered nearby.

"Who's going with Abercrombie?" he asked.

About a third of the men raised their hands. Dempsey was one of them—his hand up, but his gaze toward the ground. Hewitt was not. Pershing and his sons, Doc Tuller, and Tanner also kept their hands down.

Esther clutched Daniel's arm, tears streaming down her face. They stood on the edge of the group. Daniel hadn't put his hand up, but Mac didn't count on him to stay.

Mac was silent, thinking. There were enough men and wagons for safety in each group. He considered tossing in the sponge and following Abercrombie, but he feared for Jenny at the pace he knew Abercrombie would set. Abercrombie wouldn't stop for a baby. Mac didn't want to be alone with Jenny—or even Jenny and the Tullers—for the last stage of the journey.

"I wish you well," Mac said. "Those of you going to Whitman, we'll set out at dawn."

The group dispersed, some muttering, some quiet. Had they expected Mac to put up more of a fight? Frankly, he thought the company would be better off without Abercrombie, except for his hunting prowess. But he would miss most of the other men and their families.

When he and Jenny were alone, he pulled out his journal and wrote:

> *September 13, 1847. The company parts ways at dawn. Abercrombie heads for the Columbia across the plateau with a third of the wagons, while I take the rest to Waiilatpu.*

"Are you worried?" Jenny asked.

"About Abercrombie?" Mac shook his head. "The guides will take us to Whitman's place. Then all we have to do is follow the river to Oregon City."

Mac slammed his notebook shut. He wouldn't admit it to Jenny, but he did worry.

When he awoke on Tuesday, Mac could see his breath, but the sun sparkling through the rain-soaked evergreens promised better weather than the day before. He sounded reveille and the emigrants made their meal and hitched their teams. Mac ate breakfast slowly, giving Abercrombie the chance to leave first.

As Abercrombie got his group into line, Daniel removed a trunk from one of the Abercrombie wagons. Esther stood beside Daniel holding a pile of bedding.

"Pack up, son, we're heading out," Abercrombie shouted.

"I ain't going with you, Pa," Daniel said.

"What in tarnation are you talking about? Put that trunk back in the wagon."

"Esther can't leave her family."

"Wife follows her husband. Bible says so."

The entire company gathered around father and son. Samuel was already mounted and towered over Daniel and Esther.

Samuel's face was brick red, and spittle formed in his beard as he shouted, "Do as I damn well tell you, boy. Like I raised you." Samuel raised his whip and cracked it at Daniel's feet.

Daniel flinched. Esther screamed, dropped the quilts, and stepped between Daniel and his father as she buried her head in Daniel's chest.

"I can't, Pa," Daniel said, putting his arms around Esther. "I hope to see you in Oregon."

Chapter 69: On the Way to Waiilatpu

Jenny's heart jumped to her throat during the confrontation between Daniel Abercrombie and his father. Afterward, the elder Abercrombie bellowed at his followers and led them at breakneck pace down the mountain. It would be a wonder if his horse didn't break a leg.

After the Abercrombie party left, she went to find Esther. "That was very brave of Daniel," she said.

Esther's face still showed traces of tears. She nodded silently.

"Can I help you pack?" Jenny asked.

Esther shook her head, lips pursed. Then she sighed. "Just hold Jonah, please, while I make room for our things in Pa's wagon." Esther threw her muddy quilts into one of the Pershing wagons and climbed in after them.

Jenny sat on a crate and bounced the baby on her lap—what little lap she had. Soon she would be holding her own child.

In a few minutes Esther clambered out. "Took me all night to convince Daniel to stay," she said. "But don't you tell anyone I made him do it."

"I won't." Who would she tell? Mac already didn't approve of Esther—no reason to tell him Esther could make Daniel do whatever she wanted. Though Jenny was glad Esther and Daniel had stayed with the Pershing family.

Mac came to get her. "Come on," he said. "Let's put you on Poulette. The Abercrombies are far enough ahead now."

The last descent out of the Blues was long and steep. Every step Poulette took sent waves of pain through Jenny's back. Her stomach felt hard as a rock. She ached all over—maybe she had picked up a chill from the rain.

The company reached the Columbia Plateau around noon, a high basin filled with grass drying in the late summer. After they ate, Mac was ready to help Jenny back onto Poulette.

"Please let me ride in the wagon," she begged. "We're off the mountain now. It's safe. Horseback hurts so."

"You barely ate anything."

"Not hungry. I think I have the ague."

"I'll have Doc take a look at you."

"Just let me rest," she said. "I'll be fine."

Mac lifted her into the wagon. "Get in the back. I'll get Hatty to help you."

Soon Jenny heard Hatty Tanner call to her. "Captain McDougall says me'n Otis should stay with you. Lead your wagon. If Otis is too noisy, I'll send him back to his pa."

Jenny dozed through the afternoon. The warm sun beating on the wagon cover took away her chill, but made her feel feverish and sluggish. Her baby wasn't moving. For so many months it had poked and prodded her, and now it was still. Was her child all right?

By the time they stopped at dusk, she couldn't breathe without hurting. A vise gripped her around the middle. She didn't stir from the wagon.

"What's wrong, Miz Jenny?" Hatty asked her.

"I don't feel well," Jenny murmured.

"I'll get Captain McDougall."

After a moment, Mac appeared. "What's wrong?"

"I'm sick," Jenny said.

"You want Doc?"

"I guess I'd better," she said. She sat up slowly, trying to make herself climb out of the wagon.

"Stay there," Mac ordered. "I'll get him."

Doc and Mrs. Tuller both climbed into the wagon with Jenny.

"I hurt everywhere," Jenny said. "Must be an ague." She wiped her hand across her forehead. "No fever, but I hurt. Especially my back."

Doc Tuller felt her back and her stomach. "Is the baby moving?" he asked.

"No!" Jenny said in alarm. "Is it dead?"

The doctor shook his head. "You're fine. Baby's moved into position. Won't be long."

"It's coming?" Her voice rose in panic. She couldn't do this. She didn't want to have a baby.

Doc Tuller chuckled. "Could still be a couple days. First babies take their time."

"I'll stay with you tonight, dear," Mrs. Tuller said. "But first, Hatty and I'll get you something to eat."

"I'm not hungry," Jenny said.

The Tullers climbed out of the wagon.

"What is it?" Jenny heard Mac ask.

"Baby's coming soon," Doc said. "How far are we from Waiilatpu?"

"A day or two," Mac said. "Will we make it?"

"Don't know."

"How is she?" Mac asked. He sounded worried.

Jenny didn't hear the doctor's mumbled answer.

While she waited for her supper, she wrote:

Tuesday, September 14ᵗʰ—Doc says my child will come soon. I wish Mama and Letitia were with me. I am so afraid.

Jenny sipped the broth Mrs. Tuller brought her, but it didn't sit right in her stomach. Soon she was retching into a chamber pot. She lay in a stupor all night, vaguely aware of Mrs. Tuller beside her.

She felt no better in the morning. Mac left her in the wagon and had the company underway before the sun peeked over the Blue Mountains behind them.

Mrs. Tuller sat on the wagon bench while Jenny lay in back. The older woman hummed, creating a dull buzz in Jenny's head. Jenny wasn't sure whether her daze came from the monotonous rolling of the wagon or from the calming sound of Mrs. Tuller's voice.

At noon Mrs. Tuller coaxed Jenny out of the wagon. "Do you good to walk a bit."

Broad yellow hills surrounded the emigrants in three directions, with the Blue Mountains to their backs. Creeks ran in ravines between the rolling hills, verdant with grasses, and the sky was huge overhead.

She tried to choke down what Mrs. Tuller gave her, but the cup of milk from Esther was all she wanted. "I can't eat—like morning sickness again."

"It'll all be over soon," Mrs. Tuller said, helping Jenny back into the wagon.

Jenny wanted it over now. Through the afternoon her back hurt more and more. Finally, she could not stop a sob from passing her lips.

"Are you having pains, dear?" Mrs. Tuller asked.

"It just hurts," Jenny said. "It never stops."

"No contractions?"

"No. It hurts all the time."

"Would you like some water?"

"No, thank you. Nothing." Jenny tried to sleep, but the squeaking wheels and bouncing motion kept her awake. It wasn't fair—she had done nothing to bring this baby on. Yet here she was in a wagon a thousand miles from home about to give birth.

She heard Mac ask Mrs. Tuller how she was. "Baby's taking its sweet time," Mrs. Tuller replied.

There was nothing sweet about it. She didn't want the baby, she didn't want Mac, she didn't want Mrs. Tuller. She wanted to crawl into a hole and die.

The wagons kept traveling, though the sun lowered in the sky. Mac came by again and asked, "Will she make it through the night?"

"Hard to say," Mrs. Tuller replied.

"Should we stop or press on for Waiilatpu? Guides say we can make the mission in another hour or two."

"Won't nothing happen in the next two hours," Mrs. Tuller said. "If the rest of the folks are willing to keep going, we might as well."

On and on the wagon jolted. Jenny was in a stupor, aware only of pain and motion. She thought Mac looked in on her from time to time, but she wasn't sure.

Night had fallen when Mrs. Tuller said, "I see a light! That must be the mission."

A sudden spasm gripped Jenny. She cried out as warm liquid gushed between her legs.

Chapter 70: Whitman Mission

Mac heard Mrs. Tuller shout. "What is it?" he asked, riding Valiente over to his wagon.

"Her water broke," Mrs. Tuller said.

Mac didn't understand. "What?"

"Baby's coming. Get the doctor."

Mac found Doc and told him what Mrs. Tuller had said.

Doc swore. "Couldn't she have waited a bit longer? Let's get to the mission."

Mac spurred Valiente forward to where Zeke led the wagon train on horseback. "Jenny's having her baby. Ride ahead and tell the mission," Mac shouted. Then he rode back to his wagon. "Should we move faster?"

Mrs. Tuller laughed. "Baby won't come that quick."

They arrived at the mission half an hour later, oxen in a lather. Mac looked in his wagon. "Can you stand?" he asked Jenny.

She nodded, her face white.

"Let's get you inside." Mac lifted Jenny out of the wagon and yelled, "Where can I take her?"

An Indian woman pointed to a whitewashed adobe building. Mac carried Jenny into a room that was bare except for a lumpy mattress on the floor. "Here?" he asked.

"I've delivered in worse," Doc said from behind him.

Mac laid Jenny on the mattress. "What do we need?"

"Blankets," Doc said.

Mac ran back to retrieve Jenny's bedroll. After handing the blankets to Mrs. Tuller, he ran his hands through his hair, not knowing what to do.

"Go see to the company, son," Doc said. "Mrs. Tuller and I'll take care of her."

Mac went outside and surveyed the mission. A two-story white house sat near the low building where Jenny lay, surrounded by fields and barns. His company's wagons circled in one of the fields.

A tall, heavy white woman walked toward him. "Good evening," she said.

"Good evening, ma'am. I'm Caleb McDougall, captain of this company. Jenny—my wife—is in labor."

The woman smiled and offered her hand. "Narcissa Whitman. You're welcome here. Is your wife being cared for?"

"Yes, ma'am. We have a doctor. I understand your husband is also a doctor. Is he available?"

"Dr. Whitman is away. If I can assist you, please let me know."

Doc joined them, saying, "I'm sorry not to make Dr. Whitman's acquaintance, ma'am. We'll need some water."

Mrs. Whitman called a young half-breed. "John, bring a bucket of water."

Doc sent Mac back to his wagon. Hatty Tanner brought him a plate of food. "Eat," she said. "It'll be a long night."

Esther came over and asked, "How's Jenny?"

Mac shrugged. "Doc's with her."

Esther patted his shoulder. "You take care," she said.

When he finished eating, Mac returned to the room where Jenny lay. "Should I stay?" he asked.

Doc looked up from his supper. "Ain't nothing you can do."

Mac went back to his wagon and pulled out his notebook:

September 15, 1847. At Whitman Mission. Jenny's labor has begun. Mrs. Whitman is most hospitable.

Pershing came and sat beside Mac, lighting his pipe on a twig from the campfire. "She'll make it. She's young."

Mac was silent. Pershing's wife hadn't made it.

He worried about how he should act. The baby meant nothing to him—only another body to take care of. A new father should probably feel more, but he wasn't the child's father. Jenny wasn't his wife.

He wanted this night over and the wagons away. He wanted Jenny safe at the mission.

While he sat with Pershing, a scream split the night, louder than the panthers in the Blue Mountains. Mac jumped to his feet and ran toward Jenny.

"What's wrong?" he shouted at Doc.

"Contractions getting stronger," the doctor said as he bent over Jenny's small form. "But she's still got a long way to go."

"Can't you stop the pain?"

Doc squinted at Mac. "Not much I can do but watch. Help the baby, when it comes."

Mac stood silently. What about Jenny? He wanted Doc to save Jenny. "Doc, can I talk to you? Privately."

The doctor joined him at the door. "If it comes to Jenny or the baby," Mac said, "save Jenny."

Doc snorted. "She just told me to save the baby."

"No," Mac said, grabbing Doc's arm. "Save her."

"Let's hope it don't come to choosing. Get some sleep. We'll call you when the baby's here."

Back at his wagon, Mac stretched out but couldn't sleep. Wails of pain sounded from the building where Jenny lay. He covered his head with a blanket, but it didn't help. The screams grew louder and more frequent.

It was after midnight, or so Mac thought. The moon was not quite half full. He must have dozed off, because Mrs. Tuller woke him by tapping his shoulder.

"Captain McDougall," she whispered. "Jenny wants you."

"Is the baby here?" he asked, shaking his head to clear it.

"Not yet. She's having a hard time."

Mac bolted up, fear snaking through his gut. "What do you mean?"

"She's exhausted and weak. But she wants to see you."

Mac followed Mrs. Tuller into the adobe building. The blanket covering Jenny was bloodstained. "Why the blood?" he asked Doc.

"She's bleeding some. Baby's too big for her." Mac's stomach rose at Doc's surly tone. "Damn fool girls marrying so young."

"Mac." Jenny's whisper stopped Mac from shoving Doc against the wall.

Mac knelt beside her. She was so pale. He smoothed her tangled hair out of her face. "What is it?"

"Remember your promise."

"Promise?"

"To take care of my baby." She tried to lift herself on an elbow.

"Stay still," Mac said, pressing her down gently. "You'll take care of the baby yourself."

"Promise me," she said, grasping his arm with surprising strength.

"You'll be fine, Jenny."

"Promise me."

Mac brushed another damp curl off her cheek. "All right, I promise."

Jenny sighed and lay back. She seemed to wilt into the blankets, and her eyes closed.

"Jenny!" Mac tapped her cheek. "Wake up, Jenny."

Her eyes shot open as another contraction gripped her, and she screamed.

"Shh," Mac soothed, taking her hand. Jenny crushed his fingers in hers. Mac looked at Doc. "Can't you give her some relief?"

"All we can do is wait."

"And pray," said Mrs. Tuller behind Mac, patting his shoulder. "You should go now."

"I'm not leaving," Mac said. "I brought her this far. I won't leave now."

"It'll only distress you," Doc said. "Seeing her pain. Husband ain't meant to watch."

Jenny cried out again, thrashing on the bed. Mac kept his grip on her hand. "Come on, Jenny. You can do it."

The contractions went on for hours. Mac was sweating and his hand ached from Jenny's clasp. But he didn't let go. He talked to her almost non-stop, about everything and nothing. About Boston. About their journey so far. About the home she'd have in Oregon.

Jenny dozed between contractions. At one point Mac thought she passed out, because she was still for several minutes.

Doc shook her. "She's got to keep working," Doc said. "Can't let the baby get stuck."

So Mac kept talking to her.

The sun shone brightly in the window when Doc told Jenny, "Almost here. Push."

"I can't," Jenny moaned.

"Yes, you can," Mac urged. "Let's get this baby out." He sat behind her and lifted her shoulders.

Jenny wailed with the next contraction. Then went limp.

"One more time," Doc urged. "Don't quit on me now."

"Save her, Doc," Mac said. "I don't care about the baby. Just save her."

"Come on, Jenny. One more time. Here it comes."

Jenny leaned back against Mac, her eyes wide, and she groaned from deep in her belly.

"Got it," Doc said. "You ready?" he called to his wife.

Mrs. Tuller took a red lump from Doc. Jenny slumped unconscious on the bed. "Jenny," Mac said, shaking her.

Doc pushed Mac out of the way and worked over Jenny. "Got the afterbirth," he said after a few minutes. "All right. Let's wake her up." He sponged Jenny's face with a damp rag.

Her eyelids fluttered. "My baby?" she asked.

"It's a boy," Doc said. "Let me check on him."

Mac hadn't heard a sound from the baby. He didn't much care. Jenny was alive, and he smiled at her. "You did it," he said.

"My baby?" Jenny sounded hysterical.

"He's breathing," Mrs. Tuller said. "Let's see if we can get him to cry." She held the red baby upside down and tapped him on the back.

"Let me have him," Doc said. He stood over the infant and thumped its chest. Finally, a weak mewl sounded.

"My baby!" Jenny cried, tears streaming down her cheeks.

Doc thumped the baby again.

A hiccup. Then a stronger cry.

The doctor wrapped the baby in a blanket and handed him to Jenny. "Doing all right," he said with a chuckle.

Jenny cradled the baby in her arms. She smiled through her tears at Mac. Feeling stupidly happy, he grinned back at her.

"What's his name?" Mrs. Tuller asked.

Jenny looked at Mac. "William? William Calhoun. It was my papa's name."

"William Calhoun McDougall." Mrs. Tuller smiled. "That's a fine name. Little Will."

Doc clapped Mac on the back. "Go show off your son, while we get Jenny cleaned up."

"Me? He's not—" Mac backed away.

"He won't break." Mrs. Tuller thrust the baby at Mac. He clutched it tightly. William gazed at Mac with furrowed brow and eyes that saw right through him.

"Go on," Mrs. Tuller pushed Mac out the door. "He's got an audience waiting. I told 'em you have a son."

Mac stumbled outside. Applause sounded.

Esther rushed forward first. "Oh, let me see! What's his name?"

Mac managed, "William." And quickly gave the baby to Esther.

Back at his wagon, Hatty Tanner handed Mac a cup. "Real coffee," she said, smiling. "From the mission store. To celebrate your new son."

"Thank you," Mac said, collapsing by the fire.

"Hard birth," Hatty said, as she scrambled eggs and potatoes. "Miz Jenny all right?"

"Hmm." He was too tired to talk.

"I'll take some vittles to the Tullers." Hatty busied herself about the fire.

Mac knew he should see to his company, but he slept. It was afternoon when he awoke.

Doc stood over him. "We need to talk."

Mac sat up. Seemed like only a few minutes since Mrs. Tuller had awakened him in the night. "Is Jenny all right?"

"As well as can be expected."

Mac relaxed.

"Don't you want to know about the baby?"

Mac shrugged. "Sure."

"I ain't never seen a father less interested in a firstborn son. Is he yours?" Doc stared at him, bushy eyebrows frowning.

Mac stammered, "Wh-what did Jenny tell you?"

"I ain't asked her. I'm asking you."

"Shouldn't you ask Jenny?"

Doc's voice was mild. "Why bother her when you can answer me? Is he your child?"

Mac gulped. "No."

"She your wife?"

"N-no." Mac stammered again. "Sh-she was in trouble. Needed help."

The doctor raised one eyebrow. "You planning to marry her?"

Marry her? Jenny had needed somewhere to go, someone to take care of her. Mac had needed to look married. But he'd never intended to marry her in fact. He would find her a home—preferably here at the Whitman Mission. Then his responsibility to her would be done. "Doc, I did Jenny a favor bringing her to Oregon."

"I ain't asking what you done, boy. I'm asking what you're going to do." Doc sat on a barrel beside Mac. "Measure of a man changes each time he acts. What's your next act?"

"Thought I'd leave Jenny and the baby here. Maybe some of our other families will stay, too."

"And you?"

"I'll get the company to Oregon City. Come back through in the spring. See how she's doing."

Doc squinted at Mac. "You're making this up as you go, ain't you?"

Mac stared at the ground.

"See here, McDougall." Doc's voice turned steely. "Jenny's a fine girl. I don't know what happened back East. Between you, or before you met. She and her child need you now. Are you man enough to figure out what to do?"

Doc pushed himself to his feet. "I'm beat. Need to sleep." And he walked off.

Hell, Mac thought. Jenny didn't want to marry him. She hadn't even wanted to pretend at marriage. She'd had enough of men in Arrow Rock. She was still so young. And after what he'd told her about Bridget, she wouldn't want him.

Mac thought of Bridget. What would he have done if he'd learned Bridget was carrying his child before she died?

Chapter 71: Resting at the Mission

Friday, September 17th—I welcomed my son William Calhoun yesterday at Whitman Mission.

Jenny lay in the cool adobe house. She had slept all afternoon and night after William's birth. Her body still ached, and she shivered, remembering her panic and exhaustion. It had been worth it. Now William rooted at her breast with little grunts. She ran a finger over his soft cheek. He turned toward it, opening his eyes in surprise. They would face whatever came next together.

Mac had stayed with her through the worst of her labor. She would have died without him—given up. He had saved her again, and William, too. She owed him so much she couldn't repay.

Hatty brought her a bowl of soup. "Eat this, Miz Jenny." Hatty took the baby so Jenny could sit up. "My, ain't he a fine boy. Handsome, like his pa."

Jenny's smile fell. Who was his father? "He looks like my papa," she said.

"You doin' all right?" Hatty asked. "No fever?"

Jenny sighed. "Poor Mrs. Pershing. I surely miss her."

Esther came in carrying Jonah. "Thought we should introduce these boys. And soon we'll have my baby, too. They'll all be friends in Oregon."

Mrs. Tuller joined them. "Don't let Jenny and William get tuckered out. When she finishes her soup, it's time for a nap."

Jenny didn't want them to leave. "What's the mission like?" she asked.

"I didn't see anything when we arrived."

"It's a nice place," Esther said. "If all farms in Oregon are so prosperous, we'll have plenty."

"Everything costs so much," Mrs. Tuller said.

"Because of a drought this year," said a voice from the door. "May I come in?"

"Mrs. Whitman," Esther said, bobbing a small curtsy.

A tall, robust woman entered. "Narcissa Whitman," she said, smiling at Jenny. "It's about time we met." Mrs. Whitman took William from Hatty. "What a lovely baby," she said, cradling him to her shoulder. "I lost my daughter several years ago. Drowned in the river." She closed her eyes. "My only child. Until we adopted emigrant orphans. Are you comfortable, Mrs. McDougall?"

"Yes, ma'am. Thank you."

"You are all welcome to stay the winter. We have housed emigrant families the past several years. Your food in exchange for labor. Between what we raise and the Cayuse trade, we'll make do."

"That's very kind, Mrs. Whitman," Mrs. Tuller said. "But most of us aim to move on."

"But you and your baby are staying." Narcissa Whitman smiled at Jenny. "Your husband asked."

Jenny's spoon clattered in her empty bowl. Mac was casting William and her aside. He didn't want them. What had she expected? She'd been a burden for him long enough.

"Jenny looks tired," Mrs. Tuller said. "She and William should rest."

Hatty took the soup bowl and left, and Esther carried Jonah out. Mrs. Whitman handed William back to Jenny with a pat and followed them.

Mrs. Tuller sat beside Jenny. "Captain McDougall hadn't told you?"

Jenny shook her head. She could barely breathe.

"I'll send him to you."

Jenny's hands shook as she stroked William's head. The baby seemed to sense her despair and wailed. She was more helpless now than before William was born.

Mac didn't come see her until afternoon. "How are you?" he asked, stopping in the doorway.

"Fine." She would make him tell her, she decided.

"And the baby?" He stepped into the room, but stopped short of her bed.

"Come see." She pulled the blanket back from William's sleeping face. His rosebud mouth sucked on his fist.

Mac knelt beside the bed.

"Do you want to hold him?" Jenny thrust the baby at Mac.

Mac touched William's cheek, but didn't take the child. "Jenny, we need to talk."

"Look at his little fingernails. Have you ever seen anything more precious?"

Mac stood and moved to the window. "I've decided you and the baby should stay here. Mrs. Whitman is willing." Silhouetted against the window, Mac's back was rigid.

"You've decided." Jenny's throat swelled and her jaw clenched.

"The birth was hard. He's too small for the trail."

"Jonah's fine. William will be, too." Jenny kept her voice quiet.

"Jenny, you aren't listening. I think it's best you stay here."

She couldn't stay calm any longer. "You think!" she shouted. William startled and cried. "What about what I think?" She patted the baby's back rapidly as she said between her teeth, "I want to go on. With the Tullers. And Esther. And you. I won't be left here with the other orphans."

"Now, Jenny—"

"Don't you 'now Jenny' me. I'm not a child. I'm old enough to have this baby, and I'm old enough to know what's best for him."

"I can't stay with you, Jenny," Mac said tersely.

"I know you'll leave. But you said you'd get me to Oregon, and that's where I aim to go."

"We're in Oregon."

Tears filled her eyes. She couldn't keep them back. "You'd leave me here alone? Without the friends I've made?"

He knelt beside the bed and took her hand. "It's best, Jenny. The Columbia's ahead, biggest river yet. You hate the water. You're safe here."

"Mac, I—"

"I'm sorry." Mac stood and left the room.

Jenny buried her face in William's blanket and wailed more loudly than her baby.

Jenny cried herself out and drifted off to sleep. Mrs. Tuller dropped by at dusk. "I'm sorry, dear," the doctor's wife said. "Captain McDougall said you took it hard."

"I'm not staying," Jenny said.

"He's your husband. You have to do what he thinks best."

"He's not . . . " But Jenny thought better of telling Mrs. Tuller the truth. If she knew the truth, the older woman would want Jenny and William to stay behind for certain.

Jenny changed and fed William and ate the food brought to her. By evening she was restless, wanting out of the room she'd been in since her arrival. When Esther brought supper, Jenny asked for clothes. Esther returned with garments and shoes. Jenny dressed, wrapped William in a blanket, and the girls headed outside.

Esther pointed. "There's the Whitman house. And the blacksmith's shop. Tanner's been repairing wagons all day."

They walked past a vegetable garden and a pond. "Looks like a Missouri farm," Jenny said. "Except for the sagebrush on the hills beyond."

At the river babbling past the fields, Esther whispered, "That's where the Whitman baby drowned. Indians found her. Just like Mr. Mercer." Esther's voice took on a ghoulish tone. "No telling what really happened."

They returned to camp, and Jenny carried William over to Mac's wagon. "Shouldn't you rest?" he asked.

"Mrs. Dempsey was up within hours after her baby was born."

"You had a rougher time of it."

"I'm not staying, Mac."

"We've been through this." Mac turned away.

"Are you leaving me Poulette?" she asked.

He faced her, eyebrows raised. "Of course. She's yours. I wouldn't take her back."

"You took back your word on getting me to Oregon City."

"Jenny, I'm doing what's best."

"If you leave Poulette, I'll ride after the wagons."

"You're in no condition to ride."

Doc walked into their camp frowning. "We should leave in the morning," he told Mac.

"Why?"

"New company arrived today. With measles. Their Indian guides are sick, too. Don't want our folks to catch it."

Jenny hugged William closer to her. People in Missouri had died from measles. Some who survived were left blind.

"You can't leave Jenny and William here. Newborn could die." The doctor left, shaking his head.

Jenny looked at Mac, trying not to gloat.

Mac sighed. "Guess you're going to Oregon City after all. Feel up to leaving tomorrow?"

She nodded. "I'll be ready."

Later she wrote:

> *September 17ᵗʰ, evening—Mac wants to leave me at the mission. He will take me to Oregon City only because there are measles here. I could not bear to be left behind, friendless again.*

Jenny and William stayed in the wagon that night. She was afraid Mac would leave without her if she slept in the mission room. She woke often to feed the baby and change him. The wonder of William's presence was almost more than she could bear. His tiny fingers and toes, the way he gazed at her while he suckled, the total calm with which he slept. And his anger when she didn't know what he wanted. Would she ever learn to be less clumsy with his diapers, to feed and burp him the way he liked?

She was crying when Mac looked in the wagon. "What's wrong?"

"I miss my mama and Letitia," she sobbed.

His mouth grew thin. "Then stay here. With Mrs. Whitman."

She shook her head.

"Write your mother. Tell her about the baby. Someone headed East will take the letter, if not now, then in the spring."

"Aren't we leaving?"

Mac shrugged. "Tanner's still working on one of our wagons. Won't be done for a couple of hours."

Jenny tore a page out of her notebook and wrote:

Chère Maman,

I am at the Whitman Mission, in Oregon Territory, where I was delivered of a son on September 16, two days ago. I named him William Calhoun, after Papa. Soon we continue our journey to Oregon City.

I have thought of you often, wondering whether I have a brother or sister. My prayers are with you, your child, and Letitia.

Our travels have been perilous, the wilderness frightening, with high mountains and fast, deep rivers. Still, with God's grace we have survived this far. I have had many good companions along the way—our first captain, Franklin Pershing, and his family, though his wife died after childbirth; the Pershings' daughter Esther, who has become my dearest friend, and her husband, Daniel Abercrombie; Dr. and Mrs. Tuller, who helped me through my confinement; and the new captain, Caleb McDougall, who has been most kind. . . .

Jenny stopped, not knowing what more to say about Mac. She could not lie to her mother by saying she and Mac were married. Nor could she write of Mac's generosity without implying a relationship that did not exist.

What was Mac to her? She knew him better than anyone she had ever known, and yet she barely knew him at all. A man of contradictions—caring, yet he had callously planned to leave her behind. Always proper in his behavior toward Jenny, yet he'd abandoned Bridget pregnant with his child.

At some point after they reached Oregon City, Mac would leave her. But she would stay with him as long as she could. She trusted him more than anyone else in her world.

Jenny ended her letter to her mother and posted it at the mission store.

She clutched William as she walked, afraid the measles would find him. The day was hot, but she had swaddled the baby tightly against the dread disease. He cried as she returned to camp.

"My goodness," Mrs. Tuller laughed when she saw William. "You'll roast that baby."

"I don't want him to get measles."

Mrs. Tuller's expression turned sad. "It's every mother's fear. Nothing you can do to prevent them from getting sick or injured. Like poor Mrs. Whitman, whose little girl drowned." Mrs. Tuller didn't mention her own sons' deaths, but Jenny knew the older woman thought of them.

"Now, let's let the boy kick his feet." Mrs. Tuller unwrapped William, held him on her lap, and cooed at him.

"Where's the doctor?" Jenny asked.

Mrs. Tuller shook her head. "Doing what he can for families with measles. All he has is a little chamomile lotion. Don't know where he'll get more supplies so far from home."

Chapter 72: Fort Walla Walla

It was almost noon Saturday before Mac got the company underway. He thought about staying at the mission another day, but the threat of measles and rumors of the Whitmans' strict Sabbath practices made him anxious. If they didn't leave Saturday, they could be stuck until Monday, while the risk of measles increased.

The men had spent the days at the mission repairing wagons in the blacksmith shop and sawmill. "Worth the detour," Tanner declared to Mac. "They got real tools here."

Unfortunately, the shelves in the mission store were mostly empty. The emigrants hadn't found plentiful provisions since Fort Laramie. They survived mostly on what they scavenged or hunted off the land.

The route along the Walla Walla River twisted through a valley between rolling hills covered in golden grass. The teams grazed as they pulled newly repaired wagons. Mac rode back and forth along the wagons, checking in with Jenny occasionally. Hatty or Mrs. Tuller stayed with Jenny and William.

Mac still fretted about whether he should have left Jenny and the baby at the mission. Jenny had thought he was abandoning them, but he only wanted to keep them safe, to do the responsible thing by her.

Saturday night the emigrants camped beside the babbling Walla Walla, then traveled on, reaching the fort at the junction of the Walla Walla and Columbia early Sunday afternoon. Mac called the day's halt at the fort, not wanting to tire Jenny with a long day. He was thankful Abercrombie wasn't there to complain.

The Hudson's Bay Company fort at Walla Walla had timber walls enclosing a small stockade, with lookout towers at the four corners. After making camp, many in their company went into the trading post. Prices weren't much different than at Whitman Mission, but the post had salmon and potatoes available.

Mac asked the British agents in the guard station for advice on the route down the Columbia. Pershing and Zeke went with him.

"Float all the way to Vancouver from here," one man said as he lit a pipe. "Load your belongings into Indian canoes. We rent you the boats and Indian guides."

"What about our teams and wagons?"

The man puffed on his pipe. "Sell 'em here, buy more in Vancouver. Or some of your men can drive the animals down the shore."

"Can wagons travel along the Columbia?" Mac asked. He dreaded telling Jenny they would float all the way from here to Vancouver.

"Only to The Dalles," a man cleaning his gun in the corner said. "Got to switch to boats then. Cliffs go right down to the water. Wagons can't get around."

The first man blew another puff of smoke and nodded. "Huge rocks in the river. Portage the canoes right below The Dalles."

A third man whittling near the door spoke up. "Barlow cleared a road around Mount Hood. He's taken wagons all the way to Oregon City."

"That's new," Pershing commented.

The man shaved off a curl of wood. "Road opened last year. This summer's its first real test. Not many folks taking it."

"What's it like?" Mac asked.

Another wood sliver fell to the floor. "Ain't seen it myself. Hear it's steep. But it ain't the river."

Mac looked at Pershing. "What do you think?"

Pershing shrugged. "Let's look at the canoes."

They wandered down to the riverbank where a group of emigrants loaded canoes with boxes and barrels.

"Canoes aren't very big," Mac said. "Can they hold all our belongings?"

Pershing scratched his beard. "Probably have to leave some things here. Sell 'em. Or store 'em, come back in spring."

One canoe floated away from the shore, four men with paddles and a steersman guiding it into the current. The boat sat low in the water, only inches to spare between river and gunwale. Jenny would be scared to death in such a precarious craft. "If we take the wagons to The Dalles," Mac asked, "what do we do there?"

A man working on the bank said, "Build yourself a raft below the cascade, or wait for room on the Fort Vancouver ferry."

"I think we should take the wagons as far as we can," Mac stated. He looked at Pershing. "Any objection?"

The older man shrugged. "You're captain. Let's take 'em to The Dalles. Decide there."

Mac nodded.

They returned to camp and told the men they would head out along the Columbia first thing in the morning.

That night Mac wrote:

September 19, 1847. At Fort Walla Walla, a rude outpost at the juncture of the Columbia. The Columbia is over half a mile wide—clear, swift water coursing over a rocky bottom. We will drive our wagons to The Dalles, hoping that the sparse grass is sufficient for the teams.

Warm sunshine replaced the cold weather they had encountered in the Blues. Only the shorter days hinted at autumn's approach. The travelers were eager to undertake the last leg of their journey.

Provisions were low. The emigrants had grumbled about high prices at the mission and fort, and some were flat broke. Mac had bought shirts and a knife from others in the company with his gold, so they could re-provision. He didn't need what he bought, but he had cash and others did not. They would take care of each other until they reached Oregon City.

The teams were faltering, many animals with festering sores from yokes and harnesses and tender feet after so many miles of pulling over rough land. Some were malnourished, unable to find enough grass. Emigrants who could afford it had replaced their weakest animals at the forts. But some families had butchered their sickest oxen and pulled the wagons with fewer pair, which increased the burden on the remaining animals. The wagons also looked shabby—covers torn and dingy, cracked side boards despite repairs at Whitman Mission. The men talked daily about whether the teams and wagons would make it to Oregon City.

Monday the travelers rolled along the south shore of the Columbia. They saw occasional Indian villages on the north bank, but the south side offered only rocks, sandy soil, and stubby grass.

"Never thought I'd miss the tall prairie grasses," Zeke said to Mac as they rode their horses along the wagons.

"Kansas Territory doesn't seem so bad now, does it? Nor the Platte," Mac said, grinning.

Zeke shrugged. "Columbia's purtier. Platte weren't nothing but flowing mud."

Mac pushed his hat up on his forehead to get a breeze on his face. "Let's wait until we see the rocks at The Dalles. Then you can tell me how pretty the Columbia is."

"You planning on building rafts there?"

"Don't know," Mac said. "I hate to abandon the wagons."

Zeke chuckled. "What you hate is telling Miz Jenny she and your son have to float down the river for days on end."

"That, too," Mac said with a smile.

The men took turns leading the wagons on the rugged, narrow path along the river. Cliffs rose above them almost straight from the shore. All they could do was avoid the worst of the rocks and sand.

They nooned at the mouth of a steep gorge that spilled a small creek into the Columbia. Two tiers of black stone bluffs rose more than five hundred feet above the creek. After they ate, Jenny wandered beside the river, William cradled against her shoulder. Mac tramped over to her and heard her crooning as she paced the riverbank.

"Delightful, isn't it?" he said.

"Fearsome," Jenny said. She stared at the vast Columbia, blue as the cloudless sky above. "As big as the Mississippi and twice as swift." She snuggled William under her chin.

"It's not as wide as the Platte." Mac knew she worried about rafting the Columbia, but he couldn't reassure her. He didn't know what they would do at The Dalles, and he didn't want to raise false hopes.

"Maybe not," Jenny said. "But it's so fast."

"Not as fast as the Snake." He sounded defensive, even to himself.

"It's the biggest river we've seen so far." Jenny turned away from the water, biting her lip.

He might as well say what she wasn't saying. "You're scared."

Jenny glared at him. "Of course, I'm scared. You know I hate the water. And now I have William."

"We'll be fine. I'll take care of you."

Jenny brushed a hand across her forehead, whisking a wisp of hair out of her face. "You can swim. You don't have to carry a baby." She clutched William closer.

"I'll get you down the river safely. William, too."

"We can't go overland?"

"Most folks take the river." No use mentioning Barlow Road until he'd decided.

Jenny walked away.

He stepped after her and touched her arm. "Don't worry, Jenny. You know I won't let any harm come to you. Or William."

She looked at him, her eyes glistening. "And how do I know that, Mac? You wanted to leave me at the mission. You don't feel responsible for us."

"Damn it, Jenny." He took his hat off and slapped it on his knee. "I'm captain now. It's my job to get everyone safe to Oregon. Of course, I'm responsible for you."

She shook her head. "You care about the whole company. You'll do your best for everyone. I'm all William has. I have to think just about him, what's best for him. Not about everyone."

Chapter 73: Along the Columbia

Monday, September 20ᵗʰ —The Columbia is terribly swift and deep. Soon we will abandon the wagon, my only home, to float at the mercy of the water. I dread the churning current, not only for myself, but for William.

Jenny sat on a stone beside the wide Columbia as the orange setting sun spread across the silver water. She held William on her lap, and her journal lay on the ground next to her. The baby's lips sucked silently as he slept. It still amazed her how quickly her son had become the focus of her life.

She hadn't wanted to show her fear when she talked to Mac. But she was a mother now, responsible for William. She'd seen rafts floating past them, some made only of wagon boxes and driftwood. She quailed at the thought of stepping onto such a rickety craft with her son in her arms.

All Mac worried about was how to move the company from one camp to the next. Her throat tightened. She didn't want to cry. Then she glanced down at William. He was so small and helpless. If she lost her grip on him on the raft—a sob escaped.

Footsteps crunched the rocks behind her. She wiped her eyes and turned to see Mrs. Tuller.

"How do you bear it?" Jenny asked.

"Bear what, dear?" Mrs. Tuller sat on a rock beside Jenny.

"Being so anxious. About your child."

Mrs. Tuller smiled. "What choice do we have?"

Jenny sobbed again, freely, not caring what Mrs. Tuller thought.

The older woman put an arm around Jenny. "Just cry it out, dear. Nothing else you can do."

After a sleepless night with William, Jenny dragged herself out of the wagon Tuesday morning and lifted the baby down after her. She stumbled about camp making breakfast, burning a thumb on the skillet as she fried meat for Mac.

"Drat!" she said, shaking her hand. William screamed from his blanket behind her. She couldn't hold him and cook, too.

Mac turned from hitching the teams. "What is it?"

"Would you please pick up William?" she asked, her voice shaking. She hated to ask for help with the baby.

"What's wrong?"

"I'm cooking, and he's crying. He needs to eat, but I can't feed him now." She felt her milk start to flow. Her cheeks flamed, but she was too exhausted to care. Mac had to know she nursed the baby.

"I'll fry the meat," he said, taking the skillet away from her with a gloved hand. "You tend to the baby."

Jenny took William into the wagon and nursed him. He made greedy little grunting sounds as he sucked. If only she could stay here, safe in the wagon, with just William. But Mac needed her to cook and wash up and to drive the wagon, while he commanded the company. She had to pull her weight. She burped William, laid him on a pallet, and climbed out of the wagon.

After eating the breakfast Mac had prepared, Jenny asked, "Shall I drive?"

"What about the baby?"

"He'll sleep for a while."

He nodded. "Pull into line behind the Tullers. Call Doc or me if you need anything."

No trees broke the monotony of the barren, sandy land along the Columbia. More black crags loomed above them. Jenny shivered, wondering if Indians hid behind the rocks. Around noon they arrived at the Umatilla River. Mac halted the wagons with a wave of his hat. "We'll eat, then cross," he shouted.

Jenny started their meal and fed a fussy William. As she sat by the fire, rocking William in Mrs. Tuller's loaned chair, Esther wandered over. "Made a loaf of molasses bread," she said. "Bought molasses at the fort for a treat. I was so tired of eating the same food." Esther cut a slice. "It's mighty good."

"Mmm," Jenny sighed as she bit. "Bring me some butter, please. It's in that box." She gestured.

Esther spread the butter on Jenny's slice and on another for herself. "How's William?"

"Fussy, sleeping or wet. Or feeding."

"Jonah's lifting his head now. I swear he's bigger every day."

Jenny cut another slice of the sweet molasses bread and put it aside for Mac. "Mac's scouting the Umatilla crossing," she said. "Probably need to go upstream where it's shallower. I hope the current's not too fast."

"You still scared of crossings?" Esther laughed. "We been through so many."

"It's worse now," Jenny admitted. "With William. And soon we'll be on rafts."

"Pa says there's a road at The Dalles. We might not need to float the Columbia at all."

"A road? Mac didn't tell me there was a road."

"Well, they ain't sure what to do. Might float, might take the road. It's Captain McDougall's call."

"What's your papa think?"

Esther shrugged. "Didn't say."

"I'll ask Mac." Maybe she could persuade him to take the road.

Mac returned to the wagon and ate standing up. As he handed his empty plate back, without a word about the tasty molasses bread, he told Jenny to load up. "We found a ford upriver," he said. "Should be an easy crossing."

"Mac, about the Columbia—" she began.

"Not now, Jenny. I need to get the wagons in line."

Jenny didn't want to wait. She would worry about rafting the Columbia until Mac agreed they didn't have to. "But, Mac—"

"We'll talk tonight." Mac mounted Valiente and rode off.

They splashed across the Umatilla with little trouble. Jenny was so intent on talking to Mac about the Columbia she forgot to worry. In truth, the stream was a babbling brook, hardly worthy of the term "river." The only challenge was the steep bank on the west side, but by the time Jenny drove across, the wagons ahead of her had worn the sand into a smooth, if slippery, path.

William squalled in the wagon behind her as she tapped the whip on the oxen's backs. With a pang, she suddenly feared him rolling out of the wagon. Next time, she'd have someone ride with her to hold the baby.

After the crossing, the shore along the Columbia widened, but there were still no trees, and the warm September sun beat down on the travelers. Jenny dozed on the bench, until she snapped awake at William's cry. She ducked under the cover to nurse him, then clambered to the front to bask in the balmy light.

By the time Mac halted the wagons on a flat expanse beside the Columbia, rivulets of sweat ran down Jenny's spine. The swift river flowed past their camp, carrying with it all manner of logs and brush. Where the logs came from, Jenny couldn't say—there certainly weren't any trees nearby for the water to have swept up. She filled a bucket at the river and gazed downstream as the sun cast long shadows on the rushing water. It was beautiful, though the wild current scared her. With a sigh, she returned to camp to fix supper.

"Mac," she said later, when he sat eating by the fire. "I hear there's a road to Oregon City now."

He frowned. "Where'd you hear that?"

"Esther. Her papa told her."

"We haven't decided which route to take."

"We? I thought you were in charge."

"I'll listen to what the other men want."

Hands on her hips, Jenny said, "What about what the women want?"

"Now, Jenny—"

"Don't 'now Jenny' me." She barely kept from stomping her foot. "I don't want to take William on a raft. It'd scare the breath out of me."

"Now, Jenny—"

"Please take the road." She wasn't proud of begging, but she panicked at the thought of floating down the wild river.

"I can't promise anything. We need to talk to men at The Dalles. That's still several days away."

"So I'm supposed to fret until then?"

Mac turned to his plate. "No need to fret. Just trust I'll do what's best."

Jenny sighed, and took William into the wagon to nurse him again. Then she pulled out her journal and wrote:

Tuesday, September 21ˢᵗ—There's a road to Oregon City to avoid floating the Columbia, but Mac won't agree to take it. I doubt I shall sleep, worrying. Of course, William does not permit me much rest anyway.

Chapter 74: Willow Creek

September 21, 1847. Crossed the Umatilla, small compared to the royal Columbia. Jenny worries about rafting the river, but I cannot let her desires determine what we do.

Mac sat beside the campfire watching the sun drop. High, thin clouds turned pink and orange, then gray, before fading into the dark sky. He couldn't tell Jenny they would take Barlow Road. Not unless the company agreed. His youth and inexperience were disadvantages enough as he tried to lead the group. He'd be happy to let someone else captain, but no one else stepped forward, not since Abercrombie left. The men seemed to trust him to hold them together. He had to honor their trust.

"You're thinking deep," Zeke said, squatting beside Mac.

Mac grunted, not wanting to discuss his dilemma with Zeke.

Zeke rolled a cigarette, struck a match on a rock, and smoked lazily, giving every indication he might sit there all night.

"I don't know whether to take Barlow Road or the rafts," Mac said.

"Don't have to decide yet, do we?"

Mac sighed. "Jenny doesn't want to float the river."

"Ah." Zeke took another drag on his cigarette.

They sat in silence for several minutes, Zeke smoking, Mac staring at the stars. "I don't want her to worry," Mac said.

Zeke puffed again, without a word.

"But I can't let her tell me what to do," Mac argued, to himself as much as Zeke. "I have to decide what's best for the company."

Zeke stubbed out his cigarette. "Miz Jenny's a mighty fine woman," he said as he stood. "I've said it before—you're a lucky man." He walked off, leaving Mac to gaze at the sky.

The next morning was cool but bright, promising another warm afternoon. Mac led the travelers across a bend in the river. When the trail hit the Columbia again around midday, they took their noon halt, then continued along the river's shore.

Jenny didn't talk to him again about the road. Mac saw her frown at the river several times, but she didn't speak to him.

Mac tried not to think about their conversation the night before. He focused on the wagons and the route, riding Valiente back and forth along the wagons. In midafternoon they reached Willow Creek, which flowed through a small ravine with grass in the bottom for the animals.

"We'll stop here," Mac said. He was glad Abercrombie wasn't there to argue. They could have traveled farther, but Mac wasn't rushing to The Dalles. Once there, he'd have to make a decision. He hoped the choice would be clear.

September 22, 1847. Camped on Willow Creek, named for the trees on its banks. Good grass.

At dawn Zeke and Joel came to see Mac. "Road's purty rough on the other side of the ravine," Zeke said. "Might need to go up the creek a ways. And we don't know where to cross the John Day River."

"How far is it?" Mac asked.

Joel shrugged. "We ain't ridden ahead that far."

"Best lay by here for a day," Zeke said. "Joel and me'll scout. Come back tonight with the route."

"All right." Mac nodded. "We'll rest today."

Some men grumbled. "We're so close," Dempsey said. "I'm itching to claim my land."

Mac saw smiles on the women's faces. Willow Creek was a peaceful spot, and they relished a day without travel.

Mac led a small hunting party. They shot enough ducks for every wagon to get enough. "Zeke and Joel back yet?" Mac asked Jenny as he swung down from the saddle in late afternoon.

"No."

The women plucked and roasted the birds. The sun was setting by the time the scouts returned.

"What did you find?" Mac asked.

Zeke dismounted, then shook his head. "Road's rough everywhere we looked. It's a steep climb out of this canyon here, then rocks and sand along the river. Or upstream, then out of the canyon, with more rocks and sand on the plateau."

"What about the John Day?" Mac asked.

"Didn't get that far," Joel said.

Franklin Pershing joined them. "Can we make it along the Columbia?"

"There's room," Zeke said. "But it's tight."

Pershing shrugged. "Why go south then? Frémont made it on the river."

"We'll be heading straight into the wind," Joel said. "Sand flying everywhere. Our horses 'bout balked on us because of the grit." He chuckled. "They sure were glad when we started back."

"We'll stay on the Columbia," Mac declared.

A strong, gusty wind howled through the river gorge Friday morning. After breakfast the oxen and mules strained to pull the wagons out of the ravine. When they headed downriver, the wagon wheels slogged in heavy sand. In some places the cliffs dropped straight to the water, and the teams had to pull the wagons up the bluffs to the bleak plateau above the Columbia.

The wind blew so hard the women and children bent double as they walked. Mac saddled Poulette and led her to Jenny. "Ride the mare," he said. "No reason to tire yourself out."

"William—"

"Tie him in a sling. You shouldn't walk, and it's hard on the oxen if you're in the wagon."

"That's why I'm walking—"

"That's why you have Poulette." Mac took William, helped Jenny into the saddle, and handed the baby to her. "Go on. I need to stay with the wagons." He slapped Poulette on the rump, and the mare trotted off.

Even with Jenny on Poulette, Mac worried. The trail was so steep and narrow wagons could barely pass. Poulette and Valiente were sure-footed, but even Mac didn't like looking at the sheer drop to the river below.

They camped that night on another small stream beneath the craggy buttes. The grass was adequate, but not as plentiful as at Willow Creek.

Jenny approached Mac after supper. "About the rafts—"

"I told you, Jenny. I can't decide until we get to The Dalles."

"I simply wanted to tell you—"

Mac's impatience got the best of him. "I know how you feel—"

"You don't. You don't know how I feel. You won't even listen."

"We'll talk about it at The Dalles."

He left and walked to the Pershing wagons. Esther and Daniel sat by the campfire with Jonah. Esther leaned back on Daniel, who sat behind her with his arms around both Esther and her baby brother.

"Where are Zeke and Joel?" Mac asked.

Daniel waved toward the river. "Took the young'uns for a walk."

"Captain Pershing?"

"In the wagon," Esther said.

"Sleeping?"

Esther shrugged.

Mac poked his head in the back of the wagon. Franklin Pershing snored. Mac sniffed. No scent of alcohol.

"Think I'll go find Zeke," he said.

Mac walked through the circle of wagons, nodding at families as he passed. It was a quiet evening, a brilliant sunset over the river. Why was he so uneasy? Must be his role as captain, he thought. The others could rest, but he couldn't. Jenny nagging him about the rafts didn't help. Just when he thought they were getting along, she pushed at him.

And yet, he owed her his life.

At the river's edge, Zeke and Joel skipped rocks into the vast Columbia with the younger Pershings. They all laughed and splashed along the shore. Rachel had grown on this trip—as tall now as Jenny, though that wasn't saying much.

Mac started to call out to Zeke. But what did they really need to talk to about? It could all wait until morning. He turned and went back to camp. Jenny and William were already in the wagon. He heard the baby grunting and Jenny humming.

Mac sat by the fire and took out his journal:

September 24, 1847. Wind in our faces all day, blowing sand that stifles the breath. We hope to reach the John Day tomorrow.

Chapter 75: Crossing the John Day

Friday, September 24th—I tried to tell Mac I would trust him about the rafts, but he wouldn't listen. He has kept me distant since William's birth.

Jenny closed her journal and climbed into the wagon when William started to fuss. She would nurse him and go to sleep. She loved the quiet times with William, when she didn't have to worry about cooking or washing or tending the wagon, when she could focus on her baby. She counted his fingers and toes, marveling at their tiny pink nails. Dark lashes lay on his cheeks as he suckled. Sometimes he fought fiercely for every swallow, but tonight he drifted off to sleep, then startled and sucked again.

She had talked to Mrs. Tuller during the noon halt. While they cooked, Jenny poured out her concern about taking William on a raft.

"Do you trust Captain McDougall?" Mrs. Tuller asked.

Jenny owed her life to Mac. He had been with her at every crucial moment of their journey. She wished Mac talked to her more. She wanted him to show more interest in William. But she couldn't fault him for those things. And she couldn't tell Mrs. Tuller she wasn't married to Mac and Mac wasn't William's father. So she simply stated the truth, "Yes, I trust him."

Mrs. Tuller patted her hand. "Sometimes a man needs to hear you say it."

Jenny frowned. She didn't understand what Mrs. Tuller meant.

"Tell him you know he won't put you and your child on a raft unless it's necessary. Just let him know you trust him to do what's best."

Jenny's shoulders sagged in relief. She didn't have to talk Mac into doing what she wanted. She could trust him. "All right," she said, nodding at Mrs. Tuller.

That's what she had wanted to tell Mac. But he had stormed off, refusing to let her speak.

Through the night Jenny nursed William whenever he fussed, which was every couple of hours. She tried to feed and change him quickly, so Mac, who slept beneath the wagon, wouldn't wake. He needed to be alert during the day.

When Jenny climbed out of the wagon at dawn, Mac was gone. He returned to grab breakfast and hitch the oxen. She didn't try to talk to him about the river. She merely smiled and asked if he wanted more potatoes.

Jenny saddled Poulette and walked the mare to the Pershings' camp. "Want to ride today?" she asked Esther.

"What will you do?"

"I'll walk beside you," Jenny said.

"What about William?"

"I can carry him. It's a nice morning."

"Will you give him to me when you get tired?"

Jenny nodded.

Mac rode by on Valiente as the wagons pulled into line. He glanced at the girls and frowned.

The route followed the Columbia for a few miles, then ascended a bluff. As the path grew steeper, Jenny panted in the heat. When she paused to catch her breath, Mac wheeled Valiente around in front of her.

"Why'd you give Poulette to Esther?" he asked.

"She's tired," Jenny said, hugging William, who wailed in protest. Jenny hadn't told Mac Esther was pregnant, and she didn't know if he'd heard it from anyone else.

She thought Mac swore under his breath as he reached down. "Give me the baby," he said. "We'll all ride Valiente." He took William in one arm, then lifted Jenny behind him with his other arm. "Hang on."

The sun shone on Jenny's bonnet, and Mac's back was warm against her cheek. William stopped fussing and went to sleep, rocked by Valiente's easy gait. Jenny almost dozed herself after her sleepless nights.

"Why are we climbing?" she asked.

"John Day River. Need to find a place to cross."

"Who's scouting?"

"Zeke and his father."

"How's Captain Pershing doing?"

Mac shrugged. "Fine, as long as he doesn't get any whiskey."

Around noon Zeke appeared. "We can eat at that meadow," he said waving at a bare patch of dry grass.

Mac chuckled. "That's what we're calling a meadow now?"

Zeke grinned. "Teams'll appreciate the grass, even if you don't."

After their meal Mac told Jenny to ride Poulette. "And tie the baby to you," he said. "The canyon down to John Day is steep."

Another hour of travel brought them to the brink of the John Day gorge. The stream below roiled over rocks as it flowed north to the Columbia. Zeke led the wagons down the route he and his father had picked out.

Jenny took William and Jonah with her on Poulette, William in a cloth sling strapped to her chest, and Jonah in another pouch on her back. Esther walked beside them using both hands to scramble down the canyon.

At the bottom, Jenny watched the men hitch teams behind the wagons to control the descent. Boulders on the trail caused the wheels to cant and rock, but none of the wagons overturned. When they reached the ravine floor, a few men started wading the John Day. Slippery rocks on the river bottom made for treacherous passage.

"Everyone on horseback or in a wagon," Mac shouted. "Too slick to ford on foot." He guided Poulette across with Jenny and the two babies. Daniel put Esther behind him on his horse.

Once across, the women started to climb the western bluff. "You ride now," Jenny told Esther. "I'll walk."

"Captain McDougall wanted you to ride."

"Well, I want you on Poulette. I'd rather walk." Jenny was tired of swaying on Poulette as the mare swung from hip to hip on the steep slopes. They strapped the babies to Esther, and Jenny boosted her friend into the saddle.

By the time they reached the plateau on the west side of the John Day, it was evening. The first arrivals set up camp while others drove the last of the wagons.

Jenny loosened her sunbonnet and lifted her face to the late afternoon sun. "At least we're south of the Columbia," she said to Esther. She pointed to the north bank. "Bluffs on the other side are even higher."

Esther took Jonah and went to start supper. Jenny started a pot of stew simmering, then fed William. Finally, she had a moment to take out her journal:

> *Saturday, September 25th—Crossed the John Day. The cliffs and rocks and dry grass never end. I must speak with Mac.*

Jenny waited for Mac to finish assisting the last of the wagons. He dropped wearily to the ground beside their fire.

"Here," she said, handing him a dipper of water. "I'll dish up the stew." Meat, potatoes, and greens swam in a savory sauce. She ladled a plate for Mac.

He wolfed down half his food, then glanced up. "Aren't you eating?"

"In a minute. May I tell you something?"

Mac looked at her, his brow furrowed.

Jenny rushed her words. "I won't bother you about rafting the Columbia. If you decide that's best, I trust you." She stopped and smiled. "I mean it." She dished herself a plate and sat down beside him.

He ate in silence, frowning whenever he looked at her.

Chapter 76: Talk About Marriage

Although the next day was Sunday, the emigrants continued along the Columbia west of the John Day River. Mac led a brief prayer in the morning before they set out. He thought his words sounded stilted, unaccustomed as he was to making up prayers.

Mac found himself riding Valiente beside Doc's wagon, which led for the day. Mrs. Tuller wasn't there—she must be walking with other women. Jenny rode Poulette with William. It irritated him when she let Esther ride the pony. He'd bought the mare to make the trek easier for Jenny.

They traveled beneath a high ridge that loomed a thousand feet above the Columbia. Across the wide river more hills rose like camel backs, one after the other as far upstream and downstream as Mac could see. To the west was a huge shimmering mountain, covered with snow and barely visible against pale blue sky.

Mac pointed out the mountain to Doc. "Mount Hood," he said.

The doctor grunted.

"Pershing says we're coming up on the Columbia gorge. About where we hit the Deschutes River."

Doc looked out toward the horizon.

Mac quit trying to make conversation. He was about to ride back along the wagons when Doc spoke. "You been thinking about what I said at Whitmans' place?"

"What?" But Mac knew what Doc meant.

Doc fixed a steely eye on Mac. "The mission at the Dalles is run by a Methodist preacher."

"Jenny doesn't expect me to marry her."

"What's so all-fired important you need to go back to Boston? I ain't heard you talking about a job. You ain't said much about family. Nothing about a sweetheart." Doc's hands twitched on his reins.

"My brother wants me to join his law practice."

"That what you want?"

Mac shrugged. "It's a good life."

"You could have a good life in Oregon. You done well leading this company. The West needs educated men like you."

Mac stared at the sky. How had he been roped into this conversation? The Tullers wouldn't let Jenny come to harm. Nor would the Pershings. Why was Doc making this so hard? "She has friends now. Which is more than she had in Missouri. Even her mother didn't want her there."

"You think I'll give you an easy out, McDougall?" The doctor's voice grew harsher. "Tell you we'll take care of her? Damn it, she deserves better. She deserves a husband and family."

"She doesn't want a husband, and I doubt I'd be good for her," Mac said.

"You got anyone else you're planning on marrying?"

"No."

"Then it's a matter of will, son, whether you'd be a good husband. Ain't you man enough to do the right thing?"

"Have you told Mrs. Tuller about Jenny and me?" Mac asked.

"Not yet. I'm thinking on it."

"Jenny hasn't said anything to Mrs. Tuller?"

"Not that I know of."

"I need to go check on the other wagons." Mac turned Valiente and started off.

"I ain't letting this go, boy," he heard Doc call after him.

Doc's words echoed in Mac's mind all morning. He watched Jenny when they stopped at noon. She handed him a plate of warmed up stew with a smile. "Not much new to eat," she said. "Will we find provisions at the Dalles?"

Her face glowed when she smiled. She'd have a handsome figure, too, once she lost the weight from carrying a child. He felt an attraction to her. But marriage? She was so young. Had she turned fifteen yet? He didn't even know her birthday.

Jenny still flinched when he touched her unexpectedly. It hadn't even been a year since she was raped. He'd told Doc she didn't want to marry him—Mac didn't think she wanted to marry anyone.

And Mac hadn't planned on marrying either. Not yet. He wanted to finish this adventure to Oregon and return to Boston.

She'd done her share of work through the journey—cooking, cleaning, driving the wagon when needed. She'd saved his life when he had cholera. He'd saved her, and she'd saved him. Didn't that cancel any debts between them?

Still, he'd taken Jenny away from her home, brought her into the wilderness. Did he owe her an offer of marriage? Doc was right—it was the honorable thing to do.

She trusted him. She'd said so the night before, though he didn't know what had brought that on. He was sure she still worried about the rafts— she'd been afraid of rivers the whole journey, and the Columbia would be their greatest challenge. But she wasn't complaining any more.

When Mac finished eating, he stood. "Pack up," he said. "We need to move out."

The afternoon took them through more high cliffs, dry grass, and sand. Once the company was underway, Mac rode Valiente beside Jenny on Poulette. William nestled against her chest in a sling.

"Who's minding our wagon?" she asked.

"Zeke," Mac said.

"Pretty day, isn't it?" Jenny lifted her face to the sun.

"Have you seen Mount Hood?" Mac asked. He pointed out the white peak.

"*Que c'est belle!* And enormous."

"Oregon City is on the other side. We take the river north or the road south." He waited for her to argue for the road.

"Mmm," was all she said.

"Pershing says it's covered with snow all year," Mac said. "We'll be lucky if we don't get fresh snow before Oregon City."

"Snow in September." She shivered.

"Have you enjoyed the journey, Jenny?" Mac asked.

"Enjoyed?" She glared at him. "I've been through rivers and sickness and death and childbirth. No, I haven't enjoyed it. I'm glad I have William.

I'm glad for friends like Esther and the Tullers. But leaving home?" Her voice caught. "I wouldn't have come, if I'd known how hard it would be," she whispered.

"Despite what you left behind?"

Jenny nodded.

So where did that leave them? Mac wondered. She wasn't happy so far from home. "Do you want to go East with me in the spring?" he asked.

She laughed, short and hard. "Do this all over again? With William now? No." She shook her head.

"Do you want to get married? I'd stay here." The words burst out of his mouth. A sense of relief swept through him as he made the offer. They would do what Jenny wanted. The decision was in her hands.

Her face paled. "Married?"

"I didn't think you wanted marriage. That's what I told Doc."

"Doc? You told Doc about us? Lord have mercy." Which was as close to a curse as Mac had ever heard Jenny utter.

"He guessed William wasn't mine. That we weren't married."

"Does Mrs. Tuller know?"

"Doc says he hasn't told her."

"Heaven help me." Jenny held William tightly to her breast.

"I meant it, Jenny. If you want to get married, we will. I'll stay in Oregon."

Jenny lifted her chin. "I don't expect you to stay. Just a few days ago you were going to leave me at the mission. William and I will be fine."

"Does that mean you don't want to marry?"

She shuddered. "I can't marry you. Nor any other man."

Another wave of relief passed through Mac, along with a little wistfulness. She didn't want him. "We'll have to decide what we tell people when I leave."

"Tell them whatever you want, Mac." She sounded weary. "I don't want to lie any more."

"You don't mind people knowing we're not married? That William isn't mine?"

"I didn't ask for any of this. My friends will still care for me. And for William, too."

Zeke rode up. "Indians ahead."

"We'll talk later," Mac said, and rode off with Zeke.

Chapter 77: More Talk About Marriage

Sunday, September 26th—I hardly know what to think after talking with Mac. What should I do?

Jenny sat with William in the wagon after supper. That afternoon they had bartered with Indians for potatoes and fish. Mac was now negotiating with the Indians to guide them across the Deschutes River.

Mrs. Tuller poked her head in the wagon. "May I join you?"

Jenny smiled and nodded, and the doctor's wife climbed up.

"How's our precious baby?" Mrs. Tuller asked.

"Hungry and sleepy," Jenny said. "I wish he ate more and slept less during the day. He fusses all night long."

"Ain't fair women have all the work of babies, when men got the pleasure of making them. Has Captain McDougall changed a diaper yet?"

"I don't expect him to," Jenny said.

"Doc changed quite a few for our boys. I made sure he did. You should work on the captain."

"He has the whole company to worry about. William's my responsibility."

"There's a reason a baby has two parents. You let the captain help."

The words came out without Jenny meaning to say them. "Mac isn't William's father."

Mrs. Tuller gasped.

Jenny blurted out the rest of the story. "Evil men in Missouri. One of them's the father. I had to leave. Mac rescued me, but he doesn't want

William. Or me. It's all just a lark to him."

Mrs. Tuller's arms came around her as Jenny wept. William, caught between the two women, wailed his discomfort.

"Doc," Mrs. Tuller called, "come get the baby."

Doc took William, and Jenny cried into Mrs. Tuller's shoulder.

"Now tell me about it, child," Mrs. Tuller commanded gently.

"Three men. Before Christmas. They were after me again. Mac killed one, I shot another, and we ran away. I couldn't go back. Mac wouldn't leave me, so here I am."

"William's the result of these men hurting you?"

Jenny nodded, still sobbing. "I love William, but Mac can't. He can't love me either."

"But he married you—"

Jenny shook her head. "We're not married. He told Captain Pershing we were, so we could join the company."

Mrs. Tuller stiffened. "You're not married?"

"No, ma'am."

"And you've been living together all this time? Captain McDougall saw you birth the baby?"

"Yes, ma'am."

"Well, I never."

"He asked me to marry him, but I can't. He hasn't touched me. We've been proper."

"Nothing about this is proper. How on earth have you kept quiet so long?"

"Mac's a good man. He hasn't done anything wrong. It's all me."

"Oh, hush, child. You didn't cause any of this. But you've certainly got yourself in a pickle. Now what are we going to do?" Mrs. Tuller held Jenny's shoulders and looked her in the eye. "Does Doc know?"

"Mac said Doc guessed."

Mrs. Tuller clucked her tongue. "And he didn't tell me?" She got to her feet, ducking so she didn't hit the wagon cover. "Come with me. We'll get you back with William. Doc and I will talk tonight and decide what to do."

All night Jenny tossed and turned. William roused her frequently, but even without the baby, she wouldn't have slept. What would happen now that the Tullers knew?

Early Monday after nursing William, Jenny peeked out of the wagon, looking to see who might be about. She didn't see Mac or the Tullers, so she climbed down and prepared breakfast.

Mac stopped by the campsite to eat.

"Have you talked to the Tullers?" she asked.

"Why?"

"I told Mrs. Tuller everything. I didn't mean to."

"So now they both know."

"She said she'd talk to the doctor. They'd decide what to do."

"No one can decide what to do except us." Mac scowled. "You said you didn't want to get married. Don't let anyone push you into doing something you don't want."

Jenny grimaced. "Easy for you to say. You're a grown man."

"And you're a grown woman. Don't act like a little girl."

"Women never get a say in what happens to them." Her throat choked, and unshed tears pricked her eyes.

"Women do what they damn well please often enough." Mac looked exasperated. "This is your decision."

"Don't swear at me."

"You know what'll happen, don't you? The Tullers will tell us we should get married. You said you didn't want to. Have you changed your mind?"

"I don't want to get married," Jenny said, thinking of the Johnson men and Bart Peterson. "Do you?"

"I won't let us be forced into anything." Mac slapped his hat on his head. "I have to go. Indians are taking us to the Deschutes."

Jenny set out walking beside the wagon, lost in thought. Mac was a good man, she knew, but marriage? The thought of any man touching her made her cringe. She couldn't be a good wife to Mac—nor to any man.

Esther joined her in midmorning, carrying Jonah. "Walking today?" Esther asked.

Jenny smiled. "It's a nice day. How are you doing?"

"Got morning sickness bad. Probably for a few more weeks, Mrs. Tuller says. It should pass about the time we get to Oregon City."

"You saw Mrs. Tuller today?" Jenny tried to ask calmly.

"First thing. She and Doc were talking with Captain McDougall after breakfast. Looked serious. You know what they was talking about?"

"No." Jenny could guess, but she wasn't going to tell Esther.

"My, this boy's getting heavy. And he ain't much more'n two months old." Esther shifted Jonah to her other shoulder. "Daniel says the Deschutes is a bad 'un to cross."

"Why?" Jenny asked.

Esther shrugged. "That's what the Indians told the men last night. Daniel was there. Mac, too. He didn't tell you?"

"No."

"You two sure don't talk much. I make Daniel tell me everything. Daniel says we'll have to ferry the wagons across. Too deep to ford."

Normally, Jenny would worry about the crossing, but with everything else on her mind, she couldn't get too worked up about it. "We've ferried the wagons before."

"But the Deschutes is fast."

Jenny sighed. "I guess we'll see when we get there."

"By midafternoon, Daniel said."

The two girls walked awhile carrying the infants. Jenny glanced sideways at Esther. "You like being married?" she asked.

Esther giggled. "All but the morning sickness. Daniel's so handsome. And strong and kind. I'm glad his father's gone. Daniel gets along with Pa fine now. It's perfect. Except Ma's not here." Her face sobered.

They walked on in silence. Esther was so full of her own bliss that Jenny had nothing to say to her.

"Aren't you happy, Jenny?" Esther's voice broke into Jenny's misery.

Jenny sighed. "I love William. I have friends in this company to replace the family and friends I left behind. I should be happy."

"And you have Captain McDougall. If I didn't have Daniel, and the captain weren't yours, I'd fancy him myself."

"He's not mine. Not like you and Daniel."

"You two must have had a tiff." Esther chuckled. "Anyone with an eye can see how much he cares for you."

Jenny shook her head. "I don't think so."

"Well, it's plain as the nose on your face. He treats you so well, always helping you into the wagon. Riding with you along the trail."

"You don't know everything, Esther."

"He doesn't beat you, does he?" Esther's voice was full of horror.

"Of course not." Jenny was shocked Esther would think Mac hurt her.

"Well, some husbands do, you know. Of course, Daniel wouldn't dream of it. Though I wonder about his pa." Esther shifted Jonah to her other shoulder. "I got to go put Jonah down. He's heavy." Esther headed toward her wagon, leaving Jenny and William alone.

Mrs. Tuller must have been waiting to find Jenny by herself, because she appeared as soon as Esther left.

"I talked to the doctor," Mrs. Tuller announced. "We think you and Captain McDougall should get married at The Dalles."

"I don't want to get married," Jenny said. "I've told Mac no."

"Don't you want your baby to have a name?"

Jenny lifted her chin. "He has a name. William Calhoun. He can use that, or McDougall, if Mac doesn't mind."

"Everyone thinks you and the captain are already married. When he leaves, you can't simply change your name back to Calhoun. And you can't keep using his name."

"Why not?"

"What if he marries someone else?"

"Who'll know if he's in Boston and I'm in Oregon?"

"Don't you want to do the right thing, child?"

"The right thing?" Jenny said in a choked voice. "Who's done the right thing by me? I was raped. Had to leave my home. William's the only good thing that happened to me this year. William, and the friends I've met in this company."

"William needs a father."

"Mac doesn't care for him like a father should."

Zeke rode up to the women. "Deschutes River a mile ahead. We'll eat, then cross. We found a place to ford."

Chapter 78: Celilo Falls

The wagons sat on the east side of the Deschutes River where it joined the Columbia. The Deschutes was a hundred yards wide with a rapid current. High cliffs rose above both sandy banks.

Mac rode Valiente over to Franklin Pershing, who stood listening to the Indian guides argue among themselves. "What's going on?"

Pershing scratched his beard. "Some think we should ford, others want to float the wagons." He pointed at a sand bar where the Deschutes pushed into the Columbia. "If we ford, we cross to that island, then to the far side. Can't go direct across. Too deep."

"Sand looks too soft to bear the wagons. What if we cross upriver?"

Pershing shook his head. "Zeke and Joel rode a few miles south to look. The rapids are too steep and rocky. River drops twenty feet in thirty yards. And above the cascade, there's deep pools. Best to cross here."

"All right." Mac nodded. "Empty a wagon and try the ford."

"We'll take one of mine." Pershing walked off, shouting orders at Zeke and Joel.

Mac helped the Pershings unload their wagon. Zeke drove it to the sand bar, an Indian guide wading ahead. The wheels sunk in the sand, but the team pulled the wagon over the bar, into the churning water beyond it, then on to the west bank.

"Let's try a wagon half full, with extra teams," Mac said.

The second wagon made it across as well, though the teams strained to get the load across the wet sand.

"It'll take all afternoon to haul everything," Pershing said. "Two trips for every wagon."

Mac shrugged. "What choice do we have?"

He ordered one platoon to unload on the near side of the river, another to reload on the far bank. By now the travelers were expert at tackling these tasks. Some women tended large stewpots and brought plates to feed the men, others minded the children or crossed the river to sort wet provisions and repack wagons.

Mud from churning wagon wheels and animal hooves was visible well into the Columbia's current. By late afternoon all wagons had crossed. None had capsized, though one of the few remaining barrels of flour had fallen into the water and been lost.

Men's shirts stuck to their backs with sweat and their chests heaved from the grueling work. Oxen hung their heads, blowing and snorting. "We'll rest here," Mac decided.

"There's a better camp at the top of the hill," Joel said.

"It's steep, and we're tired," Mac said.

"Better grass above. More space to spread out."

Mac squinted at the slope of the hill. "We'll have to double team the wagons again." He turned to the men. "Do we have another hill in us?" he asked.

A few nods, no verbal dissents.

"All right. Let's go."

The sun had almost set when the last wagon reached the plateau. As Joel had promised, the grass was thicker, but wind howled down the Columbia River gorge. "Take care with fires and tents," Mac told the sergeants as he headed to his wagon and Jenny.

She handed him a plate of stew when he dropped to the ground beside her.

"It's what we ate at noon," she said. "No time to cook anything new."

"I'm too tired to care."

Cool air gusted across the plateau—a sign of autumn. Brilliant stripes of red and white light rose in the sky beyond the Columbia. "Northern lights," Mac said, pointing out the luminous display to Jenny.

"Mmm." She paused, then whispered, "Mrs. Tuller talked to me again."

"I told you, Jenny, no one can make us get married if we don't want to."

"Do *you* want to?" she asked. "Really, what do *you* want?"

Mac exhaled slowly. He should have given her money and left her in Independence. Money would have helped her avoid the stigma of being alone and pregnant. She would have been all right. "Jenny, I made you an offer, and I meant it. I will marry you and stay in Oregon if that's what you want. I became responsible for you when I took you away from your home. We've done well together. Most men and women can't say any more than that."

"Do you love me?"

Love? He'd wondered that once or twice himself. She was a pretty thing. He liked her well enough, better than most girls he knew back East. She worked hard. He remembered her soft, cool hand on his forehead at Ash Hollow. How she pestered him about caring for her baby if she died. Her smile and windblown hair as they stood together on the banks of the Snake. "I find you pleasing. We could make a good life together."

"You'd want to bed me."

Mac knew how she felt about men, but bedding was part of marriage. "Yes."

"You could bed me without loving me?"

"Most men can." He had with Bridget.

"I can't," she said, her voice choked. "I don't know if I could even if you loved me. I won't marry a man who doesn't love me. And William, too."

"Then you've decided."

"But the Tullers are set on us marrying."

"What's the worst can they do? Tell the rest of the wagon train?"

Jenny's eyebrows shot up her forehead. "You think they would?"

"What difference does it make?"

"No difference to you." Jenny's voice cracked. "You're leaving come spring. I'll be in Oregon with these people."

"I'll talk to the Tullers." Mac sighed. Jenny was right. He had to make sure she wouldn't be pilloried once he left.

In the morning Mac found Doc. "Jenny talked with Mrs. Tuller yesterday," he began.

"So I heard." Doc quirked his eyebrow while lighting his pipe.

"Jenny doesn't want to marry me."

"Did you ask her right?"

"What do you mean?"

"Did you ask her like you meant it?"

"I did mean it. I told her we could make a good life. I told her I'd stay here with her. I can't lie and say I love her. She still said no."

"So you've done your best, McDougall?" Doc puffed on his pipe.

Mac nodded. He'd taken Jenny away from a miserable situation in Missouri, and she had become his responsibility. He'd tried to do the right thing. What more could he do? "It'll be all right if you and Mrs. Tuller don't tell anyone."

Doc squinted, his brow furrowed. "Don't you know us better than that by now? We won't hurt Jenny. Nor her child."

Mac saddled Valiente and ordered the wagons to fall in line. They were following the Columbia again, west toward The Dalles.

Zeke rode up to Mac. "Celilo Falls straight ahead. No room past 'em on the bank. We'll have to climb the hills."

Mac cupped his ear. "Is that what I hear? I thought it was the wind."

Zeke shook his head. "Nope. It's Celilo."

"Have you found a campsite for tonight?"

"Not yet. Joel and I'll ride ahead. Doubt we can make The Dalles tonight. Take another day."

"Let me know what you find," Mac said.

Flashing a grin, Zeke saluted and rode off.

Mac was eager to reach The Dalles so he could decide on the route to Oregon City. But for now, he would spend the afternoon with Jenny, he decided, heading Valiente back toward the wagons.

"Jenny," he called when he approached their wagon. "Let's go see the falls. I'll saddle Poulette."

"What about William?"

"Put him in the sling."

Jenny smiled and gathered up William.

Mac left Pershing in charge and escorted Jenny through the hills toward the river. Esther and Daniel went with them, Esther carrying Jonah. It was as nice a day as when the four of them had ridden to the natural rock bridge, back in mid-June, over three months ago.

So much had happened, Mac mused. Esther and Daniel married. Jonah born, Mrs. Pershing dead. Pershing displaced, and Mac now leading the wagons. Abercrombie and his platoon gone. William. What more would happen before they reached Oregon City?

"*Mon Dieu!*" Jenny exclaimed at the edge of the bluff above the falls. Mac could barely hear her over the roar of the water.

The Columbia, a mile wide in some places, here squeezed between rocks only sixty feet apart. The rushing current cascaded between basalt cliffs in a roiling froth of spray and waves, eddying at the bottom in large whirlpools.

"People float through that?" Jenny asked.

"Pa says people portage around the falls," Esther said, her voice filled with awe.

"A body couldn't possibly survive those rapids," Daniel said, wiping a hand across his face. "And the falls beneath The Dalles are worse."

Mac grunted. He hoped the Barlow Road would be the better option, for Jenny's sake. But he had to reserve judgment.

"Look!" Esther said, pointing at Indians fishing in the churning waters. They balanced on rocks in the water or on rickety wooden scaffolding cantilevered over the raging current, spears in hand. "How do they keep their footing?"

"Don't know," Mac said, "but I hope they'll sell us some salmon."

They rode along the plateau above the river until they came to another stretch of rapids where the Columbia again narrowed and fell amidst large boulders. Spray shot up to the heights where they rode. Jenny pulled the sling more tightly around William as the wind blew mist into their faces.

"We'd best get back to the wagons," Mac said, grinning. "Don't want them to think we've drowned."

They turned away from the river. Zeke rode toward them. "Camp's just ahead," Zeke said. "Site's got grass, but we'll have to haul water from the river. I left Joel there."

Mac decided to find Joel, and took the touring party with him, letting Zeke return to the wagons alone. The campsite was above a pool of water right below the rapids they had surveyed. More Indians fished in the pool.

"Let's go talk to them," Mac said to Joel. "Daniel, you stay with the women."

Mac and Joel picked their way down to the Columbia and hailed an Indian brave. "Fish?" Mac asked, describing a salmon with his hands.

The Indian nodded and pointed at Mac's shirt. They reached agreement, and Mac took off his shirt in exchange for the salmon.

In the evening, after more bartering between Indians and emigrants, the travelers dined in comfort.

"If only the wind didn't blow so badly," Jenny said, rocking William beside their campfire. "This could be a heavenly place."

Chapter 79: Reaching The Dalles

Jenny had just nursed William the next morning, when Mac told her to hurry breakfast and pack up.

"What's the rush?" she asked.

"Pershing says The Dalles is only three or four miles ahead. I want to get there by noon."

Jenny sighed and took out a skillet to fry a piece of the salmon from the Indians. She didn't feel well, her chest tight and her head pounding. Had she sickened on the ride to Celilo Falls? William was only two weeks old—was childbirth fever still possible? She didn't want to talk to Doc. He would tell her to marry Mac. Maybe the fever would pass.

Jenny washed up after breakfast with water Mac hauled from the river, then climbed into the wagon. She didn't have the energy to ride Poulette. She wasn't sure she could even hold William. She left him on a blanket in the wagon while she sat on the bench.

They bounced along through the morning. Jenny's back ached with the strain of sitting upright. She crawled under the wagon cover to feed William, then let him fuss when she returned to the bench.

Esther walked over midmorning with Jonah. "May I join you?" she asked, her foot and one hand on the wagon wheel before Jenny could stop her.

"I have a fever," Jenny said. "Better keep Jonah away."

Esther's face paled. "I'll get Doc."

"No," Jenny said.

But Esther was already gone.

Doc arrived, and motioned Jenny to pull her wagon out of line. "Hear you're sick," he said, climbing up beside her. "Let's take a look."

He felt her forehead, asked some questions.

"Not childbirth fever," he said. "Can't tell what it is. Drink lots of water and stay quiet."

"Thank you, Doc," Jenny said.

He glared at her. "You and McDougall are damn fools."

"What do you mean?" Jenny asked. Her head throbbed. She didn't want to argue.

"Only way out of this mess is for the two of you to marry."

"He doesn't want to marry me," Jenny whispered. "And I don't want to marry anyone." She shuddered.

"McDougall's a good man." The doctor's voice was gentler. "Not like the bastards who raped you."

"I know."

"Think on it, girl. Your baby needs a father."

The doctor left, and Jenny sat shivering on the wagon seat. She couldn't think about anything, let alone marriage. The hot sun beat down on her sunbonnet, but she couldn't get warm. William fussed through the morning. She fed him, but otherwise left him alone in the back.

In late morning the wagons descended from the hills to the rude buildings of the Methodist Mission at The Dalles.

"It's called Wascopam," Mac told Jenny. "Must be an Indian name."

Jenny stayed by the wagon, too sick to want to look around. Mac and others went into the mission. They were soon back.

"Not much here," Mac said. "A school, a barn, and a couple of houses."

"A school?" Jenny asked. She hadn't seen a school building since they left Missouri.

"For the Indians. And some huts where the Indians live. Don't know where Doc got the idea there was a preacher here."

"No preacher? Then we couldn't have married."

"We wouldn't have anyway, Jenny." Mac sighed. "But there's no chance of it now. Preacher's gone. He sold the mission to the Whitmans. Dr. Whitman is here. Doc's talking to him now."

"What do they say about floating the river?" Jenny hoped they would lay by for a couple of days. Maybe she'd feel better after a rest.

Mac shook his head. "River's low now, so the rapids are bad. We'd have to portage around the falls. And there's a wait to build rafts, but we need to check at Chenoweth Creek. That's about five miles downstream."

"How about the road? What was it called? Barlow?"

"It turns south right around here." Mac waved his hand toward the hills. "I'll take some men down to Chenoweth this afternoon. See what's there. Then we'll decide." He saddled Valiente. As he mounted he looked at Jenny. "You all right? You look peaked."

Jenny nodded. "Doc says I'm fine."

Mrs. Tuller came over after Mac left. "Let me take William," she said. "You rest."

"I should do laundry," Jenny protested. "The diapers—"

"You need to keep your strength up to care for your son."

Jenny climbed in the wagon and took out her journal.

Wednesday, September 29ᵗʰ—At The Dalles. The mission here is shabby and rude. The heat is oppressive, and I am sick.

Jenny slept until late afternoon. She heard William crying and stuck her head out of the wagon. "I'll take him, Mrs. Tuller."

"Feeling better?" Mrs. Tuller handed her the baby.

Jenny sat under the wagon cover to nurse him. "A little. My head still hurts. And my throat."

"Men aren't back yet. Esther and I've been wondering why they're gone so long. Five miles is an easy ride." Mrs. Tuller climbed up on the wagon bench.

As Jenny finished feeding William, a shout sounded from downstream.

"The Abercrombies!" Esther cried.

Jenny looked out. Mac and a large man—Samuel Abercrombie—rode horseback ahead of a small group of wagons.

Daniel ran to meet them and pumped his father's hand. "You're back!" Daniel shouted.

The Abercrombie party worked their wagons into the company's camp. By the time they were settled, a large crowd had gathered, Jenny among them.

"What's the story?" Doc asked.

"Goddamn English don't know what they're doing," Abercrombie bellowed. "Can't build enough rafts to get folks to Oregon City."

"Is that true?" Jenny asked Mac when he walked Valiente over beside her.

"There's a long wait for rafts. The Abercrombies had been waiting a week already."

"Running out of flour and everything else." Abercrombie continued to shout at anyone who listened. "Got my name on the list for a raft. But I might as well hear what y'all have to say about taking the goddamn road around Mount Hood. At least it's run by Americans."

Pershing and Zeke rode into camp after everyone else was settled. Jenny saw the captain stagger as he got off his horse. Zeke reached out a hand to his father, but Pershing waved him off.

Chapter 80: Deciding on the Route

When the commotion over the Abercrombie platoon returning died down, Mac sought out Doc. "Can we talk?" he asked.

The doctor gestured at a dusty rock near his fire. "Have a seat."

"What do you think about taking the river or Barlow Road?" Mac exhaled deeply. "Neither way's easy." He wanted to take the road for Jenny's sake, but he couldn't make decisions for the whole company based on her fears.

"Why ask me?" Doc pulled out his pipe and a small pouch of tobacco.

"Can't ask Pershing. He's in no shape tonight."

"Drinking?" Doc frowned, his bushy eyebrows furrowing.

Mac nodded. "I smelled it on him. Wish I knew where he got the liquor. Zeke and Joel say they don't know. Must have been the English."

"Talk to him. He still knows more'n the rest of us." The doctor tapped tobacco shavings into his pipe bowl and lit it. "What'd they say at Chenoweth?"

"They want to sell us rafts."

"Abercrombie seems set on the road." Doc puffed on the pipe.

"That's because he's disgusted with the wait for rafts. He'll change his mind if it suits him later." Mac sighed. "I don't know whether I'm glad he's back or not." He looked at the doctor. "So what do you think?

"Hell, I don't know. I'm a doctor, not a trail captain. Talk to Pershing. Drunk or not, the man won't put his children in harm's way."

"All right. I will." Mac stood and brushed the dirt off his trousers. "We have to decide tonight. Abercrombie'll be chomping at the bit to be underway tomorrow."

At the Pershing wagons, Mac asked Zeke, "Where's your father?"

Zeke waved toward the back of the wagon, where Mac found Pershing cleaning his boots. He could smell stale whiskey, but the man didn't seem drunk.

"What do you think about Barlow Road?" Mac asked, squatting on the ground beside the older man.

Pershing looked up, then returned to scraping his boots. "Don't know any more'n you. Goes around Mount Hood, straight into Oregon City. Saves rafting down the Columbia, then up the Willamette." Pershing put one boot down and picked up the other. "River's low, so rafting is dangerous. But we could get snow in the mountains."

"How bad's the river?"

"Let's go look." Pershing pulled on his boots, stood, then called to his sons, "Zeke, Joel, come on."

The four men walked to the shore of the Columbia. Pershing gestured with a sweep of his arm. "We're at The Dalles. Means 'rapids' in French."

"Rafts have been floating down this all day," Mac said. "Most aren't having any trouble."

"I saw one overturn," Pershing said. "Man and two children died. Downstream, the river's worse."

"How bad?"

"See that rock?" Pershing waved at a boulder in the middle of the Columbia.

"The smooth one with moss on its side?" It was larger than a horse.

"We'll be dodging even bigger rocks for hours down river."

Mac squinted at Pershing. "Then why would we take the river?"

"Used to be the only way. Even now, some folks has had enough of mountains."

"What do you think we should do?"

Pershing rubbed the toe of his newly cleaned boot in the mud. "Winter could come on any time. But I reckon the road's still safer. A body's got more control on firm land than in the water. 'Tain't natural to ride a boat if we don't have to." He shook his head. "All the way to Fort Vancouver on a raft—ain't how I want to die."

"Then Barlow Road it is," Mac said. "I'll call the men together."

383

"Listen up." It was almost dark, and Mac had gathered the men. He held up a hand and waited for the chitchat to die down. He awkwardly bounced William in his other arm to keep him from crying. Jenny was exhausted, and Mac had taken the baby to give her a rest.

When the men quieted, he announced, "I've decided on Barlow Road."

"River's quicker." Abercrombie spat out the words, followed by a long stream of tobacco juice. "Ain't no rafts now, but once we git 'em, they'd be faster. You know much about this road, McDougall?" As Mac had suspected, Abercrombie changed his tune—just to be contrary.

"Be snow in the mountains right soon," Dempsey said. "Fresh snow on the peaks already." So Dempsey was with Abercrombie.

Mac nodded. "We could get snow. But with the wait, the river won't be faster, and it's too dangerous."

"Raft overturned this afternoon," Pershing said. "Two children drowned, and their pa with them."

"Here's what I've heard," Mac said, facing the group. "Barlow Road's been open a year now. Most of the stumps are cleared away. We should make good time around Mount Hood."

"If it don't snow," Dempsey interrupted.

"If we take the river," Mac continued, "It'll take a week or more to build rafts. That's what Abercrombie found out." He nodded at Abercrombie. Maybe that would mollify him. "Then we have to portage around the rapids. Or we drive the wagons as far as we can. In either case, below the rapids we rebuild the rafts or wait for the Vancouver ferry. Could take weeks, if the ferry's backed up like the raft builders are."

"Least we won't freeze on the river." Abercrombie punctuated his comment with another hiss of tobacco juice.

Doc stood in the back of the group, smiling, his arms crossed across his chest. "What do you think, Doc?" Mac asked, jostling William faster.

"You're captain, McDougall. Your call."

Abercrombie snorted. "Only because you made it happen, Doc."

"He was voted in, Abercrombie." The doctor's voice was composed, but steely. "You can't object now. Particularly not after leaving us."

"Maybe I should call for another vote." Abercrombie's hands folded into fists, though he didn't move into a fighting stance.

"Now, Pa." Daniel put a hand on his father's arm. "We ain't got far to go. Let's get to Oregon and claim our land."

Abercrombie turned to his son. "You've taken Pershing's side ever since you married his girl. Never thought I'd see my boy henpecked."

"Now, Pa—"

"Son, you better decide which side your bread's buttered on. Going to work for me or that drunk Pershing?"

"Hold on!" Pershing sprang up from his seat on a log by the fire. "I'd still be leading this company, Abercrombie, except you stuck your nose in where it don't belong."

"Come on, men," Mac said. He was losing control. He couldn't concentrate while jiggling the fretting baby. "Barlow Road is our best option. Nobody's convinced me otherwise."

"Ain't that what your little gal wants?" Abercrombie sneered. "You're as bad as Daniel. Letting your wife lead you by the nose."

William let out a poorly timed wail. Mac patted the baby's back, while turning toward his wagon. "Jenny?" he called. "Come get the baby. I can't talk while he's crying."

Jenny appeared and silently took William. She wheezed, as if trying not to cough.

"Mountains or river, neither's a cakewalk," Abercrombie said. "Y'all think young McDougall here can get us through? I say we vote him out."

Pershing stepped forward toward Abercrombie. "You been spoiling for a fight since we left Missouri. You had your chance. Twice you was voted down. You left. If you want to stay this time, shut your trap."

"Last time was rigged. Doc and Hewitt counted the ballots. They was both backing McDougall."

Hewitt sprang to his feet from the log where he sat. "You saying I cheated? Say it to my face, Abercrombie. Flat out. I'll show you who cheated."

Mac held up a hand. "Fighting won't get us to Oregon City. Let's stick to deciding our route."

"He's asking for it," Hewitt muttered.

Mac looked around. Zeke and Pershing stood next to Hewitt—all three men's fists clenched. Abercrombie stood with his chin thrust out, his hand near the knife on his belt. Daniel's gaze darted back and forth from Mac to his father.

Abercrombie was the problem. Still. Mac pointed at him and said, "Abercrombie, you've been chomping at the bit the whole way, wanting to move faster. Well, I'm convinced Barlow Road is the fastest path to Oregon City. And the safest."

Abercrombie didn't relax his stance, but said nothing.

"Any questions?" Mac asked.

Most of the men shook their heads. Others stared at the ground.

"Pershing," Mac asked. "You with me?"

Pershing nodded. "Road can't be worse'n the river."

Zeke nodded as well.

"Doc?"

Doc waved a hand. "You're captain. Whatever you say, I'm with you."

"Hewitt?"

Hewitt still glared at Abercrombie. He turned to Mac. "I'm with you," he said through his teeth.

"How about the rest of you?" Mac asked, looking around the circle. "Anyone still want to argue for the river?"

"Barlow Road's fine with me," Daniel said.

Abercrombie spat on the ground and stalked off.

Chapter 81: Heading for Barlow Gate

Friday, October 1ˢᵗ—We start for Barlow Road today. I am thankful we will not float the Columbia. My fever and cough persist.

Jenny looked up from her notebook. The morning was cool, but the clear sky promised another beautiful autumn day. She relished the dry air and brilliant sun, though the wind still blustered through the river gorge.

After breakfast Mac saddled Poulette. Jenny didn't feel up to walking. "When will we reach Barlow Road?" she asked Mac.

"It's all Barlow Road from here," he said. "But it'll take us a couple of days to get to the toll gate."

The wagons climbed through sandy soil covered with dry, sparse grass. Soon they were in hills requiring slow ascents and careful descents. The climbs were longer than the downhill stretches, and they left the Columbia behind. The grass gave way to heavily wooded slopes, much like the treacherous Blue Mountains.

The oxen were exhausted after months on the trail. Even sure-footed Poulette stumbled. Jenny wondered if she would be safer walking, but she was too tired to suggest it. Coughing used up all her energy. So she simply hung on, William strapped to her chest.

At noon Esther and Jenny prepared dinner together, the babies beside them. Jenny tried to hide her coughing, but Esther noticed.

"You still sick?" Esther asked. "But I'd rather hear you hacking than Mr. Abercrombie yelling." She shook her head. "Daniel's so happy to have his family back, but his pa just shouts at him."

"How's your papa?" Jenny asked.

Esther pursed her lips. "He's poorly, too. Zeke says he's been in the wagon all morning."

Mac had told Jenny Captain Pershing bought whiskey at The Dalles. But she didn't mention it to Esther. "You'll have to take him some soup."

After the noon meal, they climbed higher into the mountains, the ground damp as if it had rained recently. Poulette's hooves skittered over slippery wet rocks. In midafternoon Jenny dismounted and walked beside Poulette, carrying William in the sling. She sometimes grabbed the saddle for balance, but at least the mare didn't have to bear her weight.

Late in the day Mac rode Valiente over to Jenny. "Why aren't you riding?" he asked.

"Poulette's tired."

"Aren't you tired?"

"Yes, but—"

Mac got off Valiente. "Get on." He lifted Jenny and William onto the mare. "And stay on. Camp's only a mile ahead. Don't get off Poulette until we stop."

Jenny was glad she'd decided not to marry Mac. It was bad enough how he ordered her around now. If they were married, he'd have a right to tell her what to do. She fumed as Poulette picked her way down the hill to the creek.

She was still angry when Mac returned to their wagon for supper. "I wish you wouldn't tell me what to do," she said, handing him a plate of salmon and potatoes.

Mac took off his hat and rubbed his forehead. "Sometimes you ask me what to do. Now you tell me not to. What do you want from me?"

Jenny put her hands on her hips. "If you can't tell the difference between asking if you want to get married and deciding for myself whether to walk or ride, then I don't want anything from you." She wanted to stalk off, but there was nowhere to go, and she had to feed William. She picked up the baby and climbed into the wagon, coughing as she did so. Mac wouldn't follow her if he thought she was nursing William.

But he did. She had unbuttoned her blouse when Mac stuck his head into the back of the wagon. She quickly lifted William's blanket up to cover her breasts.

Mac ducked out of the wagon. "Sorry," he said. "But we need to talk."

Jenny paused. What did he want to talk about? "All right," she said. "Let me get William to sleep first."

She took her time nursing William. When he dozed, she rocked him while she hummed a lullaby. She couldn't sing without coughing, but humming soothed her throat. When the baby was a solid weight in her arms, she placed him on a blanket and climbed out of the wagon.

"Yes?" she said to Mac.

Mac didn't look at her. He simply stared at the fire, his journal on his lap. "We can't keep on like this, Jenny."

"What do you mean?"

"Upset with each other. I'm doing the best I can, but you're always angry with me."

Jenny's eyes filled with tears. "I'm sorry." But Mac had no right to order her around.

"What were you so mad about at supper?"

It seemed silly to put into words. "You ordered me to ride Poulette."

Mac stood and threw up his hands. "You're making yourself sick, walking when you have the mare. I can't worry about you and manage the company both."

"Do you have to keep telling me what to do?"

"You don't have enough sense to take care of yourself."

Jenny stared at him. "Do you really believe that?" Then why was he leaving her alone?

Mac gazed into the fire. "No," he said. "But I worry about you."

"I'm not your problem. You're not going to stay." As she said the words, she realized the truth—she really was on her own. She was all William had in the world, and she would have to make a life for herself and her son in Oregon. Without Mac.

Mac was silent a moment, then said, "Let's just get to Oregon City."

Jenny turned on her heel and climbed back in the wagon. She grabbed her notebook and wrote in the fading light:

October 1ˢᵗ, evening—I am coughing, and both Poulette and I are worn out. No matter. I must be strong. I am all that William has.

In the morning when she awoke, Jenny ached all over. She didn't know if it was from coughing or fever. Rain drummed on the wagon cover, and she was careful not to touch the canvas so the water wouldn't soak in. She nursed William and prayed he would not catch her illness, rocking him as she sat in the wagon shivering.

Mac had Poulette saddled when Jenny got out of the wagon. She held her buffalo robe over her head and shoulders to stay dry.

"Ride Poulette today," Mac said. He tipped her chin up so she had to look at him. "Please." His finger brushed a raindrop off her cheek.

Jenny nodded. "I'll get breakfast."

She didn't bother with a fire. The wood was too damp. She served Mac cold salmon and leftover biscuits, then washed the dishes quickly.

Jenny held the buffalo skin tightly around herself and William as they rode Poulette through the hills. Mac rode beside her on Valiente.

"We should reach the Barlow gate by day's end," he said.

"That's good," Jenny said. She clenched her teeth to keep them from chattering. Her skirt and shoes below the buffalo hide were soaked.

"Pershing says we could have crossed the Deschutes near here," Mac said. "Would have been easier than at the Columbia. But then we wouldn't have gone through The Dalles."

"Mmm," Jenny couldn't talk. She could barely cling to Poulette and keep William covered. Her head throbbed, and she stifled a cough.

All morning they climbed. More sage covered the land along the trail, with occasional scrubby pines in sheltered dells between the hills.

Mac called the noon halt near the top of a ridge. There was no shelter from the wind and rain, and no water other than what fell from the sky.

"Zeke and Daniel have found a campsite for tonight," Jenny heard him tell the men. "We'll have water and grass for the teams then."

"Will it quit raining?" someone asked.

Mac laughed. "Can't promise that."

Jenny tried to build a fire under the edge of a tarp she strung between two wagons, wanting a hot drink at least. The wet wood smoked, causing her to cough violently. The fire hissed and spat steam as she fried meat and boiled water, its meager heat barely warming her. Chilblains on her feet itched and pulsed in her wet shoes.

Water dripped off the back of Mac's hat onto his coat when he returned to the wagon, but he didn't seem bothered by it.

"Why are you limping?" he asked.

"My feet hurt," Jenny said, swallowing a cough.

"How can your feet hurt? You've been riding all morning."

"They're cold." She knew her tone was terse, and she didn't mean it to be. But if she spoke more than a few words, she'd set to coughing.

Mac took his plate from her, put it on a crate, and sat her on a barrel. "Let's see," he said, taking one of her feet in his hands. "Your shoe's soaked through! The sole's split. How long has it been like that?"

Jenny shrugged. "A week or two. Shortly after we left Whitman Mission."

"Why didn't you say something?"

"Nothing you could do." A huge cough wracked her chest, causing her to double over.

"And your cold is worse. You're in the wagon this afternoon."

She looked at him. "I told you not to order me around."

Mac sighed. "Would you please ride in the wagon this afternoon?"

A wave of exhaustion overcame Jenny. It wasn't worth arguing about. "All right."

Chapter 82: Ascending Barlow Road

October 2, 1847. Reached the east gate of Barlow Road. $5 per wagon—more price gouging, but cheaper than paying for rafts. Jenny is sick, and her shoes have holes. Heavy rain all day.

Mac sat under a tarp beside the wagon. The rain had eased, but everything was wet. Jenny and William were in the wagon. He heard her coughing and the baby fretting. Why hadn't she said she was ill? He couldn't have done anything, but he wanted her to talk to him.

He finished writing and pulled his blanket around him. The ground was muddy, but he couldn't fix that either. Everything was dirty. How much longer would this journey last? He thought they were about two weeks from Oregon City, but he wasn't sure.

The man at the gate had shrugged when Mac asked how long the road would take. "Depends."

"Depends on what?"

"Rain. Snow. Strength of your teams. Weight you're pulling. Whether you break an axle." That wasn't news—all along, their progress had depended on the weather, the animals, and the wagons.

Mac asked another question. "What's the road like?"

The gatekeeper shrugged again. "Rough. Most trees felled, but if you get off the blazed trail, you'll have to cut your own way through. Not much grass. Too many companies been there already this year."

Mac sighed. They called it a road, but it wasn't like the toll roads back East. The man explained that no one had maintained it since Sam Barlow hacked his way through the forest two years earlier. The emigrants would have to cope, whatever condition the road was in.

"Best lighten your loads before you head up," the man continued.

Lighten their loads? Most families had been discarding belongings since they left the Platte. What was left to give up? Mac had few personal possessions, but he wasn't planning to stay in Oregon. Jenny also hadn't brought anything, though she had acquired clothes for herself and William along the way. But most emigrants had brought what they could from home to start their new life in the West.

Mac took the message back to his company. The men shook their heads when he told them to leave what they could behind. Later he saw Doc eyeing the rocking chair his wife had brought from Illinois.

"Going to leave it?" Mac asked.

Doc shook his head. "Brought it this far. Guess I'll keep it, unless it falls off the wagon."

Now, as Mac sat beside his fire, he wondered what perils still awaited them before they reached Oregon City.

The rain ended, but the next day dawned cool and cloudy. They filtered past the toll gate, each man paying for his wagons and livestock.

All day the travelers headed up a rolling grassy plain, laughing as they rode or walked. The route was clear, the trail easy, the rain gone. As they climbed, evergreens pressed in on the wagons, but the company had seen much worse. If this was as bad as Barlow Road got, they had made a good choice compared to rafting down the Columbia's rapids.

Mac worried about Jenny's health. She wasn't any better. He rode Valiente beside her as she carried William on Poulette. "Shall I take William for a while?"

Jenny handed William to him. "You want the sling?"

"Can't I just carry him?"

"If he doesn't tire your arms. He gets heavy."

Mac looked down at William. "This little mite?" He wasn't even three weeks old. He couldn't weigh more than seven or eight pounds. He was a boneless lump, at least when asleep. But Mac remembered when the baby had squirmed and cried while Mac talked with the men.

Jenny muffled a cough in her shawl.

"You feel any better?" Mac asked.

"It's only a cold."

"Have you talked to Doc?"

"I will tonight, if I'm not any better."

Mac reminded himself to find the doctor when they stopped—Jenny wouldn't do it on her own.

"Look! The mountain!" She pointed.

He glanced at a break in the clouds on the horizon. A snowcapped, sunlit peak rose symmetrically to a point high above the hills beneath it.

"Mount Hood," he said. "That's what we're traveling around."

"My stars!" she whispered. "It's huge."

They nooned at the base of a steep hill under a pine-scented forest canopy. After they ate, Mac led the wagons up to a small plateau, where another hill awaited. They skirted that mound, traveled to a small creek, and up the creek to a meadow large enough for the company to camp.

"Water's down the hill," Zeke said. "Not far. Lots of grass."

"Not picked over like the gatekeeper said?" Mac asked.

Zeke shook his head.

"What's our route look like?"

"Daniel and I didn't get far. Gets steeper. We'll set out early ahead of the wagons tomorrow."

Mac found Doc treating one of the Pershing twins for a splinter in his toe.

"Why isn't the boy wearing shoes?" Mac asked.

"Too small," the lad said before the doctor could answer. "I gave 'em to Noah. They's too big for him, but Esther stuffed rags in the toes."

Doc sighed. "All the children need new shoes. Half are going barefoot, and the other half have blisters. Good thing we're almost to Oregon City."

"If there's anything to buy there. And if anyone has any money left." Mac shook his head. "Several families spent their last dollars on the toll. Some got through with barter or credit."

"What you need?" the doctor asked.

"Would you take a look at Jenny? She's been coughing."

Doc patted the Pershing boy on the head and sent him off. He took a hollow, wooden tube out of his medical bag, then followed Mac.

As they walked, the doctor asked, "You thought any more about marrying her?"

"She made the decision," Mac said. "That's the end of it."

Doc sat Jenny down on a log. He put one end of the wooden tube against her chest and the other against his ear, then listened to her breathe. "Not pneumonia," he said. "At least, not yet. Keep your clothes and head dry."

"Then let's hope it doesn't rain," Jenny said smiling.

"Don't laugh, girl. A chill in these mountains can turn to pneumonia quick."

Jenny's face blanched.

"I'll keep her in the wagon tomorrow," Mac said.

"It's getting steep," Jenny said. "What if the oxen can't pull William and me?"

"You ride until they can't," Mac said.

A heavy downpour awoke the company in the morning. Rain fell in sheets and streamed from the trees. The gurgling creek below their camp now foamed over the rocks.

Mac sat under the tarp, huddled in his coat, with William napping beside him. He wrote while Jenny fixed a cold breakfast.

October 4, 1847. Our first day on Barlow Road was easy enough, but the trail is becoming steep. Rain again today. Zeke and Joel have left camp to scout.

He heard a shout and looked up. Joel trotted into camp, water dripping off the brim of his hat.

"What's wrong?" Mac called.

"Fallen tree across the trail." Joel pulled his horse to a stop and dismounted. "Need men to move it."

"Have some breakfast," Jenny offered. She handed Joel a biscuit with a slice of meat in the middle.

Joel nodded his thanks, then said to Mac. "Road gets rough right above here. Can't hardly tell where it's been cleared."

"Can the wagons make it?"

"I think so. But we'll need men ahead to saw up the trees blocking the trail."

"Will two men be enough?"

Joel shrugged. "We'll see."

"Take Daniel and Tanner. If we need more, Abercrombie and I'll join you."

"All right." Joel crammed the last of the biscuit in his mouth and remounted. He tipped his hat at Jenny, which sent a rivulet of water onto his horse's withers.

The morning route paralleled the creek bed. The road was so narrow trees brushed the sides of the wagons as they squeaked along over stumps of felled pines. Mac rode at the head of the wagons and stopped to inspect a freshly sawn pine in the middle of the trail. The trunk was six feet in diameter. The portion that had blocked the trail had been sawed into rounds a foot high and pulled off the road. The rounds bore the marks of the chains needed to haul them.

"Big tree," Pershing said, as he rode up beside Mac.

"Biggest damn trees I've ever seen," Mac said.

Pershing chewed on his pipe stem. "Hope we don't have to clear many more."

But within an hour, they had passed another stump as large as the first, and caught up to the scouts who were sawing yet another tree blocking the path.

"What's it look like ahead?" Mac asked Zeke.

Zeke stopped sawing and mopped his brow. He was soaked to the skin. "Ain't gone any farther," he said. "We've stopped each time we've found a log to clear."

The travelers made slow progress through the day, stopping frequently to clear trees. Mac gave up trying to keep scouts ahead of the wagons and set every able-bodied man to sawing and hauling.

In midafternoon he paused for a drink at his wagon. Jenny and William were inside. Jenny handed him a towel as he drank a dipperful of water from the barrel.

"Staying dry?" he asked.

"It's fine in the wagon," she said. "Will we have to cut down trees all the way to Oregon City?"

"Don't know." Mac sighed. "Nothing has been what we expected so far.

Guess we got off easy yesterday."

Jenny coughed.

"You still sick?" Mac asked.

"Mrs. Tuller brought me some syrup to clear my chest."

"I need to get back to work. Take care of yourself."

When dusk hid the clouds from view, Mac called a halt. "Not much space to camp," he told the men, "But we have water and shrubs for the animals to eat. This is as good as we'll find today."

"How much farther to the summit?" Abercrombie asked.

Mac shrugged. "We've spent all our time felling trees, so we haven't done any scouting. The pines are too dense to see ahead."

"We oughta be scouting," Abercrombie insisted, spitting a dark stream of tobacco juice.

"Then you can scout tomorrow." Mac was too weary to argue.

Before he slept he wrote:

October 4, 1847, evening. Only made eight miles. Chopped trees all day. Abercrombie fights me at every step.

Chapter 83: Trouble Near the Summit

Monday, October 4th—My 15th birthday, and not even Mac knows. I am still coughing, and we are nearly out of food.

After feeling sorry for herself on her lonely birthday all day Monday, Jenny slept well that night, drugged by the medicine from Mrs. Tuller.

Tuesday morning she scraped the bottom of the flour barrel to make biscuits. "Our only grain left is a little cornmeal," she told Mac. She pulled her cloak tighter around her and coughed.

"Any meat?"

"Dried venison and one smoked salmon. And some potatoes from The Dalles."

"I can't hunt. I have to cut trees."

"Why don't you send Mr. Abercrombie? He could hunt and scout ahead."

"You want to lead this company?" Mac chuckled.

Jenny felt her cheeks flush. "I'm sorry. I shouldn't be telling you what to do."

"I'm teasing. You're right. I'll ask Abercrombie." Mac left, shaking his head.

The wood smoked and spat, but the fire put out fragile warmth. While William slept peacefully in the wagon, the adults shivered as they went about their chores. Rain seeped through the cracks in Jenny's shoes.

Esther joined Jenny by the fire. "Golly, it's wet," Esther said, putting Jonah in the wagon by William. "I couldn't get a fire started this morning.

How'd you manage?"

"Started it under a tarp, then moved the tarp," Jenny said. "But I can't hardly bear to cook, it's so smoky."

"The smoke makes me gag," Esther said. "Captain McDougall told Mr. Abercrombie to lead a hunting party. I'm glad to have him gone. He complained all day yesterday how slow we were moving."

"I hope he finds some game. We're about out of food." Jenny shook her head. "I'd hoped Barlow Road would be easy, but it isn't." She coughed.

"Sit down," Esther said. "Let me finish the biscuits."

Jenny sighed as she sank onto a barrel, but the sigh turned into another cough. "Your morning sickness still bad?" she rasped.

Esther shrugged. "It's getting better. Most days I can eat some breakfast. I'm ravenous all afternoon. I have to sneak some of my dinner into my pocket so Mr. Abercrombie don't know I'm eating afore supper."

Once the travelers were underway, Jenny huddled under the wagon cover with William. The oxen didn't need any guidance. The trail was too narrow and the vegetation along the edges so thick the teams couldn't leave the path. The road climbed through the morning, and the company nooned along the trail, not even stopping to build fires. There was plenty of wood, but no way to dry it out.

"You warm enough?" Mac asked when he returned to the wagon.

Jenny nodded. If she said anything, she would cough. She handed him a plate of dried venison and a biscuit left over from breakfast.

When they moved out after dinner, Jenny huddled in her buffalo robe, tucking William in with her. The oxen heaved with every step as they lugged the wagon. Occasionally, the trees and shrubs thinned enough to show the steep pitch of the mountain slope.

Jenny passed the afternoon dozing. Her back ached from the wagon's jostling over stumps and rocks. She roused herself only when William needed feeding or changing.

A sudden scream split the air. "We're going over!"

Jenny climbed out of the wagon to see what had happened.

"Wagon overturned," a man shouted.

Ahead of Jenny, a wagon had tumbled off the trail and down the slope. Two oxen lay on the ground bleating in pain. Other oxen still yoked to the fallen beasts bellowed. People and animals milled about.

"Who is it?" Jenny asked Mrs. Tuller.

"One of the Abercrombie wagons."

"Was anyone hurt?"

"Don't know yet."

A shot rang out, then another, and the bleating ceased. The other oxen bellowed louder.

Jenny clutched William so tightly he cried. Mrs. Tuller took the baby and bounced him on her shoulder to soothe him.

"Why'd they kill the oxen?" Jenny's voice broke. They were such placid, pleasant beasts.

"Broken legs, I expect." Mrs. Tuller patted Jenny's arm, as if Jenny needed consoling like William.

Mac's voice rose over the pandemonium. "Let the other wagons go on by. Then we'll salvage what we can."

Mrs. Tuller handed William back to Jenny and they walked on. As they passed the fallen wagon, Jenny turned her head away, but not before glimpsing the dead oxen and broken wagon parts strewn down the steep ravine beside the trail.

Esther stood silently next to the trail holding Jonah. "Are you all right?" Jenny asked.

Esther's face was somber, but she nodded. "Jonah and I were in the other wagon with Mrs. Abercrombie and her granddaughters. Only Douglass and his wife were in the one that fell. Douglass jumped out, and Louisa just cut her cheek. Mrs. Abercrombie is caring for her now."

"But all your things!" Jenny waved her hand down the hill at the boxes and barrels now broken and covered with mud. "And what will Mr. Abercrombie say?"

Esther shook her head. "Heaven only knows. Douglass was driving. Thank goodness Daniel was with his father and can't be blamed. I'm staying here. To gather up what we can."

"Shall we take Jonah?" Mrs. Tuller asked. "Jenny and I can watch him while you work."

Esther nodded and handed her baby brother to Mrs. Tuller.

"Let's get in your wagon, Jenny," Mrs. Tuller said. "You're getting soaked. It's not good for your cough."

Jenny shivered. "I don't want to. Not after seeing the wagon fall. It isn't safe."

"Shall I get the doctor to saddle your mare?"

Jenny looked at the steep path ahead of them, then down the ravine that fell away from the trail. Muddy rivulets already flowed over the Abercrombies' spilled belongings. "I'd rather walk," she said. Mrs. Tuller took Jonah to her wagon, leaving Jenny and William alone.

For the rest of the afternoon, Jenny trudged up the hill carrying William under her heavy buffalo robe. A small patch of sodden sky showed between the high evergreens, barely visible through the heavy mist. Mostly, she kept her eyes on the ground, focusing on every step.

She slid down the muddy trail almost as often as she scrabbled ahead. Her split shoes were caked in dirt and pine needles and squished each time she set her foot to ground. Pungent smells of rotting wood and wet animals filled her nose.

"How much farther?" she asked Mac when he walked beside her for a while.

"We'll be at the summit by nightfall."

"Three days of this so far," Jenny sighed.

"You wanted to take Barlow Road."

"Each hill steeper than the last."

"It'll get easier once we're at the summit," Mac said.

"I suppose it's better than the river." Jenny brushed her hand across her forehead. Her sunbonnet was soaked. "I keep thinking about Mrs. Pershing."

"Why's that?"

"How she must have felt jolting along in the wagon after birthing Jonah."

"You didn't get any fever after William. Just a cough." Mac sounded impatient.

"No. No childbirth fever. And I didn't die." No matter how much she coughed and ached, no matter how weary she was, she was alive, and so was William. But it was hard to appreciate her blessings when she was cold and wet and sick.

"You want to ride in the wagon?" Mac asked.

"I keep seeing the Abercrombies' belongings all over the ravine. I'll walk. Did they salvage their wagon and provisions?"

"A broken wagon wheel. Douglass and Tanner are trying to patch it together. They found most of their things. Everything'll need to be scrubbed to get rid of the mud."

"Poor Esther," Jenny sighed.

"You want to ride Poulette?" Mac asked. The mare was tied behind the wagon.

Jenny trembled. "I'm afraid of her falling. The trail is so steep."

Mac snorted. "That Indian pony? She won't fall."

"I worry about dropping William."

"Well, then, walk. But I can't stay with you. I need to check on the others."

She nodded, then watched Mac stride ahead. His long legs easily climbed the upward slope.

She was on her own. Alone, she would have to carry William to the top.

Jenny walked, step after step, pulling herself up the hill, trying to shield the baby from the rain. William was in his sling, but her arms ached cradling him under the buffalo skin. Her legs cramped and her back spasmed as she scrambled to keep her balance.

Hour after hour they climbed. Rain beat down through the afternoon, and the trail meandered back and forth across the side of the mountain, always uphill.

Late in the day Jenny slipped and shrieked, grasping a tree branch with one arm and clutching William closer with the other. The baby squalled. How much farther did she have to go?

Gasping, she heaved herself upward, one more time, and saw the horizon beyond. Through her exhaustion, she was dimly aware she had reached the summit. She had carried William to the top.

Mac appeared beside her. "You all right?"

She nodded, too short of breath to speak. Of all the mountains they had climbed, this was the worst. The Blues had been nothing compared to these Cascades.

"She's done in, poor thing," Jenny heard Mrs. Tuller say. "I'll take the baby." She felt William's weight lifted away.

Jenny coughed, wheezing in and out. She slumped to the ground, not bothering to step off the muddy trail. She felt arms—Mac's arms?—lifting her, and then she slept.

Chapter 84: Laurel Hill

They camped in a large meadow near the summit. Mac sat near Jenny, who slept, but moaned and thrashed as she lay wrapped in her buffalo skin under a tarp covering the wet ground. He wrote:

October 5, 1847. Camped at Barlow Pass. Grass is good, but we are all low on food. One of Abercrombie's wagons overturned, many provisions lost. He questions my authority daily. Jenny collapsed from fatigue.

It had been a hellacious day. Mac had ridden Valiente back and forth along the poor excuse for a road. Douglass and his wife Louisa were lucky they were not seriously injured when the wagon fell. Doc put a couple of stitches in Louisa's cheek. Once she was over her hysterics, she regaled the other women with her account of the calamity.

The Abercrombies lost all the food they had in the wagon, and their clothing and bedding were caked in mud—some things would never be clean again. Several family treasures were smashed beyond repair. Louisa mourned the loss of a porcelain plate the most. "It was my grandmother's from England!" she wailed clutching its pieces.

When Samuel and Daniel Abercrombie returned from hunting, a deer carcass slung behind each saddle, Samuel yelled for half an hour. "God damn it, Douglass!" he shouted, "I leave you in charge and you drive our wagon off the mountain! It's a sorry thing you were ever born."

"But, Pa," Douglass protested. "The near ox stumbled. Weren't nothing I could do."

"Any son of mine oughta be smarter'n a damn ox!" Then Abercrombie turned on Mac. "What kind of captain are you, boy? Weren't you watching? I knew I should've stayed at The Dalles, waited for the rafts. Instead, I let you talk me into climbing this infernal mountain."

"We all agreed to come this way," Mac said.

"Were you sitting with your namby-pamby wife and baby?" Abercrombie roared, spittle gathering in his beard. "You're no better'n that drunk Pershing."

"Now see here, Abercrombie," Zeke said, fists clenched.

"He can shout all he wants, Zeke," Mac said. "It won't change anything." He faced Abercrombie. "We'll see to it your family doesn't starve."

"Damn straight, you will," Abercrombie sneered. "I've been feeding this company since Kansas Territory. See if I share today's game with the rest of you." He drew his butcher knife and ran a thumb along the edge.

"Put the knife away, Abercrombie." He couldn't show any fear, or Abercrombie would continue to bully him. "I said we'll stick by you. But if I hear any more guff from you, we'll throw you out. Right here on the mountain. Go help your family sort out your belongings."

Mac had stalked off to his wagon. He couldn't have prevented the accident, but Abercrombie would have it in for him for the rest of their journey.

Jenny stirred beside him under the tarp. "William?" she asked.

"Hush," Mac whispered. "Mrs. Tuller has him."

"I need him," Jenny said, rising on one elbow.

"Mrs. Tuller can take care of him. You rest."

"No," Jenny said more urgently. "I need to feed him." Her wan face turned red.

Mac looked at her. The front of her dress was soaked. He jumped up. "I'll get Mrs. Tuller."

The older woman hurried back to the campsite with him, carrying William. "There, there," Mrs. Tuller told Jenny. "We'll have you cleaned up in no time." She glanced at Mac. "Does she have another dress?"

Mac found a dress in the wagon, handed it to Mrs. Tuller, then left.

The Pershing men and Daniel huddled under a tarp near the Pershing wagons.

"Has your father calmed down?" Mac asked Daniel.

Daniel shook his head. "He's still yelling at Douglass."

"How bad's the trail ahead?" Zeke asked.

Daniel shrugged. "We didn't stay on the trail while we hunted. It looks like a steep descent after the summit."

"How's your family fixed for food?" Mac asked. Abercrombie hadn't given Mac a chance to ask.

"Folks are trading potatoes and camas for the meat we got today," Daniel said. "No one has much grain left. We'll manage."

"And clothes?"

"What we have on. Lot of folks don't have much more. Esther's things were still in her pa's wagon. Womenfolk in other families are giving us what they can."

"So we keep going?" Zeke asked.

"Nothing else we can do," Daniel said. The other men nodded.

"Will you lead tomorrow, Zeke?" Mac asked. "I want to stay with Jenny."

Zeke agreed.

Mac returned to his wagon to find Jenny with William in her arms. The baby suckled greedily under a blanket.

"You better now?" he asked, sitting on an upended bucket beside her.

She blushed and nodded. Mac thought again how pretty she was. Her figure was thinner now than when they had first met. Lack of proper food, he suspected. He could have loved her, if she had wanted marriage.

"This is like the first night we spent together," he said. "Rain. Sleeping under a tarp. Remember?"

Jenny smiled. "But we didn't have William." She stroked the baby under the blanket.

"You know I'll stay with you until you're settled," Mac said.

"I'll be all right."

"Stop saying that!" Mac hissed. He wanted to shout, but someone might hear. "You're not all right. You're sick, and you're exhausted."

Jenny's eyes grew large as a kicked puppy's. "You're busy with the company. I have to take care of William. I can't simply lie about all day."

"You and William will ride with me on Valiente tomorrow. Zeke'll lead the wagons."

"I'll have to manage without you next spring."

"But not tomorrow," Mac said, and he stalked off to end the argument.

Mac awoke the next morning—Wednesday he thought it was—to Abercrombie bellowing at Zeke. "You ain't leading today. If McDougall won't do it, I will!"

Mac kicked out of his bedroll and strode over to where they argued. "What's the problem?"

"The problem is you ain't doing your job." Abercrombie stood so close his beard brushed Mac's chest, but at least he hadn't pulled his knife. "I lost my wagon on your watch yesterday, and now you're letting young Pershing here lead."

"Your son was driving the wagon," Mac said mildly. He wouldn't back down from Abercrombie's sneers. "Zeke's a good scout. He can lead."

"And where will you be, purty boy?" Abercrombie asked. "With your wife?" Abercrombie made the word "wife" sound like an insult.

"Lay off, Abercrombie," Zeke said. "Miz Jenny's been ill."

"That ain't no call for a man to shirk his duty."

"Go on," Mac said to Zeke. "Get us underway. I'll relieve you later." He turned on his heel and went back to Jenny.

"You'll be sorry, boy," Abercrombie yelled after him.

Mrs. Tuller had made their breakfast, and Mac and Jenny ate in silence. When they were ready, Mac mounted and pulled Jenny up behind him. Mrs. Tuller handed William to Jenny, who put the baby in the sling.

"You comfortable?" Mac asked when Jenny shifted against his back.

"I'm fine," she said. "At least the rain's gone." Mac felt her relax, William squirming between them.

"Can't see much sun with the trees so high," Mac said. "But at least we know it's there."

Later in the morning Mount Hood peeked through a gap in the trees. "Is that fresh snow?" Jenny asked.

"Most likely," Mac said. "If it rained here, it probably snowed on the peaks. Could snow on us any day."

When noon approached, they halted. Despite her cough, Jenny insisted on helping Mrs. Tuller with the meal.

Mac rode ahead to find Zeke, who sat on his horse at the top of a steep hill.

Zeke shook his head as Mac approached. "Look at this damn hill. It's worse'n anything we've seen so far. Must be Laurel Hill. Man at the gate said it was a ball-buster."

Mac stared down the slope, his heart sinking. The top of the hill was covered with evergreens, but the hillsides were so steep they were mostly bare, only a few laurels clinging to the mud. A narrow path had been cleared down the hill—this was obviously part of Barlow Road. Erosion had etched deep ruts in the trail, so deep Mac wondered if the wagon bottoms would scrape as the wheels slid down the grooves. Or the wagons could tumble end over end down the slope, as the Abercrombie wagon had the day before.

Mac rubbed his chin. "Grade must be sixty percent. We'll need chains and ropes."

"We'll need prayers," Zeke said, slapping his hat on his head.

The two men rode back to the company and described the challenge.

"I ain't going first," Abercrombie said. "I've already lost a wagon."

"We'll take mine," Mac said. He had to show he wasn't afraid, or the others wouldn't follow. "Make camp at the top of the hill. We'll start down in the morning."

At first light on Thursday Mac gathered the men to plan their descent. Jenny seemed to have recovered from her collapse on Tuesday and moved around the campsite without complaint. He worried about her, but he had to focus on getting the wagons down Laurel Hill—the greatest test of his leadership yet. He feared the company could not handle the terrain.

"We got down Windlass Hill with ropes and pulleys," Abercrombie said. "This ain't any worse."

"Then how come you won't go first," Zeke said, grinning.

"We could slide 'em down," Pershing said. "It's so steep I don't reckon the oxen can hold the wagons back."

"Or we put three teams behind to brake, and one ahead to steer," Daniel said.

Abercrombie glared at his son and spit a thick stream of tobacco juice. "I ain't putting my oxen ahead of the wagons. We lost our strongest team in the accident."

"We can use trees for brakes," Daniel said. "Plenty of those. Use 'em to snub the wagons."

"Let's try it," Mac said.

Mac hitched his lead pair of oxen to the wagon and pointed them down the trail. Others helped him chain a heavy log behind the wagon. Then they attached two ropes to the log and looped each rope around a tree trunk on opposite sides of the trail. Men positioned themselves on the ropes, several on each side, ready for a tug of war with gravity.

Mac stood next to the oxen. He stared at the drop ahead of him and panicked for a moment, swallowing hard. "Let's go," he said.

As Mac started to lead his team down the hill, he saw Jenny off to the edge of the trail hugging William. "Be careful," she called, her face pale.

He grinned and waved at her, then concentrated on the slope ahead.

"Snub it tight. Hold her!" men behind him yelled. Others grunted and groaned with the strain of keeping the wagon from careening down the mountain.

He was about half way down when a cry rang out. "Tree's going!"

"Mac!" Jenny screamed. "Jump!"

Mac dove into the bushes beside the trail, scraping his face and arms. He looked back at his wagon. It listed to the left, that rope hanging loose, the tree securing it uprooted from the muddy soil.

The right-hand rope held firm, fraying from the additional load now imposed on it. Abercrombie stood anchoring that remaining line. The bear of a man didn't budge, though his eyes bulged and his arms strained.

Other men rushed to take more of the weight. Dempsey chocked the log to keep the wagon from slipping farther.

Mac stood and brushed himself off. He caught Abercrombie's eye and saluted the man. "Anyone hurt?" he yelled up the hill.

"Naw," Zeke shouted back. "Just rope burns."

"Snub the rope to another tree," Mac said. "Let's get her down."

After his wagon reached the bottom, Mac climbed back up the hill and offered Abercrombie his hand. "Thank you," he said. "You saved my life."

Abercrombie shrugged and spat. "You'd have done the same. I don't like you, McDougall. But I won't see you die."

They lined up another wagon and lowered it down, then another. When several wagons were at the bottom of the hill, the women and children walked down, traversing back and forth across the steepest part of the trail.

"Too bad the road weren't built to switchback the wagons down," Zeke said as they rested while the walkers descended.

Mac sucked in a deep breath of cool mountain air and blew it out, grunting in assent. His lungs heaved after the morning's work. When he could speak, he clapped Zeke on the back. "Come on, we have more wagons to move."

The men took turns leading the oxen and holding the ropes. By the time all the wagons were down Laurel Hill, the trees at the top were scarred inches deep from ropes and chains, their bark worn away. They had uprooted four evergreens with trunks over a foot in diameter.

Mac sat in camp that evening writing:

October 7, 1847. Descended Laurel Hill, steeper than Windlass. It about killed me. I might be dead, if not for Abercrombie. But we did not lose a wagon, nor any oxen. I wonder if Father would think this an achievement.

Chapter 85: Descending the Zigzag and Sandy

Thursday, October 7th—Mac was almost crushed coming down Laurel Hill. Please God, don't let me lose him to death.

Jenny glanced across the fire at Mac. She could not have made the journey without him. Of course, she would never have left Missouri if he hadn't insisted. She had told Mac she regretted coming on the trek, but did she really? The travel from Missouri had been the hardest months of her life—even harder than her father's illness and death. But she cringed at the thought of staying with her mother and Mr. Peterson. Or alone in Independence. She could not imagine giving birth without the Tullers and Mac beside her. She had made good friends along the way. Of her friends, Mac was the best, she realized. The most reliable person she had known, other than her old nurse Letitia.

"Think I'll turn in," Mac said, slapping his journal shut.

"What's ahead tomorrow?" Jenny asked, reluctant to have him leave the fire.

Mac grinned. "Downhill all the way," he said. "But I hope the descents aren't as steep as today."

On a clear Friday morning the travelers broke camp and trekked down the valley beneath Laurel Hill.

Esther brought Jonah over and walked with Jenny and William. "Zeke says we'll have an easy day," Esther said. "We're past the worst of it."

Mac hadn't seemed quite so sure, Jenny thought. "What's Daniel say?" she asked.

"Daniel's just trying not to cross his pa. Mr. Abercrombie is still cussing Douglass for overturning the wagon."

"He didn't do it on purpose," Jenny said.

Esther sighed. "Mr. Abercrombie surely is hard on his sons."

Mr. Abercrombie was hard on everyone. He had shouted at Esther for making stew for the Pershings out of his vegetables. He had yelled at Jenny also. He was not a forgiving man. "Are you and Daniel going to settle near his parents?" she asked.

"Daniel says we'll have to see what the land is like. I want to be near Pa, so's I can help with the young'uns." Esther hugged Jonah. "Pa and Rachel can barely handle the twins, Ruth, and Noah. Jonah will probably live with Daniel and me."

"What about Zeke and Joel?"

"They're talking about moving on. Maybe California." Esther sighed.

"California! Whatever for? We aren't even to Oregon City yet." Why would they want another long journey?

"Our family's just not the same without Ma. We're all coming apart."

Jenny was silent. She understood what Esther meant. After Papa died and Mama remarried, Jenny hadn't felt like she had a family. Now she had William to look after, but no one looked after her. Only Mac, and he would leave. Maybe it wasn't so strange that Zeke and Joel also wanted to leave.

Through the day the travelers splashed back and forth across Zigzag River, as they had crossed so many rivers in the last six months. The Zigzag was a mountain stream, fast, with whitewater tumbling over rocks. But the fords were shallow and easy.

Tall pines and firs loomed over the wagons as the emigrants bounced along the log-strewn trail. Occasional breaks in the trees provided glimpses of Mount Hood, a ghostly presence barely visible in the hazy autumn sky.

Though they were lower than they had been, the wagons still dodged rocks and stumps and fallen logs. The mud was horrible. Jenny had spent the prior evening soaking and scraping Mac's clothes to remove the worst of the dirt from Laurel Hill.

In midafternoon, after four crossings of the Zigzag, Mac halted the company. "No sense pushing it," he said. "We'll camp by the river. Go hunting and fishing."

Fresh fish! Jenny thought. She had been so tired of fish along the Snake, but now it sounded wonderful. Soon Tanner brought her two large trout.

Jenny had fried the fish when Mac returned from scouting the river valley. "What'd you find?" she asked.

"Not much. Man at Barlow Gate told us the Zigzag runs into the Sandy, but there's no sign of it yet. I sent Joel ahead."

"Have you heard Zeke and Joel might go to California?"

"They're talking," Mac said with a shrug.

"I hate to see their family split up." Jenny sighed.

"Sorry you left Missouri?" Mac asked.

"Sometimes." She took a deep breath. "Nothing for me there. But I don't know what I'll do in Oregon."

Mac touched her shoulder. "I'll get you settled."

"I know." She smiled at him.

Late in the wagon she wrote:

Friday, October 8th—Crossed the Zigzag four times, with more tomorrow. Our journey is almost over. Will William and I be happy where we settle?

The next morning an overcast sky threatened rain. When the emigrants got underway, there was no horizon to watch—tall evergreens blocked most of the sky, and clouds veiled any mountain views. Jenny's focus once more turned inward.

Mac would find her a place to live, and he couldn't travel until spring. They would have a few months in Oregon before he left.

But she couldn't rely on him forever. She had to provide for William on her own. Having friends would help—she needed to settle near Esther and the Tullers.

The Zigzag valley widened and flattened. The trees marched almost to the riverbank, except for a narrow swath cleared for the wagons. But travel was easier on the level trail than in the mountains.

They crossed the river again before noon, slipping on mossy rocks, trees along the shore dripping with condensation from fog over the valley. They nooned in a damp meadow on soggy ground. The animals had plenty of grass for forage, but the emigrants' provisions were low.

"How much longer to Oregon City?" Jenny asked Mac as he plopped down beside her and she handed him a plate of food.

"A week or so?" He took a bite. "Man at the toll gate said we'd be on Barlow Road about two weeks. That was nine days ago." Mac grinned at her. "But who's counting?"

Jenny laughed. "We're all counting the days now." Then she sobered. "What will we find when we get there? We'll need shelter before winter."

"If we don't find something, we'll build." Mac didn't seem worried. But Oregon would be her home, and she wanted to be settled.

In the afternoon they reached the juncture of the Zigzag with another river. "Zeke says it's the Sandy," Esther told Jenny. "But it looks rocky to me, not sandy."

The Sandy was wider than the Zigzag, with stony islands in the middle where uprooted trees snagged and collected debris. White water rushed around the islands and gray mist rose above the froth.

"I want to settle near you and Daniel," Jenny said.

Esther smiled at her. "Oh, how wonderful! We can raise our children together," Esther said, throwing an arm around Jenny. "Jonah and William and my baby. If I can't have Ma around, I want you and Mrs. Tuller."

When they camped beside the Sandy, Jenny took out her notebook.

Saturday, October 9th—On the Sandy. We are making plans beyond the journey, though we don't know yet what Oregon will offer.

When they set out the next day, Mac directed the wagons to a ridge of hills above the Sandy. "Why can't we stay on the river?" Jenny asked as Mac saddled Poulette.

"Zeke says there's quicksand. That's why it's called the Sandy." He took William, boosted her into the saddle with one arm, then handed her the baby. "You and William be all right?"

Jenny nodded.

"I'll try to ride with you later," Mac said. "I need to get the wagons up the hill first."

Esther walked beside Poulette. "Probably our last Sunday on the trail," she said.

"Our last." Jenny's heart both sang and fell. Oh, to be done with the trail! But what would Oregon bring?

The trail followed the Sandy about two-hundred feet above the stream. They rode in and out of trees and meadows. When Mac joined Jenny and Esther, Jenny asked him, "Won't we have to descend these hills on the other end?"

"Yes," Mac said. "But look at the river." He waved his hat at the water below. "See how swampy the banks are? And the sand bars."

"What's it like at the other end, Captain McDougall?" Esther asked.

"Ask your brothers when they get back from scouting," Mac said. "They're searching for the way down."

"We're so close," Jenny whispered.

"You ready to settle down?" Mac asked her, smiling.

"Oh, yes," Jenny said.

"We all are," Esther said. "Won't you and Jenny build near Daniel and me? I'd dearly like to have Jenny and William near me. And you, of course."

"We'll see," Mac said. Jenny didn't know what he was thinking. And he wouldn't tell her with Esther there.

They ate their noon meal at a clearing in the hills. The families pooled their food into a communal dinner. "We don't have much to offer," Jenny told Mac. "Only the last dried venison."

"Good thing Tanner and his son went fishing," Mac said. "They caught a string of salmon."

"Hatty gathered pine nuts, and the Dempseys still have potatoes from The Dalles," Esther said, placing a corn pudding on the table. "We'll do all right."

"I'll send Abercrombie hunting tomorrow," Mac said. "Lots of deer in these hills."

Jenny maneuvered Mac to sit with William and her a little apart from the others as they ate. "Can we settle near Esther?" she asked him in a low voice.

"You mean, you and William?" Mac asked. "I won't be there come spring."

"Yes, but you'll be there for the winter."

"I want you near the Tullers," Mac said. "So Doc can watch out for you."

"Can't we all be together?" Jenny said. "Please."

His face softened. "I need to leave you where you'll be safe. But I want you to be with friends."

Chapter 86: Down the Devil's Backbone

October 10, 1847. Our final days on the trail. Tonight we camp above the Sandy on Devil's Backbone—another high ridge, like the one with the same name near Red Buttes. Families talk of where they will settle. There will be no settling for me—I have another journey home in the spring.

As Mac wrote by the campfire, he watched Jenny coo and smile at William. He remembered surprising her in the wagon as she fed the baby. It had embarrassed both of them, though she had tended Mac through cholera and he had seen her in childbirth. He had never seen a lovelier sight than Jenny nursing William, her round cheek dipped toward the baby's forehead, the child's fist clasped around her finger.

And the curve of her breast by the baby's mouth.

A part of him wanted to keep her with him. But she didn't think of him as a lover—he doubted she ever would. Plus, she was so young.

Mac wanted to settle Jenny near the Tullers, if only because they knew of his and Jenny's situation. They held Mac accountable for taking care of Jenny appropriately. Mac snorted. There was nothing appropriate about their situation. He knew that now, but he could not change the past. He had asked Jenny to marry him, and she had refused.

If she had accepted, they would have muddled along. But Jenny wasn't ready for marriage, and Mac doubted he was either. He had fulfilled his commitment to her, and now he was free for the next adventure in life.

He had unfinished business in Boston. This trek had taught him that he could lead and that he could act honorably. Now he had to convince his parents—he was no longer an untested and callow youngest son.

Jenny climbed in the wagon with William. A few minutes later Zeke wandered over. "What you thinking about?" Zeke asked.

"Dreaming, I guess."

"Seems odd to be so near the end." Zeke brushed dirt off his trousers with his hat. "We've been traveling so long."

"Be hard to know what to do when we stop," Mac said.

"Oh, there'll be plenty to do," Zeke said. "Stake out claims. Build houses for the winter."

"You staying? I thought you and Joel were going to California."

Zeke shook his head. "Not me. Joel might go. I'm staying with Pa and the young'uns. Someone's got to care for them. Pa's barely getting by."

"What about Esther?"

"She's got her own family to raise."

"You'll stay near the Abercrombies?"

Zeke grinned. "Didn't say that. And maybe if I'm here, Esther won't have to stick close to Daniel's family for support."

"Doesn't seem right for you to give up your life."

"I'm the eldest. It's my responsibility." Zeke rolled a cigarette. "And I like farming."

There was something Mac needed to ask Zeke, but he wasn't sure how. "Zeke?" he said, then hesitated.

"What?" Zeke lit a twig from the fire, then lit his cigarette.

"If I'm gone, will you watch out for Jenny? And William?"

Zeke puffed, then said, "You ain't planning to die after making it this far, are you?"

"I'm only saying, if something happens, will you take care of her? She doesn't have anyone else."

Zeke looked into the fire. "I won't let anything happen to her." He took a long draw on the cigarette. "You know how lucky you are, don't you? You got the purtiest girl in the company for your wife. And the nicest."

"Yeah," Mac said. "I'm lucky."

The travelers spent most of Monday crossing Devil's Backbone. As they moved west, the pines thinned out, replaced by brilliant alders that blazed yellow against the crystal blue autumn sky.

They descended to the banks of the Sandy in midafternoon. Zeke had found a ford, but they had to shovel gravel into the river to make it solid enough to hold the wagons. Even so, the wagons swayed as they jerked over the rocks. One wagon fell into a hole the swift current had scoured around sunken boulders. The women and children riding inside screamed when the wagon tilted precariously.

"Can't budge it," Tanner yelled, as he and Daniel threw their shoulders against the wagon.

"Hold on," Mac called. "We'll bring more oxen."

They carried the riders and perishables in the wagon to dry ground, then the men worked the wagon out of the hole using three extra yoke of oxen.

Jenny shivered when Mac joined her on shore. "I should be used to these river crossings," she said. "But I'm no less afraid than in Kansas Territory." She nuzzled William close to her face.

"Maybe you have more to lose now than you did," Mac said, puffing after the hard work.

"It's true. I have a lot more to live for now than when we left Missouri."

"Will you be happy in Oregon?" Mac wanted her to be happy. He would feel better about leaving.

Jenny looked up at the sky. "I think so. I have William. If I'm near Esther and the Tullers."

"We'll look for a place for you near them." He would do what he could.

After crossing the Sandy, the company hauled their wagons up a hill on the west side. Mac looked back east over the route they had traveled. He could see the Sandy below and the Devil's Backbone beyond. Above it all, Mount Hood rose in snowcapped glory above the trees and valleys.

"Look," he pointed out the view to Jenny.

"So beautiful." She smiled, inhaling deeply as if to absorb it.

"We don't see the splendor when we're mucking about in the mud."

They camped that night on a small creek beyond the Sandy. The creek babbled behind Mac and brilliant fall leaves fell into the stream as he wrote:

October 12, 1847. Crossed the Sandy. We'll reach Oregon City in a day or two.

Chapter 87: Foster Farm

Tuesday, October 12ᵗʰ—Mac says he will find me a home near Esther or the Tullers. William and I will not be alone.

Jenny sat near the wagon writing, William on a blanket beside her and Mac across the fire. She smiled in contentment. Soon she and William would have a home. She wondered whether Mac would find peace in Boston.

Would she ever be as happy as she had been as a child? She had William, she had friends, but she had no family. She shrank from the thought of marriage, even to a good man like Mac.

Even women married to men they loved faced trouble. Mrs. Pershing followed her husband and died. Mrs. Tuller left her children's graves in Illinois, and Hatty left a son dead along the trail. Esther had Daniel, but she had to put up with Mr. Abercrombie and care for her younger siblings.

No, marriage didn't guarantee happiness, and Jenny could not imagine herself married.

She would have to make her own happiness. Or rather, happiness for herself and William. She glanced down at her son and smoothed his downy head. Her heart ached when she looked at him, he was so beautiful. Even at a month old, he resembled her dear papa. She didn't want to know which evil man had fathered him. Better to believe William had no father—only her for a mother.

The emigrants were almost giddy as they set out on the trail beyond the Sandy the next day. The dangers of the journey were past, and they had land to claim and homes to build in the Willamette Valley.

Esther and Jenny walked ahead of the wagons, each holding an infant. "How will you handle both Jonah and a new baby?" Jenny asked.

"Ma had twins. I'll manage." Esther tossed her head and smiled. "I've told Daniel we need to settle near Pa. Then Rachel can help."

"Mac says he'll settle me near you, too."

"Settle you? Where will he be?"

"Settle *us*, I mean," Jenny said hastily. She had been so careful for so long not to let on she and Mac weren't married. "Though he might go back East." Maybe she should plant the seed that Mac would leave.

"Back East?" Esther looked at Jenny with wide eyes. "After this long, long trek, he'd go back East? What will you do?"

"Oh, he wouldn't stay," Jenny stared at the ground. She couldn't look Esther in the face and lie. "Lots of men go back to get their families."

"Why would his folks want to come to Oregon? I thought they were rich." Esther shrugged. "But then, Pa says Oregon is the best farmland anywhere." Esther prattled on about how her father described Oregon. "The land just has to be cleared and planted. All we need is water nearby and high ground for a house."

They traveled through wooded land along a cleared path plenty wide enough for the wagons. The terrain was almost level, the trail surrounded by green pines, bright orange maples, and red alders.

"Almost like autumn at home," Mac said when he rode up beside Jenny and Esther.

They had gone about five miles when Jenny heard a shout from the front of their company. "A house!"

Mac galloped ahead. Jenny and Esther grinned at each other and ran, clutching the babies. At the top of a slight rise they looked out over a valley. Mac, Zeke, and Abercrombie raced their horses downhill toward a farmhouse, followed by many of the children. A man rode out from the farm to meet them.

"We're here," Esther cried, hugging Jenny, tears streaming down her face. "Oregon. We're here."

Jenny sobbed as well, hiding her face in William's neck. She glanced up to see Mac shake hands with the farmer. Mac gestured at the wagons on the hill, and the farmer nodded.

Mac trotted back to Jenny and Esther, his face beaming. "That's Philip Foster. It's his farm. He has a field where we can camp. And fresh food. A home-cooked meal for fifty cents a head."

Mac turned to the wagons behind them and shouted. "Dinner is my treat tonight. We made it!"

Mac took William from Jenny, then pulled her up behind him on Valiente. "Let's go make camp," he said. He rode beside their wagon and prodded the oxen down the hill. The emigrants followed Foster into a clearing and circled the wagons. Another wagon company was already camped in the field, but there was space for everyone.

They ate supper that night in the farmhouse—a rude, wooden building, not much better finished than the barn beside it. But it had room for a long table and benches, like the tavern in Arrow Rock. Mrs. Foster and two other women fed the travelers in shifts. Fresh beef, buttery mashed potatoes, biscuits with jam, and crisp coleslaw. And real coffee.

After supper Mac and Jenny sat near their wagon. "Good dinner, wasn't it?" he asked.

She smiled and nodded, sated with the home-cooked meal.

"They have a store. We'll buy whatever you need tomorrow. Lay by until Friday."

"Won't it be expensive?" She wondered how much money he had left. He always seemed to have plenty.

"I want to stock up before we arrive in Oregon City. And get you new shoes."

"What did Mr. Foster tell you about the town?"

"Over five hundred people. Stores, churches, houses." Mac grinned. "Biggest settlement in Oregon."

Jenny sighed. It sounded like home.

"It's only ten miles from here," he continued. "We cross the Clackamas River at the bottom of this valley, go over a small range of hills, and we're there. The town is at the falls on the Willamette. Boats have to stop where the falls are, so that's where folks settled."

"Where will we stay?"

Mac shrugged. "Foster mentioned a field right outside town where we can camp until we find places for the winter."

"But no more traveling." Jenny cuddled William close and smiled.

"Esther says Captain Pershing and Zeke are staking out farm claims. And she and Daniel will also. Can we file a claim near them?"

"How will you manage a farm? Wouldn't you rather be in town?"

"I'd rather be near Esther and the Tullers. Where are the Tullers going? Doc both farmed and doctored in Illinois."

"Don't know. I'll talk to him."

Jenny climbed in the wagon to nurse William. When the baby slept she took out her journal, its pages almost full now, and wrote:

Wednesday, October 13th—At Foster's Farm. Good beef and vegetables for dinner. Only ten miles to Oregon City. I hope I find a place to call home.

Jenny went with Mac to Foster's store in the morning. The building was as big as the barn, built with the same open rafters. Many shelves behind the counter were empty, but there were barrels of provisions on the floor.

"Not much here, is there?" she whispered.

"It's late in the season," Mac said. "Foster says he has more dry goods at his store in Oregon City. Prices won't be any cheaper in town, so pick what you want here. Footwear on the far counter." He gestured.

They bought potatoes and flour and boots for Jenny. "Look how white it is!" Jenny said of the flour. She hadn't seen flour so fine since Missouri. "And carrots and cabbage. We'll have fried beef and cabbage at noon, and beef stew this evening. No more venison."

Jenny spent the day cooking and washing with other women. In midafternoon, when the wash was hung to dry and the stew on the fire, Jenny and Esther sat in camp with the babies beside them on the buffalo skin. The October air was crisp beneath a clear blue sky, the trees golden and green, Mount Hood rising beyond.

"Now that we're here, Mr. Abercrombie may be less cantankerous," Esther said. "He and Pa talked last night. Neither of 'em got mad."

"Will you all live together?"

"Close." Esther grinned. "But not together. Daniel and I want our own land."

"And you'll keep Jonah?"

Esther nodded. "At least until my baby comes and Pa is settled."

"You don't mind Jonah's not your own child?" Jenny asked.

"No." Esther touched her brother's cheek. "He's like having a part of Ma with me."

Maybe blood made a difference, Jenny thought. Esther felt tied to Jonah. Mac wasn't any relation to her or William, and didn't love them. Jenny kept thinking about Mac leaving. She could raise William alone, but she would miss Mac dreadfully.

After supper Doc and Mrs. Tuller stopped by. "We're almost there," Mrs. Tuller said, taking Jenny's arm.

"Yes." Jenny smiled, hugging Mrs. Tuller. "I can't wait to be done with the wagon."

"Where will you settle?" Doc asked Mac.

"Not sure." Mac poked at the campfire. "I'd like Jenny and William to be near you. She'll need friends. What are your plans?"

"You're still returning to Boston?" Doc's mouth was grim.

Mac nodded. "In the spring."

"You're going to live with her through the winter?"

Mac looked at the doctor. "We've come this far."

Doc snorted. "Wagon train's one thing. Cozy cabin's another."

"I don't want to get married," Jenny said firmly. "I can raise William by myself. And Mac doesn't care if we keep using his name." She tightened her grip on Mrs. Tuller's arm. "But I want to be near people I know."

Mrs. Tuller patted her hand. "Of course you do. It'll all work out."

"Do you plan to stay in town?" Mac asked the doctor.

"Have to see if the town needs a doctor, or if I can do more good in the country."

"Rest assured," Mrs. Tuller said. "We'll find a place for Jenny nearby."

Thursday, October 14ᵗʰ—Our journey ends tomorrow.

Chapter 88: End of the Road

October 15, 1847. This morning we leave Foster's farm. Tonight in Oregon City.

Mac called the wagons into line one more time. "Oregon City or bust!" he yelled as he waved his hat to signal the start. The faces around him mirrored the excitement he felt.

He walked Valiente next to Jenny on Poulette. "Our last day," she said. "Did you think we'd get here?"

"Of course." Mac grinned. "Never a doubt. Well, except when I was laid low by cholera. And maybe at Laurel Hill."

"I worried the whole time. The whole six months."

"I told you I'd get you here."

"We lost so many along the way." Jenny sighed. "We are blessed to have survived."

They splashed across the Clackamas River and climbed its west bank, then wound through hills and forded small creeks. In midafternoon Mac sat on Valiente on a bluff above a river churning in a wide cascade.

Below them—a town! Not large, smaller than Independence. About like Arrow Rock, Mac thought. Three streets ran north to south, and several side streets crossed in between. Their long journey was over.

"Oregon City!" Mac shouted. He dismounted and helped Jenny and William off Poulette. They stood on the hilltop staring at the Willamette valley.

Jenny had tearstains on her cheeks. "What's wrong?" he asked.

"It's real," she said, wiping her hand across her face. "We're here.

424

We're safe."

"Happy?" Mac asked.

She nodded through her tears.

After they camped in a field north of town, Mac led Jenny and William along the muddy main street, past a Catholic church, a few scattered houses and stores, a jail, and a Methodist church. They reached a ferry and a grist mill beside the falls. The river dropped thirty-five feet between boulders to a pool below the mill.

"It's lovely," Jenny said, gesturing at the river view. "And a watermill. No wonder the flour at Mr. Foster's farm was so fine."

The town had not impressed Mac until he saw it through Jenny's eyes. The streets were muddy, the wood buildings small and ramshackle, the noise of the falls unceasing. It wasn't Boston.

"Do you like the town?" he asked.

Jenny smiled. "It's more than we've seen since we left Missouri. People are making homes here."

Franklin Pershing walked over to them as they surveyed the falls. "Zeke and I are looking at land outside of town tomorrow. Abercrombie and his sons, too. And Doc. You want to come?" he asked Mac.

Mac looked at Jenny. She nodded, beaming. "All right," he told Pershing, then turned back to Jenny. "We'll find a place near the others." Her face brightened even more.

Mac and Jenny returned to the wagons, stopping along the way to inspect a few places with "Room to Let" signs. Mac couldn't see the three of them spending the winter in a dark cramped room. He would have to find a house, build one in town, or file a land claim and build there. If he filed a claim now, what would happen when he left? Could Jenny maintain a homestead?

As they ate supper, Mac asked, "How will you manage if you're on a claim by yourself outside of town? You've never run a farm."

She stuck her chin out as she did when she was being stubborn. He had learned so many of her ways in the past six months. "I lived on a farm in Missouri. I'll hire a man to work for me."

"Most men want their own places. They came to Oregon for free land."

"What about Tanner? Negroes can't file claims."

That might work, Mac thought. He'd feel better if Jenny had good people like the Tanners living with her. "Let me see what land is available, and I'll talk to Tanner. He might want to set up a shop in town. For carpentry and blacksmithing."

After supper they sat a while, William on a blanket between them, until the sky darkened and a fiddle started a lively tune. Esther and Daniel walked past. Esther called over her shoulder. "Come on. There's music."

Mac pulled Jenny to her feet and picked up William. "Let's celebrate," he said with a smile.

They strolled to a grassy field where a bonfire blazed. A fiddle and a banjo played, and couples danced. Zeke twirled his little sister Rachel in a country jig. Esther and Daniel passed by also. And to Mac's surprise, Franklin Pershing escorted the widow Mrs. Purcell out to the field. Even Tanner and his wife danced on the fringe of the crowd.

"Shall we?" Mac asked Jenny, offering his hand.

"I can't. I have William."

Mac saw the Tullers near the fire. "Mrs. Tuller might hold him."

Jenny handed her son to Mrs. Tuller and put a hand on Mac's shoulder. He took her other hand, and they reeled about the field. Jenny's face shone in the firelight and she smiled up at him.

"You've grown," Mac said to her.

"No, I haven't. I'm as short as always."

"I mean inside," Mac said. "You wouldn't dance with me early in the trip. You were scared of your own shadow."

"I was scared all the way here."

"And now you're brave enough to live by yourself."

"I have William. I have to take care of him."

Mac looked down at Jenny's determined face. "You'll do fine. You know you will."

She nodded. "I don't have a choice."

Jenny knew what she had to do and put her mind to doing it, Mac reflected as he spun her around.

And what about him? He'd begun the journey by running from his problems in Boston. He'd taken on responsibilities reluctantly, but found confidence and self-assurance in helping Jenny and in leading the wagon company. He took real pride in getting them all safely to Oregon.

His last task now was to find a place for Jenny and William to live. He would stay in Oregon if Jenny needed him, but she didn't. She didn't want marriage. She had people who cared for her. She would make her way without him. It seemed odd, seeing Jenny more settled than he was—she was so young.

When Mac left Oregon, his challenge would be to find a home of his own in the world. He hoped to find a place where he could exercise freedom and authority as he had on the trail. Probably Boston, but perhaps he'd find another use for his talents. Somewhere his father could not interfere.

He had the winter to think. Come spring, surely he'd know what to do.

The dance ended, and they returned to get William. Mac cradled the infant in one arm and held Jenny close with the other, smiling down at her. He didn't know what the next few months would bring. But for the moment, he was content.

THE END

Author's Note and Research Methods - Updated for Second Printing

This book is a work of fiction. Although its events are imaginary, I have tried to stay true to the geography and customs of the Oregon Trail as it existed in 1847.

A few historical personalities pass through these pages. Most notably, Narcissa Whitman was present at the Whitman Mission in September 1847, though her husband Marcus was away at The Dalles. I set my novel in 1847, because I wanted Mac and Jenny to meet Narcissa (a childhood heroine of mine). The Whitmans were killed by the Cayuse in November 1847.

Other historical figures in the book include the ferry operators (Joseph Papin and his wife Josette, Louis Vieux, and Captain Higbee) and Philip Foster (who owned the first farm the emigrants encountered in Oregon). I have put these historical characters in scenes of my own imagination.

Fort Laramie was named Fort John in 1847. However, I have called it Fort Laramie in this book to orient today's readers.

John Frémont journeyed west for the Army in 1842 and 1843, but the character of Franklin Pershing is imaginary. Frémont's cartographer, Charles Preuss, published seven maps of the Oregon Trail route in 1846, under the title *Topographical Map of the Road from Missouri to Oregon*. I have Mac and Pershing using these maps, which showed the major rivers and many tributaries and landmarks along the trail. However, the maps were far from a daily guide. Frémont's lengthy report to Congress, published in 1845, provided much more detail. I gave Mac a copy of that report also. I followed Frémont's route in 1842, though there is a better record of Army men accompanying him in 1843. (In the first published version of *Lead Me Home*, I had Pershing travel with Frémont in 1843; this second printing of *Lead Me Home* changes this to 1842, to be more historically accurate and to be consistent with *Forever Mine*.)

My characters ride in their wagons more than most real emigrants did. Even bedridden people made the arduous trip, traveling in the wagons the entire time. But able-bodied travelers walked most of the way, rather than ride in the jostling wagons. Also, people guided oxen by walking alongside the teams, not with reins as horses and mules were. My characters sometimes drive from the wagon bench, which makes their conversations easier.

I tried to be accurate in depicting the life of emigrants and their travel along the Oregon Trail. I relied as much as possible on the Frémont maps, pioneer diaries, and other first-hand accounts in describing landmarks as they appeared in 1847, as well as in determining distances traveled, locations of campsites, and the weather each day along the route.

I also used Google Maps to trace the route the emigrants took, making allowances for natural and manmade changes to the topography over the last 170 years. It's amazing how many places through the West still bear names like "Emigrant Road." The Oregon Trail remains traceable along much of its route.

There are numerous books and online resources available on the Oregon Trail. I recommend the following books in particular:

- *The Oregon Trail*, by Francis Parkman (1846) (the classic first-hand account of travel along the trail—if anyone doubts whether Mac would have made this journey for adventure, then read Parkman's book)
- *The Oregon Trail: A New American Journey*, by Rinker Buck (2015) (a first-hand account of traveling the trail by covered wagon in the 21st century)
- *Oregon Trail*, by Ingvard H. Eide (1972) (excerpts from pioneer diaries describing points along the trail, accompanied by beautiful photographs)
- *Traveling the Oregon Trail*, by Julie Fanselow (2nd ed. 2001) (a guide for travelers seeking to follow the trail by road today)

I take responsibility for any historical errors in **Lead Me Home**.

Discussion Guide

These questions are intended to help book clubs and other reading groups discuss *Lead Me Home*. Students might also use them as essay topics.

1. What surprised you about travel along the Oregon Trail?

2. What part of the Oregon Trail seemed the most difficult to you?

3. What more would you like to know about the Oregon Trail?

4. How would you have reacted to the dangers of the journey to Oregon? Would you have seen them as an adventure or a hardship?

5. How did roles of men and women differ in the wagon trains? How did their roles overlap?

6. What were the different attitudes toward Native Americans, African Americans, and other minorities expressed in this book? Were they realistic for the 1840s?

7. How do the characters think about marriage? What were marriages based on in the 1840s?

8. Who led whom in this novel?

9. Who are the Samuel Abercrombies in your life? How do you deal with them?

10. How do the characters handle loss and grief?

11. Where and what is home for each of the characters? Does the meaning of "home" change for some of them during the journey?

12. What choices did Mac and Jenny make that you disagree with?

13. How did the characters change and develop during the journey?

14. How do you feel about the relationship between Mac and Jenny at the end of the book?

If you enjoyed **Lead Me Home***, you might also enjoy the sequel,* **Now I'm Found***, available on Amazon and Barnes & Noble, which continues Mac's and Jenny's experiences on the western frontier.*

Forever Mine*, another novel in this series, tells the story of Esther Pershing and Daniel Abercrombie and will be available in February 2018.*

Acknowledgments

Many thanks to my critique partners in the Sedulous Writers Group and Homer's Orphans, to readers of early drafts of this book, including Sylvia, Ellen, and Norm, and to recent readers Pam, Sally, Al, Jen, and Linda.

Thanks as well to members of Write Brain Trust, who have taught me much about publishing and marketing.

All of you have improved this book tremendously.

About the Author

Theresa Hupp's interest in the Oregon Trail began in childhood. She grew up in Eastern Washington near the Whitman Mission, and Narcissa Whitman was her heroine. Theresa also lived in the Willamette Valley as a child, and now lives in Kansas City, Missouri. Thus, she knows both the beginning and the end of the trail well.

Theresa is the award-winning author of novels, short stories, essays, and poetry, and has worked as an attorney, mediator, and human resources executive.

Since its publication, *Lead Me Home* has been a #1 bestselling novel about the Oregon Trail in Amazon's Kindle Store. The sequel, *Now I'm Found*, published in 2016, follows Mac and Jenny through the California Gold Rush. It, too, was a bestselling novel about the Gold Rush. And *Forever Mine*, to be published in February 2018, tells the story of Esther Pershing and Daniel Abercrombie's courtship.

Theresa has published another novel—a bestselling financial thriller—under a pseudonym, as well as an anthology under her own name, *Family Recipe: Sweet and saucy stories, essays, and poems about family life*. In addition, Theresa has published short works in *Chicken Soup for the Soul*, *Mozark Press*, and *Kansas City Voices*. She is a member of the Kansas City Writers Group, Missouri Writers Guild, Oklahoma Writers Federation, Inc., and Write Brain Trust.

Please follow Theresa on her website, http://TheresaHuppAuthor.com, where she often posts about the topics in her novels. You can also follow her Facebook Author page, http://facebook.com/TheresaHuppAuthor, and her Amazon page at http://www.amazon.com/TheresaHupp/e/B009H8QIT8. Theresa writes a monthly newsletter—please subscribe to that through her website.